Going on Red

by Lyn Gardner

Dedication

To Nikki –

Once upon a time, there was a novice writer who reached out for a beta reader. The writer had never dared put words on paper before, and the beta had never attempted proofreading before, but regardless, they joined forces. One wrote, while across the pond, the other read, and before too long, chapters were posted to a fan fiction site. It was well-received, except one day, hateful comments began to appear. Posted by the henchwomen of the dictatorial administrator, they were hurtful, they were crude... and if it weren't for you, Nikki, I would have quit writing long before that story was ever finished.

You see, that advice you gave me that day changed my life. You told me to put my head down, and I did. You told me to disregard the ugliness of those petty people, and I did. And you told me to keep writing no matter what...and I have.

There are not enough words to truly express my gratitude for that advice, but more importantly, for your friendship. Out of the kindness of your heart, you helped a fledging writer find her path, and along the way, I found the courage to be myself, too.

And for that, I will forever and always be grateful.

Lyn xxx

Chapter One

If she heard the term understaffed one more time, Kate Monroe was going to scream. With the year rapidly winding to an end, it made perfect sense that those with families would request time off. Kate just didn't need to be reminded of it each and every time a request was made for her to work over her allotted hours.

Kate adored her job. As a Detective Inspector stationed just northeast of London, Kate spent her days solving crimes and assisting those in need, but after ending her fifth twelve-hour shift in as many days, Kate was now the one in need. All she wanted to do was go home, soak in a tub until her skin pruned, and then climb into bed and not wake up until Monday.

The drizzle and wind of the December evening showed no signs of stopping, and Kate kept her head bowed as she made her way to her car. Unlocking the door, she flung her handbag onto the passenger seat before slipping behind the wheel. As she started the engine, Kate took a deep breath, the tension of the day draining from her shoulders as she exhaled. Pulling out of the parking space, Kate was looking forward to pouring herself a healthy glass of wine when she got home, but then a call came over the radio. A few miles away, a burglary had occurred, and even though Kate was technically off duty, due to the proximity of the break-in, she knew the file regarding it would be on her desk when she returned to work the following week. Kate filled her lungs again, and putting on her turn signal, she checked her mirrors and made a safe and legal U-turn.

Ten minutes later, Kate tapped across the marble-floored lobby in her sensible pumps, stopping to get her bearings once she reached the middle of the space. Like most office buildings in the area, this one had been modernized over the years, the old interiors of paneled walls and planked floors giving way to checkerboard tile and crisp, sleek furniture with chrome accents and stylish upholstery. Toward the back, centered between two corridors leading to the elevators, was the reception desk, and given the time of the year, it was flanked by Christmas trees glutted with baubles of gold and silver.

Kate took a few more steps, the click of her heels echoing in the emptiness, and when she heard voices coming from one of the corridors, she stopped and waited. It wasn't long before two men appeared, and by the uniform the shorter one was wearing, Kate guessed he was the night guard for the building. She didn't need to guess who the taller one was. "Hiya, Elliott. Working the late shift, I see."

Elliott Thackery looked in Kate's direction and beamed. "Hey there, Kate," he said, holding up his finger. "One second."

"Take your time."

Kate's fondness for Elliott showed on her face, and it had absolutely nothing to do with the man's handsome face, chiseled chin, or large, expressive eyes.

Less than one-third of all police officers in England were women, and just because discrimination was illegal in the workplace, didn't mean sexism didn't exist. From superior attitudes to covert objectification, nearly all women would agree that while not overt, chauvinism was still very much alive and well. Kate had been on the receiving end of such anatomy-based bigotry for more times than she could count. Sometimes it was cloaked in a joke that wasn't *really* a joke, and sometimes it was hidden behind a leer that would be laughed off when challenged. Gawks had come her way as well, those slow once-overs that made her feel like a piece of property instead of a fellow officer, and earlier that day, when the break area became a bit messy, the men looked to her to clean it up just because she occasionally wore a skirt to work.

If Kate had felt any of the instances were worth reporting, she would have, but attempting to point fingers at a bunch of male chauvinists who had equally chauvinistic men supporting them would have only rocked the boat, and Kate didn't like to rock the boat. She preferred to sail smoothly through her job, advancing in rank if the opportunity came while causing not one ripple of attention. That was Kate's way and had been for as far back as she could remember.

Thankfully, there were a few men Kate worked with who didn't fit the pattern, and Elliott Thackery was one of them. In the three years they had known each other, Elliott had always treated Kate with the utmost respect. He had never objectified, never leered, and never made Kate feel anything but valued. And more than once, when Elliott had a station filled with seasoned officers from which he could glean direction, he had sought out Kate to ask her opinion on something he'd run across while doing his job.

With a work ethic matching Kate's, whenever a special assignment was posted, Elliott was always the first to apply, so his recent promotion to sergeant was well deserved and a surprise to no one, least of all Kate. She had often wondered if the man had a life outside the Met. Then again, who was she to talk?

As the night watchman headed back to the reception area, Elliott made his way over to Kate, his smile growing larger as he approached. "What in the world are you doing here? It's just a simple burglary."

"I just left the station when the call came in. I figured I'd get a jump on next week's paperwork, and if there are any witnesses to question, I may as well do it now while it's still fresh in their minds."

"Well, there's not much to report," Elliott said, glancing at his notes. "Someone tried to break into an office on the eighth floor. The person who called it in was working late, but we've got no real description, and the night guard couldn't help us either."

"What about those?" Kate said, pointing to a camera mounted on a wall.

"Believe it or not, their whole system is down tonight for maintenance. None of the cameras for the building are working. There are two across the street, but those offices are closed until Monday, so we can't ask to see the film until then, but I'm not sure it's going to really matter."

"Why's that?"

"Like I said, we've got no description, and by the looks of it, the witness surprised whoever it was before he could do anything other than break the glass in the door. It doesn't even appear like he had the time to get inside. I'm just waiting for the psychiatrist who leases the space to show up so we can make sure that's the case. After that, I can finish up with the witness, and then head back to the station," Elliott said, looking at his watch. "My shift was supposed to end about twenty minutes ago."

"Oh, I've been there," Kate said with a laugh. "Well, how about you wait for the doctor, and I'll go talk to the witness? That way, we can both get home at a decent hour?"

"You don't have to ask me twice." Elliott handed his note pad to Kate and pointed toward the lifts. "Eighth floor. Spaces by Shaw on the door. You can't miss it."

"Thanks," Kate said, and moving through the lobby, she stepped into the elevator, pushing the button for the desired floor as the doors noiselessly slid closed.

Kate sighed as she glanced at her reflection in the stainless steel walls of the cubicle. When she awoke that morning, she had taken a shower, applied just enough makeup to make a difference, brushed her hair until it shined, and put on a freshly pressed suit. Thirteen hours later, her suit was wrinkled, her hair was windblown and damp from the rain, and the only bit of eyeliner remaining had settled into the corners of her eyes. Clearing it away with the tip of her finger, Kate pushed her hair behind her ears, took a deep breath, and when the lift chimed and the doors opened, she stepped out into a tiled hallway.

Light streamed through the glass on the door to her right, and seeing *Spaces by Shaw* etched into the frosted surface, Kate went over, opened the door, and walked inside. The reception area was small and carpeted, with a modest desk just inside the door and four rather comfortable-looking overstuffed leather chairs scattered around the rest of the space. Hearing a noise, Kate turned her attention toward it and saw a long-legged woman with short black hair smiling back at her from a doorway.

***

In her life, Brodie Shaw had spent many an interesting Friday night, but mind-blowing sex with strangers, although an adrenaline rush, was no comparison to an attempted burglary. In the midst of finishing up a preliminary design for a client, instead of taking the work home with her, Brodie had hunkered down in her office and worked until nearly eight. While it wasn't usually the way she wanted to head into the weekend, this particular client had two other condos requiring renovations, so spending one Friday night *not* drinking and shagging until dawn seemed a small price to pay.

After remaining hunched over her worktable and computer for hours, with still more work left to do, Brodie had stretched her five-foot ten-inch body across the sofa in her office, figuring a short kip would give her the energy she needed to finish. Within seconds, she had dozed off, and she remained that way until a loud pop woke her up. She looked around, and seeing nothing out of order, she got up and prepared to finish what she had started, but before she reached her drafting table, there was another pop, and Brodie stiffened. Turning off the small desk lamp, she crept to the door and peered into her outer office. Seeing nothing out of the ordinary, Brodie tiptoed over and turned the latch on the door leading to the hallway. She heard the faint click as the lock slid back into its keeper, and quietly opening the door, she peeked through the crack and saw him instantly. The glass in the door in front of him was now cobwebbed with cracks, and while Brodie couldn't remember making a sound, when he turned in her direction, she pushed the door closed, threw the latch, and ran to call the police.

An hour had passed since then, and as Brodie glanced at her watch again, her annoyance was building. No longer able to concentrate on work, all she wanted to do was go home, get a stiff drink, and fall into bed, but the baby-faced policeman who had taken her statement and said he'd be right back, apparently had yet to learn how to tell time. Brodie was about to start pacing again when she heard a sound in her outer office, and grabbing her coat, she went out to greet the cop, only to find that *he* had become a she and a rather nice looking *she* at that.

Not normally a woman whom Brodie would have given a second glance, much preferring tall, blonde, and beautiful, while the woman failed in two of the categories, as far as Brodie was concerned, she owned the last. Her lips were pouty and pink, softening the stubbornness of her square jaw, and under perfectly shaped eyebrows were luminous eyes of blue. There was a faint dusting of freckles over the woman's small, straight nose, adding a touch of wholesomeness to an otherwise porcelain complexion. And even with her sandy brown hair askew from the wind and her nondescript black trench coat, rumpled and speckled with rain, the woman across the way was the prettiest woman Brodie had ever seen. Without giving it a second thought, Brodie blatantly continued to admire the view even after the woman's eyes met hers.

Blessed with good skin and a face that was carved, yet delicate, Kate knew she wasn't unattractive. She had had her fair share of boyfriends over the years, and while she bristled at the misogynistic ogling at work, when Kate walked into a pub and heads turned her way, she wasn't offended. It was part of the territory, part of the reason why droves of young and old alike flocked into neighborhood bars looking for something *more* than just a drink, and up until now, all the looks of interest sent in Kate's direction had one thing in common. They had all been done by members of the opposite sex. Tonight, however, standing in an office eight floors above the street, Kate found herself being undressed by the dark brown eyes of a woman who appeared content in mentally removing everything Kate was wearing…right down to the very last stitch.

The room suddenly felt warmer than it had a few seconds earlier, and breaking eye contact, Kate fumbled to open Elliott's pocket notepad. Frowning at the man's sloppy handwriting, she raised her eyes. "I'm looking for…um…Barbie Shaw."

"I'm *Brodie* Shaw," Brodie said, taking a few steps before extending her hand "And you are?"

It was a simple gesture, but Kate hesitated for a split-second before returning it. "Detective Inspector Monroe," she said, shaking the woman's hand.

Although not usually put off or made nervous by a stranger, between the way the woman was continuing to stare at her and the fact she'd held Kate's hand longer than necessary, put Kate on edge. That wasn't an easy task, yet this woman had done it without even trying.

Kate set her jaw and pushed the feeling aside. "Sergeant Thackery says you witnessed the break-in down the hall."

"Not exactly," Brodie said, and leaning against the desk, she crossed her arms and her ankles as her smile remained in place.

Kate found herself getting annoyed. She had had a very long day and a very long week, and the last thing Kate needed was cocky. She didn't like it at work. She didn't like it in a pub, and she certainly didn't like it while she was trying to do her job. Kate lifted her chin as she folded her arms across her chest. "Well, why don't you explain it to me, so I can wrap this up, and we can all go home?"

Brodie was still grinning like a cat with yellow feathers in its mouth, and analogies being what they are, ruffling this bird's feathers was definitely something she'd like to do. But the woman's body language was signaling a change of emotions, so Brodie straightened her posture, uncrossed her arms, and very politely began to explain the events of the evening. "I was working late, and I heard a noise. Since nothing in here seemed out of place, I unlocked the door and looked down the corridor. I saw a bloke, dressed in a dark hoodie, trying to break into the shrink's office down the hall, so I came back in and called the police."

"Did you see what he looked like?" Kate asked, jotting down some notes.

"No, the hood covered his face. It was either black or dark blue, and he wore jeans. I didn't notice anything else."

"And it says here you believe he left directly after you interrupted him?"

"Well, I can't be sure it was him, what with the frosted glass in my door, but I definitely saw the shape of someone running past while I was on the phone."

"I see," Kate said, looking down at the notepad again. "Do you know if he took the lift or the stairs?"

"Stairs, I think," Brodie said, doing nothing to hide the fact she was staring. "I didn't hear the lift chime."

"Can I ask what you were doing here?"

Brodie raised an eyebrow, and leaning back against the deck, she reassumed the position of cocky. "Working."

"And what do you do here, Miss Shaw?"

Brodie wasn't a boastful person. She had worked long and hard to get where she was, and with a pound of talent and a few ounces of luck, she'd been able to build a rather lucrative career for herself. But there was something about the petite Inspector that made Brodie want to push buttons just to see the results, so in a tone dripping with arrogance, she said, "Well, for starters, I own this company."

"Is that so?"

"Yes," Brodie said, her eyes roaming over Kate's figure from toe to head. "Care to hear more over a drink?"

In Kate's mind, Brodie Shaw had just moved from cocky to obnoxious. She had met men, pissed out of their minds, who didn't hold a candle to this woman's ego, and Kate had had enough.

Kate reached into her pocket and pulled out a business card. "You know what, Miss Shaw? I've had a very long week, and you've just capped it. If there is anything else you can think of concerning what happened tonight, please give me a call." Pushing the card into Brodie's hand, Kate turned on her heel, making it to the door before the woman called out to her.

"Oh, there is one more thing," Brodie said as she read the card, memorizing the name in an instant.

Kate turned around. "Yes?"

Brodie's eyes sparkled with merriment. "I just have to say, Kate, I think you're positively gorgeous."

Kate's lips thinned, and with a scowl to end all scowls, she stomped across the room, ripping the card from Brodie's fingers and replacing it with another she had pulled from the notepad. For the briefest of moments, Kate locked eyes with Brodie Shaw, believing her disgust would make the woman cower, but instead, Shaw's face grew even brighter. Kate's cheeks began to heat, and with a huff, she turned and stormed out of the room.

Brodie glanced at the card in her hand and sniggered when she saw the name *Elliott Thackery* staring back at her.

*****

Other than a quick trip to visit her mother on Christmas, the last day of the year and the first of the next went without notice for Kate. She worked a few extra shifts and spent her nights alone, pushing away thoughts that were nagging her like a toothache. A toothache in the form of a sensual stare she could not forget. Heading into another weekend with no plans, when her best friend suggested they spend Friday night after New Year's binging on takeaway food and boxed wine, Kate leapt at the chance. If she couldn't erase the thoughts running through her head, she'd drown them in alcohol and who better to do it with than Gina Parker.

They had met in college when they were assigned to share the same dorm room, and their friendship grew slowly. Kate had always second-guessed herself when it came to studying, so she spent long hours poring over books and lessons while Gina glided from semester to semester with a pristine academic record. Kate rarely left the school grounds, generally preferring to use whatever free time she had in the library. Gina, on the other hand, would disappear after her last class on Friday and not reappear until Sunday afternoon, shuffling into their room looking knackered, yet happy.

One Friday during their third semester, Gina disappeared as she always did; however, in the wee hours of Sunday morning, she stumbled through the door, making enough noise to rattle the windows. Startled, Kate turned on the light and gasped. Gina was standing in the middle of the room with torn clothes and a bloody, tear-stained face. Between sobs, Gina confessed she had gone home to tell her family she was a lesbian. Although Kate was surprised by the announcement, she didn't let it show, but when Gina confessed her split lip and bruises were courtesy of her mother, Kate cried, too.

Disowned and shattered by the people who were supposed to love her, the vibrant blonde with the light blue eyes and the natural smile had ceased to exist. In her place was a sobbing woman, a woman pained, and a woman scorned, and a woman Kate pulled into her arms in an instant. Through hugs and whispered assurances that all would be okay, and amidst the tears and sniffles they both shed, their friendship was born.

Gina sat in Kate's lounge, staring off into space. She had arrived at Kate's promptly at seven, carrying a box of Chardonnay and a bag filled with an assortment of Indian food. Over meat samosas, lamb kebabs, and chicken curry, Gina had filled Kate in on her recent holiday to Spain. Usually, when they got together, they prattled on until their jaws grew tired, but tonight Gina had carried practically the entire conversation.

Gina raised her eyes when Kate returned from visiting the loo. "So, what's going on in your life?"

"What do you mean?" Kate said, stepping around Gina to sit on the sofa.

"You didn't say much over dinner. Anything exciting happening with you?"

"Nope," Kate said, picking up her glass. "Same old, same old. Go to work. Come home. Repeat."

"It sounds like you're stuck in a rut."

"It is what it is," Kate said. "It'll change eventually."

Gina's face turned rosy as she gazed at Kate. "So...do you want to know what I think?"

"Can I stop you?"

"No."

Kate snorted out a laugh. "Then go ahead."

"I think you seriously need to get laid."

"Why is sex the answer for everything with you?" Kate said, eyeing her best friend. "Just because I may be a bit on edge doesn't mean I'm horny."

"Since when?"

Kate paused, trying to remember why they were best friends, and then it came to her just like it always did. Gina was Gina. Open, honest, beautiful, and unafraid to voice her opinion on almost any subject, under the heading of best friend in Kate's dictionary would forever and always be a picture of Regina Parker.

"Look, just because you screw everything with two legs, doesn't mean I have to," Kate said before finishing what was left of the wine in her glass.

Gina grinned. "Not everything."

"I stand corrected," Kate said, holding up a finger. "Everything *without* a Y chromosome."

"Thank you."

"You're welcome."

Gina watched as Kate got up and gathered their empty glasses. "So, you haven't had a date in weeks, have you?"

"I had a lunch date just the other day."

"That was with your sister," Gina said, uncrossing her legs so Kate could walk by. "By the way, how is Devon?"

Even if Kate wasn't a Detective Inspector, the fact that Gina had a massive crush on her sister was as plain as the nose on her face. "She's great, and she's still straight, so stop drooling."

Gina snickered as Kate went into the kitchen. "I was just asking."

Kate reappeared after refilling their glasses, and handing one to Gina, she returned to her place on the sofa. "I can't believe, after all these years, you still have a crush on my sister."

"Sorry."

"You've never tried to—"

"Kate, I told you years ago. I'd never do anything to risk our friendship. Devon is straight. Devon is your sister, and Devon is off-limits. End of subject."

"But you still think of her that way, don't you?"

"Kate, I can't help how I feel. Now, can we please change the subject?"

Gina's thoughts drifted. The last thing she needed to be thinking about—*again*—was Devon. Like Kate, Devon was a natural beauty who did little, if anything, to enhance it. A few inches taller than Kate and three years younger, Devon preferred jeans over skirts and kept her shoulder-length brown hair forever pulled into a ponytail. Yet, under the baggy clothes Devon wore, she was all woman, and she was a woman Gina found irresistible.

"Did you ever think of me that way?"

Brought back to reality by Kate's question, it took a second for Gina to get her thoughts in order. "What? Think of you as...um...hot?"

"Yes."

"Sure. It doesn't take two good eyes to see you're beautiful, Kate, or were you just looking for a compliment?"

"No," Kate said, shaking her head. "I mean like...um...like—"

"Like wanting to shag your brains out?"

Kate felt her cheeks redden, and she took a quick sip of wine. "You know, in college, I always thought your bluntness was just a phase. Boy, was I wrong."

"You love it, and you know it," Gina said with a wink.

Kate nodded as a few giggles escaped. "Well, did you?"

"In school, there were a few weeks where I would have given anything to get into your trousers, but I got over it."

"I never knew that."

"Some things are better left unsaid. You forget, for quite a while, you were the only friend I had, and that meant more to me...that *means* more to me than anything."

"Thanks," Kate said as she leaned over and kissed Gina on the cheek. "I like you, too."

"So, any prospects on the horizon?"

"Huh?"

"Dates. You remember dates, don't you? When the fellow picks you up at the door, takes you to dinner, dancing and maybe drinks, and then brings you home, where he tries to snog you, and hopefully, you let him. Ring a bell?"

Kate rested back against a stack of throw pillows. "I've been busy."

Gina frowned. "Don't you miss being the center of someone's attention, having someone give you that certain look?"

"That actually happened a few weeks ago, and it made me very uncomfortable."

"Why?"

"Because it was a woman doing the looking."

"What!" Gina jerked to attention. "A *woman* was hitting on you? You're kidding—right?"

"Is it *that* hard to believe?"

Gina leaned back into the soft cushions of the sofa and smiled. "Not hard, but *definitely* interesting," she said. "So, come on. Don't leave me in suspense. Tell me what happened. Who is she? And don't leave anything out."

"She's no one, Gina," Kate said, shooting her friend a look. "She's just some overconfident, brash woman. That's all."

"Overconfident? In what way?"

"Well, for starters, she *wouldn't* stop staring at me," Kate snapped. "It was like she was…I don't know…it was just unnerving and not to mention rude."

"Okay, so how'd you meet her?" Gina said before taking a sip of wine. "And where'd you meet her?"

"It was just before Christmas. I was heading home, and there was a call about a burglary. I figured I'd check it out to see if they needed any help. She was the one who called it in."

Gina tilted her head to the side. Kate's expression was pinched, the blue veins in her temples easily seen through her ivory skin. "What in the hell did she do to get you this wound up?"

"I am *not* wound up," Kate said, whipping her head around to glare at Gina.

"The hell you aren't. If you hold onto the stem of that glass any harder, you're going to break it."

Kate lowered her eyes and saw her knuckles were now white. Relaxing her grip on the goblet, she took a sip of her wine before setting the glass on the coffee table.

"That's better," Gina said. "Now, come on. Spit it out. What's got your knickers in a twist?"

"I just don't like it when someone knows they're attractive and assumes, because of it, they can pull anyone they want. She stood there, staring at me like I was a piece of meat, and then she had the audacity to say..." Kate stopped and took a deep breath, trying for the umpteenth time to push the thoughts of that night out of her head.

"Bloody hell, don't stop there. For Christ's sake, woman, what did she say?"

"She said I was gorgeous."

A second later, Kate nearly jumped out of her skin when Gina's boisterous laughter suddenly filled the room. "I am *so* glad you think this is funny," Kate said. "And here I thought we were friends."

"We *are*, but Kate, have you listened to yourself? You're miffed because an *attractive* woman, your words, not mine, called you gorgeous."

"She had no right to say it."

"It was a bloody compliment for God's sake."

"It was wrong!"

Gina flinched. "Why? Because she was a woman?"

"Yes."

"Kate, a few minutes ago, I said the same thing to you, and you had no problem with it."

Kate drew in a breath and let it out slowly. "It's not the same."

"Why not?"

"Because *you've* never looked at me the way *she* did."

***

"Christ, I need a shag," Brodie said, running her fingers through her hair as she watched her friend, Cassidy, pull her new laptop from a box.

Cassidy grinned, setting aside some Styrofoam packing. "Well, don't look at me."

Brodie smiled and walked away, returning a minute later with two bottles of beer and an ashtray. Lighting a cigarette, she pushed the pack toward Cassidy. "Are you sure I can't interest you in a quickie?"

"If you're talking about the fags, no thank you, and I thought you quit."

"I did, but if you're not going to give me what I want, I have to replace it with something."

"God, you're horny tonight," Cassidy said, and reaching over, she snatched Brodie's cigarette and stubbed it out.

Brodie sighed. "It's been almost three weeks."

"Three weeks?" Cassidy quickly did the math. "Shit, are you saying you haven't gotten laid since before Christmas?"

"Yep."

"Isn't that a record for you?"

"Don't be cheeky."

"Well, it's true. Isn't it?"

Brodie took a gulp of beer and debated on lighting another cigarette knowing full well if she did, Cassidy would put it out again. Resting into her corner of the sofa, she crossed her legs and glanced over at Cassidy. "Why *haven't* we slept together?"

"Because we're friends, and if we fall into bed together, that could ruin it...and you know it."

"We'd still be friends," Brodie said, shrugging. "Just with benefits."

Cassidy chuckled as she pulled the sleek, state-of-the-art laptop from its plastic wrapping. "Brodie, you're just saying that because you're randy. You're a shag'em and leave'em kind of woman, and that's not what I'm looking for."

"You still in the closet?"

"God, I hate that term," Cassidy said, hanging her head.

"Well, are you?"

"You know I am," Cassidy said, raising her eyes. "Look, Brodie, I appreciate you're all out and proud, but it's just not that easy for me. I only came to terms with it a few years ago, and before that, I was married to a *man*. I doubt that my friends or my family would understand, and for right now, it's just easier to—"

"Live like a nun?"

"Jesus Christ! Look, why don't you just go get laid and let me do my work," Cassidy said, flipping open the laptop. "This is going to take some time, so go to a club, find a woman, and get it out of your system. I'll lock up when I leave. Okay?"

Brodie pursed her lips. She had pestered Cassidy for days about getting the new laptop set up, and when Cassidy called to say she had time to do it that night, Brodie jumped at the chance, but she hadn't thought it through. Other than three days spent with her family over Christmas, Brodie had worked almost non-stop during December. Her usual Friday night jaunts to the clubs had taken a back seat to the demands of clients and rapidly approaching deadlines, but the rush was over, and the last place Brodie wanted to be on yet another Friday night was stuck in her flat. She *was* randy, especially after setting eyes on Detective Inspector Kate Monroe. "Are you sure?"

Cassidy chuckled again. While she had only known Brodie for a few years, it didn't take her long to realize the woman was a player, and tonight, Brodie definitely wanted to play. "Yes. Get out of here."

"Thanks, you're the best," Brodie said, jumping to her feet. She leaned down and kissed Cassidy on the cheek. "You know, you could come with me. Leave this for another day."

"I'm not into bars or picking up strange women in them, and besides, three's company." When she saw Brodie immediately waggle her eyebrows, Cassidy shook her head. "Don't even *think* I'd go *there* with you. Now, get the hell out of here before I change my mind and force you to watch me set this bloody thing up."

Chapter Two

Chase Wakefield was a doctor and a great catch, except when it came to Chase, Kate wasn't fishing. She wasn't even trying to bait the hook.

They had dated on and off for a few years, but their relationship wasn't going to lead to anything, and Kate knew it. He was busy running a clinic in Northern England and hated the hubbub of London. She loved the velocity of the city, and even though she didn't frequent clubs, the thought of living in the country sent shivers down her spine. But when Chase called to say he was in town, Kate eagerly agreed to see him. She had an itch, and she was sure, at least for one night, he could scratch it.

Chase adored Kate. She was attractive, smart, and funny. While the sex wasn't incredible, and he knew she loved the city, he refused to accept that their relationship couldn't grow into something more. Chase was a country doctor, living a country life, and he wanted a wife...a wife named Kate.

They caught up over curried duck and Chardonnay, talking for hours about their careers and lack of social lives. They both knew the evening would end in Kate's queen-size bed with the floral duvet, so rushing through dinner, drinks, and dancing wasn't necessary. They took their time, holding hands occasionally, tossing innuendo about to gauge the other's reaction and holding each other close while they danced. And when they finally arrived back at Kate's flat, she didn't need to ask him inside. Chase followed without a word.

They had slept together before, so the night brought no surprises for either of them. Chase knew Kate preferred the lights off, and she knew he liked the window open. She knew he liked to have a glass of water by the bed, and he filled a wine glass for her, setting it on the nightstand to the right. They undressed in silence, and it wasn't until Kate was wearing only a bra and knickers when Chase touched her. His hands were large and somewhat rough, but his touch was gentle, and when he pulled her into his arms, Kate went willingly.

The next morning, Kate woke up hating herself like she knew she would. Over the years, several men had been in her bed, yet she never enjoyed waking up with any of them, and this morning was no different. Chase was snoring. The room was cold, and Kate felt more alone than if the house were empty. Kate drew in a breath and let it out slowly. She had used him to try to quench a need, and he had done his best to satisfy her, but now Kate wanted him gone. She wanted to be alone to shower and putter through the day. Kate wanted to run her errands and then come home to change into comfy old clothes and snuggle down with a good book. And later that night, when the need would return like it always did, Kate would fulfill it…like he could not.

Quietly, Kate padded to the bathroom and took a quick shower, managing to get herself dressed and into the kitchen before Chase woke up. When he finally came downstairs, dressed in only boxers and a T-shirt, he gave her a wet, sloppy kiss, and it was all Kate could do not to cringe. *This* was going to be a very long day.

***

Cassidy tiptoed into the darkened flat and promptly scrunched up her face as the overpowering aroma of gardenias invaded her senses. She peered through the darkness, and when she saw Brodie curled up on the sofa without a stitch of clothing on, Cassidy smothered a laugh. Placing a paper bag on the coffee table, she grabbed a throw from a nearby chair, draping it over Brodie before she knelt by her side. "Earth to Brodie."

There was no movement, not even a hint.

"Hey, Brodie. Time to wake up, champ. Face the day and all that."

Brodie dragged herself out of the fog of sleep and tried to work moisture back into her mouth. Opening one eye, her brow knitted. "Why are you here?"

"Because you wanted to go shopping for a new telly. Remember?"

"It'll wait," Brodie said, and with a grunt, she rolled over to face the back of the sofa.

Cassidy stifled another laugh and opening the bag, she pulled out two cups of coffee. Setting one on the table, she held the other near the back of Brodie's head, allowing the aroma of the Americano to do what she could not.

Brodie took a deep breath, and before she had exhaled, she flopped back to face Cassidy. She squinted at the sunlight streaming through the windows, and propping herself up on her elbow, she took the coffee from Cassidy and sipped a bit through the hole in the plastic lid.

"Better?" Cassidy said.

"Getting there," Brodie croaked. "Thanks for the coffee...and the blanket."

"Yeah, about that," Cassidy said, her eyes traveling over the half-naked woman in front of her. "Is there any particular reason why you're starkers and sleeping out here?"

Brodie did her best to remain covered as she pushed herself into a sitting position. "I was too knackered to shower last night, and I didn't want to stink up my bed with all this perfume."

"It is a tad strong," Cassidy said, glancing toward the bedroom. "Oh, shit. Did you bring her back here? Should I leave?"

Brodie screwed up her face. "Bloody hell, you know me better than that."

"Then why—"

"Because my bleeding clothes reek of it," Brodie said, pointing to the pile on the floor. "I think I'm going to have to have them professionally cleaned."

Cassidy's curiosity got the better of her. She picked up Brodie's discarded blouse and took a sniff, and a second later, tears began stinging at her eyes. "Jesus Christ," she said, tossing it back on the floor. "I know you like all types, but this tart was a little over-the-top even for you. Wasn't she?"

Brodie gathered the throw around her body and stood up. "Yes, she was, but she was also tall, blonde, and stacked."

"Not to mention hungry," Cassidy said, seeing a few love bites on Brodie's neck. "So, where'd you find this one? The perfume counter at John Lewis?"

"No. The Loft."

Cassidy's jaw hit the floor. There were several gay clubs in the area, but The Loft was not one Brodie visited often. More like a biker bar than a nightclub, the owners had designed it with one thing in mind—sex. On two levels, the upper one featured small, private lounge areas where the clientele could get to know each other away from the prying eyes of those gathered around the bar one floor below. Dark and loud, if you wanted a quick, down and dirty shag, The Loft was the place to go.

"Why in the hell would you go there?" Cassidy said, but before Brodie could answer, Cassidy held up her hands. "Okay, I know *why* you went there, but seriously, Brodie, you can pull any woman you want, and there are a lot nicer clubs around than that one."

"Because I wasn't interested in a date or a relationship, that's why," Brodie said, wincing as she was enveloped in the reeking flowery bouquet. "And I'm not sure if this is lilies, wisteria, or gardenias, but whatever the hell it is, I need to go wash it off before it becomes permanent."

"All right," Cassidy said, heading to the kitchen. "And I'll seal your clothes in a rubbish bag, so they stop smelling up the place."

"Thanks," Brodie said as she headed to the bedroom. Once she was safely behind the screens dividing the rooms, Brodie let the throw drop to the floor, and going into the bathroom, she turned on the shower. A few minutes later, she was standing under the hottest spray she could handle, and as Brodie scrubbed the perfume from her skin, she let out a sigh. Cassidy was right. Ordinarily, Brodie was much choosier about whom she allowed to put their hands down her trousers, but last night she had needed raw sex...and that's precisely what she got.

She hadn't even finished her first drink when a towering redhead with tattoos covering both her arms tapped Brodie on the shoulder and offered to buy her a drink. Walking billboards had never been Brodie's type, but the woman was attractive and had ample curves in all the right places, so drinks were purchased. They stood at the bar, casually sipping them while they had a meaningless conversation until the redhead tipped her head toward the ladies' room.

Just like the upper level, the loo was designed to serve more than one purpose. The lighting was dim, and the music erupting from the speakers was loud enough to cover any sounds coming from the row of stalls lining one wall. The room smelled of soap and sex, and as Brodie allowed herself to be led into a stall, her body was already pulsing with what was to come.

Before the latch was thrown, Brodie found herself being pushed against the partition walls. Usually one who liked to take the lead, tonight she didn't. Tonight, Brodie didn't want to lead. She didn't want to talk. She didn't even want to think. All Brodie wanted was sex, and so did the redhead. Soft caresses and foreplay weren't necessary as each took what they wanted. Brodie plundered the stranger quickly, taking her to climax with calculated precision, and when it was time for the redhead to return the favor, although it took a bit longer, Brodie's release finally came. It wasn't earth-shattering. It wasn't even close, but as she zipped her jeans and opened the door to the stall, Brodie glanced at her watch. The night was still young.

They went their separate ways as soon as they exited the ladies'. The redhead disappeared into the sea of bodies, and Brodie headed back to the bar to order another drink. Before too long, with a fresh scotch in her hand, Brodie made her way through the crowd to the stairs leading to the upper level. She took her time as she climbed them, scanning the room as she did. Her preference was blondes, easily spotted even in the darkest clubs, but as her eyes darted over the possibilities milling about, none held her interest. Reaching the loft, Brodie found an empty sofa and settled into the worn leather. She sipped her drink and looked out across the club, watching as women of all shapes and sizes meandered below her.

An hour later, Brodie was casually sipping her second scotch when she saw her, and Brodie wasn't alone. More than one head turned as the platinum-haired woman glided across the club like a beauty contestant. She was wearing a short, black leather skirt and knee-high boots, and her breasts were barely being contained by the black bra she wore under her sheer white blouse. She didn't acknowledge a single gawk as she made her way to the bar, and ordering a drink, she waited patiently until her dirty martini arrived. She plucked the first olive from the cocktail stick with her teeth, and after enjoying the flavor of the Spanish Manzanilla, she emptied the glass in one swallow and ordered another. She lazily ate the remaining two olives while she waited, and turning to scan the room again, she found herself face-to-face with a woman with chocolate brown eyes and a dazzling smile.

"Can I buy you a drink?" Brodie said, leaning against the bar.

The woman gave Brodie a quick once-over and liked what she saw. "Martini. Dirty."

Brodie called over the bartender, and as she waited for their drinks, she sized up the woman again. She wasn't the most beautiful woman Brodie had ever seen, but she did fit all of Brodie's other criteria quite nicely. "My name's Brodie," she said, holding out her hand.

"Talia," the woman purred as she took Brodie's hand. "Where can we be alone?"

Brodie picked up her drink and led Talia to the second floor, returning to the sofa Brodie had occupied a short time earlier. Surrounded on three sides by heavily beaded curtains, the only open area faced the lower level, and with the sofa pushed toward the back, it offered them a small bit of privacy.

Brodie sat first, and leaning into the corner of the sofa, she motioned for the woman to join her. Talia threw back her head and made a sound reminiscent of enthusiastic swine before she removed the toothpick of speared olives from her glass. She set the glass aside and nonchalantly pulled the olives, one by one, from the plastic spear, consuming each as if they were the finest she'd ever had. Her eyes never left Brodie's until the last olive was gone, and then hiking her skirt, Talia straddled Brodie's lap, allowing there to be no confusion as to what she wanted.

Brodie's libido had been awoken when she had seen Talia at the bar, and the evocative consumption of the briny fruit had put it into overdrive. She leaned in for a kiss, fully intending on plundering the woman's mouth with her tongue, and that's when the potency of Talia's perfume enveloped her. In the crowded bar, it had mixed with dozens of others, diluting the strength of the flowery scent, except there was no avoiding it now. Brodie's first thought was to pull away to escape from the overpowering smell until Talia pressed her mouth against Brodie's and forced her tongue inside. Brodie's body pulsed, and when Talia's hand traveled south and roughly cupped Brodie's sex, the woman's perfume no longer mattered.

The music seemed to grow louder with every plunge of Talia's tongue, and even though the stench of her perfume had been a turn-off, what Talia was doing with her hands was not. With one hand on Brodie's breast and the other settled between Brodie's legs, Talia was squeezing, tweaking, pressing, and rubbing Brodie toward ecstasy.

Brodie broke out of the kiss and held Talia at bay. "Not here. Let's go to the loo and —"

"No. I want you here," Talia said, pressing her palm hard against Brodie's center. "*Now.*"

"That's not going to happen, love," Brodie said, shaking her head. "Not my style."

A secret smile spread across Talia's face, and grabbing Brodie's hand, she forced it under her skirt. "You wanna bet?"

Brodie sucked in a breath. Talia wasn't wearing knickers, and between the Brazilian wax and the copious amount of need oozing from the woman's center, Brodie's hand was coated in a second. "Jesus."

"So, what'll it be, *love*?" Talia said through a leer. "Here and now…or do we just call it a night?"

***

Brodie stood in her bathroom, taking her time as she applied antibiotic cream to the bite marks that had broken through her skin on her neck and shoulders, and another she discovered under her right breast. Capping the tube, she tossed it aside and catching sight of her reflection in the mirror, Brodie groaned. She looked like she'd been in a paintball war without any clothes. Circular bruises left behind by a voracious woman dotted her torso in a dozen places, and she knew if she turned around, she'd see a dozen more.

Unable to deny Talia what she wanted, Brodie had conceded and taken her to orgasm on the worn leather sofa, but when Talia tried to reciprocate, Brodie grabbed her hand and practically carried her to the ladies' room. Once inside the stall, Brodie found herself being attacked by the insatiable woman. Within seconds, her blouse was open, her bra was dislodged, and her jeans and knickers were pushed down her legs. It was then Brodie discovered the blonde enjoyed inflicting a touch of pain when giving pleasure. Wherever Talia's mouth traveled, she left a mark, and Brodie did nothing to stop her. Talia was getting Brodie where she needed to be, and even though pain hadn't been on Brodie's mind when she walked into the club, by the time she left, it was. Sore and in desperate need of a shower, a little after two in the morning, Brodie exited the club, exhausted yet sated.

***

"I didn't know you liked it so rough," Cassidy said, looking over her shoulder as Brodie came into the lounge. "Learn something new every day."

"I don't, and it didn't start out that way," Brodie said, and snatching up her coffee, she downed most of what remained of the lukewarm Americano.

"Well, by the looks of those marks, it sure as hell ended that way. Where'd you go? Her place?"

Brodie furrowed her brow. "No."

One beat of her heart was all the time it took for Cassidy's eyes to bulge. "Oh my God. You shagged her in the loo, didn't you?"

"I wasn't looking for something long term."

"Do you ever?"

Brodie quickly finished her coffee and plunked the cup down on a nearby accent table. "Cassidy, I know you mean well, but honestly, I have never met a woman who I wanted anything else to do with besides sex. Okay? They're either politically-fixated lesbians, stomping their feet at all the injustices in the world or vegetarians, shocked that I like meat. They have agendas and immediately want to start popping out babies, and I, my dear friend, am not looking for that."

"What *are* you looking for?"

Brodie thought for a second and then laughed. "I have no bloody idea, but when I figure it out, you'll be the first to know. Until then, I'll just keep doing what I'm doing because trust me, it does the trick."

Chapter Three

Kate slammed down the phone and slumped in her chair. What had started out as one date and one night had turned into an entire weekend, and since leaving her house on Sunday night, Chase had called her more times than Kate had fingers. It wasn't that she hadn't tried to get him to leave. Kate had dropped a few hints on Saturday and several more on Sunday morning, but not wanting it to look like she'd used him just for sex, which, of course, was the truth, Kate had spent two days trying to avoid the slap-and-tickle tendencies of Chase Wakefield. As if that wasn't enough, he had also poured on the attention, complimenting her to a point where if Kate heard she was beautiful one more time, she was going to hurl. And when Chase *finally* left on Sunday night, Kate debated on getting the locks changed…even though he didn't have a key.

With the holidays now over and two new Detective Inspectors on staff, Kate's workload had lessened, so when Friday rolled around, she could leave the station at a decent hour. She exited the building and quickly pulled up the collar on her coat to block the icy wind whipping down the street. A dusting of snow had fallen throughout the day, and although the roads were clear, the walks were not, so Kate took her time getting to her car, mindful of the slickness under her feet.

A few minutes later, Kate pulled out into traffic and driving down the road, she glanced at the markets along the way already knowing what she'd see. It happened all the time. At the first mention of snow, people would stampede into the stores, snatching up supplies as if the blizzard of the century was about to bury the United Kingdom in snow and ice, and Kate had no intention of joining the throng. Instead, finding an open spot a few blocks away from an Italian restaurant, Kate parked her car and trudged up the street.

Kate entered the small eatery and blinked at the brightness of the fluorescent lights. The front room was filled with tiny, round tables, and all were occupied by people eating pizza or sitting and sipping soft drinks while they waited for their takeaway orders to be filled. A glass-fronted counter ran down one side, and behind it, men with big bellies and chubby cheeks tossed dough high above their heads as they joked with the customers standing in the queue. Kate's shoulders fell when she saw the number of people waiting in the line, but going to a crowded market wasn't an option. She was tired, her feet hurt, and she did *not* want to cook. She didn't even want to think about it.

The door to the restaurant opened again, and Kate welcomed the chilly air as it washed over her. She wasn't all that surprised when she was jostled by the person coming inside. Kate was last in the queue and nearest to the door, so putting on her best smile, she turned to offer an apology for the cramped situation. A second later, the temperature in the room seemed to grow even warmer. Not only was Kate staring up at Brodie Shaw, but she was also well into the woman's personal space. Kate took a quick half step backward, and her nostrils flared when she saw Shaw grinning shamelessly back at her.

"DI Monroe," Brodie said, her eyes slowly traveling over Kate's body. "You're looking as lovely as ever."

For a nanosecond, Kate's smile reappeared, and then it swiftly died. Without saying a word, Kate turned her back on the cocksure woman.

Brodie relaxed her grin, and pausing only for a second, she tapped Kate on the shoulder.

With a huff, Kate spun on her heel and planted her hands on her hips. "What?"

"Sorry. Maybe you don't remember me. We met a few weeks ago. There was a burglary in my building."

Remembering Brodie Shaw was not a problem, and it hadn't been for almost a month. Kate remembered the black trousers Brodie had worn. She remembered the gray V-neck sweater with sleeves pushed up to reveal tanned arms, and she remembered the smell of her goddamned cologne. There wasn't much Kate couldn't recall about Brodie Shaw, and it annoyed the hell out of her.

"I remember you, Miss Shaw. You were the witness in that case. Now, if you don't mind, I'm busy." With nothing more to say, Kate turned her back on Brodie again.

Rudeness wasn't something Brodie usually tolerated; however, when it came to DI Monroe, there was a thin line between rude and downright cute. Brodie liked the fact that she, through ordinary conversation, seemed to be able to wind the woman up, throwing her off balance just enough so the staunch exterior of the Detective Inspector gave way to a flustered woman. A drop-dead gorgeous flustered woman at that.

Brodie leaned down, so her mouth was an inch from Kate's ear. "You know, you're going to be waiting for your food for quite a while."

Amidst the smell of tomato sauce and garlic, the fragrance of Brodie's cologne invaded Kate's senses, and the hairs on the back of her neck stood on end. Kate pressed her lips together, and taking a deep breath, she reeled around to face the cause of her irritation. "Well, it looks like *you* will have to wait even longer since *you're* standing *behind* me."

Before Brodie could utter a word, a waitress approached. "Your table's ready, Brodie," the woman said, gesturing toward the opposite end of the restaurant. "Come on back."

Brodie nodded her acknowledgment, and as the waitress walked away, Brodie glanced in Kate's direction. "I've got a reservation, so I'm afraid I shan't be waiting as long as you," she said, her eyes crinkling at the corners. "That is, of course, unless you'd like to join me?"

"Thanks, but no thanks," Kate said, and pivoting back toward the counter, she focused on the menu on the wall.

"Suit yourself."

With neon beer signs hanging in the windows, an Italian flag painted on the front door, and the smell of all things delicious wafting from its exhaust fans, from the outside, Calabria looked like just another pizza joint. But at the back of the restaurant was an intimate dining area, dimly lit by wall sconces and candles pushed into empty Chianti bottles. It was quiet and secluded, and it was where Brodie spent her Friday nights whenever she planned to hit the clubs. Carbs being carbs, and all that.

Having been given her usual corner booth, Brodie glanced around the room and smiled hello to the regulars. She perused the menu, and when the waitress returned, Brodie ordered some wine and asked for a favor.

Even though cold air had rushed in each time the door behind Kate had opened, it was no match for the heat emanating from the pizza ovens. As Kate shifted her weight from one sore foot to the other, she began opening the toggle and leather fasteners of her duffel coat, deciding the lesser of two evils was to carry it instead of passing out from heatstroke.

"Excuse me, miss."

Kate turned, and when she saw a waitress holding out a glass of red wine, Kate held up her hand. "I'm sorry, but I didn't order that."

"I know, miss. The woman in the back thought you might like some Chianti while you're waiting."

Kate's eyes narrowed. "Well, you can tell her for me that I am *not* interested."

Startled by Kate's abruptness, the waitress barely bobbed her head before she scurried back the way she came, leaving a very red-faced Kate Monroe standing in a queue that hadn't moved an inch in over ten minutes.

With sweat starting to dampen her hairline, Kate took off her coat, and draping it over her arm, she let out a long, slow breath. By nature, Kate wasn't a rude person. She was brought up in a strict household where respect was always shown, but Brodie Shaw pushed buttons Kate didn't even know she possessed. She had done it the first night they'd met, and by what had just happened, Shaw had not lost her touch.

Kate mentally shrugged off her thoughts, and pulling out her mobile, she decided to check her email while she waited.

"Um...excuse me, miss."

Kate raised her eyes and found herself looking at the same waitress, except this time, the woman was holding a glass of white wine.

"I'm sorry to bother you again, but she thought...she thought maybe this would be more your flavor?"

In an instant, the heat radiating from the ovens paled in comparison to the fiery blood rushing to Kate's cheeks. Taking the glass from the woman, Kate marched to the back of the restaurant. Even in the dim light, it took only a second to see Brodie Shaw sitting in the corner, and Kate stormed to the booth. "What the hell are you playing at?"

Brodie slowly looked up from the menu in front of her. "Sorry?"

"Where do you get off sending me a drink?" Kate said, placing the glass on the table.

"I was trying to make you comfortable while you stood in the queue," Brodie said, setting the menu aside. "But since you've obviously changed your mind about waiting for takeaway, why don't you rest those tired feet of yours and have dinner with me?"

"What makes you think I've changed my mind about takeaway?"

Brodie looked past Kate to the front of the restaurant. "Because you lost your place in the queue when you came back to see me, and since you've been standing here, I've seen at least four people walk in the door."

Kate turned, and when she saw the line at the counter, her shoulders fell, and her blood pressure went in the opposite direction. Whipping back around, she glared at Brodie. "You did that on purpose, didn't you?"

Brodie couldn't contain her amusement. "All I did was buy you a drink. You're the one who left the queue, so the way I see it, you can either go back up there and wait another hour to get your food, or you can join me and be eating in less than twenty minutes. It's *totally* your choice."

Kate's first impulse was to stomp back to the queue just for spite, except her tired feet and grumbling stomach were casting votes as well. Seconds ticked by as she stood next to the table, trying to decide what to do.

"Look," Brodie said, sensing Kate may be wavering. "I promise I won't say a word. We can just share the table. Okay?"

Kate cast her soon-to-be dinner companion a stern look, and tossing her coat into the corner of the booth, she sat down.

Without saying a word, Brodie handed Kate a menu, and after sliding the glasses of red and white wine to within Kate's reach, Brodie returned to looking at the menu in front of her.

As far as Kate was concerned, there wasn't a choice, and picking up the glass of Chianti, she began reading the long list of entrees, clueless that opposite her, Brodie was trying her best to control the smile that kept sprouting on her face.

Brodie waited while Kate browsed the menu. She had yet to look up, and even though the waitress had approached twice to take their order, Brodie had waved her off. It wasn't until several minutes had passed when Brodie finally decided to test the waters. "You know, I come here a lot. If you'd like any recommendations, all you have to do is ask."

Kate's first thought was to admonish Brodie for breaking her promise until she looked up and saw the woman gazing back at her. Kate had expected to see a cocky smirk and eyes gleaming with smugness, but instead, Brodie's features had softened, and her expression was warm and friendly. "It all looks so delicious," Kate said, looking back down at the choices.

"That's because it is," Brodie said. "And it's really quite simple. You just need to decide how you want to feel when you leave here tonight."

Kate's eyebrows squished together. "What do you mean?"

Brodie grinned. "Well, if you want to feel full but not overly so, then I'd recommend any of the chicken or veal dishes. If you want to feel like you're ready to explode, and you've added inches to your waistline, then, by all means, order the pasta. It's marvelous, but they serve it in these enormous bowls, and when you leave, you'll definitely be waddling. However, if you'd like to leave here tonight feeling proud of eating somewhat healthier, the antipasto is to die for, but be warned, it's more than enough to feed two." When Brodie saw Kate nibble on her lower lip, she decided to throw caution to the wind. "And by the way, I love antipasto. So, if you want to share, that works for me."

Kate flinched. "I don't even *know* you."

"Are you implying I have some sort of communicable disease?"

"No, of course not, but sharing a dinner seems a bit odd given the fact we're practically strangers."

"I see," Brodie said before taking a sip of her wine. "Well, I've got nothing to hide, Detective Inspector, so what would you like to know?"

Even though she felt Brodie was bordering on being hubristic, Kate found it hard not to admire the woman if only for her charisma. There was a playfulness about her Kate hadn't noticed before, an almost boyish charm in the way she spoke softly, her eyes seeming to smile even when one didn't appear on her face. "Fine," Kate said, putting the menu aside. "Why do you look at me the way you do?"

"You're the detective. I'm sure you can figure it out."

"I asked you a question, and you said you had nothing to hide...so answer it."

Brodie chuckled. "I think you're gorgeous."

"Do you say that to a lot of women?"

"No, I don't."

"Are you gay?"

"Yes, I am."

"I'm not."

"Pity."

"I think I should leave," Kate said, reaching for her coat.

"Am I making you uncomfortable?"

"Yes, you are."

"Why?" Brodie said, resting back in her seat. "You can't tell me that men haven't said the same thing to you. Why is it so different when I say it?"

"You're a woman."

"So, therefore, I can't admire another woman's beauty? Is that it?"

"Of course not."

"Then what's the issue?"

Kate sighed. "I just don't want you to think...I don't want you to assume—"

"I'm not assuming anything," Brodie said, leaning slightly toward Kate. "I'm not going to hit on you if that's what you're worried about. I don't chase women who don't want to be chased, Detective. It's not my style. Just because you're straight and I'm not doesn't mean that we can't share an antipasto, unless, of course, you're homophobic."

"I most *certainly* am not," Kate said, straightening her spine.

Before the conversation could go any further, the waitress approached again, and Brodie looked at Kate for guidance. Seeing her nod as she picked up her Chianti, Brodie smiled at the waitress. "Angie, we'll have the antipasto."

***

For well over an hour, they dined on the assorted meats, cheeses, olives, and peppers served over a bed of lettuce. They chatted in between bites, and by the time the platter was empty, Kate's opinion of Brodie Shaw had changed. At first, the conversation was light, the usual suspects of weather, music, and headlines making appearances until Kate's curiosity got the better of her. Remembering Brodie had said she didn't have any secrets, Kate asked her about her life, and without blinking an eye, Brodie touched on some highlights.

Her formative years had been spent in a seaside town on the southern coast of England, and after her mother died, she and her two brothers were raised by their father. At fourteen, Brodie came out to her family, and the news didn't sit well with her father. Believing it was his inability to properly raise a girl that had led to Brodie's waywardness, Harrison Shaw spent several years blaming himself for something he had nothing to do with. Luckily, by the time Brodie went off to college, after numerous talks and umpteen assurances her persuasion had nothing to do with her father's parenting skills, Harrison came to accept her lifestyle, just like his sons had done years before.

Even though Brodie had graduated with honors, like all budding architects, her career started at the ground level. After taking a position at an engineering firm in London, she spent several years designing parking lots and fast-food restaurants before the death of her grandfather changed her life. And at the tender age of twenty-five, Brodie found herself the proud owner of three empty warehouses.

A contractor by trade, her mother's father had run a small yet profitable construction business for most of his life, and through the years, he had flipped his fair share of houses as well. The money saved over his lifetime, he split amongst his three grandchildren, leaving a slightly larger portion to the youngest to ensure a tuition-free education, while to the oldest, he left his company, complete with trucks, tools, and an office trailer. But Brodie's career was already chosen, so instead of extra cash or a company she didn't want, he left her his dream. The old man had purchased the deserted buildings in hopes of turning them into condos, and who better to do that than an up-and-coming architect.

Brodie joined forces with her older brother Ethan to make her grandfather's dream come true. Forming a partnership and utilizing her designs, the first warehouse was entirely renovated and leased in less than two years. Not quite a year after that, Brodie resigned her position at the engineering firm and started Spaces by Shaw.

Kate hung on almost every word Brodie had spoken, yet there were a few moments when Kate's mind would drift as would her eyes. Weeks before, standing in the outer office of Spaces by Shaw, Kate had intentionally avoided giving Brodie attention. The woman's overt ogling had been as unnerving as it was unexpected, but now, with Brodie sitting only a few feet away, it was hard for Kate *not* to look.

With cheekbones high and pronounced and a nose, long and straight, Brodie had an aristocratic air about her without even trying. Her eyes were the color of cognac, and they were framed by the longest and thickest lashes Kate had ever seen. Unconsciously, she told herself it was because of some high-end mascara because no one should have lashes that lush, but Kate knew makeup had nothing to do with Brodie's lips. Full, but not so much to take away from the rest, they completed a face, angular and handsome. Her ebony hair was styled in a no-nonsense razor cut, slightly longer on the top than it was on the sides, and as Kate admired the hairstyle, she noticed hints of gray coming through the black at Brodie's temples.

Brodie wasn't a self-conscious person, and she wasn't stupid. Twice she had raised her eyes only to lower them again when she noticed Kate studying her, but with no food left to be eaten, Brodie looked up again. It was easy to see what had caught Kate's attention. "Admiring my gray?"

Kate's cheeks heated instantly. "Um, no," she said, picking up her wine. "I was just thinking most women your age would color it."

"First, you don't know my age, and second, I'm not that vain. My father was totally salt-and-pepper by forty, so I figure in two years, I'll be the same. And in case you missed it, that makes me thirty-eight."

"I didn't miss it, and I've always believed age is just a state of mind."

"I couldn't agree more, but when I feel like I'm twelve and I skip down the street, people do have a tendency to stare." Brodie's face lit up when Kate smiled. "You have a nice smile," Brodie said, quickly holding up her hands. "And before you get all huffy, that wasn't a pickup line. It's just a fact."

"Is that so?" Kate said, eyeing her dinner companion.

"Well, *technically*, it could be a pickup line, but not right now."

"Good."

The conversation stopped when Angie came over, and clearing away the plates, she was about to place the bill folder on the table when Brodie handed her a debit card.

Kate reached for her handbag as the waitress walked away. "How much do I owe you?"

"Dinner's on me."

"No, it's not," Kate said, opening her wallet.

"Well, not literally," Brodie said with a laugh. "But it's my treat."

"That's not necessary," Kate said, setting her jaw. "I'm more than able to pay my own way."

"I'm not asking you to marry me for Christ's sake. I'm just paying for dinner. It was my idea, and it was my fault you lost your place in the queue."

Kate arched an eyebrow. "Earlier, you said it *wasn't* your fault."

"Okay," Brodie said with a twinkle in her eye. "So maybe it was a little my fault."

Kate couldn't help but smile. Although the woman didn't lack confidence, throughout dinner, she had been nothing less than pleasant, so when Angie brought back Brodie's card, Kate put her own away.

They both slid out of the booth, and before Kate could react, Brodie reached around and grabbed her coat, opening it so Kate could put it on. Hesitating for the briefest of moments, Kate allowed the act of chivalry to be completed all the while trying to remember the last time a man had done the same.

Not another word was spoken until they exited the restaurant, and both hunched their shoulders in unison at the brisk wind whipping down the street. Reaching into her pockets to pull out her gloves, Brodie said, "Did you take the Tube or drive?"

"I drove. I'm parked a couple of blocks that way," Kate said, pointing past Brodie. "And you?"

Brodie gestured with her head at the metallic blue Jaguar parked on the street in front of the restaurant.

Kate looked at the automobile and then back at Brodie. "Nice car."

"What can I say?" Brodie said with a shrug. "I like nice things."

Their eyes met, and in an instant, Kate knew the words weren't meant only to describe the high-end automobile. "Well, I had better be going," she said, and pulling on her gloves, she took a step in her car's direction.

"I'll walk you."

"That's not necessary. I'm parked just up the street."

"Yeah, but it's dark, and I'd feel better knowing you got to your car safely."

"Miss Shaw, in case you've forgotten, I *am* a police officer. I think I can take care of myself."

"I'm sure you can, but I am not going to change my mind," Brodie said, looking Kate square in the eye. "Now, either we can both stand here and freeze our tits off while we argue about it, or you can allow me to escort you to your car."

***

Kate liked living alone, returning to her house knowing that food remained in the refrigerator, and everything was as she had left it. She liked knowing her magazines and books were stacked neatly on the coffee table, and she enjoyed the peace and quiet after a long day. But as Kate came inside, flicking on a few lights to guide her way, it was almost too quiet. Except for the tick-tock of the clock on the mantle, the house was still, and Kate felt more alone than she had ever felt before.

Dropping her coat and bag on a chair, she went upstairs and changed into warm flannel pajamas, slipping her feet into fuzzy slippers before going back downstairs to fix a cup of tea. Taking it to the lounge, Kate stared at the darkened fireplace, wishing she had a stockpile of wood because tonight she wanted a fire. She craved the warmth of it, believing that the coziness and comfort it would produce could somehow make the house feel more like a home.

Kate snuggled into the corner of the sofa, and sipping her tea, she thought about her day, or rather her night. When she left work, she was worn out and irritable, but now her belly was filled with delicious food, and her mind was filled with thoughts of a woman. She was intrigued by Brodie Shaw. First believing her to be arrogant, tonight she had found her charming, and that fact would keep Kate awake until the early hours of the next day.

Chapter Four

Arriving at work the following Monday, Kate found out that she was going to be partnered with a recent transfer from another borough. Although it wasn't standard protocol for Detective Inspectors to work in pairs, Kate had never questioned her Chief's decisions, and she wasn't about to start now. Instead, she simply smiled and firmly shook her new partner's hand...and her week proceeded downhill from there.

Frank Daggett had been a DI fifteen years longer than Kate, and he made sure she knew it. Boasting about all the arrests he'd made over the years, he gave her a patronizing wink and assured Kate that whatever ropes she needed to be shown, he'd be the man to do it.

Although supposedly a good detective, Kate found Frank Daggett to be chauvinistic and condescending, and within minutes after being introduced, Kate felt as if she needed a shower. Tall and broad-shouldered, Frank seemed to enjoy using his height to his advantage. From always looking down his nose at Kate to hovering over her while she worked at her desk to reaching over her head to push open a door or grab a file, the man was as oppressive as a hot summer day in a rainforest. It didn't take one ounce of Kate's detective skills to know that if the man were transported back to prehistoric times, pounding his fists on his chest would come quite naturally to Frank Daggett.

Monday had been spent at the station, going over paperwork and familiarizing her new partner with the current cases, so it wasn't until the next morning when Kate realized she'd only seen the tip of Frank's machismo iceberg.

As they walked to the parking area on Tuesday, Frank stated he'd be doing all the driving, and seeing no reason to argue about it, Kate went to hand him her keys. His loud guffaw echoed down the street, and shoving Kate's hand away, Frank's chest swelled as he pointed to his car. A second later, Kate deflated like a pin-pricked balloon.

When it came to automobiles, Kate leaned toward practical. Her Toyota Yaris was reliable, reasonably spacious given its size, and economical. It wasn't really that fun to drive, but it got Kate where she wanted to go, and that's what mattered. At least, that's what mattered to Kate. Frank, on the other hand, wasn't about practical or economical or even spacious. Frank was all about muscle, and what better way to prove he had it than with a 2007 Ford Mustang Shelby GT.

It wasn't that Kate couldn't appreciate the sporty car with its pristine black paint and polished chrome, but she didn't want to spend her day in something that rumbled and roared. Thankfully, as she approached the Ford, she noticed there wasn't a scoop on the hood or racing stripes down the middle, so Kate put her initial reaction aside. After all, first impressions aren't always spot-on. Maybe Frank wasn't as macho as she first thought. Maybe Frank was just trying to show off to her like he probably showed off to all his pub mates. Maybe Frank wasn't aggressive or brash or swollen-headed. Then again...maybe Frank was.

Kate couldn't find fault with Frank's knowledge of the streets of London. It was obvious he knew where he was going without the help of GPS. A few times, Kate learned a shortcut she hadn't been aware of while Frank drove them around the city working new cases and questioning witnesses, but whatever appreciation Kate gained for Frank's sense of direction was quickly trumped by something else.

More than once, Kate had to suppress a gasp at Frank's lack of driving etiquette. Driving faster than necessary, changing lanes without signals, and making illegal U-turns just because he had a warrant card, no matter how good a detective he was, Frank Daggett was the most dangerous driver Kate had ever met.

For the rest of the week, Kate occupied the cracked leather seat of the passenger side of Frank's Mustang, breathing in the smell of stale cigarettes and mustiness that seemed to hang inside the car like a wet blanket. She had blanched as they sped down roads, scrambled to hold onto anything she could while Frank took corners at breakneck speed, and although the seats in the Ford were probably quite comfortable when it had rolled off the assembly line over a decade before, they weren't any longer.

***

On her way home on Friday night, as Kate passed Calabria, she remembered that Brodie Shaw had mentioned she ate there often. Pulling into the first parking spot she found, Kate trotted up the street and entered the bustling eatery. Just like the week before, the tables were filled with patrons while even more stood in the queue waiting for their turn. Circumventing the crowd, Kate made her way to the dining room in the back and scanning the room, her shoulders fell.

"She's not here."

Kate turned and recognized the waitress immediately. "Oh, I just thought…she said she ate here quite a bit."

"Yeah, almost every Friday, but knowing Brodie, she most likely just hit the clubs early tonight," Angie said with a snort. "That woman can't go without her fix of females. That's for sure."

As if Kate had attended The Frank Daggett School of Driving, when she pulled away from the curb a couple of minutes later, she left behind two tracks of burned rubber. She darted in and out of lanes without signaling and spewed road rage adjectives to unsuspecting drivers, except they were innocent. They hadn't done anything to annoy Kate. *That* misdeed belonged to someone else.

***

A week later, Angie came from the dining room of the restaurant, and noticing her favorite customer standing at the register, she went over and smiled. "Friday night and not eating in?"

"No. I've got a shitload of work to do, so it's takeaway tonight," Brodie said as she opened her wallet.

"Well, enjoy. Catch you next time." Angie began to walk away when she stopped and turned back around. "Oh, by the way, that friend of yours came in last week. I think she was looking for you."

"What friend?" Brodie asked as she slipped her wallet back into her pocket.

"That woman you had dinner with a few weeks back. Short, cute...you had the antipasto."

"Really?" Brodie said, a grin creasing her face. "Is she here tonight?"

"No, I haven't seen her since then. She seemed a bit peeved when she left though."

"Peeved? Why?"

Angie shrugged. "I'm not sure. She asked if you were here. I told her you weren't, and since it was Friday night, you were most likely out clubbing like you usually do." Noticing Brodie wince, Angie's eyes widened. "Oh, shit, Brodie. Did I just cock something up? She's not your girlfriend, is she?"

Brodie took her time processing the information as she grabbed the bag from the counter. "Relax, Angie. You didn't do anything wrong. She's not my girlfriend. At least, she isn't yet."

**

Gina traipsed into Kate's dining room and began rearranging the three place settings to make room for one more.

It was rare Gina didn't work at her club on Saturday nights. It was the busiest night of the week, and even with two other bartenders pouring shots, mixing drinks, and scurrying to keep up with the wait staff serving the tables, having a third guaranteed they'd have a lucrative night. Gina had realized early on that to have a profitable club, she needed not only a dance floor, good music, and finger food, she also needed to ensure that her thirsty customers never waited too long for their next round. But tonight some of Gina's customers were going to have to wait a wee bit longer because tonight Kate was making lasagna, and if Kate was making lasagna, Gina knew Devon would be there.

Since they didn't travel in the same circles, whenever an opportunity presented itself, Gina jumped at the chance to see Devon, except tonight Devon wasn't coming alone. Tonight, Devon was bringing a date, and whether he was short and round, blond and tall, or dark and handsome, Gina already hated him. She knew she didn't have a *right* to be jealous, to be resentful of a nameless, faceless stranger who had done nothing wrong other than exist, but some things are easier said than done.

Gina gave the table one last look of disgust before heading back to the kitchen. "Table's set—*again*."

"Thanks," Kate said as she finished wrapping the garlic bread in foil.

Gina went over and yanking the cork from the bottle of Chianti, she topped off her glass. "So…who's Devon's plus one?"

"I haven't a clue," Kate said as she put the bread in the oven. "She texted to say she'd been working all day, and she wanted to know if there was enough for four."

"Oh."

Kate took off her apron and put it aside. "Something wrong?"

"No. Just wondering."

"Okay, but I don't think you'll need to wonder for long. They should be here any minute," Kate said, heading toward the stairs. "I'm going to run up and use the loo. Listen for the bell. Devon always forgets her keys."

"Yeah. No problem. I got it."

"Thanks."

Gina took a gulp of her wine, and then she took another, and staring at her now half-empty glass, she was about to top it off again when the doorbell rang. Taking a deep breath, Gina stood tall and making her way to the entry, she opened the door. "Hey there, stranger," Gina said, grinning like a fool at Devon Cassidy. "Long time, no see."

"Yeah, it's been too long," Devon said, and coming inside, she gave Gina a quick peck on her cheek before turning to the woman standing next to her. "Gina, I'd like you to meet a good friend of mine, Brodie Shaw."

While the woman next to Devon was definitely tall, dark, and extremely handsome, she was also the wrong gender to be Devon's *date*, and Gina's glee showed on her face. "Very nice to meet you," she said, holding out her hand. "Gina Parker."

If it hadn't been for the fact Devon had given up her Saturday to consult with Brodie and her clients over the latest and greatest in smart home technology, Brodie would have turned down Devon's spur-of-the-moment invitation for dinner. The only sustenance Brodie was interested in consuming was found in the clubs she hadn't been able to visit the night before; however, Devon *had* spent the entire day with Brodie. She had looked over Brodie's designs and listened to the homeowners' needs, and in the end, she had come up with suggestions that weren't only brilliant, they were profitable as well.

As Brodie shook Gina's hand, she couldn't help but think that the night wasn't going to be a total waste after all. Even though a certain Detective Inspector had appeared in her dreams more than once, Brodie much preferred reality, and reality was standing *right* in front of her. Brodie was about to turn on the charm when she heard a floorboard creak. She looked toward the sound and saw Kate Monroe, dressed scrumptiously casual in tight jeans and an even tighter sweater, standing at the bottom of the stairs. "D. I. Monroe," Brodie said, drinking in the view. "What a nice surprise."

"You two know each other?" Devon and Gina chimed in unison.

Kate nodded as she tried to find her voice, praying that once she had, it wouldn't sound like she'd just inhaled helium. "Yes. Miss Shaw was a witness on a burglary case a few months back."

Gina glanced at Kate and then at Brodie Shaw, and when she saw the look Brodie was giving Kate, everything slotted into place. *This* was the woman who had called Kate gorgeous, and *this* was the woman who had wound Kate up tighter than Gina had ever seen her. Gina held back her amusement, but just barely. "Talk about a small world," she said, her eyes darting back and forth between the two women.

"Yes," Kate said, folding her arms across her chest. "Care to tell me how you know my sister, Miss Shaw?"

Brodie frowned. "Um...she works for me. I mean, she sets up all the techno stuff for my clients. Why?"

"I just didn't think she knew someone like you, that's all."

Gina and Devon quickly looked at each other before Gina took charge. "Why don't we go into the lounge," she said, hooking her arm through Brodie's. "Devon, how about getting your friend something to drink?"

"Sure," Devon said, watching as Kate stomped into the kitchen. "Be back in a tick."

Devon went into the kitchen and hovered over Kate as she pulled the lasagna from the oven. "What in the hell is going on with you?"

"What are you talking about?" Kate said, turning off the timer.

"You were a bit rude, don't you think?"

"Was I?"

Devon leaned back in her stance. "Kate, she's my friend."

"Such a great friend, you never thought of mentioning her to me?"

"Kate, I have a lot of friends I don't talk to you about, and like Brodie, some of them are people who hire me to do work for them. What's the problem?"

"She's a player, Devon," Kate said, tossing the oven mitt on the stove. "And you shouldn't have anything to do with her."

Devon's mouth dropped open as she stared at her sister. "Why? Because she likes to have a good time? So what?"

"What?"

"Kate, I've known Brodie for a few years now. I know she likes to go clubbing, and I know she enjoys a good time, and it's no big deal."

"Well, it is for me."

"What has gotten into you?" Devon said, staring at her sister like she'd grown another head. "You've never judged my friends before. What makes Brodie so different?"

Kate took a deep breath and let it out slowly. "Can we just drop this and have dinner?" she said, yanking the oven mitts back on. "The sooner we get this over with, the sooner she'll leave."

***

Ordinarily, dinner conversation and cheekiness ran rampant whenever Devon, Gina, and Kate got together, but throughout the meal, Kate had remained virtually silent. While the other women chatted about technology, music, and movies, she sat at the end of the table, occasionally stealing glances of Brodie Shaw. Wearing a green V-neck sweater and straight-legged jeans, Brodie appeared comfortable and relaxed, and as each minute passed, Kate's annoyance grew.

Brodie had tried several times to get Kate to join in the conversation, and each attempt had been met by a steely glower leaving Brodie somewhere between perplexed and perturbed. After their dinner at Calabria, Kate's attitude seemed to have softened, yet tonight it was as cold and hard as concrete. Brodie wasn't exactly sure what she had done to once again fall out of Kate's favor, but by the time dinner was over, Brodie had had enough of the woman's boorish behavior. Although she volunteered to help clear the dishes, when Gina shooed her away, Brodie leapt at the chance for some fresh air. Grabbing her coat, she hurried out the door, and reaching her car in record time, Brodie snagged her emergency pack of smokes from the glove box. She had all but quit months before, only buckling to her past addiction when her mood was altered by alcohol or anger, and one glass of Chianti hadn't even made a dent.

Brodie ripped off the cellophane wrapper and was about to tap out a cigarette when the front door opened, and Devon appeared. Knowing if she lit a smoke Devon would put it out just as quickly, Brodie pocketed the pack and waited until Devon got closer before saying a word. "Why didn't you tell me you had a sister?"

"What are you talking about? You knew I had a sister."

"A sister named *Kathryn*—yes. Not a sister named Kate, who also happens to be a copper. It seems you left that part out, and I want to know why. I thought we were friends."

"We *are* friends. You're like my best friend, but you visit lesbian clubs all the time, and Gina owns one of the largest. I was afraid if you ever went to G-Street and started chatting up Gina, somehow you'd end up mentioning my name, and then she'd find out I was gay...and tell Kate."

"Do you have any idea how stupid that sounds?" Brodie growled. "Do you honestly think I'd go into a club, start up a conversation with the bartender, and then talk about my closeted friend, let alone mention your bloody name?"

Devon's eyes filled with tears, and she bowed her head. "Maybe it sounds stupid to you, but...oh, Brodie, I'm so scared. I'm always scared."

Brodie's face fell, her scowl vanishing as Devon's words hit home. During her last year in college, Brodie volunteered her time two nights a week answering phones at an LGBTQ help center. Her job was to listen and provide support and information and to connect those in crisis with counselors and therapists when things turned dire. It had been years since Brodie had heard a voice crack with emotion from the fear of being outed, but all those voices came back to her as she stood in the cold, moist night air watching as Devon trembled in front of her.

"Jesus, come here," Brodie said, and pulling Devon into her arms, she held on tightly. "I'm sorry. I shouldn't have said that. I forgot how scary it can be."

"No, I'm sorry," Devon said, breaking out of the hug. "I'm such a coward."

"No, you're not," Brodie said, resting her hands on the woman's shoulders. "You're gay in a world that isn't always that accepting; in a world where people like you and me lose friends and family every day because the homophobic idiots can't get past their own righteousness or misguided beliefs. Cassidy, I've been out for so long, I sometimes forget how terrifying it is to live in that stupid closet."

"I hate that word," Devon mumbled.

"I know you do," Brodie said, smiling. "So...apology accepted? We're good?"

"Yeah, we're good," Devon said, and sniffling back the last of her tears, she looked around. "So, what are you doing out here anyway?"

"I came out to calm down. In case you hadn't noticed, your sister has been less than pleasant all night, and I thought she and I had gotten past that."

"Past it?"

The quiet of the night was interrupted by the sound of a door slamming, and both women looked toward the house to see Kate marching down the walk. "Gina's washing, and *you're* supposed to be drying," Kate said, pushing a dishtowel into her sister's hand. "That was the deal."

"Oh, yeah, right. Sorry, I forgot." Devon took the towel, giving Brodie a half-glance before she headed back to the house. "See you inside, Brodie."

Brodie waited until Devon got to the porch before she pulled out her cigarettes and lit one.

As soon as Kate saw her sister go into the house, she whipped back around and took a step in Brodie's direction. "What the hell are you doing?"

Brodie's nostrils flared, and she took a deep, slow drag of her cigarette. "What does it look like I'm doing? I'm having a fag."

"Don't be cheeky. You know what I mean."

"Actually, DI Monroe, I haven't a clue."

Kate leaned in close and spoke through clenched teeth. "Leave my sister alone."

Brodie tipped her head to the side. "Sorry?"

"I said, leave my sister *alone*."

"What the hell are you talking about, and where do *you* get off telling me who *my* friends can be?"

"She is *my* sister," Kate said, jamming her hands on her hips. "And I don't want you teaching her any bad habits."

"Bad habits?" Brodie said, glancing at the cigarette. "Cassidy hates fags."

"Her name is *Devon*, and I'm not talking about the bloody cigarette. I'm talking about clubbing, and about...and about...sleeping around."

"Jesus! Is that why you've been such a rude cow all night?" Brodie said with a laugh. "You think I'm going to take Cassidy out and show her how to pick up women?"

Kate opened her mouth, closed it, and then opened it again just as quickly. "My sister is *straight*, and you aren't to touch her!"

Brodie wanted to die, and it was all she could do not to cringe at her mistake. Minutes earlier, she had called Cassidy stupid for believing Brodie would ever out her, and now Brodie had almost done just that. Brodie took a slow drag of her cigarette as she gathered her wits. "I know she's straight. It was a slip of the tongue, and Cassidy is my friend. I'm not interested in her in that way."

"Well, that'll be a first."

There wasn't a muscle, bone, or tendon in Brodie's body that didn't stiffen. "What in the *hell* are you talking about? And where do you get off saying that to me? You don't even know me."

"I know enough," Kate said, waving her hand in the air. "Hell, even the bloody waitress at the restaurant said you liked to...liked to..."

Brodie's face flushed as her hands turned into fists. All evening she had tried to be the gracious guest, tried to converse, tried to assist, and now she knew she'd been doomed from the start. She was being judged, and Brodie hated being judged. Kate had just pushed a button, and Brodie had *every* intention of pushing back.

"What? I like to shag? Is that what all this is about? You have a problem with me because I like sex?" she said, leaning in toward Kate. "I have an idea. Why don't you try it sometime? It might make you a bit more *flexible*."

Brodie stopped Kate's slap attempt inches from her face. Gripping Kate's wrist, Brodie pulled her close and allowed her temper to overflow. "What? Did I hit a nerve, Detective Inspector? Can't you handle the fact I like to fuck? Standing up or lying down, in a loo, in a car, or in a bed...I *like* it. I like the taste of women. I like the feel. I like the scent. I like it *all*, and I won't apologize for that—*ever*. I've never fucked your sister, and I never will. She's my *friend*, although I doubt you know what that means because ever since the night in the restaurant, that's all *I've* tried to be with *you* and look where it's got me."

Brodie let go of Kate's wrist and glared at the woman. "And now, I'm going back inside to say goodbye to my *friend* and to Gina, and then, perhaps, I'll go to a club and live up to my bloody reputation."

***

When Brodie had returned inside to say her goodbyes, Gina had seen the fury in the woman's eyes, and pulling her aside, she suggested they meet for dinner. Brodie agreed, and on Wednesday night, Gina met Brodie at an Asian fusion restaurant a few blocks over from her club. The food was delicious, and the waiter was attentive, but the conversation was stilted.

"This isn't working, is it?" Gina said as she picked up her glass.

Brodie smiled. "No, but then again, I'm not all that surprised."

"You're not?" Gina said before taking a sip of her wine.

"I'm not sure why you asked me out on a date when you're interested in someone else."

It was all Gina could do to swallow the wine in her mouth, and setting down her glass, she shook her head. "I don't know what you mean."

Brodie snickered. "Does Cassidy know?"

"What?"

"Oh, sorry," Brodie said, shaking her head. "Does *Devon* know how you feel about her?"

The blood drained from Gina's face. "Oh, God. Please don't tell her. You can't tell her."

"It's not my place to tell her. It's yours."

"I can't do that."

"Why?"

"Because she's my best friend's sister, and she's straight. Kate would never forgive me if I made a move on Devon."

One of the most essential parts of any friendship is the ability to keep secrets. Confidences revealed over drinks, dinner or work are held close, never to be disclosed to others for the friendship is too valuable, and Brodie valued Cassidy's. It wasn't a conscious decision to keep her circle of friends small. It was just part of the territory when you're someone who likes sex without any commitment. So, when it came to people who she could depend on and who'd be there for her no matter what, Brodie only had her family...and Devon Cassidy.

Brodie inwardly sighed as she looked into Gina's sad blue eyes. "That's a tough problem to have."

"Yes, it is," Gina said, studying her dinner companion. "So, I have a question for you."

"Okay?" Brodie said, picking up her goblet of wine.

"Do you like Kate as much as I think you do?"

Brodie stopped the glass a millimeter from her lips. She felt her cheeks begin to heat, and after taking a healthy sip of the Chardonnay, she placed the glass back on the table. "That clear, is it?"

"Crystal, except Kate doesn't have a clue."

"Sounds like you and I have the same problem then."

"Not exactly," Gina said. "I've got a crush on a woman I can't have, and you've got a crush on a woman you can."

"Oh, you're daft. Kate hates me."

"Kate may feel a lot of things for you, but hate isn't one of them."

Brodie snorted. "You didn't see her outside the house. She was livid. So much so, she almost slapped me in the face. If that's not angry, I don't know what is."

"Try jealousy."

"Jealousy?" Brodie said, rocking back in her chair. "How in the hell could she be jealous of you and me? We only just met."

"No, not of me," Gina said, giggling. "Look, a few weeks ago, she went back to that restaurant where you had dinner with her."

"I know. The waitress told me she stopped by."

"And that same waitress is probably the one who told Kate you were out clubbing."

"So?" Brodie said with a slight shake of her head. "Wait. Are you saying she's jealous because I was getting some and she wasn't?"

"No, I'm saying she was jealous because it wasn't *her* you were getting it from."

Brodie burst out laughing, the sound of which echoed in the restaurant causing several patrons to look her way. "Gina, don't take this the wrong way, but I think you've slipped off your trolley."

"No, I haven't. I've known Kate for a long time, and after you and Devon left on Saturday night, I hung around. Once everything was cleaned up and she was done slamming every bloody cabinet door in the kitchen, she opened another bottle of wine, and she and I had a bit more to drink. When Kate drinks, she can become somewhat chatty, and she also has a tendency to let her guard down."

"And?"

"And all she was doing was talking about you. She went on and on about you being attractive and being able to pull any woman you want, which led to her going off the deep end about your clubbing activities, and that led to an all-out *explosion* when she brought up the number of women you've probably slept with. I can't remember exactly what she said, but it was somewhere along the lines of you being able to fill a bloody stadium with all the women you've put on your team...so to speak."

Brodie did nothing to hide her amusement at the analogy. "Well, when you put it that way, I sound positively dreadful. Don't I?"

"Except, Kate doesn't see you as dreadful, and that's what has her so wound up." Gina grinned when she noticed Brodie's eyebrows slowly becoming one. "Brodie, you've gotten under Kate's skin, and whether she'll ever admit it or not, that's *exactly* where Kate wants you to be."

***

"You're home early."

Brodie came to a stuttered stop when she saw Cassidy standing in her lounge. "What are you doing here?"

"You said you wanted to add some gadgets to turn this place into a smart home, so I thought I'd make a list."

Brodie scraped her fingers through her hair and headed for the kitchen. "Devon, it's late. Go home."

"Okay, what's wrong?" Devon said, closing her iPad.

"Nothing's wrong. Why?"

"Because you just called me Devon, and you never call me Devon."

Brodie sighed as she yanked the cork from the bottle of Cabernet on her counter. "I'm just tired, and I'm not in the mood for company. Okay?"

"It seems like that's not the only thing you're not in the mood for," Devon said, glancing at her watch. "It's Friday night, and you're home before eleven?"

Brodie carried her wine into the lounge, and after kicking off her shoes, she sank into the sofa. "I just have a lot on my mind."

"Anything I can help you with?" Devon said as she sat down next to Brodie.

For over two hours, Brodie had sat at the bar in The Loft, nursing her scotch while she turned down offers for free drinks, invitations to dance, and several propositions to meet in the loo. Her mood had nothing to do with Gina's hunch that Kate liked Brodie more than she was saying and everything to do with the woman sitting next to her on the sofa. A woman who was as brilliant as she was beautiful, and a woman who was living a solitary life...out of fear.

Brodie swiveled and tucked one leg under her. "I want to ask you a question, and I want you to be honest when you answer it."

Devon's brow wrinkled. "Okay, but I'm always honest with you."

Brodie hesitated for a moment. "First, you should know that I had a date with Gina the other night."

"What?"

Devon not only raised her voice, but her spine lengthened to the extreme, and that was precisely the reaction Brodie was looking for. "Relax," Brodie said, holding up her hands. "Nothing happened, Devon. It was just dinner."

"It wouldn't bother me if it did," Devon said, dismissing Brodie with a shrug. "You're both adults."

"Liar."

"Brodie, you can date whoever—"

"Do you like her?"

"Brodie—"

"I asked you not to lie to me, now damn it all to hell, tell me the truth. Do you fancy Gina Parker or not?"

"It doesn't matter if I fancy her, Brodie," Devon said quietly. "If you like her—"

"I don't."

"What?"

"I mean, yeah, I like her, but...shit..." Brodie unfolded her legs and flopped against the back of the sofa, scrubbing her hand over her face as she came to terms with what she was going to do. It wasn't in her nature to break a confidence, but Devon was her friend, and Gina was only an acquaintance. Brodie turned to face Devon. "I'm fairly certain I already know the answer, but I need to hear it from you. Tell me the truth, Cassidy. Do you or don't you fancy Gina Parker?"

Devon's eyes began to mist over, and when she spoke, it came out in a whisper. "I do."

"Then why haven't you told her?"

"She's Kate's best friend."

"So?"

"I wouldn't want to cock up their friendship." Devon reached over and taking the wine glass from Brodie, she took a sip. "Look, I know you hate that I'm living in a bloody closet, but making a fool of myself with Gina is sure as hell not the way to come out of it."

"Actually, I think it is," Brodie said with a twinkle in her eye. "Because she likes you the same way."

Devon locked eyes with Brodie. "What?"

"When I was over for dinner at Kate's, I kept noticing how Gina was watching you, so when we met for dinner, I asked her point-blank, and Gina admitted she likes you...and *more* than just as a friend."

It took several seconds for Brodie's words to sink in, and when they did, Devon chugged down what was left in the glass and then scrunched up her face as the dry red sucked every ounce of moisture from her mouth.

"Hey, slow down," Brodie said, placing her hand on Devon's leg. "You keep drinking like that, and you'll be spending the night here."

"Not unless you have some beer. This shit is nasty," Devon said, handing Brodie the empty glass. "And you don't know what this means."

Brodie's face creased into a smile. "Well, if you play your cards right, it means you could get lucky come tomorrow night."

"Sorry?"

"Gina's having a bit of a problem with the computer at her club, so I offered your services. She's expecting you to show up tomorrow night."

"Did you tell her about—"

"I didn't tell her a thing. That's up to you to do."

"Brodie, I'm not sure—"

"Damn it, Devon. If you want her, then go for it because I'm telling you right now, Gina *definitely* wants you."

***

Twenty-two hours later, with her heart pounding and her palms damp, Devon walked into G-Street. Gina had owned it for years, but until tonight, Devon hadn't set foot in it or any other gay and lesbian club for that matter. She had never been willing to risk being recognized, being outed unintentionally to someone who knew someone else...who knew Kate.

The only woman Devon had ever been with she had met on the Internet in a chat room where false names and false faces were the norm. The relationship only lasted a few months, fizzling as reality took the place of what Devon's imagination conjured through the woman's written words. Disillusioned, Devon had left the chat room, and even though she still dabbled in social media, the appeal of using it as a dating pool had been lost, further limiting Devon's practically non-existent social life.

The strangest feeling washed over Devon as she stepped inside, and she paused. In an instant, her nerves were gone, and her heart rate slowed as she looked out across the crowded club. It was filled with women just like her, and Devon's distress morphed into comfort. They were *just* like her.

Outside, the February temperatures were hovering just above freezing, but inside the club, layers of clothes were not needed. Unzipping her bulky, blue parka, Devon tossed it over her arm before making her way to the bar. She hadn't dressed to impress, preferring her well-worn jeans and a baggy thermal over the styles worn in clubs filled with patrons on the pull, yet heads turned in her direction as she zigzagged through the throng. She was oblivious to the stares and once-overs as she passed women of all shapes and sizes, for Devon was focused solely on one of the bartenders.

Gina's grin was instant when she looked up and saw Devon standing at the bar. "Hey there!" she shouted.

"Hi, Gina," Devon said, raising her voice to be heard over the music and chatter. "Brodie said you were having some computer problems."

"That's putting it mildly." Gina looked around and dipped her head to her left. "I'll meet you over there. Give me a second."

Devon made her way through the sea of women, and by the time she reached the end of the bar, Gina was coming out from behind it. "The office is just down here."

The walk to Gina's office gave Devon yet another opportunity to admire the woman in front of her. She had stolen glances before. Clandestine glimpses of adoration bordering on lust, she had consumed each like grapes on a vine, savoring every morsel in case another chance didn't come her way. At the moment, however, since they were the only ones in the hall, Devon wasn't savoring morsels, she was enjoying a feast.

Gina was wearing an oversized cream-colored silk blouse that ended at her thighs, and the billowing sleeves were fastened at the wrist by a long line of pearl buttons. The gold chain belt she wore emphasized her slender waist, and instead of trousers, Gina was wearing leggings the color of espresso. Although the fabric was opaque, Devon could easily see the contour of the muscles in Gina's calves, pulled taut by the three-inch high heels she wore, and as she lifted her eyes, Devon cursed the length of Gina's shirt. It was far too long.

Gina opened a door and waved Devon inside. "There's the piece of crap," she said, pointing toward the desk.

Devon chuckled and tossing her parka on top of some filing cabinets, she went over and sat in the high-backed leather executive chair behind the desk. "So, what's the problem with it?"

"Everything," Gina said, and plopping down on a chair opposite the desk, she rested her elbows on her knees. "I can't get it to print. I keep getting error messages that I don't understand, and then the bloody thing locks up, and I have to restart it."

"Okay," Devon said, and pressing the button on the laptop, she waited while it slowly came to life. "Let me see what's going on."

"But Dev, it's Saturday night. Do you really want to spend it back here trying to fix that stupid thing?"

Devon raised her eyes, and her temperature rose with them. Gina's shirt had gaped, and Devon now had a view she'd *never* had before. Between Gina's cleavage and what Brodie had told her, it was all Devon could do to form a word. Feeling her face begin to heat, she looked back down at the laptop. "I...uh...I didn't have any plans tonight. Don't worry about it."

"I can just buy a new one."

"Why do that if I can fix this one?" Devon said, glancing at the laptop. "Besides, this model is only a couple of years old."

"How'd you know that?"

Devon looked up and then right back down again. "Um...because it's my job to...to know that. So, why don't you go do yours, and let me do mine?"

"Are you sure?"

"Yeah, it's cool. I just need your password."

"Oh, let me write it down. It's ridiculously long." Gina sprang up and snatching a notepad from the desk, she bent over to jot down the number, giving Devon another mouthwatering view.

"Here you go," Gina said, looking up as she handed the paper to Devon. "Anything else?"

"Um...no. I'm good."

"Okay, see you in a bit."

As soon as Gina closed the door, Devon deflated as if all the air had been sucked out of her. Fixing the computer was going to be the easy part. Coming out to Gina...not so much.

***

An hour later, Devon was doing her best to concentrate on Gina's laptop, yet each time she needed to wait for another update to come in, her eyes settled on a photograph sitting on the corner of the desk. It had been taken the day Devon had graduated from college, and to her knowledge, there was only one copy, and it sat on Kate's mantle.

It was on Devon's sixteenth birthday when she first laid eyes on Gina Parker. Kate had come home from college for the weekend with her best friend in tow to celebrate the day, and Devon's infatuation with the nineteen-year-old was instant. She had never met anyone like Gina. Her accent proper and her clothes trendy, she would chatter on about this and that, and Devon would hang on every word.

She told herself it was purely curiosity, her interest piqued by someone far more compelling than her own whimsical and rebellious friends, and Devon kept telling herself that until she met, married, and divorced Charlie Cassidy.

Devon never realized how much she talked about Gina until one night, during one of their many arguments, Charlie shouted that Devon should just shag Gina to get it out of her system. The verbal sucker punch sent Devon reeling. Escaping to the spare bedroom, she spent the night alone with her tears, and when they finally dried up, she was left with her thoughts. In the darkness, the pieces began to fall into place. Devon had dreamed about Gina before, a confusing collage of images that had made her mind race and her body pulse, and more than once, Devon had awakened from those dreams and used Charlie to try to satisfy what another had started.

Devon jumped when she heard the door open, and raising her eyes, she saw Gina coming in carrying a bottle of beer.

"Thought you might be thirsty," Gina said, handing Devon the lager.

"Thanks."

Gina moved around the desk and looked at the computer screen. "Any luck?"

"A bit," Devon said, glancing at the laptop. "You know, you really need to install updates and defrag this thing occasionally."

"Then it shouldn't give me the option to remind myself later, now should it?" Gina said, squatting down next to Devon. "So, no other surprises then?"

"Just one." Devon took a slow swig of her beer, and as she set the bottle down, she pointed at the photograph. "I thought Kate had the only copy."

Gina's heart began to pound. To the oblivious, the photograph was merely one of a college graduate. Draped in a cap and gown and clutching a diploma, Devon was looking into Kate's camera, wearing a smile that only comes from accomplishment. Yet, a brief burst of wind accompanied by Devon's elated mood had turned the photo into something so much more. Devon's hair was loose and flying in the breeze, making her appear like a model posing for the cover of a magazine. Gaiety danced in her eyes, and two tiny dimples dented her cheeks, and while Gina had already known she had fallen for Kate's sister, that day had forever sealed the deal. So, unbeknownst to her best friend, when Kate was away on holiday and Gina went over to water the houseplants, she had a copy of the photograph made...and now she had to explain why.

Intent on staring at the picture, it wasn't until Gina pried her eyes away from it that she realized Devon had leaned in closer, and Gina swallowed hard. "Um...she does have the only copy. I mean...um...I mean, she did."

Their faces were inches apart, and Devon could feel the warmth of Gina's breath as it washed over her. Somewhere in the room was a clock, slowly ticking away the seconds and the laptop hummed, downloading yet another update, but the longer she stared, the quieter the room became. Devon had never allowed herself to gaze into those eyes of denim blue before, and now she couldn't look away. Now...she didn't have to look away.

"So," Devon said, captivated by the pools of blue. "Do you want to explain why you made a copy?"

"Um...no reason," Gina said, pushing herself to her feet. "I should get back to work."

"Not so fast," Devon said, and jumping up, she grabbed Gina's hand. "We need to talk."

"Seriously, Dev. I have to get back to work," Gina said, trying to pull out of Devon's grip. "We're slammed."

Devon didn't say a word as she closed the gap between them. She looked into Gina's eyes, and when she saw the tears of truth, Devon leaned in and pressed her lips against Gina's.

The kiss started out as tentative. One was in shock, and the other was still nagged by a modicum of doubt, but it only took a few seconds before both were unable to deny what they felt. Their lips came together again and again, tasting slowly as flavors new and delicious blended. Their breathing quickened as their blood began to heat, and when Devon finally deepened the kiss, they both moaned and lost themselves in the moment.

Gina was trapped in a cyclone, the rush of desire and need pulsing through her veins stronger than anything she could ever imagine. Devon's lips were like velvet, and her taste was heavenly, and Gina wanted to revel in it forever, yet the strength of the lust-filled storm was no match for the tenacity of reality. *This* was Kate's sister. *This* was not allowed. *This could not happen.*

Gina pulled out of the kiss and stumbled backward. "We can't do this," she said, holding up her hands. "Jesus, Devon. Your sister is my best friend."

"Kate has nothing to do with this," Devon said as she walked over and touched Gina's cheek. "This is about you and me...and what *we* want."

"You...you don't know what you're saying."

"Yes, I do," Devon said, leaning in for a kiss.

"Devon, come on," Gina said, trying half-heartedly to push Devon away. "You don't know what you're doing."

"That's where you're wrong. I know exactly what I'm doing." Devon gazed into Gina's eyes as she reached down and unclasped the gold belt around Gina's waist. "Kate may be your best friend...but I'm about to become your lover."

Chapter Five

With Frank Daggett on holiday, Kate's week went by without a hitch. Managing to get two cases closed and the mountain of paperwork on her desk reduced by a few inches, she was heading into the weekend with only one thought on her mind. She needed to apologize to Brodie Shaw.

For two weeks, whenever her mind wasn't on work, it was on the night Brodie left Kate's house with fire in her eyes. Kate had tried to make excuses for their argument a hundred times, convincing herself she was only trying to protect Devon, but that wasn't entirely the truth. And the truth wasn't something Kate entirely wanted to face.

She didn't want to admit that her stomach had fluttered when she came downstairs that night to find Brodie standing just inside the doorway. She didn't want to admit that when Brodie had pulled her close during their fight, her heart began to race, and her knees had weakened. Those feelings weren't normal for Kate. She didn't do schoolgirl crushes. She didn't believe in love at first sight, and being attracted to a woman was uncharted territory, and it was territory Kate had no *intention* of investigating.

Kate had planned her life like a roadmap with each milestone precisely plotted. Her career now fully underway, by mile marker 37, she would be married and have at least one child with another on the way, and by marker 40, she would have climbed the ladder to reach the rung of Detective Chief Inspector. It didn't matter Kate had no prospects on the horizon. It didn't matter that no man had *ever* held her interest for longer than a few months. It didn't matter that none had made her swoon like the women in the romance novels she used to read, because that was make-believe and Kate preferred real life. Real-life was about decisions. Real-life was about plans, and real-life was about controlling your own destiny. Kate controlled her fate. Kate made the decisions that shaped her life, and she liked the route she had chosen. She had designed it with all the signposts aimed in one direction, and Brodie Shaw wasn't on any of them. Brodie was a danger sign…and one that *had* to be avoided.

Be that as it may, when Kate left the station late on Friday, she planned to visit Calabria one last time. She hoped she'd find Brodie at her usual corner booth with the red and white checkered tablecloth, and after apologizing for her rudeness, Kate would walk away, and their paths would never cross again. Kate told herself she could do it. Kate told herself she was resolute. Kate told herself…it was simple.

***

"You know, the more I think about it, I think Gina's right."

"About what?" Brodie said, looking up from her worktable.

"I think Kate likes you," Devon said as she ripped open the packaging of another smart switch.

Brodie's eyes narrowed. "Did they have a sale on stupid pills recently?"

"I'm serious."

"You and Gina are both nutters," Brodie said, returning to her work. "The woman hates me."

"I don't think so, and I *know* you don't hate her."

"I never said I did."

Devon sauntered across the room and looked over Brodie's shoulder. "You fancy her, don't you?"

"I am *not* having this conversation, Devon."

Devon's smile pushed her cheeks out of the way. "Oh, wow. It must be serious if you're calling me Devon again."

Brodie tossed her pencil on the table, and leaning back in her chair, she huffed out a breath. "Would it help if I asked you politely to drop the subject?"

"Nope."

"Why?"

"Because you're my friend, and I've never seen you like this."

"Like what exactly?"

"Like totally enamored."

"Fuck you," Brodie said through a weak grin.

"But it's true, isn't it?" Devon said. "You're head over heels in *like* with my sister."

"Fuck you twice, *Cassidy*."

Devon's eyes crinkled at the corners. "That bad—eh?"

Brodie let out a long breath and ran her fingers through her hair. "I don't fall for straight women, Devon, but I can't get her out of my bloody head."

"Well, I think it's mutual if that helps. I mean, Jesus, she couldn't keep her eyes off you at dinner."

"Most likely, due to the fact she didn't want me there."

Devon shrugged. "All I know is that I've never seen Kate look at any man the way she was looking at you that night."

"Perhaps that's because she didn't want to *kill* them."

"I'm telling you," Devon said, draping her arm across Brodie's shoulders. "She likes you."

"You sound just like Gina, and speaking of Gina, how is she?"

Devon felt her cheeks flame. "Gina is fine and stop trying to change the subject."

Brodie didn't even try to contain her smile. "So, you and she are—"

"Yes, we are," Devon said, feeling as if the temperature in the room had risen a thousand degrees. "But we were talking about you and Kate, not Gina and me, so stop trying to avoid the subject."

"There *is* no subject," Brodie said, and jumping to her feet, she strode out of the room with Devon on her heels. When Brodie reached the front door, she whipped around. "And I already admitted I like her. Okay? What more do you want?"

"Have you called her?"

"Are you crazy?"

"Why?"

Brodie scrubbed her hand over her face. "Devon, listen very closely. She—is—*not*—interested."

"I can give you her number if you'd like."

"Jesus, bloody Christ. You're a fucking pain in the arse," Brodie said, tugging on her coat. "If there *were* to be *any* next moves made, your *sister* would have to be the one who makes them. And even with global warming, I doubt very seriously that hell is going to freeze over anytime soon, so drop it. I am going to dinner, and then I'm going to find some tall, attractive blonde who has *no* issues and *no* slapping reflex, and I'm going to shag her until she can't remember her name."

***

"I'm told the antipasto is good."

When Brodie arrived at Calabria a few minutes before, she had sailed in with her head held high, and her confidence soaring. She didn't date straight women. She wasn't a love-struck teenager. There were lots of other women in the world, and after dinner, Brodie had every intention of sampling one or maybe even two. So, when she heard Kate's voice and her libido awoke instantly, Brodie's temples pulsed. "Thanks for the suggestion," she said as she picked up her glass of wine. "But I already ordered dinner."

Kate stood by the booth, mentally trying to force Brodie to look in her direction, and when she didn't, Kate sighed. "Look...I just want to say I'm sorry for what I said to you at my house. I didn't have the right—"

"That's right. You didn't," Brodie snapped, finally meeting Kate's stare with one of her own. "I may not live by *your* principles, DI Monroe, but trust me, I do have some of my own."

"I was wrong."

"Yes, you were."

"Will you forgive me?"

"And why in the hell would I want to do that?"

Before Kate could answer, Angie appeared carrying a huge bowl of pasta and an overflowing basket of garlic bread. Watching as the food was placed in front of Brodie, Kate waited until Angie walked away before speaking. "So, I see you're in the mood to waddle tonight."

The last thing Brodie wanted to do was smile, and she waited long enough to get it under control before gazing up at Kate. "And what, DI Monroe, are *you* in the mood for?"

The words were filled with innuendo and challenge, and Kate's body reacted to both. She was being tested, goaded into either another argument or a peace treaty, and the choice was now hers to make. Seconds ticked by as she stood there in silence. This wasn't supposed to happen. This wasn't what she had planned. This was *supposed* to be simple, except it wasn't. It wasn't even close.

"Well," Kate said, offering Brodie a tentative smile. "I think I'd like to have dinner with you."

It was the last thing Brodie expected to hear. The chip on her shoulder was suddenly teetering, and it was all Brodie could do not to scream. How could she so easily forget or possibly forgive Kate for the belligerent attitude she had displayed at her house? The woman had been a downright bitch, yet in an instant, the past no longer mattered. The woman she thought she'd never see again was standing right in front of her. Brodie pulled in a breath, taking a few seconds before she found her voice. "Then, by all means, DI Monroe," she said, gesturing toward the other side of the booth. "Have a seat."

In record time, Kate took off her coat and slid into the booth. "If you don't mind, can we drop the formalities? My name is Kate."

"Then Kate it is," Brodie said, eyeing the woman.

Angie appeared out of nowhere with another place setting, and a minute later, Brodie was filling the smaller bowls with pasta.

"So, what are we having?" Kate said as Brodie placed a bowl in front of her.

"Cappellini Primavera," Brodie said as she uncorked the small bottle of Chianti and filled Kate's glass. "It's basically just pasta and vegetables in a light garlic sauce."

"It smells delicious, but isn't this much garlic going to hamper your evening?"

Brodie cocked her head to the side, and a rock formed in her belly. "In what way exactly?"

"Um…I couldn't help but notice that you're rather dressed up just to have dinner, or am I wrong?"

Kate was spot-on, and they both knew it. With her plans for the evening including a visit to The Loft, Brodie had chosen a pair of dark gray Armani trousers and a black silk shirt which was unbuttoned far enough to show not only a fair amount of cleavage but also a hint of the black lace bra she wore underneath. To complete her ensemble, Brodie had chosen her favorite cologne from her collection. Its aroma was spicy yet subtle, and after applying it to her pulse points, she had finished with a hair gel that carried with it just a hint of cinnamon. So, when it came to alluring scents, there wasn't much left on Brodie's body that didn't have one.

Brodie's feelings were immersed in the gray between black and white. Part of her was thrilled Kate was there, and the other part was still wary, still waiting for the boorish retort or judgmental assumptions to spill from Kate's lips. Picking up her utensils, Brodie began twirling pasta around her fork. "I don't know about you, but I'm starving. We should really eat before it gets cold."

The tone of Brodie's voice was flat, almost curt, and Kate decided to follow Brodie's lead. "Oh, all right," she said, picking up her fork.

In between bites, Kate tried not to stare, tried not to appreciate the beauty of the woman across the way. It wasn't easy. The seductive undertone of cinnamon and musk had made its way across the table and above eyes defined by a pencil-thin charcoal border, Brodie had used a palette of smoky gray eyeshadow. Her look was stunning. Her look was magnetic, and her look said it all. When it came to finding a partner for the evening, Brodie was *not* going to have an issue.

Brodie ate a few forkfuls of her dinner while she pondered Kate's question. She was intrigued as to why Kate would care where she was going after dinner, especially after the argument they'd had at Kate's house. Brodie picked up her wine, and as she took a drink, snippets of conversations she'd had with Devon and Gina crept into her head. A smile began to form as Brodie realized they could be right, and then just as quickly it faded. She wasn't going to waste another night pining for a woman she couldn't have.

"I'm going to a club later," Brodie said, placing her glass back on the table. "After all, it is Friday night."

"I thought so."

"Do you have a problem with that?" Brodie said, eyeing Kate.

"No." Kate picked up her wine and took a sip, hoping it would replace the moisture in her mouth that had somehow disappeared.

"You know, you could go with me."

Kate jerked back her head. "To a *lesbian* club?"

"Does that offend you?"

"No, it doesn't offend me. It would...it would just feel strange. That's all."

Brodie rested back in the booth. "Why?"

"Well, first, people would think I was your date."

"And I'm hideous, and you don't want to be seen with me," Brodie said, and picking up her silverware, she returned to eating. "That clears that up nicely, now, doesn't it?"

"Brodie, you're hardly hideous."

As soon as Kate saw Brodie flash a devastating grin, she plunged her fork back into her meal like it was trying to skitter across the table. Mentally, Kate kicked herself a few times for her off-the-cuff compliment before she realized she had nothing to be embarrassed about. It wasn't as if Brodie didn't know she was attractive.

Two mouthfuls later, Kate raised her eyes and saw Brodie had yet to lose her grin. "Look," Kate said, putting aside her fork. "I've been to a lesbian club. Okay? In case you've forgotten, my best friend owns one, and I've gone there a few times. It's just not a place I frequent."

"You do know it's more than just a hangout for lesbians, don't you?"

"You've been there?"

"Of course," Brodie said as she folded her napkin and placed it on the table. "It has a nice atmosphere and a great dance floor."

"You like to dance?"

"Does that surprise you?"

"Yes, I mean...I mean, no."

"Which is it?" Brodie said, studying Kate. "Or are you just confused because I wear trousers rather than skirts so therefore, I couldn't possibly like to dance? I'm much too butch for that?"

"You aren't butch, and that's not—"

"Well, I hate to break it to you, but there's no such thing as a stereotypical dyke," Brodie said, picking up her wine. "Some of us like to dance. Some of us have two left feet. Some of us ride motorcycles. Some of us prefer cars or trucks. Some of us lean toward looking masculine, and some of us don't. Just like heterosexuals, we come in a plethora of varieties. There is no one-size-fits-all."

"I know that."

Brodie tilted her head to the side. "Do you?"

Kate frowned. "Correct me if I'm wrong, but I get the feeling you're still a little peeved with me over what I said at my house, and I already apologized for it. I don't know what else I can do."

"Come to G-Street with me."

"What?"

"Better yet, why don't Gina and I meet you and Devon there one night for drinks? That way, you can see it's more than *just* a lesbian club."

Kate stared at the pasta-filled fork in front of her, and placing it in the bowl, she pushed it away. "You're dating Gina?"

"We went out to dinner. Is that a problem?"

It shouldn't have been a problem. It shouldn't have been an issue, and it shouldn't have mattered, but it did. It annoyed Kate that Brodie had wined and dined her best friend. It irritated her to think of them together, intimately conversing over a glass of Cabernet, and it infuriated Kate to know her dinner companion, who had made it *perfectly* clear she liked sex, could very well have bedded Gina.

Kate picked her wine and drained what remained. "Look, what you do in your personal life is none of my business," she said, placing the glass on the table. "If you want to go clubbing and date Gina, then do it. You don't need my permission."

"So, you're not interested?"

"I told you. *I'm straight!*"

Brodie pressed her lips together, looking down at the table for a moment to silence her mirth. "Kate," she said, finally raising her watery eyes. "I was talking about going to G-Street with Devon and Gina. I wasn't asking you for a date."

Kate felt her cheeks flame and snagging the bottle of Chianti from the table, she poured the remaining drops in her glass.

On the other side of the booth, Brodie tried to act nonchalant. Kate was flustered, and Brodie had a sneaking suspicion that her heated appearance had absolutely nothing to do with the wine she was drinking.

***

Kate giggled under her breath as they walked from the restaurant. As Brodie had warned, the pasta was delicious. It was also very filling, and when the brisk night air hit her, Kate welcomed the chill.

"Where'd you park?" Brodie said as she zipped up her leather jacket.

"Down the street a bit," Kate said as she noticed the blue Jaguar by the curb. "See you got a close spot again."

"I did, but I think I'm going to walk for a few, or should I say waddle?"

"You want some company?" Kate said, buttoning her coat.

In an instant, Brodie's mouth eased into an unconscious smile. It hadn't been an invitation. Then again, did it really matter? Inclining her head in the direction she wanted to go, they began walking down the block, both casually glancing in store windows as they meandered through oncoming foot traffic.

Kate was enjoying both the stroll and the company, and lost in her thoughts, it wasn't until she looked to her left when she realized Brodie had stopped at a window a few shops behind her. Kate backtracked and stood alongside Brodie as she peered through the glass. "Looking for anything in particular?"

"No, it's just a game I play."

Kate gave Brodie a side-eyed glance. "A game?"

"Yeah. I started it when I was a kid. Dad would take us into town, and while we were walking around, I'd look in the windows and try to decide if I could have anything on display, what would it be?"

Kate sized up what the jewelry store had to offer. "Okay, so what did you pick?"

"Those, I think," Brodie said, pointing to a pair of earrings in the front row.

Kate looked at the earrings and then at Brodie and then at the earrings again. Of all the finery presented on velvet cloth, the delicate pair of diamond and emerald dangly earrings didn't really seem to be Brodie's style. "Really?" Kate squeaked.

"What? You don't like them?"

"No. No, actually, I like them a lot. They just didn't strike me as something you'd wear."

"Who said they were for me?" Brodie said, and giving Kate a quick wink, Brodie continued down the street.

Kate shook her head, and sniggering to herself, she jogged to catch up to the long-legged woman who was now stopped in front of a men's clothing store. "Need a new tie, do you?"

"No. My father's birthday is coming up."

"And you're getting him a tie?"

"No, I'm just trying to get some ideas," Brodie said, turning away from the window. "Let's keep going."

They walked in silence until Brodie paused in front of a coffee shop. "Fancy a cup?"

"You know, that actually sounds wonderful," Kate said, and opening the door, she waved Brodie inside. "After you."

A few minutes later, with their hands wrapped around warm paper cups filled with dark roast, they continued their journey in the direction of Kate's car. When they came upon a donut shop, Kate's mouth dropped open when she saw Brodie stop at the window. "Oh, you cannot *possibly* be hungry."

"I'm not," Brodie said with a laugh. "But since you're a cop, you must like donuts. What's your favorite kind?"

"Now who's being stereotypical? Just because I'm a cop, doesn't mean I like donuts."

"Point taken," Brodie said with a quick dip of her head. "Now answer the question. What's your favorite?"

"I'm not sure I really have a favorite."

Brodie flicked her eyes toward the stars. "Everyone has a favorite, Kate."

"Oh, they do, do they? So what's yours?"

"Jam-filled," Brodie said without thinking. "Now, see how easy that was? So, what's yours?"

Kate's brow furrowed as she thought about the question. "I really don't know that I have—"

"Oh, come on, Kate! Think about it," Brodie said, waving her arms about. "Someone brings a dozen donuts to work, and you rush over, hoping and praying that you'll find…what?"

Tickled by Brodie's delivery, Kate's answer came quickly. "Chocolate frosted."

"There you go. I knew you had it in you." Brodie's smile was genuine and bright until she noticed Kate now had a set of keys in her hand. A second later, the lights of a nearby car flashed, and Brodie's smile faded.

"Well, this is me," Kate said, turning to Brodie.

"So it is," Brodie saying, glancing at the subcompact. "Thanks for paying for dinner, by the way. I guess that means we're even."

"I guess so," Kate said as she moved to the driver's door and opened it. "Good night, Brodie. Enjoy your evening."

Kate slipped behind the wheel, and closing the door, she started the engine. She was in the process of checking her mirrors when she heard a tap on the passenger side window, and seeing Brodie looking through the glass, Kate rolled the window down. "What's up?"

"I wanted you to have this," Brodie said, handing Kate one of her business cards. "It has my office and mobile numbers on it, just in case you ever want company for dinner other than on a Friday night." Seeing that Kate was staring at the card as if she were holding a king cobra, Brodie snorted. "Look, we've already had this conversation. You're straight, and you're not interested. I get that. All I'm suggesting is that *if* you ever decide you don't want to cook, and it's a day *other* than Friday, feel free to give me a call. No strings. No assumptions. No expectations. Okay?"

Kate relaxed in her seat. "All right," she said, opening her handbag to slip the card inside. "I just may do that. Thanks."

"Right then," Brodie said, tapping on the roof of the car. "Off you go, and drive carefully."

The window rolled up and standing straight, Brodie watched until the car faded from view. She glanced at her watch and walked back to her car, grinning at the donut shop and jewelry store as she moseyed by. Climbing into her car, Brodie started the engine, and drumming her fingers on the steering wheel, she thought about the night while she waited for traffic to clear. It was a good night. A night of casual. A night of friendship. A night like none she could ever remember, and Brodie sighed as she pulled away from the curb and headed home. The idea of visiting The Loft and shagging a stranger no longer held her interest.

***

She arched her back, gasping as she pushed against her lover's mouth, and as that marvelous tongue lapped against her folds, she felt two fingers push inside.

"Oh God. Don't stop," Devon cried out as she rocked against Gina's hand. "Don't you *dare* stop."

Delighted by Devon's demand, Gina continued the sensual intrusion. Her strokes were deep and calculated, hard one second and soft the next, and with each push, Devon was losing more and more control.

Devon craved release, and each time Gina would slow her exploration, Devon would rock harder until she finally pleaded, "Oh Jesus...baby...oh please..."

Gina increased the tempo again, marveling at the amount of want coating her fingers. She lowered her mouth and spreading open the folds, she took several long licks before she placed her mouth over Devon's clit and began flicking it with her tongue.

Devon knew release would soon be hers, and she grabbed Gina by the hair, keeping her in place between her legs until her climax took her, and take her it did. Waves of splendor washed over her, and as her inner walls pulsated and unintelligible words fell from her lips, Devon relinquished herself to the sweetest of deaths.

Gina waited while Devon stilled, and sitting back, she gazed at the beautiful woman lying in front of her. Since the night they left G-Street together, they had spent every available minute in each other's arms, passing on dinner dates and dancing for lovemaking and whispers.

If it had been up to Devon, they would have consummated their relationship in Gina's office six days before, but after all the years of yearning and all the years of dreaming, Gina wouldn't hear of it. She wanted it to be special. She wanted it to be a night to remember for as long as they both shall live, except after Gina closed up the club in the wee hours of Saturday morning, and they returned to her flat, sixteen years of pent-up desire and hidden emotions let loose. And as Gina looked around, it was abundantly clear the honeymoon was still going strong.

Their clothes and shoes were strewn all over the lounge, and more than one piece of furniture had been dislodged from its original position. Magazines, once stacked neatly on the coffee table, were now scattered on the floor, and the only thing saving the lamp on the end table from toppling over was the weight of its base.

Gina got to her feet, and grabbing the throw draped over a nearby chair, she wrapped herself in its warmth and then gazed at the naked woman on her sofa. Devon's skin still glistened with sweat, and the tips of her nipples had yet to calm, the sight of which caused Gina's core to pulse again.

"You okay?"

Gina locked eyes with Devon. "Yeah. Why?"

"You looked far away."

"I was thinking about this past week…and us."

"Us?" Devon said, scrambling off the sofa. "Is something wrong?"

"Oh, baby, no," Gina said, lightly touching Devon's face. "I'm totally in love with you. Don't you know that?"

Devon's smile lit up the room. "I love you, too," she said, leaning in for a kiss. "So, so much."

Their lips met in a feathery kiss, and the whisper-light contact was enough for Devon's libido to ignite again, but when she went to deepen the kiss, Gina pulled away. Worry lines surfaced on Devon's face. "Okay. What's going on with you? There's obviously something—"

"We need to tell Kate."

"Huh?"

"You heard me. We need to tell Kate, Devon. We can't keep hiding this from her. It's going to make things worse."

Devon nibbled on her lip. It was a subject they had avoided almost as much as they had avoided Kate. Devon had turned down a lunch invitation on Tuesday, and Gina had done the same on Thursday, and it had to stop. "You're right," Devon said, tiny lines appearing around her eyes. "And you know what?"

"What?"

"I vote *you* tell her," Devon said, tittering like a little girl as she dashed past Gina.

Gina rushed to follow. "Why me?" she said, stepping into the bedroom. "She's your sister."

"Yeah, but she's your best friend," Devon said, opening the wardrobe.

"But she's less likely to kill you than me."

"Do you really think she'll be that mad?"

"Honey," Gina said, folding her arms. "I promised Kate years ago I'd never try anything with you. When she finds out about this, about *us*, she's going to go ballistic."

"She'll understand," Devon said, putting on a robe. "It's not like you converted me or something." When Devon heard Gina sigh, she looked over at her. "What's wrong?"

"I wish it had been me," Gina said, staring at the floor. "I wish I was your first."

Devon went over and tipped Gina's face up. "If I had known you felt about me the way I felt about you, you would have been, but I never had a clue."

Gina sighed again. "And there's a good reason for that, Devon. Seriously, Kate may have a really tough time with this."

"So what do you suggest we do? Keep it a secret?"

"Not on your life," Gina said, brushing her lips over Devon's. "We just need to choose the right time to tell her...and have an escape plan in place."

Chapter Six

Even the fact Frank Daggett was returning from his holiday could not dampen Kate's mood when she walked into the station on Monday morning. She had spent her weekend sequestered in her house due to a winter storm that brought a mixture of rain, snow, and blustery wind to most of the United Kingdom, and it was just what Kate needed. The gray skies and dreary weather took away every excuse Kate could come up with to get out of the house, and instead, she spent the weekend catching up on everything a workaholic lets slide. She cleaned and washed, polished and vacuumed, and when the sun finally set, Kate picked up a good book and relaxed the night away. She sipped dark red vintages and listened to Bach on the stereo, and when the book no longer held her interest, her thoughts returned to Brodie Shaw.

Kate had never enjoyed walking down a crowded street until Friday night. Window shopping had always seemed pointless until a game had been introduced, and when only one trinket caught her eye in a jewelry store display and Brodie chose the same one, Kate was taken aback. She couldn't deny the chemistry that existed between them no matter how hard she tried, but how could anyone know her that well so quickly? And why did Kate like it?

When Kate got to her desk, she found a beet-faced Frank Daggett glaring back at her. "Something wrong?" she said as she dropped her handbag in a drawer.

"Where you do you get off closing cases when I'm not here?"

Kate plopped into her chair and fought to keep a straight face. "Unless they changed something in the rule book, Frank, I don't need your permission to close a case when it's been solved."

"I've got seniority, or did you forget that?"

"Again, seniority or not, I don't need your permission. If you have a problem with how I do my job, then take it up with the Chief Inspector, who, by the way, reviewed those cases before I closed them. He didn't see a problem. I didn't see a problem, so if you *think* there's a problem, his office is right over there," Kate said, pointing across the room.

"I know where it is," Frank growled, and as he stood up, he leaned in close. "And I wouldn't get too comfortable if I were you. After I get done talking to him, you'll be lucky to still have a job."

As Kate knew it would, *nothing* happened. Behind the closed doors of a glassed-in office, she watched as Frank waved his arms in the air as if swatting a squadron of flies, and then he stomped a few invisible grapes until he finally yanked the door open and marched out. Defeat was not an easy pill to swallow, and Frank had no intention of swallowing *anything* until he made sure everyone in the station knew his displeasure. He proceeded to spout diatribes about Kate's inability to follow proper police procedures to everyone who would listen and several who didn't but, trapped in corners of the station, and unable to escape, they were forced to feign interest. The good old boys hung on every word, tutting and pontificating annoyance about the up-and-coming detectives half their age, and the demonstration of childishness continued even after Kate and Frank left the station. Frank griped and grumbled for four days, and between his rants, raves, and lack of driving etiquette, by the end of the week, Kate was feeling more than a bit frazzled, yet when she left the station Friday night, her smile reappeared. Kate checked her mirrors and pulling out of the parking lot, she headed toward Calabria.

***

"This is becoming a standing date, isn't it?"

Brodie stepped out of her bathroom and sent the woman sitting at her drafting table a cursory glance. "It's not a date, and don't you have someplace better to be?"

"Gina's working, and since you forgot to mention that two of your clients want home theaters *and* whole-house audio systems, either I get this done tonight or come Monday, you won't have a quote to give them."

"On second thought, stay as long as you'd like." Brodie sat on the edge of her bed and tugged on a pair of black, ankle-high suede boots.

"And now that we've got *that* out of the way, answer the question."

"I already did," Brodie said, getting to her feet. "It's not like she calls me. She just shows up, and we have dinner. That's all."

"Wait," Devon said, shaking her head. "She doesn't call you?"

"Nope."

"And you don't call her?"

"I don't have her number."

"*What?*" Devon said, rocking back on the chair. "What do you mean you don't have her number?"

"I never asked for it, and she's never offered," Brodie said as she made her way to her dresser.

"Does she have yours?"

"Um...yeah, but she's never called."

"Seriously?" Devon squeaked.

Brodie grinned as she fastened her watch. "Yes, Devon. Seriously."

"And how many Friday night dinners have there been?"

"Four, not including tonight," Brodie said as she left the room.

Devon hopped off the tall drafting chair, catching up to Brodie in the kitchen. "And then you go to a club, and she goes home?"

Brodie shuffled through some mail on the counter, refusing to acknowledge the woman who was currently tilting her head as if the world had slipped off its axis.

"Why are you ignoring me?" Devon said, crossing her arms. "You *are* going to the clubs—right?"

"I can't find my bloody keys," Brodie said, pushing past Devon. "Have you seen them?"

Devon knew a brush-off when she saw one, and it only took a minute of watching Brodie rearrange the pillows on the sofa to figure out why. "Oh my, God!" Devon said, bringing her hands to her cheeks. "You're not dating, are you?"

Brodie shot Devon a look as she stood straight. "I don't *date*," she said, heading back to the kitchen. "You know that."

"Fine," Devon said, rolling her eyes. "You can call it whatever you want, but whatever it is, you're not doing it. Are you?"

"I can't find my fucking keys," Brodie muttered, opening a few drawers.

"Is Kate the only woman you're seeing?"

"Where in the hell are my bloody—"

Devon grabbed Brodie by the arm and spun her around. "Is *Kate* the only woman you're seeing?"

"I'm not *seeing* Kate," Brodie said, giving Devon a dirty look. "We have dinner. That's all."

When Brodie tried to walk away, Devon blocked her path. "You know what I'm asking, so stop being coy and answer the question."

"Why should I?" Brodie said, taking a step backward. "It's no business of yours, so just drop it."

"This is my sister we're talking about, and I have a right to know if you've fallen for her."

"Oh yeah?" Brodie said, giving Devon the once over. "Just like she has the right to know you're shagging Gina?"

Devon hung her head. "Touché."

"Sorry," Brodie said, frowning. "That was a bit below the belt."

"Yes, it was, but you made your point."

"Look, Kate loves you, and she loves Gina, and I'm sure she'll be okay with this eventually."

"You think so?" Devon said, raising her eyes.

"Sure," Brodie said, shrugging. "Just give her ten or twenty years, and she'll come around."

"Bitch," Devon said, playfully slapping Brodie's arm.

Brodie laughed and gave Devon a quick hug. "And now, if you're done interrogating me, I really need to find my keys, or I'm going to be late."

Devon pressed her lips together and sashaying into the dining room, she grabbed the set of keys off the table. Returning to Brodie, she dropped them in her hand. "There you go."

"You could have told me, you know?"

"Where's the fun in that?"

With a huff, Brodie pocketed her keys and headed for the door. "Oh, by the way," she said as she put on her coat. "You did tell Gina about next weekend, didn't you?"

"Yeah, she knows about it."

"Great," Brodie said, opening the door. "Okay, so I'll see you when I see you."

"Wait a second," Devon said, making her way over to Brodie.

"What's up?"

"Look, you know Gina and I both think Kate likes you more than just as a friend, but she's always been very directional in her life. She's always had a plan—"

"And I'm not a part of it. Is that what you're saying?

"I just don't want you to get hurt," Devon said, touching Brodie on the sleeve.

"Devon, you don't need to worry about that. Kate's never done anything that would make me believe she wants more out of our relationship than friendship, and I've accepted that."

"I just don't want to lose you as a friend if things go south."

Brodie's mouth curved with tenderness, and leaning down, she placed a light kiss on Devon's cheek. "That's not going to happen. Trust me, okay? I'm smart enough to know that sooner or later, some bloke is going to come along, and Kate will cease to need me as her Friday night dinner companion. But, until that happens, I'm going to enjoy our time together."

"And if that happens?"

"*When* that happens, I'll move on, simple as that. I won't fall apart or jump off a bridge or anything. I'm a big girl, Devon. No need to worry about me."

***

Brodie stood at the bar and took a sip of her scotch. She hissed at the taste for the flavor was foul tonight, just like her mood. Her first stop had been The Loft, but spotting a tall blonde with an appetite for bruises and bites, Brodie left before ordering a drink and headed to Outskirts.

Upscale and trendy, Outskirts was frequented by those making a name for themselves in business, finance, and technology, apparent by the designer clothes, high-end footwear, and Rolexes wrapped around almost every wrist. Although first opened as a gay and lesbian nightclub, the word soon spread that Outskirts was the place to be and in no time at all its clientele became a mixture of gay, straight, and those somewhere in between.

The club was housed in a converted warehouse, and the interior was ultra-modern, chic, and massive. The owners, knowing their return on investment would be based on the amount of alcohol they sold, had designed the club with that in mind. Instead of offering only one bar where patrons would clamber to buy their drinks, Outskirts had three, and each had a slightly different atmosphere than the other two.

The largest, centered in the club, was rectangular with no seating surrounding it. Typically the first stop for those entering the club, drinks came fast and furious to all who wanted to get a jump-start on the evening. To the left and right of that bar were the dance floors, each covered in polished, black laminate flooring. Dozens of small droplights were scattered overhead and holding bulbs of every color, as the music blaring from the speakers changed, so did the lighting.

In the far corners of the club were the other two liquor stations. Slightly smaller than the first, they were surrounded by stools where those weary from dancing could rest between songs. High and low-top tables were scattered in every available space, and on a Friday night, few were empty.

Brodie scanned the crowd with disinterest. She had started her evening in Calabria, and for two hours, she watched as people came and went through a door with a bell hanging above it. Each time Brodie heard it ring, she'd look up, straightening her backbone and displaying her most dazzling of smiles, but within seconds, Brodie's shoulders would slump just like her smile. She had nursed a glass of wine for the first hour and finished off three cups of coffee during the second before storming out of the restaurant with her head held high. This wasn't who she was. This wasn't who she wanted to be, and *this* was over.

Brodie had planned to throw herself back into the nightlife of London and philander her way through the evening, but as she took another taste of her scotch, its flavor revolted her almost as much as her intentions. Setting the glass on the bar, Brodie pushed it away and strode toward the exit. She weaved her way through the crowd, sidestepping both undulating, lithe dancers and some who appeared as if they were convulsing, and when she spotted an opening in the throng, Brodie rushed through it. A second later, she came to an abrupt stop. The sea of people began closing in on her like a pandemic making its way across a continent, but Brodie stood her ground. Open-mouthed, she remained stock-still and watched as Kate deftly and slowly maneuvered her way across the dance floor.

"Hiya, Brodie," Kate said, raising her voice above the music.

"What are you doing?" Brodie shouted. "How'd you find me?"

"I wanted to apologize for missing dinner. I got called out on a case, and it took longer than I thought. I tried to ring you, but it went straight to voice mail."

Brodie pulled her mobile out and tapped on the screen. "Shit," she said, pressing the button on the side before returning it to her pocket. "I had a meeting today and forgot to turn it back on. Sorry."

The synthesized percussion of the electronic dance music pumping out of the speakers grew louder as the next song began, and pointing to her ears, Kate shook her head in response.

Brodie motioned for Kate to follow her, and when they reached one of the darkened corners, the volume of the music dropped dramatically.

"Wow. This is much better," Kate said, looking around.

"There are no speakers back here," Brodie said. "I figured it would be better than trying to scream over the music."

"Yes, it is."

Out of the corner of her eye, Brodie saw a couple at a nearby high-top leaving to return to the dance floor, and taking three quick steps, she snagged the table and waved Kate over. "Will this work for you?"

"Absolutely," Kate said, climbing onto the chair.

"So, can I buy you a drink?"

"After the week I've had, you might be buying me more than one."

"Doable," Brodie said, grinning. "I'll be right back."

As soon as Brodie walked away, Kate let out a long breath. Unable to reach the woman by phone, once she was done with the burglary call, Kate didn't wait for Frank to drive her back to the station. Instead, she jumped into a cab and headed to Calabria only to find Brodie had already left. Single-minded, Kate hailed another taxi and gave instructions to the driver to take her to every lesbian club in the area, and forty minutes later, Kate spotted Brodie's car parked down the block from Outskirts. The lengthy queue was the least of Kate's worries, and striding to the front, she showed her warrant card to the muscled men at the entrance, and their gold-capped teeth lit up the darkness as they opened the door to allow her inside.

The club was crowded and deafening. The dance floors overflowed with people gyrating to the latest in electronic hip-hop blasting from the speakers while others, wearing fragrances meant to attract, moved through the club in search of a partner for the night or perhaps for life. The air was thick with the smell of alcohol and cologne, and to even the most unsuspecting visitor, it was clear that the clientele of Outskirts was as varied as the aromas filling the air.

Kate stood like a statue just inside the entrance. What was she doing there? Why had she found it necessary to hunt Brodie down and apologize for missing a date that wasn't? Reality hit home when Kate looked out across the sea of people enjoying the evening with their significant others. She wasn't there to ask for forgiveness or offer explanations because she'd done that in the message she'd left on Brodie's voice mail, and she wasn't there for dinner for that's not what the club offered. Kate was there because she couldn't bear the thought of waiting another week to see Brodie.

Kate took a quick step backward, the truth forcing the air from her lungs. Her first thought was to run, to escape into the night, and allow her message to explain her absence, but then the crowd parted, and when she saw Brodie, Kate became a moth to a flame. Her eyes met those of dark brown, and the empty feeling in the pit of Kate's stomach was gone, replaced by a tickling of butterflies and an irrepressible smile.

"What's the smile about?" Brodie said, placing two glasses of Chardonnay on the table.

Kate broke out of her thoughts with a jerk. "Oh, um…nothing," she said, looking around. "This place is amazing. That's all."

"Yes, it is, although it can be a bit overwhelming at times."

"I can see that." Kate picked up her wine, and while she took a sip, she noticed more than a few straight couples nearby. "But I thought this was a gay club," she said, looking in their direction as she returned her glass to the table.

"It is, except gays don't discriminate like straights do," Brodie said, her teeth gleaming in her grin. "And when word got out about the dance floors and the bars, the well-to-do began flocking here in droves. It's amazing how non-discriminatory people can become when they want to have a good time."

"So it doesn't bother you?"

"Why would it? There are plenty of women to go around, and those walking in without blokes on their arms aren't here looking for men. Trust me. I know," Brodie said, and picking up her wine, she took a sip.

Kate shifted in her seat, and snatching up her Chardonnay, she emptied half the glass. The light-bodied wine went down smoothly, and if Kate had wanted to appreciate the flavor, she would have noticed the hint of apple and pear on her palate, but she didn't. She did, however, see an attractive woman wearing an incredibly form-fitting little black dress, making a beeline for their table.

"Well, as I live and breathe! How the hell are you doing, stud?"

Brodie's eyes flew open wide, and hurrying to set her glass down, she leapt to her feet. "Oh my, God," she said, throwing her arms around the woman. "What the world are you doing here?"

"I came into town Wednesday on business, and I wasn't about to turn around and head back to Texas without visiting a few clubs."

Brodie loosened her grip and holding the woman at arm's length, her eyes casually traveled over the woman's body. "You look great. You haven't changed a bit."

"Thanks," she said before looking at Kate. "Who's your friend?"

"Oh, Christ, where are my manners?" Brodie said, glancing between the two women. "Kate Monroe, meet Harper Adams, an old friend of mine."

"I'll forget you said old," Harper said with a chuckle as she held out her hand. "Pleasure to meet you, Kate."

Kate extended her hand, forcing a smile as she eyed the woman. Slightly shorter than Brodie and appearing to be in her late forties, Harper's age hadn't affected her beauty. Her skin was porcelain, and the few wrinkles that did exist seemed to add depth to her good looks. Her short, vibrant red hair was cut in a wispy bob and wearing a knit dress that clung to every curve, even though Harper was older than most in the room, there was no doubt in Kate's mind that the woman could pull with the best of them...and Harper Adams knew it.

No sooner had the handshake ended when Kate saw Harper lean into Brodie. She whispered something in Brodie's ear, her face brightening as she played with the gray hair at Brodie's temples, and suddenly Kate felt like a third wheel. Out of place and out of her element in a lesbian club, Kate was quickly growing annoyed at the situation, the interruption, and the fact that it was *crystal* clear that Harper Adams had once pulled Brodie Shaw.

Kate pushed her frustration aside and decided to get the most obvious question out of the way. "So, how do you two know each other?"

"Brodie and I go way back," Harper said, nudging Brodie. "Don't we, stud?"

It was all Kate could do not to curl her lip. Knowing Brodie was a player was one thing, but having it made blatantly clear by a stacked redhead in a skin-tight dress was quite another. This wasn't how she had planned to spend her Friday night, and Kate's head began to pound.

Brodie was enjoying the unexpected reunion, and it showed on her face, but as she glanced back and forth between the two women, her expression began to waver. Kate's jaw was clenched, and whenever she looked in Harper's direction, the look wasn't a look—it was a cold, hard stare. Harper, on the other hand, was displaying her biggest Texas smile, content in dancing her fingers down Brodie's arm or lightly touching her hand, and the signals were unmistakable. Brodie had seen them before. Harper was laying claim to her…whether Kate liked it or not.

A decade before, while working her way up the ladder in the advertising business, Harper Adams had been transferred to her company's office in London. Housed in the same building where Brodie worked, it wasn't long before the two women met and fell into a very comfortable, lustful relationship. Since neither wanted anything long-term, their relationship was based on parties, drinking, and sex, and they spent several years simply enjoying each other's company. But truth be known, it was in the bedroom where their relationship thrived. Healthy, adventurous, and ten years older than Brodie, Harper had several more notches in her belt than her younger counterpart, and she was more than willing to share her knowledge. And share it, she did.

Before meeting Harper, Brodie wasn't into sex toys or shags in the loo. She wasn't into loud parties, dancing until midnight, and clubs like The Loft, but the tall Texan had changed all that. Harper was the teacher, and Brodie was the student, and before long, shagging in a bathroom, or wearing a harness to please her lover, became commonplace. Although they adored each other, love had never entered the equation. During the five years she worked and lived in London, Harper dated several women, as did Brodie, but every few weeks, one would call the other, and they'd spend a few days honing their skills. It was a perfect partnership on the most basic of levels.

Harper had arrived in London in the wee hours of Wednesday morning, and after completing her work in record time, she went out and purchased the skimpiest, sexiest black dress she could find. After spraying on what she knew was Brodie's favorite perfume, Harper began making the rounds. Friday nights had always been Brodie's club night, giving her two days to recover from whatever or *whom*ever she got into, so Harper wasted no time in traveling to all their usual haunts in search of an old lover with skills second to none.

By the time she reached Outskirts, Harper had thought her night would end in the arms of a stranger until she saw Brodie sitting at a high-top. Her blood heated and her body pulsed, and for a good reason. With what Harper had in mind, they would *both* need the weekend to recover.

The rakish glint Brodie saw in Harper's eyes was undeniable. It was a silent suggestion to visit the loo or find an empty corner, car, or hotel. Demanding, possessive, and hungry, it was filled with promises of a night without sleep, and the thought gave Brodie pause. It had been a long time since she'd spent an entire evening with a woman, preferring quick wham-bam-thank-you-ma'ams, over nights that turned into mornings, and to make matters worse, even those had come to an end since she'd met Kate. Brodie knew she only had to return Harper's attention with some of her own, and the drought would come to an end, but when she looked at Kate, and their eyes met, the thought of spending the night with Harper lost its appeal.

Harper's posture sagged just a smidge, watching as the two women appeared to be mesmerized by the other. If she had targeted another that night, some random woman she didn't know or care about, Harper would have turned up the charm and gone back to her hotel with her conquest, except Brodie wasn't a trophy. She was a friend and one who owned more of Harper's heart then she cared to admit. Even though before she had reached the table, Harper knew Brodie wasn't alone, she believed the battle had already been won. Attractive as Kate was, Harper had come up against stronger competition in the looks department, and she had walked away the victor, but this wasn't about looks or even history. This was about chemistry, and in that department, it was quite apparent that Kate Monroe owned Brodie's periodic table.

Harper knew her plans for the evening had now changed, but she wasn't yet willing to bid farewell to her old friend. Noticing the wide-bowled stemware on the high-top, she said, "Since when do you drink wine, stud?"

Brodie moved her focus from Kate back to Harper. "People change, Harper."

"Yes, I can see that," Harper said, giving Kate a cursory look. "But before I go on the prowl, how about buying us a round...for old times?"

"That I can do," Brodie said, picking up the empty glasses. "Be right back."

Kate hadn't missed the lack of ear-splitting music until Brodie walked away, leaving her alone with the exquisite Harper Adams in a deafening bubble of silence. After several excruciatingly awkward seconds passed without a word between them, Kate blurted, "So...you in town for long?"

Harper smiled. "Don't worry. I'm leaving Sunday morning."

"Worry?"

"Meaning, I'm not going to try to steal Brodie away from you."

Kate sat straighter in her seat. "Oh...um...Brodie isn't my girlfriend. We're just friends."

Harper's eyes crinkled at the corners, but before she could speak, Brodie returned with their drinks.

"Here you go," she said, placing a small tray holding six shot glasses on the table. "I'm assuming you still drink tequila—yes?"

"For breakfast, lunch, and dinner, stud," Harper said, and taking a glass, she downed it in one gulp.

It was a nickname Harper had given her over one incredibly voracious weekend, and hearing it again, a slight blush crept across Brodie's cheeks, thinking back to those two days. A split-second later, Brodie remembered something else. Alcohol loosened Harper's lips, and if the Texan decided to reminisce, tonight would be the last night Brodie would *ever* see Kate. Brodie wracked her brain, trying to come up with a plausible reason to get Harper alone when Harper came to her rescue.

"How about a dance for old times?" Harper said, tugging on Brodie's sleeve. "What do you say?"

Kate smiled weakly when Brodie looked in her direction. "Go ahead. I'll be fine."

"Are you sure?"

"Yes, of course," Kate said, eyeing the tray of tequila. "It sounds like you haven't seen each other in years so, go ahead. Enjoy yourself."

Brodie took Harper's hand. "Okay, thanks. We won't be long. I promise."

Kate watched as they disappeared into the crowd, and a few seconds passed before she spotted them on the dance floor, moving together as if they were Siamese twins joined at the pelvis. Kate downed the contents of one of the shot glasses, and hissing at the burn, she slammed the glass on the table.

Kate had come to the club to see Brodie, to talk to her, and to enjoy another Friday night in her company. She hadn't planned for the evening to be interrupted by an old flame, and as she watched the two women move as one, all Kate wanted to do was go over and interrupt their reunion. She didn't like the casual touches. She hated the way they moved in perfect unison. She loathed the fact they had once shared a bed together, and if Harper called Brodie 'stud' one more time, Kate would not be held accountable for her actions. Eyeballing the drinks in front of her, Kate picked up the next.

"I like your friend. She's cute," Harper said, glancing over at Kate.

"Yes, she is."

"Do you think she'd be interested in a little get-together later on?"

Brodie scowled. "She's straight, Harper."

"So was that one in Madrid," Harper said, snickering. "But that didn't stop us, now did it?"

"Kate's not like that."

"How do you know? Threesomes can be fun, or have you forgotten?"

Brodie's expression darkened even further. "No, I haven't forgotten, but like I told you, Kate's straight so rein in your bloody hormones, Harper."

"Relax," Harper said with a laugh. "I'm just playing with you. I'll be leaving after this dance."

"What? Why?"

"Because I know when I'm not wanted."

It was Brodie's turn to laugh. "Harper, it's not like that. Kate and I are just friends."

"From where I come from, we call that bullshit."

"Well, it doesn't matter what you think it's called, because I'm telling you, she and I are just friends."

Harper studied Brodie, waiting while the song faded and another began. The tempo of the next was slow, and the thunder of the electronic hip-hop was replaced by the synthesized strings of a modern-day love song. Pulling Brodie into her arms, as they continued to move to the music, Harper whispered in Brodie's ear, "Honey, you and Kate may only be friends, but don't think for one minute I believe you don't want more. So, stop trying to convince me. It's boring, and you have *never* been boring."

Brodie's lack of response signaled she was done with the conversation, so Harper took the time to scan the room for her next victim. More than once, her eyes traveled to Kate, and each time, Harper found the woman staring back at her.

Smiling, Harper whispered in Brodie's ear again. "If she's so straight, why can't she take her eyes off of us?"

Brodie went to turn in Kate's direction only to have Harper pull her back around. "Don't look, you idiot."

"Is she really watching us?"

Harper burst into giggles, the charismatic Brodie Shaw sounding more like a love-struck teenager than a woman who could pull anyone in the room. "Oh, my God," she said. "You've got it bad, don't you?"

Brodie's jaw tightened. "I swear to God if you're winding me up..."

"I'm not."

"Well, is she looking at us, or isn't she?"

"No, she's looking at *you* and has been ever since we stepped foot out here," Harper said, and placing her hands on Brodie's ass, Harper pulled her even closer.

"What the hell are you doing?" Brodie said, trying to back away.

"Relax, stud. I'm just proving a point."

"And what point would that be?"

Harper quickly glanced over at Kate before looking Brodie in the eye. "First, I want you to kiss me."

"No."

"Why not? If Kate thinks of you only as a friend, why would it matter?"

"It matters to me, Harper. That's all you need to know."

Harper's eyes misted over, and letting out a long breath, she ran her finger down Brodie's cheek. "Honey, you and I have been through a lot together. We've had great laughs and unbelievable sex, but seeing the way you look at Kate, and the way she looks at you, well, that tells me that while you and I will always, *always* remain friends, we will never again be lovers. So, do your old friend a favor and kiss me like you mean it…for old time's sake."

Brodie stared Harper squarely in the eye, expecting to see a snippet of naughtiness stirring in the pale green gazing back at her. Instead, all she saw was sincerity and truth. Harper wasn't playing games. She was merely saying goodbye, and denying her request was impossible. Leaning in, Brodie pressed her lips against Harper's. The kiss was warm, and it was wet, a silent, tender farewell between two women who had taught each other so much.

When they came up for air, Harper's eyes twinkled, and it had nothing to do with the lights shining down on them. "And now, you'd best skedaddle back to Kate because I think she's going to need your help."

"What are you talking about?" Brodie said as she tried to look in Kate's direction. Blocked by the dancers, she turned back to Harper. "Is someone bothering her?"

"No, but how many shots did you bring to the table?"

"Six. Why?"

"And I drank one—right?"

"Yeah. So?"

"Because since we've been out here, your *friend* emptied the other five, and the bartender just brought over another tray."

Chapter Seven

Kate relished the warmth and weight of the heavy duvet over her. She also knew it didn't belong to her. It smelled of vanilla, a scent Kate liked but didn't have in her collection, and the pillowcase against her cheek was softer than any she owned. She licked her lips, trying to replace the moisture sucked away by too much alcohol, and then the taste of tequila invaded her mouth. It was all Kate could do not to hurl.

One minute passed and then another before Kate dared to open her eyes. Between the foulness of the tequila and the pounding in her head, if rays of sunlight were streaming into the room, she would hit the trifecta and lose what little she had in her stomach. Kate cautiously opened her eyes, and she let out the breath she'd been holding. The drapes were closed, and while there was some subdued lighting coming from the other side of the room, its wattage didn't cause Kate's skull to split.

Kate saw a glass of water within reach on the nightstand and picking it up, she took a few sips. When her stomach didn't protest, she drank a little more before gingerly sitting up. The sound of running water made its way through the fog of Kate's hangover, and she looked in the direction of the muted lighting across the room. Kate squinted through the dimness, blinking more than once until her eyes finally focused, and when they did, they opened wide. The light was coming from a wall, or rather *through* a wall made entirely of glass block. The rippled surface made it impossible to see what was on the other side, but it didn't take a detective to figure it out. When Kate heard the water stop, she adjusted a few pillows behind her back and resting against them, she took an occasional sip of water while she kept her eyes locked on the doorway cut into the glass.

A few minutes later, dressed in track pants and a long-sleeved T-shirt, Brodie emerged from the bathroom and smiled when she saw Kate staring back at her. "Good morning. How are you feeling?"

"Confused, embarrassed, and hungover if you must know the truth."

"I can understand the hungover part. I see you found the water."

"Yes, thank you," Kate said through a weak grin. "Where am I?"

"My place."

"Can I ask why you didn't take me back to mine?"

"Because you were too drunk to be left alone," Brodie said, approaching the bed. "But don't worry. I didn't play dress-up or anything. I took off your shoes and your jacket and put you to bed."

"And Harper?"

"I poured her into a taxi and sent her back to her hotel. I doubt she'll see the light of day until her flight on Sunday."

"So, you're not going to see her again?" Kate said, placing the glass back on the nightstand.

"No, I don't think so," Brodie said. "Can you handle a bit more light?"

"I think so."

Brodie ran her fingers down the wooden post of the headboard, and when they traveled over the contacts bored into it, the lamps on both nightstands sprang to life. "That's a little better."

"It's also very cool."

"They're touch-controlled," Brodie said, walking to the door. "And now that you can see your way around, I'm going to fix us something to eat. That is if you think you can handle some food."

Kate glanced at the water, placing her hand on her belly as she thought about the question. "Actually, I think I can."

"Good," Brodie said, heading out of the room. "Oh, and I put some things for you in the bathroom in case you want to get cleaned up. Okay?"

"Yeah. Thanks."

"No problem."

Kate took a minute to drink what remained in the glass before tossing aside the duvet and dangling her legs over the side of the bed. She smiled to herself when her feet didn't touch the floor, and sliding off the mattress, Kate stood up. The room began to spin, and Kate, holding onto the bedcovers, waited until the carousel came to a complete and full stop before shuffling to the bathroom.

The feeling of being at a carnival returned as soon as Kate stepped through the opening in the glass black. The walls of the passageway were curved, and slowly following the short but winding path, she found herself standing in a spacious and brightly lit bathroom. Kate squeezed her eyes closed, allowing a few seconds to pass before she dared to open them again, and when she did, so did her mouth.

Sunlight streamed in through a sizable glass block window on the far wall, and below it was a whirlpool tub spacious enough to hold two people or possibly three. To Kate's left was a long black marble countertop, the veins of white in the stone matching perfectly with the two white porcelain drop-in sinks. A mirror ran the length of the wall behind the vanities, and avoiding it at all costs, Kate went over to a doorway next to the wash station. Looking around the corner, she found a toilet tucked into the alcove, a much-needed convenience after all the drinking she had done the night before.

It wasn't until Kate returned to wash her hands when she noticed something else on the vanity. Between the two sinks was a pile of clothes along with some towels and a toothbrush still in its packaging.

A few minutes later, with the taste of tequila replaced by minty freshness, Kate was about to get undressed to take a shower, except when she turned to face the room, something was missing. Kate looked right. Kate looked left, and then Kate scratched her head. "Okaaay?"

Kate walked from the bathroom only to come to a stop when she saw Brodie sitting on the edge of the bed. "Um…"

"Let me guess," Brodie said, humor dancing in her eyes. "You can't find the shower?"

"How'd you know?"

"It's happened before," Brodie said, getting to her feet. "Come on. I'll show you."

As soon as they walked into the bathroom, Brodie pointed to the far corner of the room. "It's right there, and now I'd best get back to the kitchen before I burn the bacon. Enjoy."

Kate went over to where Brodie had indicated, wondering how she could possibly miss a door, and then the penny dropped. The shower *was* the corner of the room, and what she had thought was a large square vent in the ceiling was actually the showerhead, its polished surface covered in a hundred tiny holes. A long L-shaped bench wrapped the corner, its surface covered in the same gray and black tile of the floor, and because of the design, Kate hadn't noticed that quite a substantial section of the floor was four inches lower than the rest of the room.

It was easy to see why the shower didn't need walls; however, Kate did. The idea of being naked and completely exposed to whoever walked into the room was far outside her comfort zone. It would have been doable if a door existed she could lock, but it now seemed, at least in this area of Brodie's flat, the woman didn't believe in doors.

Kate sighed and returning to the mirror, she tried her best to straighten her rumpled clothing before leaving the room in search of her host.

The only thing separating the bedroom from the rest of the flat was a series of floor-to-ceiling room dividing panels. The inserts held black rice paper with an understated white bamboo design painted on the surface, and Kate's admiration for the simplicity showed on her face as she walked from the room. On the other side of the panels was the dining area, and Kate's smile grew broader. A bowed-front china cabinet filled the wall to her right, its shelves holding an eclectic collection of dinnerware in varying shades of black, blue, and white, and the rest of the space was taken up by a long, oval glass table. Six chairs stood at the ready around it, and in front of two, Brodie had arranged place settings, complete with cutlery, dishes, cups, and glasses filled with orange juice.

Kate heard a noise, and taking another few steps, she turned the corner and saw Brodie, standing in a lengthy, galley-style kitchen, placing a platter of sausage and bacon into the oven. "This is quite a place."

"Thanks." Brodie gave Kate a side-eyed glance as she shut the oven door and saw the woman had yet to get cleaned up. "What? You don't like my shower?"

"It's not that I don't like it. It's just—"

"You don't feel you need one?"

"No. It's just a bit...a bit—"

"Open?" Brodie said, picking up her coffee mug.

"Yes."

"You should try it. You might like it. Cassidy does."

"My sister takes showers here?" Kate said, cocking her head to the side.

"Yes. On the days we're working together, Cassidy schedules her morning run so she ends up here. She says she loves the freedom my shower gives her, whatever that means."

"Do you have an aversion to doors?"

Brodie snorted. "No, but most of the time, they aren't really necessary. It's just our own insecurities that make us think we need them."

Kate folded her arms. "So, you're saying I'm insecure?"

Brodie took a quick sip of her coffee, using her mug to conceal her amusement. It was rare she purposely tried to antagonize, but it seemed Kate's fuse was almost non-existent, and Brodie enjoyed the spark in Kate's eyes when it was lit. "Well," she said, placing the mug on the counter. "When it comes to showers without walls and bathrooms without doors, then yeah, I guess I am."

"We'll see about that!" Kate turned on her heel and marched back the way she came. Out of habit, as she stepped into the bathroom, Kate went to close the door that *should* have been there and then hung her head when she realized her mistake. "Shit."

Kate padded to the mirror and stared at her reflection. Her hair was a mess. Her makeup was smudged, and her clothes were hopeless. She took a deep breath, and grabbing the towels Brodie had set on the sink, Kate went over and turned on the tap for the shower. Piece by piece, her clothing dropped to the floor, and even though she doubted Brodie would intrude on her privacy, Kate couldn't help but keep one eye on the doorway. With only her underwear remaining, Kate unclasped her bra, and as she stepped out of her knickers, she made a mental note to explain the importance of doors to her sister the next time she saw her.

***

"Someone was hungry," Brodie said as she gathered the plates.

"Someone makes a great omelet."

"Thanks," Brodie said, heading to the kitchen. "I'm going to get some more coffee. Would you like some?"

"Yes, please."

Feeling as if she needed to loosen the borrowed track pants she was wearing, Kate leaned back in her chair and took a deep breath. Even though she'd had time to get used to her surroundings, she couldn't help but continue to admire Brodie's home.

Brodie's condo filled the top floor of the last of the warehouses she'd inherited from her grandfather, and it was roomy and stylish. The lounge was unlike any Kate had seen before, for other than in a ski lodge, she had never seen a fireplace staged in the middle of a room. The circular stone hearth was complete with a stainless-steel hood overhead and noticing a small pile of wood stacked neatly on a rack in the corner, Kate guessed everything was in working order. The sofas and chairs circling the hearth were covered in gray faux suede, and pillows of all shapes and sizes were scattered about. Although the furthest wall had been painted black, a color Kate would never have chosen to use in a house, with the addition of a mixture of black-and-white photographs and charcoal sketches all framed in white, it acted as a perfect accent. Natural light flooded the room courtesy of the windows filling the wall to the right, and even though the sunlight was tempered by white sheers framed in smoky gray drapes, it was more than enough brightness for the space.

Getting up from the table, Kate headed to the kitchen to see if Brodie needed a hand. Like everything else, the kitchen was modern and high-end. A galley design, one wall held both upper and lower black laminate cabinets while the other had only bases, allowing the countertop to overhang the six stools running down its length. The granite countertop was a blend of white, gray, and blue, and the stainless steel appliances were all state-of-the-art, as was the tiny wine refrigerator tucked under the counter.

"This place really is amazing," Kate said, watching as Brodie finished filling their mugs.

"Thanks," Brodie said, handing her the coffee. "It took me over a year of nights and weekends to get the design just the way I wanted it."

"Wait. You designed this place?"

"Yep. Right down to the lack of doors."

Kate laughed, and after taking a sip of her coffee, she looked past Brodie. "So, what's on that side?"

"Oh. That's where I play. Come on. I'll show you."

The door leading into Brodie's flat was directly opposite the kitchen, and if Kate had been able to pay attention when Brodie brought her home the night before, she would have easily seen both sides of the condo. But Kate hadn't been sober. She had barely been conscious, so when she followed Brodie through the kitchen and into the next room, Kate almost dropped her coffee cup.

"*Wow*," Kate said, looking from one end of the room to the other.

While Brodie had designed the lounge and dining areas for intimate dinners and conversation, the other side of the condo was designed for partying and games. One wall was covered in black and gray cabinetry with the highest units having glass doors to protect the knickknacks displayed, while the next row was open and filled with dozens of books. Below that was a sizable flat-screen television, and under it were cubicles filled with stereo equipment, gaming consoles, and more books. A semi-circular sofa in the color of ash was sitting in front of the entertainment center, and instead of having a coffee table, huge pillows were stacked on the floor atop a white, fluffy, fake-fur rug.

At the opposite end of the room was an octagonal card table surrounded by four chairs, and an electronic dartboard hung on the wall, but what really caught Kate's attention was in the middle of the room. Under a rectangular stained glass light was a regulation size pool table.

Kate went over and ran her hand over the dark blue felt. "You don't do things half-arse, do you?"

"Not if I can help it," Brodie said, walking past. "Would you like to see the rest?"

"There's more?"

"Just a bit. Come on. I'll show you."

Kate followed Brodie past the card table to an arched opening leading to a small hallway. The first thing Kate noticed was a wrought iron circular stairway winding upward, and the second was a door off to her right. "Wait. I thought you didn't believe in doors?"

"No. I said that *most* of the time they aren't necessary, but if friends or family stay over, I offer them some privacy," Brodie said, opening the door.

Kate stepped into a room equally as large as the master suite, but instead of using modern furniture, Brodie had chosen traditional. All the furnishings were dark cherry, and the four-poster bed was covered in a blue and white patchwork quilt. Noticing another doorway, Kate went over and peered into the guest bathroom. It held all the amenities, including a slightly smaller whirlpool bath.

"It's lovely," Kate said, turning back to Brodie. "But I have to ask a question."

"Okay?"

"How come I didn't sleep in here last night?"

"Because I had to practically carry you into the flat. It was late, and I was tired, and when you veered left, I veered left. I figured it was easier to pour you into my bed than try to maneuver you back here."

"That makes sense," Kate said, walking out of the room. "So, what's up those stairs?"

"The roof."

"Ha-ha."

Brodie glanced at Kate's socked feet and shook her head. "That'll have to wait for another time if you don't mind. It rained earlier this morning, and it's cold. You're not dressed for it."

"Okay," Kate said, smiling. "I'll look forward to it."

"Well, I'm looking forward to some more coffee. Shall we?"

"Sure."

A few minutes later, the two women settled in the lounge, and setting her coffee to the side, Kate said, "So...um...did I do anything stupid last night?"

"Define stupid."

Kate inwardly winced at the infinite possibilities of what she might have done. "Okay, how about...did I do anything I should regret?"

Brodie's face split into a grin. "Not as far as I'm concerned."

Kate's cheeks flamed, and she shot Brodie a look. "Are you trying to wind me up?"

"Is it working?"

"Do you really want to find out?" Kate said, straightening her spine.

"Relax," Brodie said, holding up her hands. "All things considered, you were quite...um...quite behaved for a person who drank that much tequila."

"Define behaved," Kate said, narrowing her eyes.

"Well, you didn't take off your clothes or try to dance on the tables, if that's what you're thinking. You just had a bit of fun with Harper, and then you insisted on dancing with me, and after that, I brought you here. End of story."

"I don't remember dancing with you, and what kind of fun—exactly—did I have with Harper? It's all just a blur."

With the amount of tequila Kate had consumed, Brodie wasn't surprised. Once her dance with Harper ended, they returned to the table just as the second tray of shots was delivered. As soon as Harper picked up the first glass, she insisted that Texans could outdrink anyone, and a competition was born. Brodie watched as the two women drank shot after shot of the potent liquid, and in less than an hour, Harper and Kate were pissed to the gills. After Harper fell off her stool for the second time, Brodie asked a waitress to keep an eye on Kate while she put her old friend into a taxi, and when she returned a few minutes later to take Kate home, the woman refused.

***

"I wanna dance with you."

"You're drunk, and I need to take you home."

"You don't like me!"

Kate's pout was the cutest Brodie had ever seen. "Yes, I do, and when you're sober, ask me to dance, and I will. I promise."

"One dance. *Pleeeeease.*"

"Kate, you're totally pissed."

"Am not!" Kate said, stomping her foot.

"Yes, you are."

"Fine," Kate said, and looking around, she spotted a man standing alone at the bar. "If you don't wanna dance with me, maybe he will."

Kate listed to the right as she began weaving toward the bar, only to have her progress stopped when Brodie grabbed her hand. "Okay. One dance and then we go. All right?"

"Yep."

At a snail's pace, Brodie guided Kate to the dance floor, and it wasn't until they stood under the flickering lights when Brodie realized she had made a mistake. In Kate's alcohol-infused state, she was relaxed, almost fluid in her movements, and unabashedly she pulled Brodie close as they began to dance. Brodie inhaled the faint aroma of perfume, and closing her eyes, she allowed the woman in her arms to overpower her senses. Brodie's body reacted instantly. Awakened by Kate's curves pressed against her own, the surge of awareness heated her blood and moistened her knickers. Foreign as it was to Brodie, she knew that this was love. She had fancied others, but not like this. She had craved others, but not like this. Brodie had never wanted to die in someone's arms...until now.

The song ended, and another began, and its tempo was slow and sensual. The thump of the bass matched Brodie's heartbeat, and when Kate melted into her, slipping one leg between Brodie's, a low groan rose in Brodie's throat. She stepped back to break the connection and glowered at the woman wearing a sloppy grin. "It's time to take you home."

Kate gazed into Brodie's eyes, and nodding her acknowledgment, she allowed Brodie to lead her to the door. She didn't say a word as they made their way to the car. Her head was spinning, and her knees were weak, both easily explained by the amount of alcohol in her system, but that wasn't the case...and the proof pulsed between Kate's legs.

Chapter Eight

"Here you go," Kate said, placing the tray over Devon's lap. "Just what the doctor ordered."

As soon as Devon saw the bowl of soup in front of her, her eyes lit up. "Tell me that's Mum's recipe, and I'll love you forever."

Kate smiled as she sat on the edge of the bed. "I called her last night, and she e-mailed me the recipe, along with instructions that you're to stay in bed until you feel better."

"Trust me. I don't plan on going anywhere feeling like this."

"Good," Kate said, patting her sister's leg.

"Speaking of going places," Devon said, picking up her spoon. "Brodie mentioned that you went to Outskirts last Friday."

"That's right. I met her for a drink."

Devon stole a few glances of Kate while she slurped her soup. Like a dog with a bone, she had spent three days interrogating Brodie about that night until the woman finally caved. Devon knew her sister had gotten totally pissed when an old flame showed up, and she also knew the night had ended with a dance that Brodie refused to talk about.

"You like her. Don't you?"

Kate drew back her head. "Of course, I like her. She's a nice person."

"That's not what I meant, and you know it."

Kate played with a loose thread on the duvet for a few moments before raising her eyes. "With the way we were brought up, I honestly don't think Mum could handle both of us dating women, so let's just drop it. Shall we?"

The only thing that dropped was the spoon Devon was holding, and clanking into the bowl, droplets of broth splattered over her pajamas. The color drained from Devon's face. "What did you say?"

Kate reached for the small glass tray on the nightstand and pulled out a pair of antique silver earrings. "I gave these to Gina last year for her birthday, and the leather jacket I gave her for Christmas a few years ago is hanging in your wardrobe."

Devon stared at the earrings as if they contained Ebola. Since her divorce, she had tried and failed to tell Kate the truth about herself, her fear based on so many stories from others who had lost families and friends. Devon took a deep breath. Even though she had joked about Gina telling Kate the truth, Devon knew it was on her…and the time had come. "Kate, you need to know that she wasn't my first, so please don't blame this on Gina."

"I know."

"You know what?"

"That she wasn't your first."

Devon's eyes turned to slits. "How in the hell would you know that?"

"Because I'm your sister, and I watched you grow up. You never had any boyfriends other than poor Charlie, and a few years ago, when I was on a call, I noticed you in a coffee shop across the street. I went over just to say hello and saw you with a woman. You were holding hands…and she was wearing one of your shirts."

"Shit," Devon said, resting against the pillows behind her back. "Why didn't you ever say anything?"

"I kept thinking you'd trust me enough to tell me the truth," Kate said softly. "It kind of hurt that you didn't."

"I'm sorry," Devon said, reaching for her sister's hand. "I was just so scared of losing you."

"That's never going to happen," Kate said, giving Devon's hand a squeeze. "Dev, you're my sister, and I love you. I always have, and I always will. That's never going to change. I promise."

Devon's eyes shimmered with tears. "I love you, too, Kate."

For a few moments, the room grew quiet until muffled shouting from the flat next door came through the walls. Kate frowned. "You seriously need to move out of this place."

"It's all I can afford at the moment, and it's not that bad."

"You have five bloody locks on the door."

"It's called being safety conscious."

"It's called drug deals and burglaries, both of which have gone down in this building too many times."

"Please don't start," Devon said, tossing another tissue aside. "We've been over this before. Once I manage to put away some money, I'll find a new place, and before you bring it up—*again*—I'm not moving in with you."

"Why not?"

"Kate, do you remember when we had to share a room when Mum decided she was going to paint yours?"

"Yeah. So?"

"So, we almost killed each other."

"We did not—"

"Oh, come on, Kate. I came home from school to find you had rearranged all my stuff down to reorganizing the drawers in my dresser, and you tossed out some of my favorite clothes. It was a nightmare."

"Those clothes were faded and tattered."

"And I didn't care. They were *comfortable*," Devon said, sitting up a bit. "Kate, like I just said, I love you. I love you to death, but you like structure, and I like...I like being able to kick off my shoes when I walk in the door. I like putting a bottle of spice away without thinking where it falls in the alphabet, and I like...and I like drinking milk out of the container instead of a glass."

Kate curled her lip. "You do that?"

"See," Devon said, giggling as she slapped her hands on the mattress.

"I suppose you're right," Kate said, letting out a long breath. "I am pretty controlling at times, huh?"

"You're just you, Kate," Devon said, taking Kate's hand. "And I promise, once I get enough saved, I'll move out of here. Until then, the door will remain locked, and I'll keep this copper I know on speed dial...just in case." Okay?"

"All right." Kate got up and began gathering the balled-up tissues that were scattered all over the bed. "Now, eat your soup. I'm going to throw these out and tidy up the kitchen."

"Wait," Devon said, grabbing Kate's hand again. "Don't go just yet."

"Why?"

"Because two wrongs don't make a right."

Kate's brow furrowed. "What's that supposed to mean?"

"It was wrong of me to not tell you I was gay, which makes what you're doing equally as wrong."

"I don't follow you."

"Talk to me about Brodie."

"There's nothing to talk about," Kate said, snatching her hand away. "Drop it."

"Kate, talk to me. Let it out. I know you want to."

"There is nothing to let out," Kate said, walking away.

"It's okay if you like her."

"*No*, it's *not!*" Kate said, whipping around. "I shouldn't feel this way. I don't *want* to feel this way. This isn't what I want, Devon. This isn't what I planned."

"Plans change."

"Oh, don't give me that crap," Kate said, going back over to the bed. "This isn't about buying a red car instead of a blue one. It's about...it's about..."

Devon tried to hide her grin. After stopping mid-sentence, Kate was staring at Devon as if she expected her to interject. Devon chuckled. "Oh, don't look at me. I've already done my confession for the day."

"I don't think I want to talk about this," Kate said, turning to leave.

Devon grabbed Kate by the sleeve and forced her to sit down. "Yes, you do."

"No, I—"

"I've been where you are. Don't you get that? I've been in your shoes, and right now, you don't just *need* to talk about it. You *have* to talk about it," Devon said, sitting up. "Kate, you need to get this off your chest and out of your head, or it's going to eat you alive."

Kate bowed her head. "Devon, I can't."

"Do you like her?"

"Please, Dev—"

"Do you *like* her?"

"Yes!" Kate snapped. "Yes, I like her. All right? Is that what you want to hear?"

"Do you want to be with her?"

"I don't know what that means?"

"Yes, you do," Devon said, whimsy dancing in her eyes. "Because it's probably all you've been thinking about for weeks."

Kate's nostrils flared, and she jumped off the bed. "*You* need to mind your own fucking business!"

Even with a stuffed up head and feeling as if she was in the Sahara, the sight and sound of her sister's temper caused Devon to laugh out loud. "Oh, by that outburst, I'd have to say I guessed correctly."

Over the years, like most siblings do, Devon and Kate had had their fair share of arguments, yet the ability to stay angry with her sister for longer than a few minutes had always escaped Kate, and it still did. The sound of Devon's girly titters warmed Kate's heart, and with a huff, she sat back down and swatted Devon's leg. "You're a pain in the arse. Do you know that?"

"Yeah, but you love me."

"I have absolutely *no* idea why."

Devon's smile lit up the room. "Probably because we're sisters and apparently, in more ways than one."

Kate pursed her lips. "This isn't funny."

"No, but it's true. Isn't it?"

Kate sighed. She'd been riding an emotional roller-coaster for weeks, and the ride needed to stop. She wasn't eating. She wasn't sleeping, and the more she thought about Brodie, the angrier she got. Kate didn't want to feel this way. She didn't want to dream about a woman with dark brown eyes or wake up out of breath with her body craving for release. Kate needed to take back control of her life, and the sooner, the better.

"You know what's true," Kate said, looking Devon in the eye. "What's true is that I've never been attracted to a woman before, so this whole bloody thing is just in my head. It's a stupid crush, and next week I'm going to tell Brodie I won't be joining her for dinner anymore. All I need to do is put some distance between us, and I'll be fine. She can go back to clubbing and fucking random women, and I'll find a nice man, get married, and have a few kids. That's what I've always wanted, and *that's* something Brodie Shaw can't give me."

Devon studied her sister. "Okay, but if you're so serious about this, why not just tell her tonight and get it over with. Why wait a week?"

"Because she's going out of town today, so we aren't meeting for dinner tonight."

"Oh, crap." Devon grabbed her phone from the nightstand, and looking at the time, she hurried to move the tray off her lap. "Kate, take this."

"What the hell are you doing? You haven't finished your soup."

"I've got to get dressed," Devon said, tossing aside the blanket.

"Dressed? Devon, you're sick. You need to stay in bed."

"I'm fine." Devon scrambled out of bed and made it halfway to the bathroom before the pounding in her head caused her to stop. Leaning against the dresser, she closed her eyes and waited for the ache to ease.

"No, you're not," Kate said, guiding her sister back to bed. "And what's all this about anyway?"

Devon sunk onto the mattress. "I'm supposed to be going out of town with Brodie today."

"Well, I'm sure her clients will understand."

"Oh, it's not for work."

"It's not?" Kate said, tucking the blanket around Devon.

"No, I'm her date."

Kate stood straight and parked her hands on her hips. "You're her *what*?"

Devon blanched. "Please stop yelling. It hurts my head."

"I'm sorry," Kate said, her expression softening as she placed her hand on Devon's forehead. "You're really hot."

"I know, and I feel like shit, but Brodie's going to be here in less than two hours, and I haven't even packed."

"And you're not going to because you're not going anywhere."

"Kate, I have to. I promised to be her date for the weekend."

"Okay, that's the second time you've used that word, so would you care to explain *date*?"

The coolness of Kate's tone wasn't lost on Devon, and she held up her hands. "Relax, sis. It's just make-believe."

"Make-believe?"

"Yes, as in not real," Devon said, resting back against a stack of pillows. "Her father's birthday is tomorrow, and they're having a big party to celebrate. Brodie loves her family, but every time she goes home, her brothers and father try to fix her up with someone. They end up having a house filled with single women, most of whom are either too old or totally straight, and Brodie ends up having a horrid time. So, this time, Brodie thought if she brought someone with her, they'd stop trying to be matchmakers, and she could enjoy herself." When Kate arched an eyebrow, Devon held up her hand. "In name only, I swear."

"Of course," Kate said quietly. "Well, you'd best call her and tell her you're not going."

"Kate, I don't want to let her down. She's been looking forward to this for weeks."

"Devon, you're sick. Now, pick up the bloody phone and tell her you're not going. She'll just have to find someone else."

***

Brodie glanced at her watch, and delighted to see she was on still on schedule after hitting every red light between her home and Devon's, she trotted up the stairs. Ever since Devon had agreed to the charade, Brodie had been counting the days until she saw her family. Since her brother, Ethan, ran the construction side of her business, it was rare a week would go by without her touching base with him, but she hadn't seen the others since Christmas. With her face bright and her smile wide, Brodie lightly rapped on the door and waited for her salvation to appear.

A second later, Brodie heard the latch click, and when the door opened, Brodie's mouth did, too. "Kate?"

"Hiya, Brodie."

"What are you doing here?"

"Can't a girl visit her sister?"

"What? Oh right, of course," Brodie mumbled. "I just wasn't expecting to see you today."

"That's not all you weren't expecting," Kate said under her breath as Brodie walked into the flat.

Brodie hadn't told Kate anything about her plans for the weekend. It didn't seem like a good idea to let her know her supposedly straight sister would be portraying Brodie's girlfriend for a few days, and it still didn't. An uncomfortable silence fell over the room until Brodie said, "Um...is Cassidy...I mean, Devon around? She was going to do me a favor—"

"Brodie, I'm your date."

"Sorry?"

"Devon's got a cold, so I volunteered to take her place for the weekend."

Ever since their dance at Outskirts, all Brodie had done was think about her relationship, or rather her *friendship* with Kate Monroe. Forefront in her mind was how she had felt when Kate didn't show up at Calabria that night, and after a few days of being dogged with that memory, Brodie faced facts. She was on a dead-end street, and it was time to turn around. She hadn't looked at another woman in weeks and allowing Kate to remain in her life, if only for Friday night dinners, wasn't going to work. If Brodie wanted Kate out of her heart, she needed to get her *out* of her life.

"I'm sure you mean well, Kate, but my family is expecting...well, I told them I was bringing someone...um...someone special."

"And you don't think I'll pass the test?"

"What? No. *No*, that's not what I meant. It's just that I asked Devon because she's..." The words died in Brodie's throat. Disclosing that Devon was a lesbian wasn't an option and open-mouthed, Brodie could do nothing but stare back at Kate.

Kate snickered at the befuddled look on Brodie's face. She had never seen the woman flustered before, and it was a nice change of pace. "I'll meet you at the car," she said, picking up her suitcase. "And Devon's in the bedroom if you want to say goodbye."

As soon as the door latched, Brodie let out a long breath before heading to the bedroom to peek inside. "Hey there."

"Hey yourself," Devon said, tossing aside a crumpled tissue.

"You look like shit."

"Gee, thanks."

"And looking as bad as you do, I'm surprised Kate would want to leave you alone," Brodie said, stepping into the room.

"I won't be. Gina's coming over."

"Really?" Brodie said, jerking back her head. "And how did you explain that to Kate? I mean, I would think she'd be a little curious as to why *her* best friend volunteered to play *your* nursemaid."

"I didn't have to explain it," Devon said. "Kate knows."

"She knows about you and Gina?" Brodie said, moving closer to the bed.

"Yeah. I told her today."

"And?"

"And it seems she's known for a while but wasn't saying anything," Devon said, snatching another tissue out of the box. "I guess that's why she's a Detective Inspector, and I'm not."

"Oh, thank God," Brodie said, sinking onto the edge of the bed. "I almost fucked up royally a minute ago."

"How?"

"I almost told her the reason I had asked you to go with me this weekend was that you wouldn't have a problem playing the part of my girlfriend since we're both cut from the same cloth, so to speak."

"Oh."

Brodie swiveled around. "But I still can't believe she volunteered to do this. You did tell her the truth, didn't you? I mean, she knows my family is expecting to meet my new *partner*—right?"

"I told her everything, Brodie," Devon said, pulling the blanket up to her chin. "And you better get going, or you won't make dinner."

***

Twenty minutes later, Gina let herself into Devon's flat. Her first stop was the kitchen to place the takeaway bag on the counter, and her next stop was the bedroom, walking in just as Devon was stripping the duvet off the bed. "So, did it work?"

Devon looked up and smiled. "Like a charm."

"Did you take your allergy meds?"

"As soon as they left," Devon said as she loosened the fitted sheet and pulled out a heating pad. "And your idea about using this was priceless. I was so bloody warm. I'm surprised Kate didn't call a doctor."

Gina helped Devon remake the bed and then plopped down on the freshly tucked sheets. "But do you think we went too far? I mean, you told me Brodie hates it when her family tries to play matchmaker, and here we're doing the same thing."

"All we're doing is giving them an opportunity to spend some time together. What they make of it is entirely up to them."

Devon walked around to where Gina was sitting and gazed into her eyes. "And don't take this the wrong way," she said as she lifted off her shirt and tossed it aside. "But do you really want to spend the afternoon talking about Brodie and Kate?"

Gina adored that Devon rarely wore a bra, and when two rose-tipped breasts came into view, Gina licked her lips. "Who?"

***

"So, where are we going?" Kate said as Brodie turned onto the motorway.

"My dad lives just outside of Bournemouth, about a two-hour drive give or take."

"And your entire family is going to be there?"

"Actually, I'm not sure who my brothers invited to the party tomorrow, but tonight it'll be just them and the kids."

"Kids?"

"Yeah. Ethan and his wife have two. Kyle just turned three, and Megan celebrated her eight-month birthday last week. It's actually one of the reasons I wanted to go home this weekend. Ethan lives an hour outside of London, so the only time I get to see the kids is on weekends, and then it always seems like the family has plans. I haven't seen her in over a month. She's probably grown a foot."

"I think that's a wee bit exaggerated," Kate said with a laugh. "And you like kids?"

"Well, I don't like them when they're crying and throwing tantrums, but for the most part, kids are okay," Brodie said, glancing in Kate's direction. "Why? Does that surprise you?"

"A little," Kate said, rubbing the back of her neck to calm the hair standing on end. "You just never struck me as the type that wanted to have a baby."

"Whoa," Brodie said, fanning her fingers off the wheel. "I never said I wanted to *have* a baby. The thought of pushing something that size through my vagina is *not* on my bucket list, but if ever I do find the right woman, and she wanted to eventually start a family, I wouldn't have a problem with it."

"I see." Kate looked out the windshield, losing herself in her thoughts for a moment. "Oh, speaking of your family, what do they know about me? I mean, what do they know about Devon? Oh, Christ, I'm supposed to be Devon on this little escapade, aren't I?"

Brodie snorted and gave Kate a side-eyed glance. "Relax. I never gave them a name, so you can be yourself."

"Good," Kate said, relaxing in her seat. "So, if you don't mind me asking, how many other women have you taken home to meet your family?"

"Um...none."

"None?"

"Nope."

Kate tilted her head just a bit. "Why not?"

"Well...um..."

"Wait," Kate said, holding up hands. "Let me guess. Most of the women you...uh...you *date* aren't the type you bring home to Daddy?"

Brodie's cheeks turned rosy. "Something like that."

"So, how are you going to explain me?"

"What?"

"You just said you've never taken a woman home before, and now you're going to show up with me. Aren't they going to think this make-believe relationship of ours is, well, serious?"

Matchmaking, it seemed, didn't run only in her family, and in that nanosecond of Brodie's life, the thought of murdering her best friend sounded tremendously appealing. Brodie tightened her grip on the steering wheel. "I need to take you home."

"What? Why?"

"Because Devon lied to you, and then she lied to me."

"What are you talking about?"

Brodie filled her lungs and then let the air rush out. "Kate, I made up this whole fucking charade so my weekend wouldn't be interrupted by a bevy of strange and straight women parading through my father's house."

"I know. Devon told me all about it."

"Yeah, well by the sounds of it, she forgot to mention that when I told my father I was bringing someone, I told him she was my new partner, as in *lover*. And since I know Devon told you earlier that she's gay, you'll understand why I knew she could play the part easily enough. She wouldn't have had a problem if I held her hand or gave her a hug or even a small kiss if it came to that, but that's not the case with you, and I'm not going to put you in that position. So, I'm going to take the next ramp, get you home, and then head out again."

Kate should have been thrilled. After all, she had argued with Devon for nearly twenty minutes earlier that morning, rattling off a laundry list of reasons why she couldn't go in Devon's place until Devon's you-go-or-I-will ultimatum ended the fight, and now she had an out. Kate didn't have to be a part of the farce any longer. She didn't have to play the role of Brodie's attentive partner, holding her hand or pretending to gaze lovingly when the need arose. She could just go home and spend the weekend alone. Kate *should* have been thrilled.

Kate picked at a loose thread on her coat, mindless of the minutes as they ticked by. If they turned around, Brodie would be late getting to her father's house, and even though her family believed she had a partner, would that stop them from pushing single women in Brodie's direction when she showed up alone? And if that happened, Brodie's weekend would be ruined, and Kate would be to blame. There was no getting around that. Yet, if Kate did pretend to be Brodie's partner, the woman would have the weekend she had hoped for, and Kate would be in a place she'd only visited in her dreams. Kate's palms grew damp. Did she really want to go *there*?

Kate raised her eyes as Brodie changed lanes, and seeing the off-ramp up ahead, Kate blurted, "No, don't turn around."

"What?"

"I said, don't turn around."

"Why?"

"Just give me a minute, okay?" Kate said, holding up her index finger. As they passed the off-ramp, Kate took a steadying breath and got her thoughts in order. "Are we supposed to stay at your dad's house?"

"No. I made reservations at a hotel," Brodie said, glancing at Kate. "One room, two beds, in case you're wondering."

"Then, this will work."

"Have you gone mad?

"Brodie, we can do this."

"At the risk of repeating myself, have you gone *bloody* mad?"

Kate flashed a face-splitting smile. "No, but you said it yourself. All you planned to do was hold Devon's hand occasionally—right?"

"Yeah."

"So, what's the problem?"

"The problem is I don't want you to be uncomfortable," Brodie said, knowing she wasn't just talking about Kate. It was hard enough hiding her feelings over dinners or walking down avenues filled with store windows. How in the hell would she be able to hide them for an entire weekend while playing the part of Kate's lover?

"Why, because I'm going to have to hold the big, bad, scary lesbian's hand?"

Brodie grimaced. "It sounds really stupid when you say it like that."

"Because it is," Kate said, patting her on the arm. "Trust me, Brodie. This will work."

Brodie didn't want to have hope. She didn't want that feeling of expectation, that desire for a truth she yearned to have, but hope, it seemed, was tenacious. The sensual dance they shared at Outskirts she had blamed on tequila, but what could Brodie blame this on? Why would Kate agree to this farce if she didn't want the same thing? Brodie scrubbed her hand over her chin. It was time to think with her head and not her heart, and give Kate one more chance to back out. "Are you *sure* you want to do this?"

"Yes, I'm sure," Kate said, bobbing her head.

For a few minutes, neither said a word. The landscape whooshed by and the only sound was the rumble of the tires on the pavement as two women came to terms with their own demons. One was about to take a detour from her plans, traveling down a road that was as frightening as it was surreal, and the other teetered between feeling elated…and terrified.

"Okay," Kate said, swiveling in her seat. "So, I'm going to need to know what our story is."

"Our story?"

"When they ask how we met, what are we going to tell them?"

"I suppose I'm just going to tell them the truth," Brodie said with a shrug. "It seems easier than trying to make something up."

"Agreed," Kate said, her thoughts drifting back to her first impression of Brodie. "So, you're going to have to refresh my memory a little. Your father's name is Harrison—right?"

"That's right, and he was a Professor of Mathematics at Southampton University until he retired a few years ago. Now he spends his time reading, fishing, tutoring at a few of the local community colleges, and gardening. My dad *loves* to garden."

"And your mother? I know that night in Calabria, you said she died. Can I ask how?"

"Giving birth to James."

"Oh, sorry."

Brodie glanced at Kate. "It's okay. It was a long time ago, and it was her choice."

"What do you mean?"

"None of us knew this until years later, but after my mother had me, the doctors told her she wouldn't be able to carry another child to term, let alone give birth. Dad said they had taken all the precautions after that, followed all the rules, but she got pregnant again. Even though abortion was an option, my mother wouldn't hear of it, and my dad supported her decision. He adored her, and it was what she wanted. He said that she told him her life had always been in God's hands, and now it is," Brodie said, briefly looking at Kate. "I can still remember him coming home from the hospital that night to tell us Mum had to leave us, but she had given us all a gift, and his name was James."

Kate ran her hands down her arms to calm the goosebumps that had sprouted. "So, James. Tell me about him."

"James is a Professor of Computer Science at Exeter University. He's thirty-four, single, and even though we all take after my father's side of the family, James has my mother's eyes. They're brilliantly blue. Oh yeah, and he reminds me a lot of your sister."

"Why?"

"Because they have the same taste in clothes and hairstyles," Brodie said, grinning. "And he's as nerdy as she can be."

Kate smiled. "All right, so that leaves…um…Ethan?"

"Very good," Brodie said with a dip of her head. "Ethan is my business partner. He runs the construction side of things. He's one year older than me, and up until about five years ago, he was a confirmed bachelor."

"What happened?"

"He met Lucy," Brodie said, her affection for her sister-in-law showing on her face. "And that's about it for family. I have a few aunts, uncles, and cousins scattered about, but we rarely see them. No need to bore you with those details."

"Okay, so is there anything I should know about you in case someone mentions something a partner should know?"

"Like what?"

Kate paused to think back on a few of her own family gatherings. Remembering one particular party where her sister thought it would be funny to hide fake spiders in Kate's room, she turned to Brodie. "What about phobias? Do you have any of those?"

Brodie let out a low, throaty chuckle. "Yes, taking a woman, who *isn't* my partner, home to meet my family."

"You're not helping."

"Sorry. Um...no phobias, but I'm not particularly fond of tree houses."

"Afraid of heights?"

"Not really. I just fell out of one when I was a kid. Ended up with a couple of scars."

"Oh," Kate said, perking up in her seat. "The scars, where are they?"

Brodie didn't appreciate Kate's eagerness to know her bodily defects, and she shot her a look. "Why?"

"Unless your family is different than most, once we get there I'm going to be deluged with stories of little Brodie's past exploits, and when they mention the tree house, which you *know* they will, as your partner, I sure as hell better know where those scars are. Don't you think?"

Kate's use of 'little Brodie' caused Brodie's scowl to disappear. "Right...hadn't thought about that. Well, I hit several branches on the way down, so there's one on my left hip and another under my left breast. All right?"

"Yeah," Kate said quietly, trying to keep her mind off of the scar locations. "Um...do you have any tattoos or piercings?"

"Tattoos, no. Piercings, just my ears. How about you?"

Kate shook her head. "No tattoos and no scars. Pierced ears."

"Well, I'm glad we got *that* out of the way," Brodie muttered.

"Are you angry with me?"

Brodie frowned. "No, of course not. I just never should have lied to begin with. All I wanted to do was have a nice, relaxing weekend with my family, and now I've got you lying for me. Seriously, Kate, if you want to turn around, just say the word."

Kate had never had an addiction. She had never rationalized all the wrongs to make a right until now. Going back to London made perfect sense. Ending the deception before it began was the right thing to do. Distancing herself from Brodie instead of playing the part of her lover was what Kate needed to do so she could get on with the life she had planned. There was only one problem. Brodie Shaw was a habit Kate was not yet willing to quit.

Chapter Nine

By the time they pulled up to Harrison Shaw's house, Brodie and Kate were convinced they knew enough about each other to easily play the role of partners. Over the past few years, Brodie had had enough conversations with Devon to already have a basic knowledge about Devon's and Kate's upbringing, so the last two hours had been mostly spent giving Kate a crash course in Brodie and her family.

Brodie turned off the car and glanced at her passenger. Since turning onto the side road leading to her father's house, Kate had gone quiet, and the woman was now bouncing her knee like a lottery ball in an air machine. Brodie grinned. "You sure you're ready for this?"

Kate took a deep breath, letting it out slowly as she looked over at Brodie. "Yeah, piece of cake."

"All right then." Brodie went to get out of the car, and then she saw something in the window of the house, and her grin expanded. "Stay there. Let me open your door."

"Why?"

"Because my dad, the old bugger, is watching from the house, so it looks like our game begins now." Brodie jogged around the car, and opening Kate's door, she held out her hand.

Kate rolled her eyes, and slipping her hand in Brodie's, she climbed out. Somewhat amused they were being watched like teenagers arriving home past their curfew, Brodie and Kate walked hand in hand to the house.

Situated off the main road, and found only if one traveled down a lengthy, cobblestone, tree-lined path, Kate hoped Harrison Shaw wasn't as imposing as the two-story brick structure before her. Leaded glass filled the three panels making up the entrance, the sidelights matching the door in height and width, and a thick vine traveled up the brick and over the door, its woody tentacles spreading across the façade as they climbed toward the sky. To the left and right of the entrance were bay casement units, their copper roofs now green with age, and under both windows were gardens edged in stone. Daffodils and camellias, awakened from their winter sleep, erupted from the soil, providing a colorful blanket of yellow, pink, red, and white. Far to Kate's left, an arched opening in the brick framed a thick, planked door, and noticing the wall continued for some time, Kate assumed the entrance led to more gardens behind the house.

Kate was just about to comment on the impressive home when the front door swung open, and a man, at least a foot taller than she, stepped out.

"You're late," he said in a booming voice.

Kate unconsciously gripped Brodie's hand tighter. Clean-shaven, and with a head full of wavy, salt-and-peppered hair, Harrison Shaw was as commanding as his house. Towering, with broad shoulders and a barrel chest, the arms of his long-sleeved Oxford bulged from the muscles underneath, and while she knew he was about to turn sixty, Kate had no doubt Harrison Shaw could best most men half his age. For a few seconds, his expression was unreadable and dark, and then he laughed, and whatever trepidation Kate was feeling vanished as a network of tiny lines creased the man's face.

"Christ, I've missed you," he said, pulling Brodie into his arms.

The love flowing between the father and daughter was unmistakable, and Kate stood quietly off to the side, somewhat honored to watch as they hugged and kissed and hugged again.

Harrison finally took a step back and holding Brodie at arm's length, he scrutinized her lanky frame. "You've lost weight."

"No, I haven't, so don't even start," Brodie said, narrowing her eyes.

Harrison gave Brodie a wink before focusing on Kate. "Now then, who do we have here?"

If it had been an act, Brodie would have won an award, but her dazzling smile wasn't a part of the masquerade. It was real. Until that moment, Brodie hadn't realized that for the first time, she would be able to look at Kate the way she wanted. Under the pretense of being partners, she no longer needed to conceal her admiration for the woman at her side, and Brodie couldn't believe the overwhelming feeling of pride at the words she was about to say. "Dad, this is my partner, Kate Monroe."

It was as if sunshine suddenly broke across Kate's face, and as she gazed at Brodie, Kate found it impossible not to return Brodie's radiant smile with one of her own.

When Brodie was in college, Harrison had visited often, and during those times, he had managed to meet a few of his daughter's 'friends.' Mostly tall and always blonde, they'd chatter on about parties, clubs, and concerts while draped in the latest and tightest of fashions, and Harrison wasn't impressed. They weren't deserved of the daughter he raised, but thankfully he soon recognized they were only fleeting fancies. None had held Brodie's interest for long, and he became accustomed to hearing a new name every time she came home or called.

There were nights when Harrison would sit in front of the fireplace, watching the flames dance and seeing his daughter in the sparks, silently questioning himself about the way he had raised her. Had he been too strict? Had he shown enough love? Would she ever find someone who could fill her heart and kindle her flame? Harrison's eyes darted back and forth between the two women, and an invisible grin was formed. He had just found his answer.

"Very nice to meet you, Mr. Shaw," Kate said, extending her hand. "I've heard so much about you."

Harrison tempered his strength as he took Kate's hand. "It's an honor to meet you, Kate, though I can't say I've heard that much about you," he said, giving Brodie the sternest look he owned. "Quite a secret you've been keeping—eh?"

When the only reply he received from Brodie was a shrug, Harrison huffed out a laugh as he pushed open the door. Ushering them inside, he put their jackets in the cloakroom before leading them to the kitchen. "How about I make some tea while we're waiting for the others?" he said, grabbing the kettle from the stove.

"Where is everyone?" Brodie said, looking around. "It's not like them to be late for one of your dinners."

"You just missed James. I sent him to the store to get a few things, and Ethan called and said they were running late. But not to worry, that just means we have a bit of time to get to know one another. Right, Kate?"

Kate beamed. "Right, sir, but before we do, is there a place where I could freshen up?"

"Of course, my dear," Harrison said, turning back to the stove. "Brodie, why don't you bring in your bags and then give Kate a tour?"

"Oh, Dad, sorry. I guess I should have told you. I made a reservation at a hotel for us."

"Bollocks," Harrison said, whipping around. "I'm not having you spend your nights in a drafty old hotel. I've got your room all ready and waiting. Now, do what your father—"

"But Dad—"

"Broderick Anne Shaw!" Harrison said, eyeing his daughter as only a parent can do. "I don't see you nearly as much as I'd like, and I'm not taking no for an answer. Now get your bloody bags and do what your father is telling you to do. End of discussion."

Kate bit her lip, trying not to giggle at a father's power over his child. Brodie may have been a confident, swaggering woman at work or in the clubs she visited, but in Harrison Shaw's house, she was his child...and children do what they're told.

Brodie's shoulders fell, and letting out an audible breath, she motioned for Kate to follow her. "I'm sorry about this," she said when they reached the door. "I forgot how stubborn he is."

"Imagine that," Kate said, her grin finally reaching her face.

"I'll be right back," Brodie said, opening the door.

"Want some help?"

"No, I got this. Won't be but a minute. Take a look around if you'd like."

Left alone to admire her surroundings, Kate did just that. The entrance hall was spacious, with arched openings on both sides, and heading to the one on her right, she stepped into the formal dining room. Centered in the space was an oval, cherry table surrounded by eight chairs, their backs and seats upholstered in a mauve and ivory striped fabric. A small corner hutch stood in one corner, and a modest buffet ran along another wall, atop which were assorted photographs in frames of gold and silver. The setting sun streamed through the bay window, and the light reflected off the highly-polished oak floor as well as the crystal chandelier hanging in the middle of the room.

Making her way across the foyer, Kate walked into the lounge. Like the dining room, the front wall was filled with a bay window, and the orange hues of sunset flooded the room, adding to the warmth already existing. A built-in seat ran under the bay, its surface cushioned with several throw pillows tossed about, and Kate could easily imagine spending a rainy day snuggled under the window reading a book. The back wall held a set of French doors with sidelights to match, and with the heavy drapes pulled open, she could see a wee bit of the patio and gardens behind the house.

The fireplace was just opposite the doorway, and to the left and right of the hearth, openings cut into the brick were filled with logs awaiting their demise. A thick, heavily-varnished slab of rough sawn lumber acted as the mantle and down its entire length were more family photographs.

The furniture seemed to be a mixture of old and new, the finely striped fabric on the sofas appearing crisp while the two leather wingback chairs nearest the hearth were well worn. The area between the seating and the fireplace was open, with no coffee table to clog the space, and a thick, cream-colored shag rug covered the oak flooring between the couches.

Kate returned her focus to the mantle. Curious as to which of the frames contained photos of Brodie, she went over and was about to bring one down to her level when Brodie returned.

"Shall I show you the rest of the house?"

Kate turned around, and her eyes flew open wide. Bookcases filled the walls on both sides of the doorway, and their shelves were lined with easily a few hundred books. "Wow, that's a lot of books."

"My Dad is a big reader. Actually, we all are."

"I can see that," Kate said, secretly wishing it would rain so she could enjoy one of the many classics before her.

"Shall we?" Brodie said, gesturing for Kate to follow.

"Yes, please."

A little further down the hall, Brodie stopped and opened a door. "The formal sitting room."

Kate looked inside, and she had to agree. It was indeed formal. Queen Anne furniture filled the room, and with tapestry upholstery, walnut details, and distinctive cabriole legs, it was elegant and stylish. "*Very* formal."

"Yes, it is," Brodie said with a laugh. "We hardly ever used it unless Dad needed to sit us down and have a talk, as he would say. I think he was hoping because it's so prim and proper in here, the mood would rub off on us."

"Did it?"

"Do you really need to ask?" Brodie said with a chuckle. "Come on. I'll show you where we're staying."

Brodie led Kate back to the front of the house to grab the luggage she had left by the door. "We're up there," she said, looking toward the stairs.

"All right."

As Kate began making her way up the stairs, Brodie let out a long breath. She was home. A place filled with memories of wrestling matches on the lounge floor and decorating for Christmas. A place where she had skinned her knees in the gardens, slid down the banister when her father wasn't watching, and fell out of a tree...when he was. This is where she said her first prayer, cooked her first meal, and on one cold winter night, told her family she was gay. The memories made Brodie smile, yet as she watched Kate walk up the steps, her smile morphed into a leer.

Until Kate had removed her raincoat, Brodie only knew she was wearing an olive green dress that reached Kate's knees, and it had a neckline that didn't plunge nearly far enough. After Harrison took Kate's coat, Brodie tried her best not to stare at the knit sheath dress, but now she could...and she did.

In clubs, Brodie had seen the same style worn by others, and usually, it was shrink-wrapped to their bodies, leaving nothing to the imagination, but Brodie's imagination was now working overtime. Kate was wearing the dress as intended, the soft, stretchy fabric hinting at the curves underneath without flaunting their delicious existence, and Brodie unconsciously licked her lips.

Halfway up the stairs, Kate stopped on the landing and looked through the prismatic bevels of the leaded glass window, curious to see if Harrison had more gardens behind the house. Brodie stopped one step away and unable to resist the temptation, she swung one of the suitcases and hit Kate squarely on her bottom. "Keep moving, woman. Plenty of time for sightseeing later."

Kate playfully squinted at Brodie before dashing up the rest of the stairs. With her hands on her hips, she tapped her foot and waited for Brodie to catch up. "Took you long enough."

"Yes, well, I didn't know I was going to be a pack mule this weekend. What the hell did you bring anyway? The entire clothing department of Harrods?"

"If you remember, I didn't really have much time to plan," Kate said, keeping her voice low. "I just ran home and grabbed a little of everything."

"Feels like you grabbed a lot of everything."

"Fine," Kate said, holding out her hand. "Give it to me. I'll carry it."

"Oh, sure, make *me* fetch the bags, carry them up the bloody stairs, and now that I've done all the work, you want to help. I don't think so," Brodie said, her face brightening as she held Kate's suitcase at arm's length. "What would my father say?"

Kate's eyes crinkled at the corners. "Okay, fine," she said, looking around. "Which way then?"

"Last door on the right."

Kate knew that tastes change over time, so she wasn't sure what to expect as she made her way to Brodie's childhood room. Although Brodie's flat and office were both filled with modern décor, Kate doubted she'd find the same sterile whites, muted grays, and stylish blacks, and when Kate opened the door, she found she was right...and in a big way.

Decorated in everything Waverly, the room was bright, festive, and ultra-feminine. The walls were baby blue and trimmed with glossy white woodwork, and the bed, sitting catty-corner in the room, was covered by a thick quilt displaying a bold print of blue, green, and mauve flowers. Decreasing in size, six pillows with ruffled edges were propped against the white iron headboard, and lace doilies protected the nightstands from the small, elegant crystal lamps atop each. The drapes were flowery with ruffled edges to match the pillows, and a white carpet with baby blue stripes covered the floor.

Kate's eyes sparkled with humor as she turned to Brodie. "Where's your doll collection?"

"What the fuck is this?" Brodie said, dropping the luggage.

"Quite the little lady back then—eh?"

"In your dreams," Brodie said with a huff. "Trust me. My room *never* looked like this."

Kate let out a laugh. "Um...loo?"

"Oh, sorry," Brodie said, tipping her head in the direction of the door in the corner of the room. "Through there."

"Your own private bathroom? I'm impressed."

"I was the only girl in a house full of men. Dad decided I needed my privacy before a certain issue began to arise."

"Good point."

"He thought so."

While Kate used the facilities, Brodie looked around the space that used to be her room and scratched her head. Gone was the old squeaky bed with its lumpy mattress and plaid duvet. Gone was the tall dresser that once stood in the corner, its surface scratched from years of use, and gone were the sketches that once covered the walls. Drawn on paper of every size and color, her designs of imagined homes and rooms had been taken down and replaced by watercolors of lakes and seashores, hung on walls now covered with white paneling.

As Kate washed her hands, she looked at her reflection in the mirror and let out a long breath. Within minutes of their arrival, their plans had been changed by a man as headstrong as the daughter he had produced. Even though the thought of sleeping alongside Brodie in a bed large enough for lovers but too small for friends made Kate's palms sweat, the fact Harrison Shaw had clearly accepted his daughter's lifestyle warmed Kate's heart. He had welcomed her partner into his house with open arms, and in that instant, she knew she could do this. For the weekend, Kate would leave her doubts, concerns, and inhibitions behind and become Brodie's partner in *almost* every sense of the word, because whether she cared to admit it or not, it wasn't a ruse...and it wasn't a lie.

Kate came out of the bathroom, and seeing Brodie sitting on the bed, Kate went over and plopped down next to her. Glancing over her shoulder at the full-size bed, Kate said, "At least it's not a single."

Brodie dropped her chin to her chest. "Are you sure you're okay with this?"

"Do you snore?"

"No," Brodie said, shooting Kate a look.

"Do you talk in your sleep?"

"Not that I've been told."

"Do you steal sheets or pillows?"

"Never. That's just rude."

"Then we should get along just fine," Kate said, patting Brodie on the leg.

"Are you sure?"

Melted by Brodie's compassion toward the situation, the last shred of Kate's anxiety dissolved, and her features softened as her face eased into a grin. "Absolutely," she said, and leaning over, she kissed Brodie lightly on the cheek. It was chaste. It was simple. It was friendly. It was *not*.

Kate couldn't move. She didn't want to move. With her eyes closed, for a split-second, she became lost in the softness of Brodie's skin. The smell of her cologne and shampoo invaded Kate's senses, and like an aphrodisiac, it swirled through her mind and her body before settling squarely between her legs.

The sensual throb brought Kate to her senses, and she scrambled off the bed. Unable to look at Brodie, she went across the room, grabbed her suitcase, and then tossed it on the bed. "Maybe we should unpack before things get wrinkled."

Brodie slowly opened her eyes. Having clutched the duvet when Kate's lips touched her skin, Brodie relaxed her hands and allowed the blood to return. One platonic peck on the cheek had sent a shockwave of desire through her body, and while she knew pretending to be in love with Kate would be easy, not being able to consummate it would be the hardest thing she'd ever done.

Brodie drew in a deep breath. She got to her feet, and grabbing her case, she began putting things away, never once looking in Kate's direction. She wasn't trying to be rude, but until her blood cooled and the pulsing in her core subsided, it was the safest option.

A few minutes of silence passed before Kate looked up and said the first thing that came to mind. "I like the bathroom, by the way."

"No doubt due to the use of doors," Brodie said as she hung a shirt in the closet.

It was said without thinking. Just a random thought blurted out by a woman still annoyed by her uncooperative hormones, but it was enough to ease the tension, and when Brodie heard Kate snicker, she did, too.

"By the way, you forgot to mention your first name's actually Broderick. Your parents set on a boy?"

"No," Brodie said, placing her empty suitcase off to the side. "My dad's father died a few weeks before I was born. Since the doctors had already warned my mother against having any more children, my parents decided to give me his name to carry it on. I've always been called Brodie though unless, as you saw, Dad wants to drive home a point."

Kate sunk onto the edge of the bed. "You know, I thought we did all right in the car, but there's still so much I don't know about you. I mean, up until a few minutes ago, I didn't even know your first name, for Christ's sake."

"But you know it now, and you didn't even flinch when Dad said it."

"I suppose," Kate said quietly.

Brodie frowned and going over to the bed, she knelt by Kate. "Look, how about this? If you get into trouble, call me...call me darling or sweetheart, and that'll be my clue to come to your rescue. All right?"

Kate hesitated for a second. "Okay. That should work."

"Good," Brodie said, standing straight. "But you really needn't worry. Once the grandkids get here, Dad won't even know we're around. Now, come on. Let's go see if he needs any help, and then I'll finish the tour."

***

"What can we do to help?" Brodie said as they returned to the kitchen.

"Well, I've got dinner under control, so why don't you go to the cellar and bring up a few bottles of wine," Harrison said as he stood at the sink peeling potatoes.

"Consider it done." Brodie went to a door in the corner of the room and disappeared down a set of steps.

Kate was about to ask if she could lend a hand when someone pounded on the front door, the sound causing both of the people in the kitchen to jump.

Harrison let out a loud guffaw and looked over at Kate. "That would be James. The boy never remembers his key. Could you be a love and get that?"

"Sure thing." Kate trotted to the entry and pulled open the door, smiling at the tall, lanky fellow whose arms were filled with bags. "Hiya."

James scrunched up his face. "Who the hell are you?"

"I'm Kate. You must be James," Kate said, stepping back so he could come inside.

"You're a bit young for my dad, don't you think?" James said, giving Kate a quick once over.

Surprised by his assumption, Kate's mouth dropped open, but before she could think of something to say, Brodie chimed in from the kitchen.

"Yes, but she's not too young for me."

James looked past Kate, and when he saw his sister standing in the doorway, he dropped the bags and rushed over. "Christ, it's good to see you," he said, wrapping his arms around Brodie. "It's been like forever."

"It's only been a few months," Brodie said, returning the hug. "And I missed you, too."

James released his grip on his sister, smiling back at her for a moment before he glanced over at the attractive woman still standing by the door. "Wait," he said, looking back at Brodie. "Did I hear you right?"

Brodie waved Kate over. "James, I'd like you to meet my partner, Kate."

As if he was watching a tennis match, James looked slowly back and forth between the two women several times before finding his words. "Partner? Really?" he squeaked. "You mean she's a...I mean...you and she are..."

Kate didn't know what bothered her more. James not believing she could possibly be Brodie's partner or the ridiculous questions he was asking. Deciding it was a tie, Kate tapped him on the shoulder. "To answer your questions," she said, staring him square in the eye. "*Yes*, I'm her partner. *Yes*, I am, and *yes*, we are."

Having witnessed Kate's temper before, Brodie knew the warning signs, and it was all she could do not to burst out laughing. Kate's backbone was rigid, and her chin was high, and if looks could kill, poor James would have been on his way to the morgue.

Brodie slipped her hand in Kate's as she grinned at her brother. "So...any more questions?"

Chapter Ten

"I've got a question," Brodie said as she pulled the cork from a bottle of Cabernet.

"And what would that be, my dear," Harrison said, raising his eyes.

"What in the hell happened to my bedroom?"

After their somewhat awkward introduction was remedied when James stuttered and stammered his way through an apology, Kate and James shook hands and started again. With Brodie volunteering to help in the kitchen, they were put in charge of the appetizers. Given strict orders from the elder Shaw that all breakables and sweets were to be put out of his grandson's reach, James was just placing the remaining bowls of candy on the mantle when his father's laughter rang out. "It sounds like someone's having fun," he said, handing Kate one last framed photo while he rearranged a few others.

"I've always heard that's what family get-togethers are all about," Kate said as she glanced at the photo. Appearing to have been taken on the back of a boat, three teenagers were sitting with their arms draped over each other's shoulders, and the gaiety on their faces was instantly contagious.

"I see you like that one, too," James said, seeing Kate's smile.

"That's Brodie in the middle—right?"

James snapped back his head. "I would have thought you'd have seen that one before. It's one of Brodie's favorites, and I know she has a copy."

Kate's expression froze as if dipped in liquid nitrogen. "Oh...um...well...um...she has so many. I must have just overlooked this one."

"That's odd. I'm sure Brodie has it hanging—"

"Dad said since everyone is staying here tonight, the bar is officially open," Brodie said, walking into the room carrying a bottle of beer in one hand and a glass of wine in the other. Giving James the beer, she handed Kate the Cabernet.

"Thanks," Kate said, taking the wine. "Sweetheart, James said there's a copy of this hanging in the flat, but for the life of me, I can't remember ever seeing it."

The term of endearment was not lost on Brodie. Without missing a step, she leaned closer to look at the photo in Kate's hand. "Oh, that one. Of course. It's actually one of my favorites."

"Then where is it?"

"In a drawer in the game room. Early last year, I was having a party, and someone knocked it off the wall. The frame broke, so I put it away for safekeeping. I totally forgot about it until now."

"Well, I really like it. You need to get it fixed," Kate said, handing Brodie the photo.

"Yes, dear," Brodie said, and to complete her performance, she gave Kate a quick peck on the cheek. "Anything you say, darling."

Hearing her father bellow for assistance, Brodie winked at Kate and practically skipped from the room, leaving Kate and James alone again.

James slumped into one of the leather chairs to nurse his beer, and Kate sat in the other, glancing at James occasionally while she enjoyed her wine.

Other than his sky blue eyes, the family resemblance was undeniable. His jaw was square, and his frame slender, and his hair already carried a hint of gray, just like Brodie's. The last visible family trait was his height, and although he was a few inches shorter than his father, he had a six-inch advantage on his sister.

Kate's thoughts drifted, taking her back to a previous conversation, and stealing another peek at James, she nodded to herself. He was wearing the same style of flannel shirt and faded jeans that had become Devon's norm, and just like her sister, the man kept his long hair pulled back in a ponytail. Although Kate doubted anyone would mistake the professor and the IT professional as

GOING ON RED / 126

siblings, Brodie was right. They had more in common than the thread connecting their chosen professions.

James sat in the wingback chair, sipping his beer and stealing glances of Kate when he could. When it came to the style of women Brodie preferred, the only thing James had to go on were the words used by his father when he'd return from visiting her in college. He'd mumble and grumble about the women Brodie was dating, and the things he had said under his breath painted a slightly different picture. Unless Kate had dressed down for the weekend, she was hardly flashy, and ditsy didn't seem to fit either. She hadn't tittered or blathered, or become lost in their limited conversations, and as James studied Kate, she just didn't strike him as promiscuous, so that left out tart as well. "So, Kate," he said, bringing the bottle of beer to his lips. "What do you do for a living?"

"I'm a police officer," Kate said, preoccupied with admiring her surroundings.

In the process of taking a drink, when James heard Kate's occupation, his mouth dropped open at the same time he tilted the bottle and what went in...promptly came back out. "Oh, bugger!"

Kate jumped and looking over at James, her eyes widened when she saw beer dripping off the man's chin. "Shit," she said, getting to her feet. Picking up a handful of cocktail napkins off the mantle, she rushed to his side and tried to help mop up what had landed on his shirt while he dried his face.

"Well, it's about bloody time!"

Kate and James looked toward the door in unison. The likeness was unmistakable, and Kate knew in an instant that the man striding toward them was Brodie's older brother. She straightened and held out her hand, but before she could introduce herself, Ethan took center stage.

"I'm Ethan," he said, shaking her hand as if trying to dislocate her shoulder. "And I must say even though it's taken him years to find a girlfriend, *you* were definitely worth the wait."

James quickly got to his feet. "Ethan—"

"What? Did I embarrass you?" Ethan said, looking over Kate's shoulder at his brother. "What's to be embarrassed about? She's a knockout, and you're the luckiest bloke I know. Little brother, this one's a keeper."

"I'm glad you think so," Brodie said, standing in the doorway.

Ethan turned toward the familiar voice. "There you are," he said, and marching over, he pulled Brodie into a hug. "It's not like I could mistake your car, but I thought you weren't coming."

"Why would you think that?" Brodie said, stepping out of the embrace.

"Because that's what I told them," Harrison said, coming into the room. "I didn't want your brothers trying to fix you up with another date, knowing you were bringing your own."

"You brought a date?" Ethan said, grinning like a fool. "Come on, then, stop hiding her. Where is she?"

Brodie's face took on an inner glow as she gazed at her brother. "She's right behind you."

Ethan whipped around, and when he saw Kate giving him a tiny wave, he jerked back his head. "You?"

"Afraid so," Kate said.

"Really?"

"Yep."

Ethan's cheeks turned two shades darker. "Oh, Christ. I'm sorry. I just assumed—"

"No worries," Kate said, giving James a quick look. "It's happened before."

A red-headed woman suddenly appeared at Ethan's side. She was shorter than Kate and a bit rounder, and her smile was genuine as she held out her hand to Kate. "Hi. I'm Lucy," she said, gesturing with her head toward Ethan. "I'm married to stupid. Pleased to meet you."

***

Once again, apologies were made and accepted. By the time they sat down for dinner, Kate was part of the family, and as he always did, Harrison had planned everything right down to the seating arrangement. Kyle had yet to get past the playing-with-his-food stage, so he was on one side of the table, flanked by his parents, while eight-month-old Megan's carrier was safely strapped to the chair between Brodie and Kate. Casseroles fresh from the oven had been lined up down the center of the table, unreachable by youngsters knowing no better, so plates were passed around, and portions were piled on, and any request for a small amount went unheard. Friendly banter filled the room as bites of food and sips of wine were consumed, and more than once, tears were wiped from eyes as reminiscences brought hilarity to the table.

Kate found herself watching Brodie, fascinated at how easily she tended to the baby at her side. Spooning food and wiping away dribble, Brodie smiled and cooed at the tiny tow-headed girl and Megan, happily enjoying her meal, gurgled in delight each time Brodie airplaned another spoon in her direction.

Kate couldn't deny the feelings washing over her as she sat amongst the Shaw family. She liked the warmth of the home in which she sat. She liked the way the siblings would shoot dirty looks at one another when they were on the receiving end of a memory, only to dissolve into fits of laughter moments later, and albeit make-believe, as Brodie's partner, Kate had been accepted with open arms. There was no judgment. There were no furrowed brows holding condemnation in their creases or side-eyed glances of disapproval. There was only the love of a family, and it was a family Kate now adored.

Howls of merriment found their way to Kate's ears, and she looked at Brodie to see what she'd missed. A split-second later, Kate was laughing just as hard as the rest. "Oh, my God," she said, seeing spots of strained carrots all over Brodie's face. "What in the world happened?"

"The little bugger grabbed the spoon," Brodie said, glowering at the mess covering her.

Kate, fighting to keep her mirth under control, picked up a napkin and began dabbing away a few of the larger splotches. It was a simple gesture, except when their eyes locked, simple became anything but. The look they exchanged was heated and intimate, and it was not lost on the other adults at the table. Smiles spread as brother looked at wife, and father looked at son.

"You'd best change that shirt," Lucy said through a fit of giggles. "Carrots leave beastly stains if not tended to quickly."

"Well, it appears that's your cue," Brodie said, handing Kate the spoon. "Here you go, darling. Have fun."

Brodie left the room and spinning Megan's chair to face her, Kate continued feeding the cherub-faced little girl.

"So, Kate," Harrison said, placing his napkin on the table. "You've listened all night to us going on and on about ourselves, but we don't know very much about you."

"That's easily remedied," Kate said, glancing at her host. "What would you like to know, sir?"

"Oh, I don't know," Harrison said, scratching his chin. "How about you start with what you do for a living, and how you met my daughter?"

As Kate continued to feed the babbling infant, she filled the Shaw family in on her career and how she met Brodie after an attempted burglary in her office building.

"So, it was love at first sight?" Lucy said, perking up in her chair.

"Not exactly," Kate said through a grin.

"And why not?" Harrison said, looking at Kate. "My daughter is a fine-looking woman and has a lot to offer the right lady."

"That she does," Kate said, chuckling under her breath. "She can also be a bit cocky at times."

Ethan exploded with a laugh so loud it sent all the others in the room an inch off their chairs. He had worked alongside his sister for several years, and he knew all about her swaggering streak. He had seen Brodie stare down the most stalwart subcontractor as she discussed their inability to meet deadlines or their lack of quality control, and brawny men with sun-weathered faces would end up limping from the room like whipped pups. "Talk about hitting the nail on the head," Ethan said, wiping the tears from his eyes. "I couldn't have said it better myself."

Lucy reached over her son and slapped Ethan on the arm. "That's enough out of you," she said before focusing on Kate. "But you obviously gave her a second chance. How did she change your mind? When did it get...you know...serious?"

Kate suddenly found herself in a strange place. She knew pretending to be Brodie's partner would involve a certain amount of lying, but not when it came to answering that *particular* question. Kate could talk of wine and antipasto and strolls down a street, window-shopping. She could tell them about Friday night candlelit dinners where hours would be spent chatting about their days, their dreams, and their jobs. Or Kate could speak of a night when she sat alone while Brodie danced with another, and how her stomach knotted with jealousy at the sight. Kate looked around the table at the eager eyes staring back at her, and she knew what she needed to do. She needed to lie.

"All right, little one," Brodie said as she ambled into the room. "I didn't bring my entire wardrobe, so no more grabbing the spoon. Okay?"

"Brodie, you're just in time," Lucy said, her face brightening instantly.

"Oh yeah?" Brodie said, returning to her chair. "Why's that?"

"I was just asking Kate when things between you two got serious, but it seems the cat's got her tongue."

"Is that so?" Brodie said, stealing a quick glance at Kate.

"Oh, come on! You've got to tell us," Lucy gushed, clapping her hands like an excited child. "I just *love* romance."

Collectively, the three men at the table groaned, and then Harrison stood up. "Well, I don't know about you boys, but I think that's my cue to start clearing the table."

"I'll help you, Dad," James said, springing out of his chair.

"Count me in, too," Ethan said, jumping up. "You ladies have fun."

Lucy watched as the men paraded from the room. "Well, that's a first," she said, focusing on the women sitting opposite her. "Okay, so Brodie...where were we? Oh, that's right. You were going to tell me when things between you and Kate got serious, and don't hold anything back. I want to hear everything."

Tickled by Lucy's curiosity and the male mass exodus, Brodie stood up. "Maybe later, Lucy, but since it appears that little Megan here is done and the men have cleaning duties, I'm going to go stretch my legs. Be back in a tick."

"I'll join you," Kate said quietly, pushing back her chair.

After grabbing their coats, Brodie led Kate to the French doors in the lounge. She flipped on the second of three switches and opened the door. "After you."

Kate stepped out onto the patio, and breathing in the chilly air, she took in her surroundings. "This is nice."

"Another of Dad's hobbies," Brodie said, zipping up her leather jacket. "I could turn on more lights if you'd like, but with the full moon, I didn't think we needed it."

"No, this is fine," Kate said, admiring Harrison's handiwork.

The slate patio was sizable, easily large enough to hold the nine-piece gray metal dining set placed in its center along with an assortment of clay pots scattered about. In several, winter snowdrops were standing tall amidst the pale yellow flowers of primrose, while in others, vibrant violets of purple were intermixed with the bright yellow of celandine.

Kate noticed an opening in the rock border of the patio, and going over, she saw a path lined with daffodils. It meandered into the lawn, disappearing into the shadows of the night, and Kate could relate. Much like the walkway, Kate's confidence in playing this part was fading. She took a deep breath and blew it out through parted lips.

"Is something wrong?" Brodie said, taking a step closer. "I can bring you out tomorrow to see the rest. No worries. We have time."

"That's not it," Kate said, turning around. "Brodie, your family is wonderful, but when Lucy asked about our relationship, I got nervous. I didn't know what to say."

"Well, I'll try not to leave you alone with them again, and if she keeps asking, I'll think of something."

"Thanks."

"Anytime."

Spring had begun the week before, and with the sun shining, Kate's thinly-lined raincoat had been enough to ward off any chill. However, the sun had long since set, so when a gust of wind came out of nowhere, Kate shivered and quickly began fastening the buttons on her coat.

Kate's actions weren't lost on Brodie. If things were different, if things were what dreams were made of, Brodie would have wrapped her arms around Kate and pulled her close. Unfortunately, Brodie knew that such an advance wasn't up to her. She wasn't stupid, and she wasn't blind. Brodie knew in her heart that Kate was attracted to her, the tequila shots had proven that, but Kate was scared. Kate was deer-in-the-headlights-scared, and until she could move past it, *if* she could move past it, there was nothing Brodie could do because she'd never been where Kate was.

Brodie had known her own sexual preference since puberty. There was never any doubt. There was never any choice. For Brodie, it was as normal as breathing, and for Kate, it was not. Brodie had questioned Devon enough to know Kate had never danced over the line. She had only ever dated men, so this attraction, unwanted yet undeniable, was no doubt as strange as it was frustrating. Brodie could empathize. She wasn't looking for love when Kate walked into

GOING ON RED / 132

her office late that Friday night, but it had found her nonetheless, and there was nothing Brodie could have done to stop it.

Brodie heard a noise behind her and looking over her shoulder, she saw James standing just outside the patio door. She stepped closer to Kate, wrapping her arms around the woman's waist as she lowered her mouth to Kate's ear. "Showtime, darling."

Kate hadn't heard the click of the latch when the door had closed. Standing under a sky filled with stars, she'd been lost in thoughts about the woman behind her. Brodie was as much a mystery as she was an open book. She had candidly told Kate about her family, her life, and in a rather heated argument, even the joy she found in sex, but it seemed that each time they were together, a new page was revealed. Tonight, Brodie cared for an infant with the tenderness of a mother. She had hugged and kissed her family and played horsey with her nephew, riding him around the lounge on her back without a care or concern. She had made jokes of many and had been the brunt of many more, and she had laughed until she cried, so when she felt Brodie's arms around her waist, Kate thought another page was about to be turned. A page that made Kate's palms sweat in the cold night air. A page that would reveal new and different, and something as equally scary as it would be welcomed.

When she heard Brodie's whispered words, reality came rushing back to Kate. No more pages would be turned that night, but the moment could still be relished. After all, they were supposed to be partners. Kate relaxed back against Brodie, allowing the woman to hold her even more tightly, and breathing in Brodie's cologne, Kate cherished the warmth radiating from the body pressed against hers.

"You two finally seem comfortable," James said, lighting a cigar. "I thought being around the family might be cramping your style."

Brodie relaxed her hold on Kate, and they both turned to face James. "You only wish you had my style, baby brother."

Kate jokingly elbowed Brodie. "Your family is great, James. Why would you think we're uncomfortable?"

"Because for partners, you sure keep your distance. When Ethan started dating Lucy, they were like conjoined twins. You two hardly make eye contact."

James was spot-on, and Brodie knew it. She'd been raised in an affectionate family and showing it had never been a problem, so she racked her brain to come up with an excuse. Even though she'd never brought a woman home before, Brodie knew her family had long ago accepted her lifestyle, so using that excuse was pointless. She could, of course, blame it on Kate, perhaps suggesting the woman was raised differently, but that didn't seem quite fair. If anyone was to be held accountable, it had to be Brodie.

"I'm afraid it's my fault, James," Brodie said with an exaggerated sigh. "You see, Kate and I had a little disagreement in the car, and she's still a bit mad at me. Isn't that right, darling?"

Kate paused for a split-second before her eyes began to twinkle. "Yes, it is, and until *you're* ready to admit you were wrong, I see no reason to kiss and make up."

It was a dare, and one Brodie had no intention of backing down from. While she was impressed by Kate's quick thinking, making the non-existent argument all Brodie's fault, by graciously accepting the defeat, Brodie would still get the win. She slowly lowered her face to Kate's. "I'm sorry, darling," she murmured, brushing her lips against Kate's.

Kate's heart had begun to race the moment Brodie leaned down. She knew what was about to happen, and she also knew that there was nothing she could do to stop it, not that she wanted to.

The kiss was soft and chaste, barely lasting a few seconds, but when their lips parted, they remained close, breathing in the scent of the other and forgetting they had an audience.

"Dessert's on the table," Lucy chirped from the doorway. "And then Dad wants to take some pictures, so you'd best be prepared to say cheese...a lot."

***

There were already dozens of photographs displayed throughout the house, and as Kate smiled for the umpteenth time, she couldn't help but wonder where these would be displayed. Just as Brodie had said, Kyle and Megan were at the center of everyone's attention until they were safely tucked into their beds, and then it was Brodie's and Kate's turn. As Harrison took picture after picture, obviously thrilled with his daughter's choice of partner, while their cheeks ached, the expressions Brodie and Kate wore were not false. Candid shots and those posed per his instructions filled the memory card of Harrison's high-end digital until the clock struck twelve. Holding up her hands,

Brodie put an end to her father's enthusiastic photo shoot, and after kissing her family goodnight, she took Kate's hand and led her upstairs.

As they walked into the bedroom, Kate let out a deep breath. It had been a long day, and one Kate wouldn't have missed for the world. She couldn't remember ever feeling this comfortable in anyone's house so quickly...and then she saw the bed.

Brodie went to the dresser, and out of the corner of her eye, she saw Kate standing near the bed. "It seems I have you to thank for this."

Broken from her thoughts, Kate turned to Brodie. "What?"

"This," Brodie said, circling her finger in the air. "I talked to my dad earlier, and he said that once I told him I was bringing someone home with me, he decided my old room needed some redecorating, and lucky me, he took Lucy with him."

"Oh, I see," Kate said through a thin smile. "Well, I think they did a good job. I like it."

"Yeah, me, too, now that the shock's worn off," Brodie said, opening a drawer to get some clothes. "I'm going to get ready for bed unless you want to use the loo first?"

"No, go ahead."

"All right. I won't be long."

Kate opened a drawer to get her pajamas, and finding herself staring at a small collection of Brodie's lingerie, Kate slammed the drawer and opened the next. After pulling out a pair of light green silk pajamas, Kate plopped onto the edge of the bed, unable to rid herself of the images of lacy bras and black knickers while she waited for Brodie to reappear.

With makeup removed, teeth cleaned, and her face washed, Brodie stared at her reflection in the mirror. "You've got this," she said, and opening the door, Brodie stepped out. "All yours."

Kate raised her eyes and swallowed hard. Praying her cheeks weren't heating as fast as the rest of her body, she muttered a quick "thanks" as she rushed into the bathroom and closed the door.

***

Early morning light streamed through the window, and the smile Brodie had worn the night before reappeared instantly. When they had gone to bed, they discovered the mattress to be marshmallow soft. Since Brodie was taller and a few pounds heavier, the bed dipped to her side, and sometime during the night, Kate had rolled downhill. Warm puffs of air caressed her neck, and when she felt Kate stir, Brodie sighed. She didn't want this to end...ever.

Kate licked her lips, slowly awakening to face the day. She thought she must be dreaming, for she had never felt this content, and Kate snuggled closer to the warmth and softness.

"Good morning," Brodie purred.

Kate's eyes flew open and finding herself staring down the front of Brodie's tank top, Kate closed them just as quickly. Assuming Brodie wasn't the negligee type, Kate had expected her to emerge from the bathroom the night before wearing pajamas. They'd be either flannel or silk, and while somewhat worn, they'd be nonetheless, stylish. What Kate didn't expect was the woman to come out wearing only a black tank top with knickers to match, and as if Brodie's lack of clothing wasn't enough to cap off Kate's evening, the squishy mattress was. It was like sleeping on a feather pillow, and no matter how hard Kate had tried, she kept sliding into Brodie, who, in turn, sniggered at Kate's predicament. Finally, exasperated by her dilemma, Kate grabbed hold of the edge of the mattress and held on for dear life. That worked...until she fell asleep.

Kate had never been one to cuddle. She had shared her bed with men several times, but once the deed was done and urges had been satisfied, her desire to cling was right up there with BASE jumping. She had yet to meet a man who wasn't a furnace, and between the hair covering their bodies and the stubble on their chins, she saw no need to sleep against sandpaper. But Brodie was soft, and Brodie was smooth, and Kate had wrapped herself around the woman like a snake.

"Sorry," Kate said, her cheeks reddening as she extracted her leg from between Brodie's. "I never do this."

"That's all right. I got used to it after about an hour or so."

"What?" Kate said, sitting up. "Are you saying I was...I was doing that all night? Why didn't you wake me up or...or push me away?"

"And why, pray tell, would I have done that?" Brodie climbed out of bed and headed toward the bathroom. "I think I'm going to take a quick bath," she said, turning around. "Do you need the loo before I do?"

"Um...no....uh...go ahead. I'm fine."

The bathroom door closed, and falling back against the pillow, Kate stared at the ceiling. The night before, Kate had allowed herself barely a glimpse of Brodie in her skimpy attire before rushing into the bathroom, but in the few seconds it just took Brodie to reach the loo, Kate didn't only glimpse, she gawked. Brodie's legs were long, muscled, and bronzed, and her hips, while slim, had just enough roundness to emphasize her gender. What Kate thought were bikini briefs were actually thongs, giving Kate more than an ample view of Brodie's bottom, and the snug tank top did very little to hide the shape of Brodie's breasts...or the woman's arousal.

Kate raked her fingers through her hair. She told herself this wasn't who she was. She told herself this wasn't who she wanted to be. She told herself she didn't want the woman now naked and soaking in the tub. There was only one problem. Her body thought otherwise, and the result had already soaked through Kate's knickers.

Chapter Eleven

Over breakfast, Brodie and Kate were told about the plans for the day. Since it was Harrison's birthday, his sons were taking him out for a round of golf, and while the women were extended a half-hearted invitation, they all declined. Ominous clouds filled the sky, and the temperature was more in line with winter than spring, so as the men paraded out of the house with golf bags slung over their shoulders, the women happily stayed behind.

With most of the preparations for Harrison's party already completed, they enjoyed a leisurely breakfast, and afterward, they settled in the lounge. While the children played, Kate, Brodie, and Lucy casually chatted as they wrapped a few remaining birthday gifts. Minutes after the last package was topped with a bow, the men returned, soaking wet and chilled to the bone, and as laughter erupted from the lounge, they grumbled and groused as they headed to their rooms for a much-needed wash.

When planning the party, Ethan, Brodie, and James agreed that having a house filled with their father's fishing and golfing buddies would end up becoming loud and crowded, and afterward, they'd spend hours putting the house back in order. So, they rented a small hall in town, hired a caterer for the food, a bartender for the drinks, and a DJ for the music. Now, the only thing left to do was get changed, pack up the cars with gifts and children, and head to the venue.

Brodie walked into the bedroom to find Kate standing near the wardrobe wearing a thigh-length, pale pink silk robe. "Oh, Christ, I'm sorry," she said, closing the door behind her. "I would have knocked, but Lucy was right behind me."

Kate quickly confirmed the belt on her robe was securely tied. "Don't worry about it," she said, returning to scrutinizing the two dresses hanging in front of her.

"Problem?"

"I'm just trying to decide what to wear."

"Do I get a vote?"

Kate glanced over at Brodie, hesitating for only a second before pulling out her choices and holding them up for Brodie to see.

One was black jersey and the other red satin, and even though Brodie's favorite color was black, she couldn't take her eyes off the other. "Um…the black is more sedate."

"Yes, it is."

"But the red is…uh…well, it's quite stunning."

"Yes, it is."

Brodie managed to pry her eyes away from the dresses, and seeing Kate grinning back at her, Brodie lowered her chin. "I'm not helping, am I?"

"No, you're not."

"Right then. I'll leave it up to you," Brodie said, and reaching into the closet, she pulled out a long garment bag. "But remember this party is for my dad, and a lot of the guests will be old codgers."

Kate's eyebrows knitted. "And your point would be?"

"The red may be a bit more than they can handle."

***

"You look nice," Lucy said, glancing up from the toddler on the floor when Brodie came into the lounge.

Brodie's smile was instant, for she had purchased her outfit with the party in mind. Even though she had a wardrobe filled with clothes, once she rummaged through it, new was the only option. Brodie's standard work attire consisted of business casual tops and jeans or chinos worn to a softness only age can provide, hardly clothes appropriate for the occasion. Her clubbing clothes, on the other hand, were stylish and modern except painted-on leather trousers, snug sweaters, and blouses barely covering her midriff, while suitable for the clubs, were not suitable for father's birthday celebration.

Brodie had chosen a lightweight wool suit in her favorite color, and lacking the stiffness found in heavier materials, the soft fabric draped beautifully over her figure. As androgynous as it was feminine, the jacket was fitted, with notched lapels and a standing color, and the pleated trousers had just a hint of flare to the leg where it reached her ankle boots. The decision on which blouse to wear wasn't made until a short time earlier. Brodie had purchased two, a basic black and a not-so-basic red. After seeing Kate's choices, Brodie packed the black away for another day. They weren't attending a wake, and at least one of them should have a splash of color. Even though the fire engine hue wasn't one Brodie frequently wore, the provocative long-sleeved blouse had caught her attention in the store. Chiffon and shimmering, with a dozen cloth-covered buttons down the front, it was undeniable sensuous, even more so now since Brodie had chosen not to fasten *all* the buttons.

"Thanks," Brodie said as she sat on the sofa and crossed her legs.

"So, where's your other half?"

"She commandeered the bathroom *hours* ago."

"She's quite lovely, by the way," Lucy said, dropping some things into Megan's travel bag.

Brodie smiled again. "Yeah, she is that," she said, glancing at her watch. "And she also has no sense of time. I told the guys we'd be there early."

"Well, then I hope I was worth the wait," Kate said, standing in the doorway.

Brodie and Lucy looked over at Kate, and while one lost the ability to speak, the other did not. "Wow, look at you," Lucy said as she picked up Megan and put her in the carrier. "Now, that's what I call a party dress."

Brodie tried not to stare, and she failed miserably. Kate had chosen the red, and it was positively breathtaking. Trendy and ending just below the knee, the satiny, off-the-shoulder cocktail dress flattered every curve Kate owned. The sweetheart neckline accentuated her breasts, and Brodie's mouth began to water as she imagined what remained hidden under the carmine fabric.

Perspectives can change with time. Three months earlier, Brodie had leered at Kate from across an office, doing nothing to hide her perusal. It was blatant, and Kate had found it annoying. She didn't any longer. Kate had seen the way Brodie had looked at the dresses. She had barely glanced at the black, but she had fixated on the red, seconds ticking by before she finally spoke again. Before Kate had closed the bathroom door behind her, her choice had been made. It wasn't based on color, and it wasn't based on comfort. It was based solely on the smoldering ardor she had seen in Brodie's eyes.

***

The party was in full swing by the time they arrived at the hall. The bar area was swarming with men in plaid trousers and sports coats while their wives, dressed in flowery spring garments, mingled like little bouquets around the room, quietly chattering on about this, that, and the other.

Ethan emerged from the crowd to help Lucy with the children, and after Brodie handed off Megan's carrier, she took Kate's hand and led her to the main table. Voices quieted as they made their way through the crowd, but within seconds, the noise level increased, and the party continued. Harrison had never hidden his daughter's preference, and most of the guests filling the hall assumed the two women walking to the family table were more than friends, and no one cared. If they had, they wouldn't have been invited.

It was a day of celebration, fun, and family. Friends toasted the birthday boy and unabashedly told stories about their mate, most of which were exaggerated by alcohol. Some laughed until they cried, some howled so loudly that all heads turned in their direction, and some sat silently, their faces redder than the wine in their goblets. Drinks were never-ending, as was the food, and it wasn't until the sun began to set when the party slowed to a dull roar.

Kate stepped out of the ladies' room and did a double take when she saw Brodie standing just outside the door. "What? Did you think I'd get lost?" she said, giving the bodice of her dress one last tug.

"No. I was just trying to protect you from the geezers."

"I think they're harmless, sweetheart," Kate said, smiling.

Brodie knew it was just a slip of the tongue. An endearment uttered without thought, undoubtedly brought on by the day's events. They had spent hours holding hands and hours acting like attentive partners, fetching drinks, and taking the occasional tidbit off the other's plate. It was an award-winning performance, yet in Brodie's heart, it was far from that.

They walked back to the dining area, and stopping when they reached the door, Brodie scanned the room. "Harmless, eh? Do you see any man in this room you haven't danced with yet?"

Kate looked out across the expansive hall. "Maybe one or two."

"My point exactly."

"Are you jealous?"

"What?"

"You heard me."

"No," Brodie said, lines forming on her brow. "Well...yes, I mean...I mean, no."

Kate snorted. "Which is it?"

Brodie frowned. "Look, *I'm* not jealous, but as your *partner*, I should be. Shouldn't I?"

"You tell me. You're the director. I'm just playing a part."

Before she could respond, Brodie felt a heavy hand on her shoulder, and turning around, she found her father standing behind her. His face almost matched the color of Kate's dress, and if his smirk were any more lopsided, he would have been wearing it on his shoulder.

"Are you ever gonna dance wiff your lady?"

Eyeing her father, Brodie's cheeks turned rosy. "I think my time will be much better spent getting you home. You're pissed."

"So?" Harrison said, waving his arms about. "It's my birfday, and I'll do wha' I want. I'm havin' a good time."

"I'm sure you are, but tomorrow you're going to have one *hell* of a hangover," Brodie said, motioning toward the door. "So, why don't you say your goodbyes, and I'll take you back to the house?"

"I'm not ready to go home, and *yooou* can't make me," Harrison said, poking his finger against Brodie's bicep. "I'm gonna get meself another drink, and you're gonna dance wiff Kate."

Brodie felt as if she'd been transported back to Outskirts, trying her best to get a tequila-laden Kate home while the woman refused to leave without a dance. Brodie sighed and looked at Kate.

Kate tried not to appear too eager because she never thought she'd have this opportunity again. After spending the night at Brodie's recovering from her hangover, when Kate finally returned to her own her home, bits and pieces about their evening at Outskirts had returned. Like a poorly edited movie, some parts were forever lost on the cutting room floor, but her dance with Brodie was not. At first, Kate was embarrassed and blaming her actions on the demon alcohol, she tried to explain them away. She told herself Harper was at fault. The intrusion of a friend far too clingy for Kate's liking seemed like a great reason to have a few drinks, and the strength of the tequila had just helped dilute Harper's existence. End of subject. Then she told herself she wanted to unwind after a long, hard week at work and one drink or maybe two had always done the trick before, and Kate had simply lost count. End of subject. Unfortunately, there was one teeny-weeny problem. Kate couldn't come up with any plausible explanation as to why she had insisted on dancing with Brodie. She owned *that* decision lock, stock, and barrel, and she knew it. Kate also knew she wanted to own it again. She wanted to feel Brodie's arms around her like they had been that night. She wanted to welcome the heat radiating from her body as they swayed to the music. She wanted to hold her so close that all others in the room would know Brodie was hers, and Kate wanted to inhale that insanely sensuous cologne...one more time.

Kate's mouth went dry as she gazed into Brodie's eyes. She became lost in the chocolate brown as she struggled to speak the truth, and when she couldn't find the courage, Kate shrugged. "It's up to you."

Brodie inwardly sighed again. She didn't want to hold Kate in her arms and feel that delicious body pressed against hers if it was only make-believe. She didn't want to smell her perfume unless she could nuzzle close to breathe deeply the scent, and she didn't want to detect the hint of Cabernet on Kate's breath if she couldn't taste it as well. As each hour had passed, Brodie's hunger for Kate had grown stronger, and she knew she was a hairsbreadth away from losing control, so leaving it up to her was like hanging the keys to Fort Knox right outside the vault.

"Well, whaz taking you so long?" Harrison said, looking back and forth between the two women. "Cat's got your dancing feet?"

Kate waited for a moment or two before taking matters into her own hands. Since Harrison wasn't backing down and Brodie had lost the ability to make a decision, Kate made it for her. "Come on, sweetheart," she said, taking Brodie's hand. "The sooner we dance, the sooner we can get him home."

"Thaz my girl!" Harrison shouted, followed by a thunderous clap of his hands. "Now, I'm gonna get meself another drink, and you two girlies have fun."

Brodie scowled as she watched her father weave his way to the bar. "I'm sorry. He's beyond pissed."

"There's nothing to be sorry about," Kate said. "It's his birthday, and he's celebrating. We've both been there."

"Yeah, I suppose."

"Shall we?" Kate asked as she squeezed Brodie's hand.

With the party winding down, the lights had dimmed, and the music had slowed. Only four couples remained on the dance floor, and as they reached the center of the room, Brodie gave in to her emotions and pulled Kate close. With their arms around each other, they moved to the music, and one dance turned into two and then into three. Neither noticed as one by one, the other couples left the dance floor until the music stopped, and the hall went quiet.

Without words, they knew it was time to leave, but as Kate started to walk away, the last song for the evening began to play.

If it hadn't been for Harper, Brodie wouldn't have known the song. She had always preferred new music. Synthesized with catchy lyrics holding within their words the energy of the day, they were forever changing as genres were added, and new artists were discovered. Harper, on the other hand, adored the ballads of old, and in their time together, Brodie had been forced to listen to more than her fair share of smooth, simple, and soppy melodies. None had caught her interest, the lyrics oozing with love undying and adoration bordering on the ridiculous, but then again, Brodie had never been in love before, and now she was. *Now*, this song made sense. *Now*, the lyrics spoke to her heart because, like the songwriter, Brodie was totally and unequivocally in love with a lady in red.

"Not yet," she said softly as she pulled Kate back into her arms. "Just one more."

With no resistance, Kate said not a word as she allowed herself to be led back onto the dance floor, and under dim lights, they began to dance.

Kate melted into Brodie, and resting her head on Brodie's shoulder, she closed her eyes. It was as if she was on a cloud far above the world, far away from doubts and worries and fears. Kate didn't want to think. She didn't want to consider tomorrow or the next day or the day after that. Kate only wanted for this moment in time to remain for a little while longer. They were two, yet they were one, and Kate felt safe and warm and loved.

Brodie lowered her head, placing her cheek gently against Kate's head, and when she heard the woman's sigh, Brodie's soul liquefied. The last chord played, and as they began to separate, Brodie gave in to her feelings and placed a soft kiss upon Kate's lips.

Kate had barely opened her eyes when they fluttered closed again. She knew what was about to happen when Brodie threaded her fingers through her hair, and Kate didn't have the strength or the desire to stop her.

At first, Brodie's lips barely brushed Kate's, but when she was met with no resistance, Brodie kissed her again. She applied a hint more pressure, and as she savored the flavor of Kate's full lips, Brodie's body began to pulse. Again they separated, and again, their lips touched, and this time, Brodie ran the tip of her tongue across Kate's lips, craving what lay inside.

From a place Kate didn't know she possessed was born a moan. Hungry and lustful, it rose in her throat, and then just as quickly, it was swallowed up by a gasp. A gasp of shock. A gasp of denial. A gasp of shame, the force of it caused Kate to take a step backward, and as she locked eyes with Brodie, the veins in Kate's temples announced themselves.

In an instant, the reality of what she had done came crashing down on Brodie. "Christ, I'm sorry," she whispered. "I shouldn't have done that."

Kate's hands turned into fists. "You're right. You shouldn't have, and *this* party is bloody *over*."

Chapter Twelve

"You *cannot* be serious."

"Sorry, Ethan. Plans change."

"Yeah, I get that, but it's raining its arse off. Hell, it took us over an hour just to get back home, so you're going to be driving all bloody night. And if you think I'm going to stand here and let you leave—"

"It's not *up* to you," Brodie said, glaring at her brother. "Kate has to get back to work, and that's that."

"Jesus, Brodie. Can't you wait until morning? They're already reporting roads flooding out and…and what about Dad?"

Brodie peered into the lounge to see her father still happily snoring away on the sofa. "What about him?"

"You're going to leave without saying goodbye?"

"I'll call him tomorrow."

"Brodie—"

"*Enough!*" Brodie said, doing her best to keep her voice down. A second later, her anger ebbed as she saw her brother's sandbagged expression. "Look, I'm sorry. I know we were supposed to stay until tomorrow, but Dad's passed out, James is busy playing on his phone, and you and Lucy have the kids to tend to. I'm a good driver, and I'll take it slowly, so stop worrying. Kate has a job to do, and she needs to get back to it."

***

They had been in the car for over an hour, and just like Ethan had predicted, they hadn't gotten far. The storm had grown worse—much worse—and even with the wipers on full and going well below the speed limit, Brodie could barely see the road. Other than when Kate demanded to go back to London, not a word had been spoken between them. Brodie hadn't dared turn up the radio, fearing a love song would play, so the sounds of the storm had kept her company. The thunder had started shortly after they had left the house, and now it seemed never-ending. One rumble after another had followed them from Bournemouth, and bolts of lightning continued to split the sky, bringing with them deafening cracks that seemed to shake the car.

For a while, Brodie appreciated the cacophony, for it helped to drown out her thoughts, but now the monotonous clamor of Mother Nature's fury was beginning to get on Brodie's nerves. She opened the window a smidge, and the storm intruded instantly, its volume intensifying as cold, damp air flowed through the crack.

"What are you doing?"

Brodie gave Kate a half-glance. "Oh...um...I just wanted some fresh air. Thought maybe I'd have a fag. That is, unless you mind?"

"Sounds counterproductive, if you ask me," Kate said, folding her arms.

Brodie sighed and rolled up the window.

"Do whatever you want," Kate snapped. "I don't care."

Brodie opened the window again, and as she reached for her lighter, a blinding, jagged bolt of lightning splintered the sky. She winced at the brightness, and out of the corner of her eye, she saw Kate flinch. "Are you okay?"

"I'm fine. Have your bloody fag already."

"Kate, look, I'm sor—"

"I came down here so *you* could enjoy time with your family," Kate said, shooting Brodie a look. "I agreed to pose as your partner, not *become* it! You had no fucking right to do what you did. None, Brodie. *None!*"

"I didn't mean—"

"It doesn't matter what you meant. It happened. Now, do us both a bloody favor and just get us back to London so we can both get on with our real lives. Can you do that?"

The next sound Brodie heard was Kate sucking in a quick breath as the front tire of the car hit a pothole and sent them veering off the edge of the road.

"Shit," Brodie blurted, and fighting to regain control, it seemed like forever before she finally managed to get all four tires back on the asphalt. "Christ, I could have done without that. Are you okay?" When Kate didn't answer, Brodie looked over and saw that the woman's eyes were bulging, and she was clutching the seat belt as if holding on for dear life. "Kate, are you all right?"

"Yes. I'm...um...I'm...I'm just a bit on edge."

The trembling in Kate's voice wasn't lost on Brodie, and she glanced at Kate again. "You don't like storms, do you?"

"Don't worry about it."

Brodie had to strain to hear Kate's reply, and she frowned. "Why didn't you say something? I could have easily found a hotel in Bournemouth for the night."

"I don't mind the rain. I'm just not a fan of lightning and thunder."

"I'm a little surprised a copper like you would be afraid—"

"It's a childhood phobia. Okay? You satisfied? I don't like thunder and lightning. Never have. Probably never will. No big deal."

"On the drive up, I thought you said you didn't have any phobias?"

Kate relaxed her grip on the shoulder belt, but her jaw remained taut. "You know what? If it's all the same to you, how about you just keep your eyes on the road and don't concern yourself with me. Okay?"

Brodie huffed out a breath. "Have it your way."

Kate stared out the window. Angry with Brodie, angry with herself, and angry at the world, her rage had carried her this far, yet the storm was rapidly diluting her fury. Her vision obscured by that which she could not face, Kate had been blinded to the danger she'd put them by demanding to go home tonight. Kate sunk in her seat. She could now add yet another mistake to her ever-growing list.

Ten minutes passed without a word between them until Kate broke the silence. "There's a car coming at us," she said, staring at the lights up ahead.

"Yeah, I see it."

"Doesn't he look a little too much in the center?" Kate said, stiffening in her seat.

"A bit," Brodie said, her focus solely on the lights. "I'll slow down."

Brodie lifted her foot off the accelerator, and as the car crept along the highway, she kept her eyes on the headlights approaching her.

"Brodie, he's in the middle of the road!"

"Bloody hell!"

Brodie swerved to the other side of the road a split-second before the headlights went whizzing past, and hitting the brakes, the Jaguar came to a stop in the grass along the edge of the highway. "Holy *Mother* of God," Brodie said, slamming her hands against the steering wheel. "What a *fucking* idiot."

Mindless of the storm growing even stronger around them, over a minute passed while Brodie got her nerves under control. Finally, slouching in her seat, she looked over at her passenger. "Kate, I'm sorry. I know you want to get home, but this is shit. We can't keep driving in it, and I know you hate me, but are you really willing to die because of it? Talk about counterproductive."

A ghost of a grin appeared on Kate's face. "Maybe we should turn around?"

"We don't have to. There's a town up ahead. I've been through it dozens of times, and I know they have a few B&Bs. Is that okay with you?"

"Yes, of course. Anything to get out of this."

"All right then," Brodie said, checking her mirrors before pulling back onto the road. "We'll just take it slow and easy."

***

"Any luck?" Kate asked as Brodie rushed to climb back into the car.

"No, we aren't alone. This storm has stranded lots of people, and everyone's filled up."

"Brodie, if the problem is you're looking for two rooms, it's only for one night and—"

"Kate, look at me. I'm soaked to the bone. Trust me, if they had a wardrobe I could have booked for the night, I would have."

Once they arrived in the town, Brodie had managed to find three bed-and-breakfasts. Each time, she was the one to run through the storm only to return a few minutes later with the same results. There were no rooms, and the rain wasn't supposed to ease up until the morning. If Brodie had been alone, she would have found a safe place to park and wait it out, but with each boom of thunder and bolt of lightning, Kate had curled further and further into her seat.

"So, what now?" Kate said, watching as Brodie put the car in gear.

"There's one more down the street," Brodie said, pulling away from the curb. "So, cross your fingers."

Fifteen minutes later, Brodie clambered back into the car and slammed the door behind her.

"Well?" Kate said.

"Now I know how Joseph and Mary felt."

"You have *got* to be kidding."

"Nope. Four rooms, all occupied," Brodie said as she started the car.

"Shit."

"Look, the bloke inside said there's another place down the road a bit. The landlines are down, and the storm is wreaking havoc with mobiles so he couldn't call them. He said it's definitely not a five-star, but since they're off the beaten path, he thinks they'd have a room."

"What do we have to lose?"

"My thoughts exactly."

***

Brodie climbed back into the car, placing a paper bag between them before smiling at Kate as she dropped three keys into her hand.

"Oh, my God, they had a room?" Kate said, looking at the keys. "Wait. You got us three rooms?"

"No, one's for the entrance. The other two are for the rooms."

"So...should I ask? What's it like?"

"The geezer had a three-day-old beard and a big old stogy sticking out of his mouth, but he guaranteed me they were clean. And quite frankly, Kate, even if they weren't, it's better than driving around in this shit."

"All right," Kate said, pocketing the keys. "What's in the bag?"

"Oh, some candles. He said the power has been going off and on for hours. We might need them."

"Okay," Kate said, and a second later, she hunched her shoulders when the sky lit up again. "So, where do we go from here?"

"The entrance is on the side. He said I could park in the alley."

Brodie guided her car down the narrow path alongside the building, getting as close to the entry as she could before turning off the engine. "You get the door. I'll get the bags."

"Don't bother. I can get my own bag," Kate said, reaching for the door handle.

"Jesus Christ, woman, could you give me a break?" Brodie growled. "I get that you hate me, okay? I *get* it, but I'm not being chivalrous. I'm already soaked to the bone, and there's no need for both of us to catch pneumonia. Now, can you please put your bloody bruised dignity to the side for just one minute and go open the door, or would you rather just sit here and argue about it all night long?"

Kate gave Brodie the evil eye before opening the door, and jumping out, she slammed it behind her before making a mad dash to the stoop.

The hostel was nothing more than the end unit of a row home that had been converted to guest rooms on one side and the owner's living space on the other. It wasn't deserving of any stars, and Brodie couldn't have cared less. All she wanted was to change her clothes, have a bed on which to sleep, and put as much distance between her and Kate as possible.

Brodie had spent most of the drive silently berating herself for what she had done. She knew she fucked up. She knew she crossed the line. She also knew she wasn't *entirely* to blame, and Kate's righteousness was starting to grate on her. It was one thing for Kate to cry foul because Brodie kissed her. It was quite another to let it happen three times and then point a finger in only *one* direction.

The alleyway was acting like a funnel, and the minuscule roof over the door offered Kate little protection from the onslaught. Wind and rain whipped pummeled her as she fumbled to get the key into the lock, and when she finally stumbled inside, Kate was soaked to the skin.

While water dripped off her useless raincoat and puddled on the floor, Kate took in her minimal surroundings, lit by a single naked bulb on the ceiling. The walls hadn't been painted in years, the once-white surface now grimy and gray, and the linoleum covering the floor had peeled in several spots. Kate shrugged. At least it had a roof.

Brodie used her foot to slam the door closed, and putting down the luggage, she grimaced. "I hope the rooms look better than this."

"That makes two of us."

"Only one way to find out," Brodie said, picking up her suitcase. "You've got the keys. Choose a room."

Kate looked at the keys and handing Brodie the fob labeled *Two*, Kate grabbed her suitcase and headed to the door with a crooked number one nailed to its surface.

Brodie unlocked her room, and feeling around the doorframe, she found the switch and flipped it on just as Kate called out from behind her.

"Hey, I don't know about yours, but mine's not that bad."

Brodie had to agree. While the hallway was a bit seedy, her room appeared to be clean and neat. Sparsely furnished, it held only a bed, a nightstand, a small dresser, and an upholstered chair, and as she stepped inside, she noticed a tiny door to her left. Going over, Brodie discovered an equally tiny bathroom. The porcelain on the fixtures was permanently stained, and the chrome on the faucets was pitted and dull, but for one night, it was doable.

Brodie returned to the bed and unzipping her jacket, she pulled out the bag containing the candles. Placing it on the nightstand, she looked across the hall to see Kate standing in the other room. "Hey, if you're going to be okay, I think I'm going to get out of these wet clothes."

Lost in her thoughts, it took a moment for Kate to answer. "I'll be fine, Brodie. Thanks."

Kate closed the door and rested against it. She wasn't fine. Kate wasn't even close. Since the kiss, she'd been unable to get the flavor of that memory off her lips or out of her head. She had reprimanded Brodie and accused her of taking advantage, yet Kate knew she was as much to blame, if not more. The dress she wore, she wore for Brodie. When hands were held, she was the one who had made the first move, and when Brodie rested her hand on Kate's bare shoulder, it was Kate who had remained motionless, praying Brodie wouldn't remove it.

Brodie had only managed to hang her jacket on a hook in the bathroom before a brilliant flash lit up the room. Within seconds, a booming crash of thunder rattled the window, and then the room lit up again. Impressed by Mother Nature's show of power, Brodie went to the window and pushed aside the drapes. There wasn't much to see other than the alley and the rain slashing against the glass until the black sky was splintered by tentacles of lightning branching out in all directions. Brodie's eyes lit up as she watched the spectacle, and she was about to drag the upholstered chair over to the window and get comfortable when the lights in her room flickered, and then everything went dark. "Well, shit."

Brodie did an excellent imitation of a gauze-wrapped mummy as she made her way across the room, feeling for the bag of candles on the nightstand. She uttered a few expletives when her shin met the metal frame of the bed before she managed to find the bag, and feeling her way to the bathroom, Brodie fumbled for the lighter in her jacket pocket. A minute later, her room now aglow with candlelight, she set one jarred candle on her nightstand and carried the other across the hall to Kate.

Brodie lightly tapped on Kate's door, chuckling when she heard Kate rattle off her fair share of curse words before the door finally opened. "I thought you might need one of these," Brodie said, holding up the candle.

As Kate reached for the jar, another resounding crash of thunder rattled the hostel and cringing at the racket, she stepped aside so Brodie could come into the room. "Do you have any idea when this shit is going to stop?"

"Um…I told you," Brodie said, placing the candle on the dresser. "It's not expected to let up until morning."

"Oh, that's right," Kate said, aimlessly looking around. "I forgot."

A blinding flash suddenly lit up the room, and as soon as Brodie saw Kate's eyes double in size, she was at her side. No longer concerned with their argument, Brodie pulled Kate into her arms. "Hey, it's okay," she said, rubbing Kate's back. "It's just a storm."

Kate listened to the rain beating against the window, but it didn't compare to the pounding of her heart. Brodie was only doing what friends do, trying to offer comfort and soothe her nerves. Kate knew it was innocent, yet with each gentle caress, Brodie was unraveling everything Kate was trying to keep hidden.

The next crash of thunder seemed to rock the hostel, and feeling Kate trembling in her arms, Brodie gathered her tightly against her chest. "Kate, there's no need to be afraid," she said, her tone hushed and calm. "It'll be over before you know it."

"I'm not afraid of the storm."

"No?"

"No," Kate said, tipping her head to look at Brodie. "I'm afraid of this."

Brodie didn't move. She didn't blink. She didn't even breathe. She merely swallowed hard as Kate reached up and touched her face. Mesmerized, she watched as Kate's eyes darted from her lips to her eyes and back again, and when Kate slipped her hand behind Brodie's neck and gently pulled her downward, Brodie offered not one ounce of resistance.

With the memories of what happened a few hours before still in her mind, Brodie allowed Kate to take the lead, and her kiss was tender, almost timid. Lips parted and then met again, heads slowly tilting to allow for new areas to be tasted, and when Brodie could no longer hold back and lightly drew her tongue across Kate's lips, this time Kate didn't pull away.

Kate moaned as Brodie's tongue slipped inside, and as she slowly explored the recesses of Kate's mouth, Kate could do nothing but offer her more. Opening her lips, she deepened the kiss, and as their tongues danced...their hearts began to race.

Brodie's body throbbed with desire, and a wildfire spread outward from her core, igniting everything in its path. Her body tingled. Her heart pounded, and her breathing grew shallow, and it took all the strength she had to pull out of the kiss. "Are you sure?" she said, gazing at Kate. "Are you sure this is what you want?"

Their eyes met, and it only took Brodie a few moments before she found her answer. Swirling amidst the passion in Kate's eyes was an infinitesimal hint of doubt, and when Kate lowered her gaze, Brodie knew the evening was over. She held Kate in her arms for a few seconds longer before placing a light kiss on her brow, and pulling out of the embrace, Brodie walked to the door. "Good night, Kate. See you in the morning."

***

Brodie sat in the thread-bare upholstered chair wearing nothing but an oversized Oxford and a pair of knickers. After she had left Kate's room, she ran a bath and sitting in the tub until the water grew cold, she hoped it would extinguish the fire in her heart as quickly as it had the one between her legs.

As she had done for the past two hours, Brodie stared off into space, scolding her heart for not listening to her head. She had become a dog chasing its tail, and she was never going to catch it. Brodie rocked back in the chair, letting out a long breath before reaching for another cigarette. They were a crutch, and she knew it, but at that particular moment, Brodie didn't give a good goddamn. Tomorrow she'd quit smoking, and tomorrow she would, once and for all, quit Kate.

Brodie had barely managed to take a drag when she heard a noise, a noise that had nothing to do with the storm. She waited, praying she wouldn't hear it again, but when someone rapped lightly on her door for the second time, Brodie rolled her eyes. "Fuck me," she said under her breath, and pushing herself out of the chair, Brodie reached the door in four long strides. Yanking it open, she hesitated when she noticed Kate was still wearing the clothes dampened by the rain. "I'm not sure why I need to tell you this because you *are* an adult, but you should get out of those wet clothes," Brodie said, staring down her nose at Kate. "And if you're looking for towels, I don't have any extras, so you'll just have to make do."

As if she was carrying the weight of the world on her shoulders, Kate slogged into Brodie's room without waiting for an invitation.

Brodie gritted her teeth, and silently counted to ten before slamming the door. "What do you want from me, Kate? Can I ask you that?" she said, turning to Kate. "One minute you're hot, and the next, you're cold, and then you have the audacity to make it all *my* fault when I misread signals that I *didn't* misread. Well, it isn't *all* my fault, Kate, and I'm done with your games. Go back to your room. You don't belong in here."

Without saying a word, Kate walked to the dresser. She stubbed out the cigarette burning in the ashtray, and while she extinguished one fire, she fanned the flames of another.

"Kate, what in the hell are you *doing*?" When she didn't answer, Brodie marched across the room until she was inches from Kate. "Kate, answer the bloody question. What are you doing? Why are you *here*?"

"Yes."

"What?" Brodie said, staring blankly back at Kate.

"Yes."

Brodie tilted her head, rewinding their previous conversation in her mind until she came to the only question Kate could possibly be answering. Her mouth dropped open, and everything she had condemned herself for doing, Brodie was about to do again. Deliberating for only a second, Brodie came up behind Kate until she was standing a hairsbreadth away from the woman. "Yes?"

For the past two hours, Kate had argued, debated, and rationalized herself in and out of Brodie's bed. Turn one direction, and her life returned to normal, turn another, and it would be anything but, yet denying what she wanted was futile. With her heart beating so fast she dared not move, Kate could only nod, and when she felt Brodie's hands on her shoulders, pushing aside the damp sweater to expose bare skin, Kate closed her eyes as her lungs emptied.

Brodie lowered her lips to skin, ivory and soft. There was no need to rush, no need not to cherish every kiss she bestowed as she deliberately moved toward the pulse beating in Kate's neck. Kate leaned her head, silently giving Brodie permission to continue, and wrapping her arm around Kate's middle, Brodie gently urged her closer. As their bodies spooned, Brodie nuzzled against the hollow of Kate's neck as her hands found the hem of Kate's sweater, and a heartbeat later, Kate raised her arms, and her cardigan was lifted off and dropped to the floor.

After the party, they had both changed into traveling clothes, but Kate hadn't bothered with her undergarments. Her bra was the color of blood. Strapless and underwire, it exposed and presented beyond Brodie's wildest of dreams, and as she ran a trail of kisses across Kate's shoulder, Brodie's eyes remained riveted on the valley between the ivory swells. Her fingers danced lightly down Kate's arms and across her belly, leaving goosebumps in their path, and when she unfastened the snap on Kate's jeans, Brodie heard Kate draw in a hissing breath. The denim, still wet from the rain, was heavy, and it took almost a minute for Kate to free herself from the damp fabric. She kicked them to the side, but as she went to turn around, Brodie held her firm.

"No, not yet," Brodie whispered. "Not yet."

Kate melted into Brodie's body, and the sensual assault continued. Brodie seared Kate's skin with a pleasurable path of delicate kisses, and when she reached Kate's ear, Brodie ran her tongue around its edge before gently nibbling on the lobe. Kate's core throbbed. She was being pushed to a place she had never been. A place where thoughts disappear and instincts take over, yet when Kate tried to turn to face Brodie, she found herself stopped again. "Please, Brodie," Kate said in a breath. "I want to see you."

Brodie smiled into the creaminess of Kate's neck. Weighed down by arousal and need, Kate's voice was breathy and low, and every word had made Brodie's body pulse with desire. No longer able to resist, Brodie raised her hands and cupped Kate's breasts.

"Oh, my God," Kate said. "Oh…God."

Kate felt passion seep from her body as Brodie fondled her through the red spandex edged in lace. Her nipples were hard and erect, and Brodie was tweaking them so flawlessly Kate couldn't help but squirm. She turned her head and found Brodie gazing back at her. Her eyes now appeared almost black, and blazing in the inkiness was a hunger that took Kate's breath away. For a split-second, she felt Brodie's grip loosen, and Kate quickly spun in her arms. Grabbing Brodie by the hair, she pulled her down until their lips met.

It was a devouring, open-mouthed kiss with not one hint of shyness or doubt, and filled with the ferocity of unrestrained emotions, once the kiss started neither wanted it to end. Fingers laced through hair, and heads leaned this way and that and until finally, with lips swollen from passion, and gasping for air, they parted.

Through heavy-lidded eyes, Kate watched as Brodie began unbuttoning her Oxford. One by one, the fasteners were freed, and as the shirt gaped, a hint of Brodie's breasts came into view.

The image should have been provocative. It should have heated Kate's blood to the point of boiling, but instead, Kate felt as if she'd been doused in icy water, and the cold, hard reality of what she was about to do punched her in the stomach. *This* wasn't something she could take back. *This* wasn't something she could ever explain away. This was a craving that, once tasted, would foul the rest of what she wanted in her life. Kate knew she was in love with Brodie, but this moment—this *act*—would forever pollute Kate's plans. It would contaminate her thoughts. It would poison future lovers. It would corrupt every minute of the rest of her life.

Kate took a half-step backward, and when Brodie followed her, Kate put up her hands. "No, don't."

"What's wrong?" Brodie said with a slight shake of her head.

"I can't do this," Kate said, shrinking further away from Brodie as her eyes remained glued on Brodie's partially unbuttoned shirt. "I can't do this."

It was Brodie's turn to step back, and as tears welled in her eyes, she struggled to take a breath. "Kate, please…not again."

"No, I can't do this," Kate said, snatching up her clothes. "This isn't what I want."

"You're just scared. It's new."

"It's *wrong*," Kate yelled, clutching her sweater to her chest to cover what Brodie had already seen. "This isn't who I am. This isn't who I want to be. I'm sorry, Brodie, but I *cannot* do this."

Brodie didn't move a muscle as Kate pushed past by her. She listened as one door slammed and then another, and in a room musty and quiet, Brodie slowly buttoned her shirt. Just under the surface simmered an emotion, and taking a ragged breath, Brodie went over and sank into the cushion of the old, shabby chair. She stared at the flame of the candle across the room, and as it drifted to and fro, she lit a cigarette. Brodie wondered if this was how it felt to be dead. She was so empty, so hollowed out that the universe no longer existed outside of this room. There was no tomorrow. There was no future. It was all black and dark, and resting her cigarette in the ashtray, Brodie bowed her head and cried for the loss of a love she would never have.

Chapter Thirteen

"Someone's busy," Devon said as she strolled into the bedroom.

"If people could make up their bloody minds, it would make my job a hell of a lot easier," Brodie muttered as she sat bent over the drafting table in the corner of the room.

"Problems?" Devon said, looking past Brodie to the papers covering the slanted surface.

"No, not really," Brodie said, letting out a long breath. "I'm just working on something for the Hirshfelds."

"I thought we finished that job."

Brodie looked up. "We?"

"Huh?"

"You said we."

Over the past few months, Devon had become well-versed in walking on eggshells around Brodie, and she held up her hands. "My bad. A slip of the tongue."

Brodie spun in her chair, shuffling through the papers in front of her before turning back around. "It needn't be," she said, handing Devon an envelope.

"What's this?"

"I have a feeling if you open it, you'll find out."

Devon didn't have to be told twice. Ripping open the flap, she pulled out a piece of a paper, and after reading what was written, she looked at Brodie. "I don't understand."

"Ethan and I have been talking. We both believe, especially in this day and age, it makes sense to branch out a bit. He can build, and I can design, but smart homes are all the rage, and they are not going to fall out of grace. Between home theaters, home technology, automation, and security systems, there's a huge part of the market we've yet to tap, and we'd like your assistance in doing just that."

"Security systems? I thought you always used Basham and Sons."

"Have you seen Basham or his sons? Not only are they never on time and never clean up after themselves, if I have to see one more of their butt cracks, I'll be forever mentally scarred. Besides, I can't imagine security systems fall that far outside your high-tech wizardry."

"They don't. It's really just a bunch of ones and zeros."

Brodie peered at Devon. "I'll pretend to understand what that means."

"Speaking of understanding," Devon said, glancing at the paper again. "I'm really not sure I understand this."

"Ethan and I would like you to become a partner in Spaces by Shaw. By signing that document, you'd give up your independent contractor status and join with us. We haven't figured out all the details, but the amount of money shown there would cover your stake in the company, and once it's all said and done, you'd be almost an equal partner with Ethan and me."

"Almost?"

"Well, we did start the company, but that doesn't mean we can't even up the split down the road. Baby steps."

A weak smile appeared on Devon's face as she scanned the contract again. "Brodie, I really appreciate what you're offering, but...but this would wipe out my savings. I'm not sure—"

"You don't have to pay it all at once, Devon. We'd work out something where a bit of your pay would go against what you owe us, and if you want to pay more toward the balance, you can. Totally up to you."

"But I'd still get paid?"

"No, I want my new, techno-brilliant business partner to live on the streets," Brodie said with a laugh. "Of course, you'll get paid. Actually, even with paying against this, you'll probably...no...you'll definitely make more than you're making now."

"Really?"

"Yes, *really*," Brodie said. "We have some things in the works, and if they come to fruition, you, Ethan, and I are not only going to be working our arses off, we're also going to be bringing in quite a bit of cash. No more living in that tiny flat of yours in that not-so-good area, Devon. No more taking the Tube because if you want a car, you'll be able to afford one, and when you want to treat that lady of yours to a special night or a special holiday, you'll easily be able to do just that...with proper scheduling, of course."

"Of course."

"So?"

"You're not going to give a girl a minute to think?"

Brodie's face split into a grin. "Take all the time you want," she said, spinning back to the drafting table. "I've got work to do."

"Okay, thanks," Devon said, pocketing the offer. "Hey, I'm going to get something to drink. Do you want anything?"

"Yeah. There's an open bottle of Malbec on the counter. Pour me a glass, will you?"

"Sure thing."

Preoccupied with a design, Brodie had no idea Devon had returned until she placed a glass of wine on the table. A second later, the contract that now had her signature scrawled across the bottom was placed next to it. "You didn't have to sign that today," Brodie said. "You could have taken it to a lawyer for review."

"Do I need to?"

"No, you don't," Brodie said, picking up her glass. "And thanks for the wine."

As Brodie took a sip of her drink, Devon looked at the sketches on the table. "That's not the Hirshfeld addition."

"No, it's a cottage in New Milton they just bought. Apparently, it was a steal, but Dori hates the kitchen, and Winston loathes the floor plan, so they asked me to come up with some ideas. I went down there earlier this week and took all the measurements, and this is as far as I've gotten."

"So, will my expertise be needed on it?"

Brodie's eyes creased at the corners. "Yes, this will be a smart home all the way. Of course, I need to lock down the design before we start talking about all the geeky stuff."

"Speaking of geeky stuff, I still can't believe you do this shit on paper when CAD is installed on every laptop you have."

"I use it. You know I use it. I couldn't do what I do without it, but in the early stages, I like old school better. It makes me feel like I'm part of the design instead of just someone pushing a few buttons and sliding a mouse around a pad."

Brodie turned back to the table, and Devon sat on the edge of the bed, sipping her beer as she thought about how her life had just changed. It would be nice being able to live somewhere without worrying so much about break-ins or neighbors higher than kites. She'd finally be able to afford something better than second-hand furniture, and after all the meals Kate had fixed her, Devon was already looking forward to inviting her sister to dinner.

Devon jerked upright. It had been almost three months since Brodie had returned from Bournemouth, and while the woman had hidden her pain from most, Devon had seen it on more than one occasion. Strong and defiant, Brodie still saddened at the sound of rain. Confidence bordering on arrogance gave way to glassy eyes when a love song played on the radio, and when her family phoned, it took Brodie days to return their calls.

Devon had soon made it her mission not to mention Kate. It hadn't been easy, and after a while, she intentionally put some distance between herself and Brodie, fearing if she slipped up, it would bring Brodie more pain. The usual invite to visit a pub hadn't happened in months. The easy banter about her day or her evening had been edited to eliminate all mention of her sister, and whenever Kate called, Devon let it go to voice mail if Brodie was within hearing distance.

Although it should never be a constant in any friendship, sometimes to protect those held dear, untruths are spoken, or words are censored. It's what friends do. Business partners, on the other hand, aren't afforded that same compassion for honesty has to come before all else. If you can't trust your business partner, they have no business being your partner.

Devon looked over at Brodie and took a deep breath. "I can't thank you enough for giving me this opportunity, but...but what about Kate?"

Brodie stiffened. "This has nothing to do with her."

"She's still my sister, and whether you noticed it or not, I...well, I've done my best not to mention her, but I can't keep that up. Not if we're going to be working together as closely as I think we are."

"I noticed, and I appreciate what you've been doing, but you don't have to any longer," Brodie said as she began fiddling with some papers on the desk. "I'm okay."

"Liar."

"Don't start."

"Then, don't lie."

Brodie spun back around and tossed her pencil on the worktable. "Devon, I'm fine. Every day gets a bit better. Okay? I'm not saying I'm perfect, and life is grand, but I'm better than I was yesterday or the day before."

Devon didn't know the details. The day following Brodie's return from visiting her father, Devon had asked how the trip had gone only to be rebuked by her friend in a rant that ended with Brodie bolting from the room, stating unequivocally it was none of Devon's damn business. Confused, she went over to visit Kate's and casually asked the same, and Kate blew her sister off with a shrug. Neither woman had mentioned the other since that day, but the door had just cracked open, and Devon would be damned if she was going to allow it to close again. Brodie hadn't been herself in months, and Devon knew in her heart, Kate was to blame.

"You loved her, didn't you?" Devon said softly.

Brodie rested back in her chair. "Yes, love is a two-way street and Kate...Kate couldn't get past the fact that I'm a woman."

"Shit," Devon said, her eyes instantly misting.

The room grew quiet, the hum of Brodie's laptop the only sound as minutes crept by until finally, Brodie found the courage to ask a question she had wanted to ask for months. "How is she?"

"She's fine. She's been keeping busy with work and..."

Brodie knew what was coming, and she hung her head. "And?"

"She's seeing someone, Brodie. I'm sorry."

"I suppose it was bound to happen," Brodie said, her voice lacking any emotion. She turned her back on Devon and stared at the drawings on her desk.

Devon sniffled back some tears and wiped her nose with the back of her hand. "Hey...um...Gina's working tonight. How about I order some takeaway, and we can shoot some pool. You know? Like old times."

"Can't. I'm going out."

"Out?"

"Yes, Cassidy, *out*, like on a date."

The room grew quiet again, almost too quiet. Brodie turned and saw Devon gawking back at her. Brodie sighed. "If you must know, Harper's in town. She called earlier, and I'm going to meet her for a drink or two."

"Oh, I see."

"Do you have a problem with that?"

"Um…no," Devon said, lowering her eyes. "I just don't want you to do anything you'll regret."

"What's to regret? It's not like I have anyone to come home to, is it? I've got no woman in my bed *or* in my life, and I'm not planning to sleep with Harper, but honestly, if the subject comes up, I can't think of one reason why I should say no. Can you?"

Devon looked up. "Rebound…maybe."

"Oh, Jesus Christ, it's been almost three bloody *months*," Brodie shouted, slapping her thighs. "No calls, no e-mails, no *nothing*. You said it yourself, Cassidy. Kate's seeing someone else, and correct me if I'm wrong, but I'm assuming that someone else is a bloke—yes?"

"Yes."

"Fine, but men aren't my flavor, women are. Women like Harper, who know *what* they want and *who* they want without making you believe one thing and then slapping you in the face with another."

Devon frowned. Although the wound in Brodie's heart had scabbed over, it was still there. In the tone of her voice, the furrows in her forehead, and the clench of her fists, it was like graffiti on a wall. "I'm sorry she hurt you," Devon whispered. "I'm truly, truly sorry."

Brodie let out a long breath and reaching across the desk, she switched off the lamp. She got to her feet, and as she made her way to the wardrobe, she stopped for a second to give her friend a hug. "I know you are, and I appreciate it. All right?"

"Yeah."

"Good, now I need to get changed, or I'm going to be late."

"I guess that's my cue to leave?"

"You can hang here if you'd like. If I hook up with Harper, we'll most likely end up at her hotel so you won't be interrupting anything. Oh, and I promise to take you up on the offer about takeaway and shooting some pool. It's been way too long."

"I couldn't agree more, and don't think I'm not going to hold you to that," Devon said as she went to leave. "See you later, boss."

"Don't you mean partner?"

Devon stopped in her tracks and turned around. "Yeah," she said, her expression brightening the room. "I guess I do…partner."

The two women exchanged smiles, but when Devon turned to leave, Brodie called out, "Hey, Cassidy."

"Yeah?" Devon said, spinning around again.

Brodie paused for a moment. "Is he a nice man?"

Devon's heart broke, and fighting to control her emotions, she bobbed her head. "He seems to be. A bit nancy for me, but Kate seems happy."

"Good."

***

The day after Kate returned from Bournemouth, steadfastly refusing to think about or speak of Brodie Shaw, she returned to work more focused on her career than ever before. As if possessed, and much to the chagrin of her lackadaisical partner, Kate took on as many cases as was allowed. She worked each, leaving no stone unturned right down to the smallest of pebbles, and on the rare occasion when she wasn't working, if friends called about dinners or drinks, Kate happily accepted. She was on a mission…a mission to forget a woman and find a man.

Having already crossed Chase Wakefield off her list, for weeks, Kate was the third or fifth wheel whenever she met with friends until one suggested she meet an acquaintance of theirs. Kate loathed blind dates almost as much as she loathed dating apps, except when you're an amped-up workaholic, your options are limited. So, on one warm summer night, Kate was introduced to Julian Fitzgerald.

Julian was an attractive man, and he knew it. His chestnut brown hair was cut in the trendy long on top, short on the side style that was all the rage, and the stubble on his chin and cheeks was forever two days old. He was only a few inches taller than Kate, but what Julian lacked in height, he made up for with a charismatic smile and a light, carefree attitude. His waist was slender, and his shoulders were square, and he had a nicely defined six-pack courtesy of his yearly membership at a gym. And even though his profession should have hardened his hands, when he first held Kate's, she was surprised at their softness.

Julian had inherited his father's business when the old man keeled over and died from a heart attack. The first thing Julian did was change the name of the company from Fitzgerald & Son to Premier Hardscapes by Julian. The second thing he did was raise the prices. It had been an ongoing argument between father and son for years, the elder believing his prices were fair while the younger thought them to be ridiculous...even though Julian had never laid a single brick, block, or paving stone in his life.

As a youngster, Julian's dream was to work alongside his father to learn the trade that would eventually become his, but at the age of eight, he was diagnosed with childhood asthma. Between the coughing and shortness of breath, his parents decided Julian couldn't be exposed to the dust, dirt, and pollen on his father's jobsites. Young Julian was not happy. He whined and complained, sending himself into more than one asthma attack as a result of his meltdowns until, on one very trying afternoon, his mother came up with an idea. She gathered up every interlocking building block she could find in Julian's toy chest and asked Julian to help design the next project. She believed it to be a game, just something to quiet a rambunctious child, so she could take care of the bookkeeping, except it wasn't a game to Julian. He worked, hunched over on the floor for hours, anxious to show his father what he created, and the game eventually became his calling. Julian's eye for design surpassed both his parents, and by the time he turned sixteen, Julian no longer wanted to work side-by-side with his father in the dirt and dust. Even though his allergies and asthma had eased as he had grown older, Julian preferred the comfort of their home office, and eventually, he was designing every project his father had under contract.

It wasn't until his mother passed away when Julian took over the company books and discovered what his father was charging, and the rift began. Their list of clients was the who's who of the upper class, yet they had almost nothing to show for it, except for the company's reputation.

If it had to do with patios, driveways, retaining walls, stonework, ponds, and fire pits, there weren't many who hadn't heard of their company or Julian's design capabilities, and after his father died, Julian used that to his advantage. He added to his employees the best from his competitors, luring them away with promises of better wages and benefits, and although the benefits he offered were only a smidge above the others, the wages were not. Julian paid his people well. He was driven to succeed further than his father could have ever dreamed, and to do that, the quality of the work produced by Hardscapes by Julian had to surpass his father's...and it did.

Ten years from the day after changing the company name, Julian had doubled his clients and tripled his money. He didn't break his back lifting bricks and pavers, nor did he sweat in the summer sun or work in the misty rain of autumn or winter. Julian did what he did best. He ran his company. He schmoozed with new customers, and putting in longer hours than his workers in the field, he came up with new, innovative designs that everyone in the business was talking about. However, when Friday night rolled around, Julian put aside his company and partied like a college freshman.

"You are *not* canceling again."

Kate rubbed the bridge of her nose. "I'm sorry, but I need to work on finishing up some paperwork."

"What about working on our *relationship*?" Julian crowed into the phone. "Because, babe, I gotta tell you, this is getting old."

Kate silently agreed. Julian's Friday night routine *was* getting old. When she first met him, Kate found him attractive and likable. A seemingly fellow workaholic, Kate believed she'd found her match, and it wasn't long before Julian ended up in her bed. It wasn't the best sex she'd ever had, and it wasn't the worst either. At least he preferred the window closed.

As the weeks passed, Kate enjoyed spending time with Julian as long as it didn't include Friday nights. Julian loved spending those in noisy pubs with his boisterous mates. They'd slam their mugs on tables as they bellowed about the football matches playing on the flat-screen TVs or challenge each other to never-ending dart games that lasted until the wee hours of the morning. It was fun at first. It was nice to be someone's other half again, to be part of a pair instead of the odd woman out at a gathering. It was nice to have plans, instead of going home alone to books, leftovers, and silence...yet Friday nights were different.

Julian was always a perfect gentleman when they went out on their own. He'd hold Kate's hand, open doors for her, and even pull out her chair, but when he was around his mates, Julian turned boastful and arrogant. He'd raise his voice to project over others around him, name-dropping his list of rich and famous clients as he spoke about his week. He would point out all the things his friends were doing wrong in their lives while assuring them he'd never made the same mistakes, and when his mates weren't listening, Julian talked about them behind their backs.

At first, Kate put her feelings aside, blaming Julian's hubris on ale and testosterone. She told herself it was what men did, and it was only one night a week. That lasted for three weeks before Kate began finding excuses to skip Julian's set-in-concrete plans because she had also noticed something else about her boyfriend. On pub nights, Julian didn't hold Kate's hand. Instead, he'd pull her close, and draping his arm across her shoulders or wrapping it tightly around her waist, with no words he made it clear she was his. Kate didn't mind being Julian's girlfriend. She actually liked it six days of the week, but his actions in the crowded pubs filled with his college buddies made her feel less like a partner...and more like a trophy.

Kate flinched out of her thoughts. Julian was still talking, and she hadn't heard a word he said. "What? I'm sorry...um...someone needed some files. What were you saying?"

"I was saying that you're my girl, and now that I have you, I want you to be with me when I'm seeing my mates. I'm proud of you, and I want to show you off."

"I'm not a prize, Julian," Kate said, straightening her backbone.

"You are in my eyes."

In an instant, Julian went from being annoying to sweet, and Kate slumped in her chair. "All right...um...listen. Let me finish up here, and I'll meet you there. How's that?"

"When?"

Like a slow-motion Jack-in-the-box, Kate sat straight again. "I don't know, Julian. I'll get there when I get there, but that's not going to happen until we end this conversation."

"Right. Fine. Then I'll see you at the pub. Just don't take all night."

With a click, the line went dead, and Kate slid her mobile back into her pocket. She glanced at four remaining folders on her desk. In each were a few forms containing information that needed to be entered into the computer. On a bad day, it would have taken Kate an hour to complete the task. Tonight, she had every intention of making it last for at least two or possibly three if she counted visits to the ladies' and the vending machines.

Chapter Fourteen

"When do you have to be at the airport?"

Harper raised her eyes. She put aside her fork and dabbed at the corners of her mouth with a napkin. "Do you realize that's the third time you've asked me that since picking me up at the hotel?"

"Is it?"

"Yes," Harper said, looking back and forth between the plates in front of them. "And my dinner is delicious, so I'm not sure why you've picked at yours for over ten minutes without taking a bite."

"I guess I'm not as hungry as I thought," Brodie said, resting her fork on the plate.

Before Harper could speak, their waitress appeared holding a bottle of wine. "Sorry to interrupt. Giuseppe's tied up in the kitchen, but he wanted you to have a bottle on the house. He was worried something had happened. We haven't seen you in weeks."

"Oh, sorry about that," Brodie said, forcing a smile. "Just swamped at work."

"It happens to us all," Angie said, gesturing with her head to the filled tables in the room. "But you're our favorite customer, so don't be a stranger. Okay?"

"I'll try not to be. I promise."

"Good," Angie said, touching Brodie on the arm. "Well, enjoy the wine."

Harper watched as Angie headed to another table and then returned her focus to Brodie. "What's all that about?"

"It's nothing," Brodie said, grabbing the bottle of Chianti. "Refill?"

"Sure," Harper said, holding out her glass. "I'm not driving."

"Neither am I."

"Yeah, I was kind of surprised you picked me up in a taxi."

"Didn't feel like driving."

Harper's eyebrow arched. Brodie had already had two glasses of wine, and the one she just poured herself went almost to the rim. "By the looks of it, you feel like getting drunk though."

"I just want to unwind."

Brodie's voice had remained flat, almost monotone since the moment she'd arrived at Harper's hotel. The only time she'd seen the woman smile was at the waitress a minute earlier, and Brodie had lost weight she didn't need to lose. She was still beautiful, but her eyes lacked the vitality Harper knew so well.

Harper reached across the table and took Brodie's hand. "Do you want to talk about it?"

"No. It still hurts a bit too much for that," Brodie said, pulling her hand away. "Besides, I've already beaten myself up enough for falling for a straight woman. I don't need to hear it from you, too."

"I would never do that, and you know it," Harper said, lovingly gazing at Brodie. "Look, I only met Kate that one night and a lot of it was lost to the tequila, but I honestly thought she was the real deal...not that it helps."

"That makes two of us, and you're right. It doesn't."

"So, what are you going to do?"

"About what?" Brodie said before picking up her wine and polishing off half the glass.

"About this," Harper said, waving her hand in front of Brodie. "You can't keep moping around, you know? One of these days you're going to have to get back in the saddle."

"I'm not really in the mood for a ride."

"Then, get ridden."

Brodie's face clouded with anger. "Harper!"

"What?" Harper said, holding up her hands. "All I'm saying is there are lots of women out there willing to give you want you need, so stop brooding about the one you can't have...and find one you can."

"It's not that easy," Brodie said, placing her glass back on the table.

"Sure, it is. Before Kate, it wasn't about love. It was about sex," Harper said, leaning forward in her seat. "Go back to the basics, Brodie. Stop thinking about love and settle for lust. It hardly ever hurts, that is...unless you want it to."

***

Kate held up her warrant card as she made her way through the police officers standing on the sidewalk, her teeth showing through her smile when she saw Elliott Thackery walking toward her.

"We have to stop meeting like this."

"Hiya, Elliott."

"Hi yourself," he said, tucking a notepad under his arm. "What are you doing here?"

"I was just leaving the station when the call came in. It sounded like all hands on deck, so I thought I'd come over and see if I could help. I would have been here earlier, but there was a fender bender that caused a ridiculous amount of gridlock."

"Blame it on that," Elliott said, looking up at the evening sky. "Bloody full moon always creates havoc."

"By the number of squad cars around here, I'd have to say you're right. It must have been one hell of a brawl."

"You could say that," Elliott said, signaling for Kate to follow. "Come on. I'll show you."

Kate shadowed Elliott down the walk, and when she stepped into what used to be a club, her jaw hit the floor. "Oh my God."

Elliott grinned. "Quite a mess, isn't it?"

Mess didn't even begin to describe it. Amidst the puddles of spilled beer and liquor, the floor glistened with what remained of mugs, glasses, and bottles, and at least a dozen stools and tables were either broken or lying on their sides. The mirror behind the bar was shattered, and the bottles of alcohol once perched on shelves had been smashed, making the club smell like a distillery. Customers who had become witnesses stood in groups around the room, waiting their turn to be questioned while medics roamed the club, assisting those with cuts, scratches, or worse.

"What in the hell happened?" Kate said, looking over at Elliott.

"Bar fight."

Kate laughed. "Ya think?"

Elliott smiled. "And I know this is going to sound totally sexist, but I still can't believe women did this."

"What?" Kate blurted. "Women?"

"Yeah. This is or *was* a lesbian hangout. It's always been one of the rougher ones, and now I can see why."

Kate looked around at the wreckage, and even though it was a sexist comment of sorts, Kate had to agree with Elliott's assessment. She'd seen the aftermath of brawls in sports bars that didn't compare to what was in front of her. As her eyes darted here and there, a group of people off to her right moved in tandem toward the door, and with her view no longer obstructed, Kate saw yet another victim of the fight...and her gasp went unchecked.

"What's wrong?" Elliott said, looking up from his notepad.

"Um...nothing," Kate said, glancing toward the door. "But since you seem to have everything under control, I think I'm going to head out."

"That's fine. We're almost wrapped up here anyway," Elliott said, returning to his notes. "Have a good night."

"You, too."

Kate made her way to the door and spotting a medic standing near the entrance, she touched him on the arm. "Excuse me, but that woman over there, the one sitting on the stairs...it looks like she's bleeding."

The portly man looked over his shoulder. "That she is."

"Aren't you going to help her?"

The man glowered at Kate. "Love, I've asked her three times if I could help her, and three times she's told me to bugger off. I can't help them if they don't want to be helped. It's the law, and I have to follow it." Without waiting for a response, the medic walked away.

Kate took a deep breath and letting it out slowly, she walked to the door, but when she reached the threshold, she stopped. "Shit."

***

Brodie's butt was sore. The treads on the spiral stairs were open grate, and she'd been sitting on them for almost an hour while the police questioned and the medics annoyed. All she wanted to do was to go home, except she was in no shape to drive. Between her pounding headache and her blurry vision, Brodie wasn't about to risk herself or others by getting behind the wheel of her car, but calling for a taxi was proving difficult. With a huff, she pulled out her mobile and tried to focus on the screen like she had done earlier. She squinted at the display for a few seconds before pocketing the phone, telling herself she'd try again in a couple of minutes.

"You really should let someone take a look at your head."

As if the jackhammer pounding its way through her skull wasn't enough, when Brodie heard the voice she never—*ever*—wanted to hear again, her temples began to throb. Refusing to look up, she growled, "Bugger off."

"I've heard you've been saying the same thing to the medics."

"And now I'm saying it to you. Bugger the *fuck* off."

"You're hurt."

"And you're a fickle tart," Brodie said, raising her eyes.

This time Kate managed to suppress her gasp. From across the room, she had seen what she knew was dried blood on Brodie's face. What Kate didn't know was that some of it wasn't dry. There was a slow, meandering trickle making its way down Brodie's forehead, some of the blood following the shape of her eyebrow and sliding down her right cheek while the rest trailed down the center of her nose and dripped off the tip.

"Jesus, you need a medic," Kate said, looking around.

"I don't need anything from you." Brodie jumped to her feet. The sudden motion flipped Brodie's stomach, and sitting down hard on the step, she winced as she swallowed the bit of bile that had risen into her mouth.

"Brodie, you need help."

"Look who's talking," Brodie said, cocking her head just enough to see Kate before looking at the floor again. "I don't need anything from you. Not one goddamned thing. Now leave me the fuck alone."

Brodie heard the crunch of broken glass as Kate walked away and closing her eyes, she took a few slow breaths, hoping they would calm her anger and her nausea. A few people were milling about, so she wasn't surprised to hear more glass being ground under shoes until one particular pair seemed to stop in front of her.

"Here. Take this."

"Jesus Christ," Brodie said, pushing herself to her feet. "You really *are* a stupid cow."

Brodie stormed past Kate, and a second later, she was on a carousel, a very fast carousel that sent the room spinning around her. She felt her knees begin to buckle, and then an arm wrapped around her waist.

"I've got you," Kate said, guiding Brodie to one of the few chairs left unbroken. "Now, sit down before you fall down."

"Go to hell."

"Brodie, either you sit the fuck down, or I'm going to let go of you, and you're going to end up on the floor. So, the way I see it, you either you do what I'm asking, or you're going to spend the next few days picking glass out of your arse. Your choice."

Brodie had to blink a few times to clear her vision enough to see the glittering clear, green, and brown shards littering the floor. "Fine," she said, slowly lowering herself to the chair. "Satisfied?"

"I will be once you let me call a medic over."

"Go to hell," Brodie said, and bowing her head, she closed her eyes, hoping when she opened them again, Kate would be gone. A few seconds later, she caught a whiff of Kate's perfume, and then she felt fingers in her hair. Brodie pulled away and ended up scrambling to hold onto the chair when the blinding pain in her skull brought with it another wave of nausea "Whataya doing?" Brodie mumbled, praying her stomach contents wouldn't soon cover the floor.

Kate's eyebrows drew together, and squatting down, she looked Brodie in the eye. "Are you pissed?"

"I haven't had a drink in over an hour, and what's it to you if I am?"

"Are you dizzy?"

"Are you a doctor?"

Kate rested back on her haunches. "Could you please give me a straight answer?"

"Straight?" Brodie said with a snort. "You know, that's *almost* funny."

"Brodie, listen. I'm just trying to make sure you're okay."

"Fuck you, Kate."

"Brodie, please," Kate said, resting her hand on Brodie's knee. "This isn't exactly easy for me, either."

"You should try getting hit with a beer bottle."

"Is that what happened? Were you involved in all of this?"

"Of course not," Brodie snapped. "I was coming out of the loo. Next thing I knew, I was on the floor covered in beer."

"And blood," Kate said, her eyes drawn to the stream, still snaking its way down Brodie's brow. "Look, will you please just let me get someone to check you over? I'm not a doctor, but you don't look well."

"I've got a fucking headache, Kate. Okay? My vision is blurry because I got blood in my eyes, and my head hurts like a mother, and you are *not* helping the situation. So, the sooner you leave, the—"

"Let me just clean you up a bit, and then I'll go. All right?" Kate said, holding out a wet towel.

"Where'd that come from?"

"I got it from behind the bar."

"Oh," Brodie said, holding out her hand. "Give it to me. I'll do it."

Kate straightened and handed Brodie the cloth. She watched in silence as the woman dabbed it against the top of her head a couple of times before setting the towel aside. Kate mentally counted to ten. "Brodie, you *seriously* need to do better than that."

"I can't. It hurts."

"I would think so."

Brodie slumped further in the chair as her eyes met Kate's. "No, I mean...I think there's glass in it."

***

Kate pulled into the driveway and turning off the ignition, she glanced at her passenger. She had spent the last three hours at the hospital while doctors and nurses tended to Brodie. From the other side of the curtain, Kate had listened while Brodie remained polite and obedient. She had answered their questions and never once protested as they stitched the gash in her scalp, but when the drape was finally pulled aside, and she caught sight of Kate, Brodie's mood swung in the opposite direction. She strode past Kate without saying a word. Her head was high and her attitude defiant until Brodie stepped outside the hospital and the world begin to spin. Kate saw her sway and offered assistance, and a fifteen-minute argument ensued before Kate finally caved to Brodie's demands...sort of.

Brodie scowled as she looked at the window. "Why are we here? I asked you to take me home."

"I have taken you home, just not to your home."

"Goddammit, Kate—"

"Brodie, the doctor said that someone needed to keep an eye on you, and since Gina's still working, Devon's no doubt asleep, and I don't know any of your other friends, you're staying here tonight."

"I don't need a babysitter. I'm an adult."

"Then start fucking *acting* like one," Kate shouted. "It's after midnight, and I'm tired. Okay?"

"I don't want to argue about this."

"Good," Kate said and stepping out of the car, she looked back inside. "Because neither do I."

The car rocked when Kate slammed the door, and by the time she reached the passenger side, Brodie was climbing out. "That's more like it," Kate said, offering Brodie her hand. "You need some—"

"I don't need anything from you," Brodie said, waving off Kate's assistance.

Kate followed two steps behind, thankful the moon was full. Brodie's swaggering gait had been replaced by a shuffle reminiscent of someone wearing concrete boots. When she reached the stairs, she stopped for a long moment, and Kate held her breath, watching as Brodie finally white-knuckled the handrail and climbed the steps. It seemed like she had shrunk in size by the time she reached the top, her entire body slouching under the weight of exhaustion, but Kate didn't say a word. She just opened the door and ushered Brodie inside.

Kate flicked on a few lights and motioned toward the lounge. "Why don't you go relax, and I'll make up the spare room?"

"I can't sit in there."

"God*dammit*, Brodie," Kate barked. "Must we argue about *everything*? Can't you just give me a break and—"

"I'm *not* arguing," Brodie said, looking down at her clothes. "But I smell like I've taken a bath in beer, and I'm covered in blood. Do you really want me sitting on your furniture like this?"

"Shit...good point," Kate said, eyeing the stains on Brodie's trousers. "How about the kitchen?"

Brodie didn't say a word as she followed Kate into the next room, and when she reached the kitchen table, she dropped into a chair and cradled her head in her hands. "Do you have something for a headache? The doctor rattled off what painkillers he recommended, but I wasn't paying that much attention, so anything will do."

"No, anything won't do, and luckily, I *was* paying attention," Kate said, setting the kettle on the stove. "I'll be right back."

Kate jogged up the stairs, returning a few minutes later with the prescribed over-the-counter painkiller. "This is what he said to take," she said, placing the bottle on the table. "Let me get you some water."

Brodie tapped out three tablets and waited for Kate to return. "Thanks," she said, taking the glass.

"If you're okay in here, I'm going to go set up the spare room. All right?"

"Yeah, I'm fine," Brodie said, setting the glass on the table.

A short time later, Kate came back just as the kettle on the burner began to whistle. "I'm going to make some green tea. Would you like some?"

"No, actually, I think...I think I'd like to get cleaned up. Get some sleep."

"All right. My spare room's just down the hall."

Brodie pushed herself out of the chair and followed Kate in silence until she was standing in the middle of the guest room. The furnishings were contemporary, and the walls were green, but other than that, Brodie didn't pay attention to anything except the state of her clothes.

Kate walked over to the dresser and pulled something out of a drawer. "I think you'll need these."

Brodie sneered at the pajamas she was being handed. "I doubt we wear the same size."

"I doubt it, too, but these belong to Gina." When Kate saw Brodie's eyes narrow, she snorted. "I have some of mine at her flat, too. For those late nights when we've both had too much to drink. It's easier than sleeping in our clothes."

"Oh," Brodie said, glancing around. "I need a bath."

"Through there," Kate said, pointing to a door. "Do you want any help?"

"The last time you saw my body, you ran from the room," Brodie said, snatching up the PJs. "And I don't know about you, but I think I can do without repeating *that* particular experience."

"Brodie—"

"Kate, please, I'm tired, and I'm done talking about this," Brodie said as she stepped into the tiny bathroom. "Now, do us both a favor and just leave."

Brodie closed the door in Kate's face, resting her head against the wood for a few seconds before going over and turning on the tap. As she watched the tub fill, Brodie took off her blouse, and as it dropped to the floor, the door opened.

"I'm sorry. I forgot to bring you fresh—"

Kate's gasp echoed off the walls, and it took a split-second before Brodie's lips curled into a knowing smile. She looked over her shoulder, and it was all she could do not to laugh out loud at Kate's horrified expression. "Oh that," Brodie said, her tone deliberately casual. "Her name's Talia...and she likes to leave marks."

Chapter Fifteen

"Who's Talia?"

"Who?" Devon said, placing her fork on her plate.

"Talia."

Devon shrugged. "I have no idea who you're talking about."

"I thought you knew Brodie's friends."

Devon looked up from her coffee, trying to keep the liquid inside her mouth. For months, Kate hadn't mentioned Brodie's name once, and now, over Sunday breakfast, she said it like she was asking for more toast. "Um...I know some of them, but I don't recall one named Talia."

Kate hesitated for a moment. "She likes to leave marks."

"Oh, Christ," Devon said, rocking back in her chair. "*That* one."

"Then you *do* know her?"

"Not exactly. I didn't even know her name until now."

Kate lifted her chin just a bit. "Care to explain?"

"No," Devon said, crossing her arms as she stared back at her sister. "Actually, I don't think I do."

"Devon!"

"What? Why do you care?" Devon said, leaning forward in her seat.

"I just want to know. That's all."

"That's not a reason."

Kate sucked in a breath, holding it for a second before letting it go. "Look, I'm not sure if you know this or not, but a couple of weeks ago, Brodie stayed here—"

"I know. It was the night she got bashed on the head. She told me you wouldn't call me."

"It was late."

"Whatever."

"Anyway," Kate said, pausing to gather her thoughts. "I forgot to give her some towels. I wasn't thinking, and I just walked back into the bathroom and...and she'd taken off her blouse, and there were bruises all over her back."

Devon chuckled. "Trust me. They weren't just on her back."

Kate blanched at the innuendo. "Brodie's into that...that pain thing?"

"No, of course not, but from what I hear, this Talia chick likes it rough, and she's up for it, if you know what I mean. So, what's a little pain when you get all that pleasure—right?"

It was intentional. Devon adored her sister, but Kate had hurt Brodie, and Devon wanted to give a bit of that back, except Kate's reaction wasn't what Devon had expected. Kate wasn't angry. She was jealous. Green from head to toe, it seeped from every pore like sweat.

Kate got to her feet and began grabbing the dishes from the table. "It's time to clean up this shite. I'm assuming you're done."

"Um...yeah," Devon said, hiding her smile behind her coffee cup. "It was great, as always."

"Good."

Devon watched as Kate busied herself at the sink. "Oh, by the way...I'm going to come out to Mum."

"You're what?" Kate said, spinning around.

"I said, I'm going to—"

"I heard what you said, but why in the hell would you want to do that? She never visits us. We visit her."

"And what's that got to do with it?" Devon said, getting to her feet. "Gina and I are planning to move in together, so I can't very well lie about a change in address, not that I'd want to."

"This is all because of fucking Brodie," Kate said under her breath, turning back to the sink.

Devon went over and grabbing Kate by the arm, she spun her around. "What are you talking about? This has nothing to do with Brodie."

"Until she came into your life, you were just fine with things the way they were."

"In case you've forgotten, I've known Brodie for a lot longer than a few months. So do you care to grasp for *another* straw because that one isn't holding water, Kate. As a matter of fact, I think it's leaking jealousy all over the floor."

"I am *not* jealous," Kate said, snatching her arm away. "Brodie Shaw is a bad influence, and if you were *smart*, you'd wise up, stop working with her, and move on."

"Well, that's a little hard to do since I'm now her business partner."

"You're her *what?*"

"She and Ethan have plans for the company. They want to branch out, and since smart homes are all the rage, they offered me a buy-in, and I took it."

"Oh, Jesus Christ, that's just great," Kate said, stomping back to the table to grab her coffee cup. "That's just fucking great."

"What in the hell is wrong with you? I thought you'd be happy for me."

Kate whipped around. "Just like Mum is going to be happy when you tell her you shag women?"

Devon rocked back in her stance, her hands becoming fists as she glared at Kate. "I shag Gina because I *love* Gina, and I don't know where all this crap is coming from, but just because you're angry at Brodie, don't take it out on me."

"This has *nothing* to do with Brodie!"

"It has *everything* thing to do with Brodie," Devon screamed, waving her arms about. "She got under your skin and screwed up your bloody plans, didn't she? She made you see that not everything is black and white and lives can't be planned down to the nth degree, and you don't like it, do you? No, you don't like it at all because you like being in control. You like calling the shots. Well, I hate to break it to you, Kate, but you don't call Brodie's shots, and you sure as hell don't call mine. Tomorrow, I'm going up to see Mum, and I'm going to tell her I'm a lesbian and if she doesn't like it—"

"Devon, we both know her bloody beliefs! Have you forgotten how she tried to cram them down our throats day after day after day?"

It was something they rarely talked about, a conscious avoidance of memories that brought with them pain and condemnation. Devon hadn't forgotten anything because, at times, she could see their mother in Kate, and that thought brought sadness to Devon's face. "I remember everything, Kate," she said quietly. "Every goddamned thing."

"Then you know she's not going to like *this*," Kate said, taking a step in Devon's direction. "And I'm telling you right now, don't come crying back to me when it blows up in your face...because it *will* blow up in your face."

"So what do you want me to do? Lie to her? Is that your solution for all of this?"

"Why not? It wouldn't be the first secret we've kept from her."

Devon's shoulders sagged. "Maybe not, but what about me, Kate? What about Gina? What about my living my life? Doesn't any of that matter?"

"What matters is the world isn't as open-minded as you think. There are lots of people who don't like gays, and it's foolish for you to put yourself out there for everyone to see, especially our *mother*," Kate said, slamming her hands on her hips. "Jesus Christ, Devon, you know Gina's visits home with me during school stopped the moment Mum found out she was gay, and you've been there when she's shut me down whenever I try to even mention Gina. You're just being stupid if you think she won't do the same goddamned thing to you."

"The only one being stupid around here is *you*," Devon said, raising her voice. "You are in complete and utter denial over your feelings for Brodie, and you're so enraged that she went out and got laid—"

"I don't give a *fuck* about Brodie Shaw!"

Devon threw back her head and laughed. "Keep telling yourself that, Kate, because from where I'm standing, there's only going to be one liar in this family now…and it sure as *hell* isn't me."

***

Brodie walked into G-Street, slowing only for a moment before heading to the bar. It wasn't her usual club night, but then again, she wasn't looking for a shag. She was looking for a friend.

As Brodie neared the bar, Gina looked up. "Hey there, stranger," she said, placing a drink on a server's tray. "Devon told me what happened at The Loft a few weeks back. How's the head?"

"Oh, it's fine," Brodie said, running her hand over her hair. "Stitches came out over a week ago."

Before Gina had a chance to speak, another server came over and handed her an order for drinks. Gina held up one finger, silently requesting Brodie to wait for a second, and after filling a few shot glasses with tequila, Gina sent them on their way and turned back to Brodie. "Sorry about that."

"Not a problem," Brodie said, reaching for her wallet. "You have some Cabernet back there?"

"Yeah, hold on."

A minute later, Gina placed the wine in front of Brodie. "So, what brings you here on a Thursday night? I thought Devon said your clubbing night was Friday."

"It is," Brodie said, glancing around the club. "But I'm not here for fun. I'm looking for your significant other. She took some time off early this week, but I thought she'd be back by now, and every time I call, it goes right to voice mail. She's not at her place either, and since I don't know where you live, here I am."

"Oh…um…give me one minute."

Gina went over and said something to the other bartender, and after waving to Brodie to follow her, before too long, they were standing in Gina's office. "It's quieter back here," she said, closing the door.

"Okay, what's going on?" Brodie said, eyeing Gina. "Is Devon all right?"

Gina groaned out a breath. "Yes and no."

"What's that supposed to mean?"

"She went up to see her mum on Monday and outed herself."

The sadness in Gina's tone was all too clear, and Brodie's face fell. "And I'm going to assume it didn't go well."

"That's putting it mildly. Typical out-of-control parent who can't see their way past the bedroom door. I'm sure you know the type."

"Unfortunately, I do," Brodie said, frowning.

"From what Devon told me, her mother went ballistic, ranting, raving, and screeching every chapter and verse she could remember from both the Old *and* the New Testaments just like my mother did when I came out. Luckily, Devon managed to escape with only a bruised cheek."

Brodie snapped back her head. "Wait. Are you telling me her mother hit her?"

"Yeah, she managed to get in one good slap before Devon got the hell out of there."

"Now I know where Kate gets it from."

"What?"

"Oh...um...nothing," Brodie muttered. "So, where's Devon now? Your place?"

"Yeah, and I'm sorry she didn't call you. She's had a lot on her mind. Apparently, she's been disowned, and after what Kate did to her, Devon needed some time to get it all sorted."

"What do you mean? What did Kate do?"

Gina pondered the question for a moment. "Look, I'm not really sure it's my place to say. I know how you feel about Ka—"

"Kate and I are done, and Cassidy is...*Devon* is my best friend. I love her to death, so please just tell me what happened. Please?"

The corners of Gina's mouth drooped. Letting out a long breath, she went over and plopped down in one of the chairs facing the desk. Patting the arm of the other, Gina waited until Brodie sat before she turned to her to speak. "Last Sunday, Kate invited us over for breakfast. I had worked until two the night before, so Devon let me sleep in, and she went on her own. While she was there, Devon told Kate she was going to see their mum and tell her she was gay, and Kate...Kate went off the deep end." Gina stopped and shook her head. "I still can't believe she reacted like she did. I mean, she basically told Devon to keep her relationship with me to herself, and when Devon tried to explain why she didn't want to do that, Kate blamed it all on you."

"On me? What the fuck did I do? I didn't even know Devon was planning to do this."

"Yeah, well, according to Devon, the whole thing started when Kate found out about someone named...um...Terry? Tracy? Tam—"

"Talia?"

"Yes, that's the one," Gina said, leaning back in her chair. "Talia."

"And what the fuck does Talia have to do with Devon outing herself?"

"Nothing, except once Kate found out that this Talia was one of your...um...*acquaintances*, her whole mood changed. She became argumentative and angry, and everything went downhill from there. It ended up with Kate making it crystal clear that if Devon did what she was planning to do, she was going to be on her own."

Brodie took a sip of her wine, processing everything Gina had told her. "Why do I think there's more to this than what you're telling me?"

"Because there is," Gina said, letting out a long breath. "When Devon got back into town, she went over to Kate's to tell her what happened. She figured by that time, Kate would have calmed down and come to her senses, offered a shoulder to cry on or at the very least a little empathy. Instead, Kate said, 'I told you so' and made it clear to Devon she wasn't planning to do anything to change their mother's mind."

"That makes no sense. That night you and I went out to dinner, you told me that Kate's always had your back."

"She *has*. From the day my mother cut me off, Kate's been there for me. She's never had a problem with my sexuality, and more than once, she's come to my defense when some wanker made an off-color remark in a pub, which makes me believe Devon's right."

"About what?"

"She thinks Kate is so wound up over you, she's taking out her frustrations on the rest of us."

"Can't she see she's driving a wedge between herself and Devon in the process?"

"Right now, I think the only thing she sees is red," Gina said, shaking her head. "I haven't talked to her all week, and honestly, I wouldn't know what to say if I did."

"Well, luckily, I do," Brodie said, and after downing what remained in her glass, she stormed out of the room.

***

Kate jerked out of a sound sleep, and for a second, she didn't know why. She blinked, and as her vision cleared, she looked around the lounge. She saw nothing out of the ordinary, and then she heard pounding. Someone was knocking on her door or rather trying to knock it down, and picking up her phone, Kate looked at the time. It was late, and in a flash, Kate was bolting off the sofa. There had to be something wrong for anyone to demand such urgent attention, and since her neighbors knew she was a copper, Kate raced to the entry and yanked open the door. A second later, Kate was trying to keep her eyes firmly in their sockets. "Brodie?"

"That's right, Kate," Brodie said, holding her head high. "It's Brodie. Remember me?"

Kate had to quickly sidestep as Brodie marched past her into the house. "What the hell do you think you're doing?" Kate shouted. "Get out of my house."

"Not until I say what I've come here to say."

"I don't give a fuck what you have to say," Kate said, crossing her arms. "Now get out of my—"

"Why didn't you have Devon's back?"

"What?"

"Why didn't you go with her when she went to see your mum?"

Kate's eyes turned into slits. "That's none of your business," she said, walking toward the kitchen. "Now, if you don't mind, it's late, I'm tired, and you're trespassing. Don't let the door hit you on the way out."

"Like your mother hit Devon?"

Kate came to a stop. Over the years, she'd always been the one on the receiving end of her mother's slaps, and it pained her to know Devon had joined the club. Kate's eyes began to mist and blinking away the blur, she paused long enough for her annoyance to replace her empathy. "Nothing I can do about that," Kate said over her shoulder. "Devon made her bed. She can lie in it."

Brodie's nostrils flared, and taking two long steps, she grabbed Kate by the arm and spun her around. "Oh, no, you don't," she said, looking down her nose at Kate. "I'm not going anywhere until you tell me why you didn't go with your sister and support her. Why couldn't you have lifted one goddamned finger and—"

"Because I have a job, and I can't just up and leave it whenever I'd like, especially when it concerns my sister acting like a bloody *idiot!*" Kate said, yanking her arm away. "Devon and I grew up in the same house. She knew exactly how our mother would react, and she was stupid to think it would end up any differently."

Brodie rocked back. "But she's your *sister*. She needed you. Do you have any idea how much courage it took for Devon to do what she did? That was her Everest, Kate, and you let her climb it all alone. Yeah, she probably knew how it would end up, but if you'd been there, supporting her decision and defending her right to live her own bloody life, maybe your mother wouldn't have been so quick to disown her or...or hit her."

"You *seriously* have no idea what you're talking about," Kate said, meeting Brodie's unrelenting stare with one of her own. "Whether I was there or not wouldn't have stopped my mum from doing what she did, and it sure as hell wouldn't have changed the fact that Devon's a...a..."

"Because she's a what, Kate?" Brodie said, and intruding on Kate's personal space, Brodie pushed her up against the wall. "Because she's a lesbian? A dyke? A fucking carpet muncher? Do you hate it...or are you just jealous because she can admit it, and you can't?"

This time, Brodie didn't see it coming, and the slap echoed through the house. Brodie's cheek instantly reddened in the shape of Kate's handprint, but refusing to acknowledge the sting, Brodie smirked. "Hit a nerve, did I?"

Kate broke out of Brodie's grasp. "Get the fuck out of my house!"

"My pleasure," Brodie said, giving Kate a slow once-over. "But just because you don't have the guts to live the life you *want*, don't punish your sister because she does." After skewering Kate with one more contemptuous look, Brodie turned and walked to the door.

"I hate you!"

Brodie stiffened, and in three strides, she was on top of Kate. Shoving her against the wall, she grabbed Kate's face and kissed her with all her might. Brodie ground her mouth against Kate's, and forcing her tongue between Kate's lips, Brodie took what she wanted as Kate half-heartedly struggled to get away.

When Brodie finally pulled back, she knew what was coming, and she welcomed the pain of it. Another slap stung her face, and this one left her lip, split and bleeding. The metallic tinge of blood invaded her mouth as Brodie headed for the door, and as she was about to leave, she looked back at Kate and wiped the blood from her lips with the back of her hand. "If you think I believe anything you've said tonight, you're wrong. The only reason you didn't stand up for Devon is that if you did, if you *had* defended her right to live her own goddamned life, it would have legitimized what you feel for me...and you're too bloody afraid to admit that."

Chapter Sixteen

After her argument with Kate on Thursday night, Brodie had worn a permanent scowl for three days. She didn't go clubbing on Friday or even leave her flat until Monday morning, preferring to spend her time mentally kicking herself for being such a prat. Brodie knew she was right in coming to Devon's defense, but the way she had gone about it was wrong, and she didn't know how to correct it. Brodie sighed, and taking a sip of her coffee, she was about to try focusing on her work when she heard a tap on her door. She looked up and couldn't help but grin, seeing Stevie standing in the doorway.

Two years earlier, with their business thriving, Ethan and Brodie agreed it was time to hire someone to manage appointments, pay the bills, and sort out all the everyday tasks that took the time they didn't have to spare. Stevie Diamond was one of the applicants they had interviewed, and while Brodie knew her brother had no issue with her sexuality, *she* had never worn it on her sleeve. Stevie, on the other hand, draped himself in it. From his turquoise platform shoes to his ultra-tight leopard-print trousers and spandex shirt, he was as gay as gay could be, and flouncing into Brodie's office the day of his interview like a feather in the breeze, he perched himself on a chair and freely spoke about himself.

Having earned degrees in Accounting and Finance as well as Business Administration, Stevie's intention had always been to follow in his parents' footsteps. The son of a banker and accountant, Stevie had grown up with numbers, and he had also grown up with two loving parents who had faced their own amount of discrimination through the years. The power of their love had carried them through it all because they adored their child, and they accepted Stevie's sexuality without batting an eye. He was their son. He was who he was supposed to be, and his parents never faulted him for it. Unfortunately, many in the job market didn't feel the same.

Even though his college record was impeccable and his manners were respectful and professional, Stevie lost out on one position after another. In his heart, he knew it was due to his flamboyance. He also knew he wasn't going to change who he was. Instead, with his parents' encouragement and support, Stevie plodded from one job interview to the next, hoping someone would eventually see past his eyeliner and effeminate ways. When he sauntered into Brodie's office that morning and saw a small Pride flag on a shelf, Stevie thought he'd finally found the person who'd look past his eccentricities. Needless to say, he and Brodie were both surprised when they found they weren't alone.

Ethan's love for his sister was unshakable. His chest was forever puffed simply because he adored Brodie for all she was and all she stood for. Yet, he had never fully understood her strength until one afternoon a few months before Stevie's interview when Ethan's eyes were forever opened.

Brodie had been running late and asked Ethan to stop by the office to meet some clients so they could sign their contract. It would have been Spaces by Shaw's largest contract to date, and Ethan was prompt and courteous. He ushered the couple into Brodie's office to sign the papers, but as they took their seats, the wife noticed a photograph on the wall. It was a picture of Brodie taken at a Pride parade a few weeks before, and in it, she was wrapped in a rainbow flag. Within seconds, the couple was on their feet, and after spewing vileness and hatred at Ethan, they tore up the contract and stormed out of the office. Ethan was gutted, and it had nothing to do with the pieces of paper littering the floor. He had never tasted judgment before, never faced the wrath of the ignorant whose beliefs were so warped he wanted to vomit. Ethan told himself then and there, from that day forward, he would make sure their clients would be open-minded, or they wouldn't be their clients, and Stevie Diamond was his answer. Not only did he have the manners, education, and intelligence they were looking for, Stevie was a billboard...and the sign he wore was proud.

Today, Stevie was wearing tight leather trousers with a long-sleeved, tailored shirt, and the bold pink and burgundy flowered print hugged his torso like a second skin. In his right ear was a row of gold studs, and in his left was a line of silver, and on his feet were suede tasseled loafers, the shade of which matched the burgundy in his shirt. He had several chains draped around his neck, and as always, his cologne was crisp, and his toffee-colored afro was perfectly styled, the loose curls on the top soft and natural while the sides were faded. Like the shade of his hair, his skin tone was a blend of his father's Jamaican roots and his mother's Swedish heritage. The amber held in its undertone a coppery hue that almost shimmered, and with eyes the color of the sky, Stevie turned the heads of many, straight *and* gay.

Stevie's eyes almost popped out of his head when he saw Brodie's face. "Oh my, Lord, what happened to you?" he said, sashaying to the desk. "Has The Loft reopened, or have you joined an after-hours fight club?"

"No to both," Brodie said with a laugh. "This was courtesy of a...hell, I don't even know what she is or *was*."

"You must be speaking about Kate," Stevie said, and flopping into a chair, he set his iPad on the desk. "She's the only slugger in your past."

"And how in the hell would you know that?"

"People talk," Stevie said, nonchalantly checking out his recently buffed fingernails. "And if you think you'll pry their name out of me, you can't. I plan to take it to my grave."

Brodie laughed again. "It was either Gina or Cassidy because they're the only ones who know Kate once tried to slap me, and honestly, it doesn't really matter."

"By that cut on your lip, it appears she finally connected, though."

"Yeah, not that I didn't deserve it."

"No one deserves to get hit. Violence is never the answer unless, of course, you're talking about whoever came up with twerking. That bastard should be beaten within an inch of their life."

Brodie's eyes creased at the corners. "I'd have to agree."

"So…" Stevie said, dangling one leg over the other. "Do you want to talk about it?"

"Since when are you my shoulder to cry on?"

"Do you want to cry?"

"No, I want to work and get this…this bloody woman out of my head."

"And out of your heart by the looks of it."

Brodie took a deep breath and leaning back in her chair, she let it out slowly. "Have you ever fallen for a straight bloke?"

Stevie splayed his fingers against his chest. "Oh, please, honey, tell me you didn't. That's the ultimate in crotch death or, in your case, vag death."

"It's not dead," Brodie said, smiling. "Just wounded…like my heart."

"I've been there, felt that, and I got past it. We all do, and so will you. It just takes time, and I highly recommend *massive* amounts of alcohol. I drowned two of my exes that way. Figuratively speaking, of course."

"And the worst part about it is, I think I ruined any chance we could ever even be friends."

"Thus, the bruise on your face?"

"Yes," Brodie said, nodding. "She did something to Cassidy I didn't like, so I went over to her place in all my holier-than-thou dyke glory, spewing fairness and equality. Instead of trying to talk to Kate or listen to what she had to say, I was literally shoving my opinions down her throat. In a way, I guess I was trying to hurt her as much as she's hurt me. By the time I got home, I'd realized I'd been a stupid cow, a total, *total* prat, and I want to apologize, I *need* to apologize, but I have a feeling it would either fall on deaf ears, or she'd arrest me for stalking."

"That's right, she's a copper."

"Yeah."

"What about Cass—Devon? I'm not going to ask what happened, but is she okay?"

"I talked to her on the phone yesterday. She's fine. Gina's keeping her busy looking at flats and making plans. She was heading down to the Hirshfeld's cottage today, and since Gina's off, they plan to make a day of it," Brodie said, glancing at the iPad Stevie had placed on her desk. "But enough about this. You and I both have jobs to do, which is why I'm assuming you came in here?"

"Yes," Stevie said, picking up the tablet. Opening the cover, he lightly tapped on the screen. "I wanted to let you know that the invoices for the Wilson's renovation have been paid, Donald Morgan called first thing and rescheduled his meeting with you tomorrow to discuss that loft conversion for two o'clock instead of three, and you're supposed to meet up with Ethan at one today over at the Patels."

"Well, it doesn't look like keeping busy will be a problem this week," Brodie said, grinning.

"Not just the week. You also have that party on Saturday, and before you try to get out of it, you made me promise not to let you."

"Damn, I forgot about that. I need to get them a housewarming gift of some sort. Put a reminder in the planner and sync it to my phone, will you please?"

"Already done," Stevie said, popping to his feet. "Is there anything else?"

"Yes," Brodie said, looking Stevie in the eye. "Thank you."

"For what? I'm just doing my job."

"I wasn't talking about that. I don't have a lot of people I'm comfortable enough with to talk about my personal life, so thanks for lending the ear...and the shoulder. It helped."

"So, you feel better?"

"No," Brodie said with a snort. "But like you said, there's always alcohol."

***

Gina opened the cooler bag and unwrapping one of the two sandwiches they had bought at a local shop, she handed it to Devon. "Here you go."

"Thanks, I'm starving," Devon said, taking the food.

"That's a nice change."

"What is?" Devon said before taking a huge bite of her sandwich.

"You've been either skipping meals or pecking at them like a bird since you got back from your mother's. It's good to see your appetite is coming back."

Devon held up a finger, chewing wildly to clear what was in her mouth. "I had a lot on my mind," she said, reaching for a napkin. "And now I don't."

"No?"

"No, because this is exactly what I needed."

"If I knew you liked BLTs so much, I would have made you one last week," Gina said, unwrapping her chicken club.

"I'm not talking about food. I'm talking about this," Devon said with a wave of her arm. "I'm talking about sitting on this beach with you, about the sun and the salty air, and about being your partner. That's why I did what I did, and I don't regret it. If Mum never comes around, which I seriously doubt she will, then she's missing out on my life. She's missing out on family holidays. She's missing out on us...maybe even grandchildren?"

The sparkle in Gina's eyes had nothing to do with the sun reflecting off the water. "That's definitely a possibility," she said, leaning over to give Devon a quick kiss. As she pulled back, her eyes lost their luster. "But what about Kate?"

"Kate's not homophobic. She's just in denial," Devon said, before taking a small bite of her sandwich. "She's in love with Brodie and—"

"Love is a pretty strong word."

"I know, and so is the emotion attached to it," Devon said, gazing at Gina. "But how else do you explain the way Kate reacted that morning. First, she got jealous over Talia, and then she tried to make Brodie out as some sort of villain as if by changing my mind about Brodie, it would somehow validate Kate's inability to accept her own feelings toward the woman. It's like what homophobes do to us, you know? Standing on the sidelines, squawking crap and pointing fingers, when behind closed doors, they're as gay as we are."

"Deniability 101."

"Exactly."

Gina unzipped the cooler bag again and handed another can of cola to Devon. "So, are you going to take the first step or wait until Kate decides to apologize?"

"I'm going to wait for Kate to come to her senses. I love her. She's my sister, and she's the only family I have now, present company excluded, but I didn't do anything wrong. She did, and once she pulls her head out of her arse, she'll see that."

"It might take a while. We both know Kate's as pigheaded as the day is long."

"Yeah, but that's not her fault. She can't help herself."

"How can you say that? Kate's an adult. She's responsible for her actions, and her actions were shit."

"I know, but some things are hard to unlearn."

"Honey, you're not making any sense," Gina said before taking a bite of her sandwich.

Devon took a long breath and setting her BLT aside, she swiveled to face Gina. "Kate's never told you about our mum, has she?"

Gina stopped chewing. Even though she had gone home with Kate on a few college weekends, Devon was right. Outside the woman's home, Kate rarely brought her up. Gina always believed it was just Kate's way. She knew Kate was a private person, and it wasn't until Gina began her relationship with Devon when she realized it was more than that. Both women called their mother once a month, and both visited a few times a year, but other than that, it was as if the woman didn't exist. Gina quickly chewed what was left in her mouth and swallowed it down. "No…but then again, you don't talk about her either."

"That's because there are some things you just want to forget, even though you can't, no matter how hard you try."

"What are you talking about?"

"You know my parents are divorced—right?"

"Yeah, that's one of the few things I do know. Why?"

"Well, after the divorce, things became strained between our mum and us. She changed. She was angry all the time, and her temper, her temper grew really short. She'd yell at us for the stupidest things, and then she'd yell about our father, how he'd never amount to anything without her, how foolish he was…how worthless he was. Doing all she could to turn us against him."

"I'm glad it didn't work."

"What do you mean?"

"You called your dad a few weeks ago on his birthday. I was with you when you bought his present."

"You're right, I did, but Kate and I didn't reconnect with our dad until we were in our twenties. When we were kids, he tried to stay in our lives, but Mum…Mum made that really hard. He'd come by and try to take us out for pizza or a movie, and Mum would bad-mouth him in front of us, saying awful things that kids shouldn't hear, and on the few occasions she did allow him to take us out, when we got home, she'd spend the next week ridiculing him *and* us for being too stupid to see he was worthless. I guess it worked in a way because eventually, his weekly visits turned into monthly visits, and when his job changed, Dad moved away. He always sent us cards and gifts for our birthdays or Christmas though. I guess it was his attempt to remain in our lives somehow, and it worked. It was because of those cards we had his address and when Kate moved to London, and I came to visit her, unbeknownst to Mum, we jumped on a plane, flew to Edinburgh...and re-introduced ourselves."

"That must have been a tearful reunion."

"It was," Devon said, smiling. "And I had forgotten how much Kate looked like him which, in retrospect, helps to explain some stuff."

"Like what?"

"I was only six when they got divorced, too young to really see that our mother was trying to turn us against our father, but Kate was nine. She was old enough to speak her mind, old enough to disagree with things she knew weren't true, *and* she is the spitting image of Dad, and I think that just escalated their arguments. When Mum looked at Kate, she saw our dad, and things would go from bad to worse in one way or another."

"What do you mean?"

"Mum liked things neat and tidy, so on most weekends while I was allowed to go outside and play, she'd force Kate to stay in, to clean the house and do the wash, and anything else Mum could think of. I guess she thought she'd wear Kate down, totally forgetting they both have the same stubborn streak, and when that didn't work, she started belittling Kate like she'd done with our dad. I have to hand it to Kate, too, because she stood up to Mum so many times, protecting me from her wrath all the while knowing she'd have to be the one to back down or...or pay the price."

"The price? Oh shit. Please don't say she hit her."

"It wasn't a daily occurrence or anything like that, but yeah, Kate got slapped around more than once. She even took one for me."

"What?"

"I was nine, and I broke one of my mother's favorite Christmas ornaments. It was an accident. It just slipped from my fingers, but I knew Mum was going to be angry, and I started to cry. Kate told me not to worry and that everything was going to be okay, and when Mum came back into the room and saw it broken, she did what we both knew she was going to do. She went off the deep end, screaming about how thoughtless we were, how unappreciative we were to the *only* parent who loved us, and when she demanded to know who had done it, Kate stepped up and took the blame," Devon said, tears overflowing her eyes. "I can still hear the sound of that slap."

"Jesus," Gina said, taking Devon's hand. "Oh, sweetheart, I had no idea."

"Well, shitty childhoods don't make for good conversation."

"Please don't joke about this."

"I'm not, and out of bad things, comes good because, after that day, Mum never slapped either one of us again."

"Why? What happened?"

"The next morning, Kate's face was bruised. There was no way Mum could have missed it, yet she never said a word. She just put a plate of eggs and bacon in front of Kate and told her to eat her breakfast...and that was it. Kate and Mum would still argue at times, typical teenager stuff for the most part, but never again did Mum raise her hand in anger...until recently, that is."

"Thank God for that."

"Yeah, but it doesn't erase how she treated us for those three years," Devon said, looking at Gina. "Don't get me wrong, Kate and I love our mother, and for the most part, we've forgiven her, but some scars go really deep. Mum's never apologized for any of it, and I know that weighs on Kate. I mean, between the two of us, Kate bore the brunt of Mum's temper way more than me, yet it's like she's still not worthy of Mum's apology, you know?"

"I never knew any of this," Gina said softly. "Kate never said a thing."

"And I'm sure if you asked Kate now about it, she'd say the past is in the past, and she's fine, and for the most part, she is. I mean, she's got a great career and good friends, but when she lashes out like she did with me, when she loses her temper because things aren't going her way, when Kate's so headstrong you want to scream, well, that's got my mother written all over it."

***

"Why do you have to be so bloody stubborn about this?"

"Julian, I'm *not* being stubborn," Kate said, raising her voice slightly. "I just think it's too soon to talk about sharing a flat together. We've only been going out for a few months."

Julian huffed out a breath. "Why are you so afraid of taking a chance on this?"

Kate shot Julian a look that could have easily planted him six feet under. Of all the things he could have said, *that* was the wrong one. Ten days prior, Brodie had stood in her house, berating Kate for being afraid of living life, and now, sitting in Julian's car as they drove to an open house, her boyfriend was doing the same thing. If it hadn't been for the fact she'd already backed out of two dates in as many weeks, Kate would have demanded Julian turn the car around. Instead, she stared out the window and counted to ten and then to twenty…and then to fifty.

"Aren't you going to answer me?"

"You know what?" Kate said, shooting Julian yet another look. "I know this afternoon is important to you, so can we please just enjoy the day and talk about this later?"

"Fine," Julian said, steering the car onto a cobblestone drive. "We're here anyway, so I guess I really don't have a choice. Do I?"

Thankful she'd put an end to traveling down a path she cared not to travel, Kate looked at the house they were approaching and smiled. She always loved Tudor homes. From their steeply pitched roofs to the half-timbers decorating the triangular gables to the large groups of rectangular windows nestled into the brick, they were almost medieval in appearance. And to make her mood brighten even further, in the place of a lawn, stepped gardens filled the front landscape on both sides of the walk leading to the arched entrance. A rainbow of color erupted from the sandstone boundaries, and as Kate admired the flowers, she realized it was the rock she should be noticing. "Oh, it's marvelous. The garden walls are beautiful, and the driveway is amazing."

Julian jerked the car to a stop and gave Kate a side-eyed glance. "Thanks, but none of *this* crap is mine," he said, and hopping out, he trotted around the car to open Kate's door. "The addition's on the back of the house. That's where you'll see just how talented *I* am, so prepare yourself to be impressed."

Kate began counting again as she climbed out of the car, her smile returning almost instantly when she breathed in the scent of the flowers. Kate loved flowers. She enjoyed visiting botanical gardens or strolling through parks on a sunny day, admiring the topiary and clusters of annuals and perennials planted around fountains and statues. Many an afternoon had been lost in greenhouses and exhibitions, and while the gardens around Kate's home were small, every spring, she took great pleasure in filling them with as much color and fragrance as space allowed. When she first met Julian, Kate thought she'd found a kindred spirit in her love for gardens until Julian invited her to tour one of the garden parks he'd recently completed.

Prior to meeting Julian, Kate never paid that much attention to the hardscapes that were Julian's pride and joy. She appreciated the work that went into building the walls of stone and brick that kept the flowers captive, and the winding paths of concrete pavers that made it easy to traverse the sprawling landscape. Even the precast concrete benches situated under the shade of trees could be admired for the rest they offered, but that's where Kate's appreciation ended, and by the conclusion of Julian's tour of the park, Kate wanted to scream.

Julian had no interest in the topiaries or flowers overflowing the beds, and he made that perfectly clear. He scrunched up his nose at the delicate fragrance of the roses, waved off the aroma of the lilacs, and scoffed at the sculpted shrubbery all the while identifying every intricate detail of his hardscapes. How the rocks were perfectly stacked, how the bricks were perfectly aligned, and how the pavers were perfectly level. At first, Kate took it in stride. She told herself there was nothing wrong with taking pride in your work, or in Julian's case, in his designs, but that was before she discovered Julian's method of advertising. Not only was the name of Julian's company etched into the surfaces of numerous pavers and bricks, but brochure boxes sprouted from the beds like unsightly weeds. The plastic was yellowed and scratched and under the lids, protecting them from the weather, were flyers about Julian's company. Kate found it tacky and disruptive. She didn't want to see propaganda littering the view of what were beautiful gardens, and it was all she could do not to voice her opinion when Julian puffed out his chest, pontificating that none of his competitors had ever been so intelligent.

Kate followed Julian up the walk, biting her tongue as she listened to his condemnations of the landscape architecture on the front lawn, and before they reached the door, Kate had made up her mind. Where Julian was concerned, the bloom was definitely off the rose.

After being cordially greeted by the happy homeowners, Kate barely had a chance to get a glass of wine before Julian was ushering her toward the back of the home. Thankfully, one of their hosts came to her rescue when she called Julian over to introduce him to a possible new client. Kate's mood changed in the blink of an eye, and sipping her Chardonnay, she moseyed through the house alone.

Like many older homes, the ceilings in the original section were low, and as Kate approached the ample doorway leading to the addition, she thought the trend would continue. She was wrong. While the height of the opening matched those in the front of the house, as soon as Kate walked through it onto a highly polished wooden floor, she nearly dropped her glass.

The ingenious architect had used a tray ceiling, and while the lowest section matched the original architecture, from there, it gradually stepped up, higher and higher until it peaked at well over ten feet. Kate was in awe of the design, and her admiration continued when she saw the conservatory to her right.

Made almost entirely out of glass, the room was alive with brilliance. Even though blinds were installed on the roof panels to prevent the sun's rays from heating the room, the glass walls allowed more than enough natural light to enter. Rattan furniture, covered in tropical-themed cushions, was placed around the perimeter, and down the center of the room was a rectangular glass table surrounded by chairs, offering a comfortable place to sit for breakfast, lunch, or even dinner. Clay pots were scattered about, some holding towering snake plants and bushy foxtail ferns, while slender orchids rose from others, their petals holding in their delicateness a myriad of colors.

Next to the conservatory was the new kitchen, and it was as uncomplicated as it was elegant. Cherry, flat-panel shaker doors covered the cabinetry, and a densely veined granite of ivory and tan served as the countertop. Drop lights highlighted the workstations and the island separating the kitchen from the rest of the addition, and a large window unit filled the back wall so those preparing meals could gaze at the rolling hills behind the house.

To the left of the kitchen area was a four-panel-wide door that led to the patio, and Kate didn't have to step outside to have her breath taken away.

"It's marvelous, isn't it?"

Kate turned to see the homeowner walking toward her. "It's amazing, Mrs. Hirshfeld. Absolutely amazing."

"Please, call me Dori," the woman said as she stood next to Kate. "It's actually Dorethea, but I'm too young to have a name that old."

Kate grinned as she looked out the glass again. "The view is stunning."

"I couldn't agree more," Dori said, admiring the landscape. "You know, when Max and I were interviewing architects, we invited them out to see the property, and as you can imagine, they spent most of their time taking measurements and photographs...except for one. It was cold that day, brisk enough to see your breath, and at the time, there was nothing behind the house except a ridiculous little wooden deck surrounded by grass and weeds. It was truly horrid, but for over an hour, she stood on that ghastly old thing, almost where you're standing now, taking in the view without saying a word. When she finally came inside, she spent another hour just talking to us about what we wanted, what we liked, and what we didn't. She didn't take one bloody measurement that day, and before I ever saw her preliminary designs, I knew she'd be the one we'd hire. She seemed so focused, so in tune, you know? Really quite an amazing woman, our Brodie."

***

"It's brilliant, isn't it?" Julian said, holding his head high. "Of course, it's only domestic cobbles. They were too cheap to use imported, or sandstone or granite slabs like I suggested, but every one of these stones is perfectly level. Not an easy task, trust me."

Kate's eye roll went unnoticed as she walked the path leading back to the house. "It's very nice, Julian."

"Nice? Is that all you can say? Look around, Kate. This is my work. This is what will put food on our table, and believe you me, it has to be better than *nice* to do that."

"Julian," Kate said, coming to a stop. "You've spent the last two hours pointing out every cobble, every stone, and every bench. It's warm. I'm thirsty, and my feet are sore. Your work is marvelous. It truly is, but I'm getting a little tired. If you don't mind, I think I'd like to head back to that bench we passed and rest for a bit. All right?"

"Honey, I don't have time to sit," Julian said, straightening his posture. "The guest list is filled with possibilities. I can't waste my time relaxing down here when there's money to be made up there."

"Then go on without me. I'll catch up."

"That's a marvelous idea," Julian said, spinning on his heel. "Thanks, babe."

Julian sprinted up the path, and smiling to herself, Kate turned around and retraced her steps. It only took a minute to come upon the bench she'd seen, and taking a seat, Kate promptly kicked off her shoes. It was a gorgeous summer day, and with not a cloud in the sky, Kate was thankful for not only the shade provided by a nearby tree but also for the light breeze that continued to blow. She was also thankful to escape her new shoes. Wiggling her toes, Kate muttered, "Next time, Monroe, buy something that *feels* good instead of just something that *looks* good."

***

Brodie's intentions had only been to attend and blend into the background, except the Hirshfelds had made that impossible. They were so pleased with her work, they insisted on introducing her to all their friends, and within a few hours, Brodie's phone was filled with the names and numbers of possible clients. Brodie hadn't planned on looking for new business that day...and she also hadn't planned on seeing Kate.

Worn out from talking, Brodie had escaped to the conservatory to have a drink, and settling into a chair, she took a few minutes to enjoy the view. As her eyes wandered across the landscape, she spotted a couple walking down one of the paths, and as they got a bit closer, Brodie narrowed her eyes. The woman wearing a lemon yellow halter dress was Kate, and she was holding hands with Julian Fitzgerald.

An avid gardener, Mr. Hirshfeld wasn't interested in someone else's opinions on what flowers he would plant. He only needed a company that could design and install the boundaries and walkways, so while Brodie's company was responsible for the layout and construction of the new wing, Premier Hardscapes by Julian had been hired by the Hirshfelds for the exterior work.

Wealth, at times, can bring with it a certain, albeit false, sense of entitlement, and Brodie, having had her fair share of affluent clients, was quite accustomed to their grandiose demands. Gold-plated fixtures, imported cabinetry, custom Italian marble inlays, wine cellars larger than her own flat, and in-home theaters able to comfortably sit eighteen only scratched the surface of what some had wanted, so Max and Dori Hirshfeld were a breath of fresh air. Although of independent means, the Hirshfelds saw no need to flaunt that fact, and through conversation, Brodie discovered they preferred simple over preposterous. They wanted a warm, inviting addition, a place for the family to gather, to laugh while meals were prepared, and to enjoy the rolling hills and soon-to-be gardens behind their home. Using this knowledge, Brodie had incorporated natural colors and light into her design and using soft wood tones and fixtures appearing modest even though they weren't, Brodie designed the Hirshfelds exactly what they wanted without conflict. Unfortunately, when it came to Julian Fitzgerald, it seemed conflict was his middle name.

Recommended by a friend, the Hirshfelds had signed a contract with Julian with the understanding that his approach would be minimalistic and uncomplicated. They didn't want anything to distract from the hills in the distance. They merely wanted a place for Max to indulge in his love for flowers, a small area where Dori could grow some vegetables, and meandering paths throughout, so at night, when the sun was setting, they could walk hand-in-hand amongst nature. Julian didn't hear a word.

Having already researched the Hirshfelds, he knew they could afford much more than minimalistic, and he believed once he impressed them with his designs, they would readily accept them without batting an eye. Two weeks later, he met the Hirshfelds and Brodie at the house and proudly displayed his intentions. He covered the table with sketches and computer-generated photographs showing pathways of imported Belgian cobble, garden walls constructed of marble and topped with slabs of granite, soaring statues, magnificent fountains, and an outdoor fire pit taking up a third of the space on the patio. The Hirshfelds were speechless. Brodie was not.

Brodie's thoughts were interrupted by the sound of voices and noticing a couple sitting down at the table with plates filled with assorted canapés, Brodie gave them a grin as she got to her feet. Heading out of the conservatory, she went back to the party, sampling a few of the appetizers as she mingled until she returned to the kitchen and looked out the window. Brodie had wanted to apologize for days, but each time she picked up the phone, the sting of her words and Kate's slaps resounded in her head. Brodie had stormed into Kate's house, filled with the rage that comes from injustice, and she left battered, wishing she could take it all back. Brodie hung her head. Whoever said love was grand was a bloody fool.

Kate slipped on her shoes when she reached the patio, and tapping across the brick toward a small table, shaded by a majestic oak, she took a seat. Again removing her uncomfortable yet gorgeous high-heels, Kate kicked them under the table, totally oblivious that she was being watched.

Like a voyeur, Brodie gazed at Kate through the glass. At first, she was just a lemony speck on a bench in the distance until she finally made her way up the walk alone. Brodie scanned the patio, and seeing Julian nowhere around, her focus returned to Kate. The breeze blew the skirt of her dress ever so gently, and her sandy hair appeared almost golden in the sunlight, and as she moved across the patio, Brodie had only one thought. When it came to beauty...God had outdone Himself.

When Kate disappeared from view, Brodie sighed, and she was about to return to the party one last time when she saw an open bottle of wine on the counter. Brodie chuckled under breath at her own fortitude. Grabbing two glasses and the Chardonnay, Brodie headed outside, praying that this meeting wouldn't be as disastrous as the last.

Chapter Seventeen

As a glass of wine was placed in front of her, Kate heard a familiar voice say, "Consider it a peace offering."

Kate swiveled in her seat, and looking up, she shielded her eyes from the sun. "And if I choose not to accept?"

"Then I'll go back inside and bring out a bottle of red."

Kate smiled despite herself. She wanted to hate Brodie. She wanted not to care, but damn it all to hell, Kate couldn't. She just couldn't.

When Brodie saw Kate smile, her day was made, and pulling out a chair, she quickly sat down and filled the other glass with wine. "I want to apologize," she said, placing the bottle on the table. "What happened at your flat, it was wrong of me to say those things and to do...to do what I did. I was a bit on edge at the time, and I took it out on you, and I'm truly sorry. Devon's your sister—"

"And she's your friend," Kate said, picking up her glass.

"Yes, but that didn't give me the right to storm into your house, and...and accost you."

Kate giggled, and Brodie relaxed a bit more. Leaning back in her chair, she gazed at Kate. The halter dress was light and delicate, and atop the white chiffon were large, lemony flowers with a hint of green here and there. It was easy to see Kate's shapely legs through the glass tabletop, and courtesy of the high/low hem of the dress, the view it afforded Brodie was generous. The fact that Kate wasn't wearing shoes hadn't been missed and glancing at the heeled footwear under the table, Brodie said, "Sore feet?"

Kate cocked her head to one side. "Do you have a foot fetish?"

"Sorry?"

"You heard me," Kate said before taking a sip of her wine. "The first time we met, that night in Calabria, you said something about my feet being sore, and now, you've done it again."

It was Brodie's turn to take a taste of wine, and as she returned her glass to the table, she said, "I was watching you standing in the queue that night, and you kept moving from one foot to the other, so I assumed your feet were sore. And now, since those cute little high heels of yours have been tossed to the side, I presume you're having the same issue."

"You would be correct," Kate said with a single dip of her head.

"I'd offer to rub your feet, but you'd probably take it the wrong way."

"Is there any other way to take it?"

"No," Brodie said ruefully. "I suppose not."

For a moment, it grew quiet, and as Kate picked up her wine again, she glanced at the house. "By the way, I really like the addition. It's beautiful."

"Thanks."

"You're very talented."

Kate knew her compliment was truthful, and she believed it to be innocent, but when she saw Brodie's tiny smirk, Kate felt her cheeks begin to heat. Desperate to find a subject change, when Kate noticed Brodie's hair being ruffled by the breeze, she blurted, "How's your head?"

"It's fine," Brodie said, running her fingers through her hair. "Thanks for asking."

"I was...um...I was surprised to find you gone when I got up the next morning."

"I was feeling better and saw no reason to stay any longer, so I called a cab."

"Oh, I see," Kate said, studying the woman. "How's your lip?"

"It's also fine. How's your hand?"

Kate frowned. "I'm sorry that I hit you."

"Which time?" Brodie said, grinning.

"Both times," Kate said with a weak laugh. "You do seem to bring out the worst in me."

"Well, then I guess it's a good thing we didn't take it any further that night in the hostel."

It was clear Brodie wanted answers, and Kate knew she deserved the truth, but fear and jealousy prevented Kate from speaking it. Brodie had returned to her life of clubbing while Kate was still fumbling through yet another dead-end relationship, and to admit that particular fact seemed counterproductive. Kate needed to appear as if she had moved on with nary a blip in her life. She needed to appear happy and content. She needed to appear like all the things she wasn't. In other words, Kate needed to lie.

"Brodie, about that night. I want to apologize for what happened. It was all my fault."

Folding her arms, Brodie snickered. "Well, it sure as hell wasn't mine."

"I made a mistake."

It was the last thing Brodie wanted to hear, and she sat straight in her chair. "Which part was the mistake, Kate? When you kissed me in your room or when you came into mine and did it again?"

"Please, don't be angry."

"Oh, darling, I got past angry months ago," Brodie said, keeping her voice low. "You pushed me away, ran from my room, and then refused to speak a single word to me from that moment on. Do you have any idea how many times I've thought about that night? How many times I tried to figure out what I did wrong?"

"You didn't do anything wrong."

"I *know*," Brodie said, sitting forward in her chair. "But it would have been nice hearing it from you *then* instead of now. Why couldn't you have just told me that night, Kate, or the next day during our excruciatingly silent drive home? Why wait until today? Why wait this long?"

"I was embarrassed, and I didn't want to hurt you more than I already had."

"Hurt me, how?"

Kate fingered the stem of her wine glass, unable to look Brodie in the eye. "Brodie, I got caught up in the charade, and I let things go too far. I am *really* sorry, but I'm into men…not women."

It was a painful death for the glimmer of hope Brodie had been desperately clinging to since she'd sat down, and an awkward silence fell over them. There was a part of her that wasn't surprised. She'd noticed how Kate hadn't looked her in the eye, and while she had laughed in all the right places, those, too, seemed strained, but hope is hope...until it's been dashed.

Brodie stiffened, the warmth of the day paling to the annoyance burning within her. Brodie knew she should leave before it rose to the surface, for if it leached out in her tone or expression, it would start yet another argument, and there was no point in arguing any longer.

Kate saw Brodie pick up her wine and empty it in one swallow, and believing the woman was ready to leave, Kate tried to restart the conversation. "So...are you here with anyone?"

"No," Brodie said, raising her chin. "But you're here with Fitzgerald. I saw you walking in the gardens with him earlier."

"Oh."

Brodie stared at the empty glass in her hand for a moment before raising her eyes. "Is it serious?"

It only took a second for Kate's mind to drift back to the night when she viewed the marks covering Brodie's back left by a vampire named Talia, and a knot formed in her stomach. "Yes, as a matter of fact, it is," she said matter-of-factly.

Brodie clenched her teeth. She reached into her trouser pocket, silently damning herself a second later for having quit smoking, so taking a deep breath, she held it for a moment before slowly letting it out. When she did, her thoughts came, too. "He's a wanker."

Kate's eyes flew open wide. "Sorry?"

"You heard me. Fitzgerald's a prat, and his ego is larger than this bloody addition," Brodie growled. "Honestly, Kate, I thought you had better taste than that."

"Oh, and *you* should talk."

"What's that supposed to mean?"

"At least he doesn't leave bruises!"

"Oh, give him time, Kate," Brodie said, sneering. "Just give him time." Seeing Kate straighten in her chair, Brodie held up her hands. "Sorry. That was inappropriate. It seems like we both bring out the worst in each other."

"Brodie—"

"Kate, if he's who you want and *what* you want, then I wish you all the luck in the world. I just hope he appreciates what he has."

"What about us?"

"There is no *us*, Kate," Brodie said, leaning slightly forward in her seat. "There can't be. You have a boyfriend now, and I seriously doubt he'll want you spending your Friday nights with me, and, quite frankly, I was getting a bit tired of Italian anyway. I'm sure you and I will bump into each other occasionally, what with Cassidy being your sister, but other than that...other than that, I think it's best we go our separate ways."

Their heads turned in unison when someone called Kate's name, and seeing Julian walking toward them, Brodie got to her feet. "I'd better be going," she said, and debating only for a moment, she leaned down and placed a light kiss on Kate's cheek. As she pulled away, Brodie's brow knitted. "You changed your perfume."

"Oh...um...yes. Julian bought this one for me. Why? Don't you like it?"

"Does it matter?"

Brodie had yet to straighten, and hearing the sound of approaching footsteps, she whispered, "You look lovely, by the way, but stay out of the sun. You're starting to burn."

"Thanks," Kate said softly. "I'll do that."

"Shaw, I've got a small bone to pick with you," Julian said as he neared the table.

With their faces still only inches apart, Brodie gave Kate a wink before standing tall and turning to face Julian. "Yes," she said, giving him the once over. "I heard it was small."

Kate choked back a laugh, and averting her face, she covered her mouth with her hand in hopes of stopping the rest welling up inside of her.

Julian's nostrils flared like a charging bull as he glowered at Brodie. "Where in the hell are my stones?"

Brodie sucked in her cheeks. "Lost them, did you?"

"I have had *enough* of your crap," Julian said, intruding on Brodie's personal space. "My stepping stones have been replaced along with all the pavers with my company name on them. Now where the fuck are they?"

"In the rubbish would be my guess."

"What gives you the right to touch my work?"

Brodie sniggered. "Trust me, Fitzgerald, I don't want to touch anything of yours," she said, slipping her hands into her trouser pockets. "However, when Dori called the other day and said she didn't appreciate your advertisements in her garden, I rang up Ethan, and he had them removed, and now I think it's time for me to leave." Brodie glanced at Kate. "It was nice talking to you, Kate. Do enjoy your day."

Julian's cheeks burned even redder as he watched Brodie stride across the patio and back into the house. "Come on," he said, looking at Kate. "I'm going to need your help."

"What?"

"The bins are on the other side of the house."

Kate's mouth dropped open, and for a second, she just stared at Julian. "Are you...are you saying you want me to rummage through the rubbish dressed like this?"

"Well, I can't very well do it myself. There are dozens."

"I'm sorry, Julian, but I think I've had a bit too much sun and—"

"It's a bloody sunburn, Kate. It'll disappear in a few days," he said, scowling. "But those stones and pavers cost me a fortune. Now, come on. Up you go...and for Christ's sake, put on your shoes."

***

Kate stepped inside her empty house and flicked on some lights. She dropped her handbag on a chair, letting out a sigh as she kicked off her shoes. Kate had no idea what direction her life was heading. She only knew that Julian Fitzgerald's number would no longer show up on her caller ID.

She slogged up the stairs and stripping off her clothes, she headed into the bathroom and filled the tub. She needed to wash off the sweat of the day and the smell of his trendy aftershave. A few minutes later, Kate sunk into the steaming water and hissed at the heat as it enveloped her. She relaxed back against the tub, immersing herself up to her neck, and as she looked up at the ceiling, she thought about the day...and about Brodie.

She missed her. She missed those dark eyes that twinkled when banter became filled with innuendo or a joke had been made at Kate's expense. She missed sharing a dinner prepared for one but eaten by two, and Kate missed that goddamned confidence that bordered on cocky.

Weeks of denial and nights of vodka dinners had done nothing to erase the feelings Brodie had stirred. They had been friends for a while, but Kate knew they could never be *just* friends again. The night in the hostel proved that. She had run from the room, frightened of the feelings that had caused her body to pulse and her heart to race. She had never been so hungry for another, and Kate's mind spun out of control at the possibilities. She was scared. She was terrified. She was in love.

Chapter Eighteen

Rhonda Monroe walked into her kitchen and almost dropped the bags she was carrying. "Kate! I thought that was your car down the street. Let me just get rid of these packages, and we can have a proper hello."

Kate stayed slumped in the chair. She was exhausted. It wasn't because she had to walk a block to get to her mother's house, and it wasn't because she'd run up a flight of stairs. It was because of thinking. Kate was *tired* of thinking.

Sixteen nights had crept into fifteen mornings with sleep coming in short spurts, and when the blaring of her alarm woke her, it would start all over again. Two opposing arguments took up all the space in her head, and if Kate had said them aloud, she would have screamed them, but instead, they remained in her mind, jabbing and pummeling at her like prizefighters. There wasn't a morning that had gone by when Kate hadn't stared into the bathroom mirror, wondering who she was and what she was, and then she'd go about her day, pretending she knew the answer. The night before, Kate had sat in her lounge, sipping wine and staring off into space, trying once again to win an unwinnable argument. No matter how many variables she added to the mix, the answer came back the same. It was time to stop running. It was time to face her fears, and it was time to stand up for her sister.

As her mother came to the table, Kate pushed herself out of the chair and gave her a quick hug. "Hiya, Mum."

"Oh, I can't believe you're here. What a nice surprise," Rhonda said, holding Kate at arm's length. "How long are you planning to stay? The county fair starts tomorrow, and we could spend all day—"

"I'm heading back later today."

"What? Oh, that's preposterous. Why drive three hours only to turn around and do it all again?" Rhonda said, waving off the idea with a flick of her wrist. "You'll stay for at least the night. I insist."

"I can't do that, Mum. I have to work."

"Call them and tell them you're sick. I'm your mother, Kathryn, and what I say goes. Now pick up the phone—"

"Mum, please stop," Kate said, motioning for her mother to sit down. "I'm here because we need to talk."

"Talk?" Rhonda said, sitting down. "Oh, my Lord. You're not sick, are you?"

"No, Mum. I'm not sick."

"Thank God," Rhonda said, splaying her fingers over her chest. "Then what's so important you drive all the way up here to spend only a few hours? I thought I taught you better than to waste your time on frivolous trips."

"Devon is why I'm here."

Rhonda's face lit up, and she clapped her hands together in glee. "Oh, I was *so* hoping you were going to say that! What do you think we should do? Do you have a plan?"

"A plan?"

"Well, of course. I'm sure between the two of us, we can come up with something to bring your sister to her senses. We could find a doctor or…or a psychiatrist perhaps, and he could—"

"Mum, Devon doesn't need a doctor *or* a psychiatrist."

"She most certainly does."

"There is nothing wrong with Devon, Mum. She's a les—"

"Don't you dare utter that disgusting word in my house," Rhonda said, jumping to her feet. "What Devon is doing is filthy. It's perverted and unnatural. It goes against everything I tried to teach you girls, *and* it goes against God. As the good Lord is my witness, Kate, that woman will never set foot in my home again if she chooses to live such a deviant life."

"You're being irrational," Kate said, standing up. "Devon's just trying to live *her* life. Be happy for her."

"Happy? *Happy*! How in the world can I be happy for something as...as appalling as the lifestyle Devon has chosen? It's vulgar, just like that bloody friend of yours. She's the reason—"

"Gina is not vulgar, and she didn't do anything wrong."

"What she and your sister are doing is *wrong*!"

Kate stiffened and lowered her eyes. In an instant, the tone of her mother's voice transported her back to her childhood, yet a few seconds later, Kate relaxed. She had spent the three-hour drive rehearsing over and over what she planned to say, and in her repertoire, she had answers for every scenario and rebuttals for every ludicrous argument.

Kate raised her eyes and straightened her posture. "That's not your place to say."

"I'm her mother!"

"Since when does that give you the right to tell us how to live? Look around, Mum. Devon and I have our own careers. We have our own lives, and whether you like it or not, you don't get a vote in whom we choose as our partners. We aren't kids anymore, Mum. We've grown into two independent women. We're self-sufficient, we think for ourselves, and we make our own decisions...and that's *exactly* what Devon's doing."

"This is *not* a decision! This is a grievous error that's going to send Devon straight to hell, and I will *never* approve of it, young lady. Never!"

"You don't have a choice."

"Oh, that's where you're wrong. Until your sister comes to her senses, *you* are my only daughter. I've already changed my will and removed her name from everything. And since I'm assuming Devon or that tart friend of yours put you up to this *stupid* attempt to change my mind, please feel free to take this message back to London with you. As far as I'm concerned, I wish Devon had never been born."

"Mum, don't say that. Devon's your daughter. You love her, and she loves you."

"I'm sorry, but I don't know anyone by the name of Devon," Rhonda said, waddling to the stove. "I think I'm going to have some tea. Would you like some?"

Before Kate had even climbed into her car that morning, she knew she had two battles ahead of her. One would revolve around her mother's ability to deny anything she didn't want to accept. The woman was an expert at it, and it had almost ruined Kate's and Devon's relationship with their father. The second was one Kate was all too familiar with. Her mother's stubbornness even bested Kate's, and many a disagreement between them had lasted for days until Kate would finally cave. But Kate couldn't cave today. Today the issue was more important than the clothes she wanted to wear, the movie she wanted to see, or even the boys she had once wanted to date. Today it was time to start righting wrongs...no matter what the cost.

Kate picked at a loose thread on the old tablecloth. It was one of only three her mother had ever used on this table, and as Kate looked around the room, she slouched. Nothing had changed over the years except for the shade of the paint on the walls. As a child, they were bright green, almost lime in hue, and as a teenager, they became the soft orange that still remained as a background for the almond laminate cabinets filling the walls. The cooker and refrigerator had been recently replaced, but the kitchen table and the wall decorations were still the same. A cuckoo clock that had long since lost its voice, a pair of ceramic rooster profiles, the red of their combs now faded from cleaning, and three copper cake molds that Kate had never seen used. The rest of the house was like the kitchen, filled with tired mementos accumulated over the years, and the furniture in the rooms was in the same place it had been throughout Kate's life. Her mother was a creature of habit. From folding laundry to setting the table to the food filling the pantry, it was the same old, same old, and Kate winced. She was becoming her mother...right down to the slaps.

"Kathryn, answer me when I'm speaking to you!"

Kate flinched and looked across the room. "Sorry?"

"*Tea*," Rhoda said, holding up a cup. "Would you like some?"

"Oh...um...no. No, thank you," Kate said, watching as her mother set the one cup aside and picked up another. "Can you please sit down so we can talk about this some more?"

Rhonda's face turned pinched, and going back to the table, she slipped into a chair. "There's absolutely nothing to talk about unless you've come to your senses."

"Me?" Kate said, leaning forward in her chair. "I'm not the one cutting off one of my children."

"I only *have* one of those," Rhonda said, peering at Kate. "And I can just as easily have *none* if you keep this up."

"What?"

"You heard. Homosexuals are disgusting creatures, and I won't have you defending them in my house."

Kate rocked back in her chair and ran her fingers through her hair. "They aren't *creatures*, Mum. They're people, just like you and me."

"I am *nothing* like them," Rhonda shouted. "And I am done discussing this horrid subject. Do you hear me? Done!"

"Well, I'm *not*," Kate said, glaring at her mother. "Devon is your daughter, and you need to stop all this crap and—"

"I only *have* one daughter, Kathryn. Look around this bloody house and tell me if you see anything that says otherwise."

Kate's mouth fell open, and for a few seconds, she stared at her mother. "You didn't. No, you bloody didn't!"

In a flash, Kate was running from the kitchen. Her first stop was the lounge, and her eyes turned glassy. The photographs on the mantle were only of Kate, and those perched on tables around the room had been reduced by half. Kate bounded up the stairs and fought back her tears as she passed the shadowy outlines of missing photos that appeared like ghosts amongst those that remained. Bolting to Devon's bedroom, Kate threw open the door, and her breath caught in her throat. The shelves once holding her sister's rugby and cross country trophies were now empty, and the keepsakes and stuffed animals that used to crowd the tops of the dresser and bureau were gone. Even the bedspread had been changed, for it was now yellow...and Devon hated yellow.

By the time Kate returned to the kitchen, all the color had drained from her face except for two splotches of red, dotting her cheeks. "What did you do with all of it?"

"All of what, dear," Rhonda said, picking up her teacup.

Kate strode to her mother, getting so close that Rhonda had to lean back in her chair. "What did you do with Devon's stuff?"

"Oh, that," Rhonda said, waving her hand. "I tossed it in the rubbish yesterday."

"Shit," Kate said, and racing to the back door, she flung it open, bounded down the steps, and rushed to the side of the house. Ignoring the recycle bin, Kate lifted the lid of the other, and her tears fell again. "You bitch," she said as she pulled Devon's trophies and childhood memories from the trash. "How could you do this? How could you *do* this?"

Kate took the time she needed to stack everything on the ground next to the bin, and struggling to keep her emotions in check, she held her breath as she lifted the lid on the recycle container. Her face brightened when she saw all the missing photographs still housed in their frames, and collecting them from the trash, Kate patted her jeans and grinned when she felt her keys under the denim.

It took her three trips to her car to get everything safely tucked away, and when Kate got back to the house, she hesitated for only a moment before quietly entering through the front door. She crept through the house, gathering anything showing her mother had ever had *any* children, and stacking it all by the door, Kate went upstairs and did the same. She piled everything on the front porch before returning to the kitchen

Kate entered the room and then stopped. She thought it would be harder than this, bordering on impossible yet as she stared at her mother, sitting at the table and sipping her tea with her pinkie sticking out like a royal, the words came easily. "I'm leaving," Kate said in a monotone voice. "And I won't be coming back."

Rhonda pursed her lips and flicked her eyes upward. "Oh, don't be so dramatic. Of course, you will. This will blow over, and you and I—"

"That's where you're wrong, because if you can't accept Devon's lifestyle, accept the fact that she's—"

"I will *never* accept it. What your sister is doing with that woman is not *normal!*"

Kate took a deep breath and squared her shoulders. "Well, it is for them, Mum…and it is for me."

***

Gina had just finished serving a customer when she looked up, and the smile she was wearing slipped from her face. "What are you doing here?"

"I thought I'd stop by to say hi and—"

"Well, you just said it, so feel free to leave," Gina said, pointing across the club. "The door's over there."

"Don't be like this."

"Like what, Kate? Like angry enough to slap the shit out of you for not defending your sister?" Gina said, snatching up a rag from behind the bar. "For letting her go to see your mother alone knowing how that woman is? For letting her face that kind of hatred *alone*? Jesus Christ, Kate. Your mother slapped her!"

"I know the feeling," Kate said quietly.

Gina's anger faded just a bit as she recalled what Devon had told her about their mother, but the weight of what disappeared, couldn't displace what remained. "I don't really give a fuck what you do or don't know," Gina said, wiping down the bar as if she was trying to remove the finish. "I thought you were my friend. I thought you were an ally, but right now, Kate…I'm not sure you're either."

"Can you please just let me explain? It will only take a—"

"You need to explain to Devon what you did, not me, and you owe her a *goddamned* apology," Gina said, and tossing the rag aside, she turned her back on Kate and began straightening the bottles of liquor filling a shelf.

A ghost of a grin appeared on Kate's face. "I've already apologized to Devon. I stopped for a late lunch on the way back and called her from a café. We had a long talk."

Gina stopped what she was doing and turned back around. "What?"

Before Kate could reply, she was jostled by a woman trying to order a drink. She stepped aside and waited while Gina tended to the customer. Once the woman walked away with ale in hand, Kate returned to her spot at the bar. "Can you take a short break, so we can talk about this in your office?"

Gina took her time mulling over Kate's request before finally turning toward the other bartender. "Chloe, I'm going to take a break. Call me if you need me. I'll be in the back."

"Sure thing, boss."

Gina grabbed a couple of bottles of lager and indicating for Kate to follow her, Gina didn't say another word until she closed the door to her office behind her. "Now, what's this all about?" she said, shoving one of the bottles into Kate's hand as she walked past. Leaning against the desk, Gina crossed her arms. "And it better be good."

Kate took a seat in one of the chairs facing the desk, raising her eyes to meet Gina's for only a split-second before lowering them again. "I went to see my mother this morning."

"Why?"

"To see if I could get through to her. Convince her that Devon being gay isn't the end of the world."

"You mean, do what you should have done to begin with?"

"Yes."

"Well, did you? Convince her, I mean."

"No," Kate said quietly. "She said until Devon comes to her senses, she only has one daughter."

"Lucky you," Gina said, following it up with a swig of her lager.

"Not exactly," Kate said under her breath.

Gina covertly kept her eyes on Kate. They had been friends for far too long for her not to know there was more to this story than Kate was telling. They had both made their fair share of apologies to one another over the years. Forgiveness asked for tardiness, misunderstandings, and the occasional broken dish had been exchanged with kind words and eye contact, but Kate hadn't made eye contact since they came into the office. Gina took a deep breath, and going over, she sat down in the chair next to Kate's. She opened her mouth to speak, and her lungs emptied in a whoosh. The dim lighting in the club had hidden it until now, but in the brightness of the fluorescent fixtures above their heads, the bruise covering Kate's cheek was vividly apparent. "Jesus, what happened to your face?"

"What do you think happened to it?" Kate said, raising her eyes.

Gina's eyes bulged. "Are you saying your *mother* did that?"

"Yeah," Kate said before taking a taste of her lager.

"But why?"

Kate forced the smallest of smiles. "Because Devon's not the only one motherless now."

"What in the hell are you talking about?" Gina said, touching Kate on the arm. "She couldn't possibly disown you simply because you stood up for your sister. That's ridiculous. She's just angry you didn't see things her way. Just give her a few days, and she'll calm down."

"That's not going to happen."

"Why not?"

Kate stared off into space for a moment before looking Gina in the eye. "She didn't hit me because I sided with you and Devon. She did it because...because I told her...because I told her if Devon wasn't normal, then neither was I."

Time stood still as Kate's words sunk in, and when they did, Gina leaned back in her chair. "What did you just say?"

Intent on peeling the label from the bottle in her hand, when Kate raised her eyes again, they were filled with tears. "You know, that's the third time I've had to say that today, and it hasn't gotten any easier. Does it ever?"

Gina slid her hand down Kate's arm and slipped her fingers through Kate's. "I'm assuming this is about Brodie," she said, gently squeezing Kate's hand. "Do you want to talk about it?"

Her voice trapped in a quagmire of confusion, fear, and a modicum of shame, all Kate could do was shrug.

"Well, I think I'll sit here until you're ready to talk," Gina said, squeezing Kate's hand again. "Something tells me you need to. You're just scared...and that's okay. We all get scared."

The office was quiet save for the thumping bass of the music in the club coming through the walls, and as the minute hand swept around the clock for the fourth time, Kate took a ragged breath. "When did you know?"

Gina's mouth curved with tenderness. "Are you asking when I knew I was a lesbian?"

"Yes."

"I was thirteen."

"I'm thirty-five."

Gina's eyes creased at the corners. "I don't think there's a time limit on it, Kate. You know when you know. That's the way it works."

"But what if I'm wrong?"

Gina tilted her head as she gazed at Kate. "Does it feel wrong when you're with Brodie?"

"I haven't *been* with Brodie," Kate said, a vivid blush staining her cheeks almost instantly.

"Sorry?"

"You heard me."

"Wait," Gina said with a slight shake of her head. "Are you telling me you came out to your mother just because you're attracted to another woman?"

"Attracted is putting it mildly."

"How mildly?" Gina said, struggling to hide her amusement.

"*Very* mildly."

Unable to contain it any longer, Gina's grin appeared. "Do tell."

In an instant, Kate snatched her hand from Gina's and jumped to her feet. With the room seeming to grow hotter as each second passed, Kate downed the rest of her drink and then began to pace. She had no idea that a few feet away sat a woman with as much love in her eyes as there was mirth.

Gina watched as Kate prowled the room like a caged animal. Over the years, she'd seen Kate go from one relationship to another, and after meeting a few of her dates, it was all too clear why. The men had always been handsome, and most had been charming as well, but they all lacked the strength and the backbone a woman like Kate required. Eventually, Kate would walk away and start again because those men offered her no challenge and no excitement. They were weak, and she was strong, but Kate had finally met her match...and Gina couldn't have been happier.

"You're in love with her, aren't you?"

The question stopped Kate in her tracks, and returning to sit next to Gina, Kate gazed at the woman while she gathered her thoughts. "When I'm with her, Gina, nothing else seems to matter. She's so bloody charming and confident, and she can always make me smile even when I don't want to. I look into her eyes and see nothing but truth and caring, and a tenderness that takes my breath away." Kate paused for a second and shook her head. "And I don't understand why when my boyfriends opened doors for me, it would always irritate me, like I was weak or something, but when Brodie and I leave a restaurant, and she puts her hand on my back to guide me through the door, it feels so bloody good. And when she kissed me, Gina...oh, God...when she kissed me, I have never felt like that before."

"So what are you waiting for?"

"What?"

Gina reached over and placed her hand on Kate's knee. "Kate, it's obvious you both like each other, and from what you just said, she definitely turns you on. So, what's the problem?"

Kate let out a long breath. "Gina...I'm not sure—"

"Oh, don't worry about that," Gina said, patting Kate's knee. "If you've got any questions, just ask. I'll tell you everything I know. I'm not an expert or anything, but I've picked up a few things over the years."

Kate stared back at Gina for a second, and then her eyes flew open wide. "Gina, I'm not talking about the...the...the *mechanics*! I'm pretty sure I can figure that part out." As soon as the words finished exiting her mouth, Kate buried her face in her hands, convinced that her flaming cheeks were going to leave behind second-degree burns. "Oh, God, I can't believe I just said that."

"Neither can I," Gina said, bubbling with laughter. "You go, girl."

"Stop!" Kate squeaked as she uncovered her face. "Please?"

"All right. I'll behave," Gina said, snickering. "But I have to tell you, red is *definitely* your color."

"*Enough*," Kate said, swatting Gina's leg. "You aren't helping matters."

"Yeah, I am," Gina said quietly.

Kate's eyes met Gina's, and she smiled. "I love you. You know that, right?"

"Yes, and I love you, too."

"I'm sorry I hurt you. I was just so confused, and...and that made me angry."

"I know. You forget, I've been your friend for a lot of years. I've seen the pattern. You have one hell of a temper when things don't go your way."

"That scares me."

"Why?"

"Because you just described my mum."

Gina leaned back in her chair. "I think you should know that...that Devon filled me on what went on after your folks got divorced."

"She did what?"

"Kate, it's okay," Gina said, sitting straight. "I was really, really angry with you, and I think Devon was just trying to give me some insight on why you are the way you are."

"Wow, that makes me sound positively horrid," Kate said, pushing herself out of her chair.

"Not in the least," Gina said, grabbing Kate's hand so she'd sit back down. "It makes you sound like you didn't have the best childhood, and you have a few scars. It makes you sound like you did the best you could, and it makes you sound like someone that, regardless of what you went through, knows the difference between right and wrong. You know what you did to Devon was wrong, and you apologized for it...*and* you stood by her. You stood by her when you took that slap for her way back when, and you stood by her today. That tells me that while you may share the same short fuse your mother has, that's where the similarities end."

Kate bowed her head. "I'm not so sure about that."

"Why?"

"Because I hit Brodie," Kate whispered.

Gina's mouth fell open. "You did *what*?"

Kate took a slow breath and raised her tear-filled eyes. "I slapped her. She has a way of getting under my skin, saying things I don't want to hear, and I was so confused about my feelings toward her—"

"Are you still?"

"Huh?"

"Confused about your feelings toward her?"

"No," Kate said, shaking her head. "No, I'm not, but that doesn't change what I did."

"Do you plan to do it again?"

"Of course not," Kate said, frowning. "As a matter of fact, the drive home gave me a lot of time to think. We have counselors at work to help us deal with stress or other issues. I'm going to see about talking to one of them because I know it's wrong, and I don't want to do it again. Ever."

"Which brings me back to what I said a minute ago," Gina said with a soft smile. "You aren't putting your head in the sand, Kate. You aren't pretending it didn't happen like your mum did. You've acknowledged it. You know it was wrong, and you're going to seek help for it, which makes you *nothing* like your mother, Kate. Nothing."

"I hope you're right."

"Trust me. I am." Gina finished what was left of her lager, and putting the bottle aside, she stared at the floor.

"What's wrong?" Kate said, noticing a look of sadness cross Gina's face.

When Gina raised her eyes, they were moist with tears. "Devon told me you knew she was gay before she actually told you, and that cut me to the core, Kate. You knew how I felt about her, yet you kept it a secret from me. Why? Why hurt your best friend like that?"

"Because it wasn't my secret to tell," Kate said, reaching over to take Gina's hand. "And yeah, I knew how you felt about her. You could never hide it no matter how hard you tried, and I knew Devon liked you, but how was I supposed to know she liked you *that* way. I didn't want to get your hopes up only to find out I was wrong. It was the lesser of two evils, Gina, and I'm sorry. I really am."

Gina mulled over Kate's apology for only a second. "You're forgiven."

"That was quick."

"It just means she and I have a lot of making up to do," Gina said, wiggling her eyebrows.

"TMI, Gina," Kate said, raising her hands. "*TMI.*"

Gina chuckled. "So…what are you going to do about Brodie?"

"I have absolutely no bloody idea," Kate said, flopping back in the chair. "She made it very clear the last time I saw her, she didn't want to see me again, and I really can't blame her. Where Brodie's concerned, I've changed my mind almost as much as I change my knickers."

"You plan on changing your mind again?"

"No. I'm done with that. I know what I want…and who I want."

"Well, then it sounds like you better come up with something good."

Chapter Nineteen

Brodie hung up the phone and rocking back in her chair, she clasped her hands behind her head. In less than three weeks, she'd received six calls from people who'd seen the Hirshfeld's addition, and an email from Dori that morning told Brodie to expect even more attention soon. Home Digest, an interior decorating magazine, would be running an article about the Hirshfeld's new addition in an upcoming issue, and Dori had made it clear she intended to sing Brodie's praises.

After taking a few minutes to celebrate in silence, Brodie reached for her calendar to jot down the appointment a split-second before Stevie sauntered into the room.

"Scrumptious, I really wish you'd let me do that," Stevie said, nearing the desk. "It is my job, after all."

Brodie looked up, her eyes sparkling at the sight of her admin assistant. He was wearing skin-tight mandarin orange trousers with an equally-as-tight mandarin orange shirt. If the man's hair were green instead of light brown, Stevie could have passed for a carrot.

"Yes, but it's *my* planner," Brodie said, pushing the calendar aside.

"Of that, we agree," Stevie said with a bob of his head. "But it seems your pretty little noggin has forgotten something."

"Oh yeah? What's that?"

"*You* never remember to put them into the computer, so I end up scheduling appointments in slots that you've already slotted."

Brodie couldn't argue the point. Just last week, she had done it twice, and to appease one of her new clients, Stevie ended up buying them a lavish lunch to express the company's apologies for the mix-up. "Be my guest," she said, pushing the planner in his direction.

"Thank the Lord," Stevie said, snatching up the calendar. "And since you've been a good girl, I'll give you this."

Brodie cautiously took the small white paper bag from Stevie. "You bought me pastries?"

"No, they were just delivered."

"Delivered?"

"Yes, along with this," Stevie said, handing Brodie an envelope. "Having a fling with the neighborhood baker, are you?"

"*He* looks like Santa Claus, so he's more your type than mine."

"Well, I like them mature, but not *that* mature," Stevie said, flicking his wrist over his shoulder as he headed to the door. "Enjoy."

Brodie set aside the envelope and unfolding the top of the bag, she reached in and pulled out a donut covered in powdered sugar. She turned it this way and that before dropping it back into the bag, and after licking the confectioner's sugar off her fingers, she tore open the envelope.

Brodie -

How do you feel about Sichuan food?
The Chengdu Empress - Friday, at 7.
Please say yes.

K

PS – Enjoy your breakfast.

***

"I hate bloody, fucking paperwork," Frank Daggett said, tossing another folder on his desk.

"It's part of the job," Kate said, opening a file to begin entering the information into her computer.

"Data entry is for lasses," Daggett said, pushing out his chair. "I'm going for a walk."

Kate looked up as he marched away and shaking her head, she got back to work. It was Friday morning, and as far as she was concerned, Daggett could keep right on walking until Monday. Kate had yet to request a sit-down with her Chief to find out why she even *had* a partner, something virtually unheard of at the Met, except Kate prided herself on following orders. Having a stubborn streak also added to Kate's patience, and she hoped that Daggett would beat her to the punch. His aversion to working with women was as well-known as his pungent aftershave, but so far, he seemed content in making her life miserable. Kate had heard some rumors that Frank had colored outside too many lines at the last borough, and since the man only had a few more years before reaching the minimum pension age, Kate couldn't help but wonder if this partnership was just babysitting duty.

Kate glanced at the phone, debating if she should call and cancel the reservation she made on Wednesday. She'd yet to hear from Brodie, and Kate feared the lack of response *was* Brodie's response. She couldn't really blame her though. Kate huffed out a breath. No, she couldn't really blame Brodie at all.

Kate looked back and forth between the documents on her desk and those on her computer, trying to see where she had left off when a pastel green box was placed on her desk.

"Fancy a donut?"

Kate looked up to see Elliott Thackery smiling back at her. "You bought me donuts?"

"Oh, I didn't buy them. The bakery delivered them a few minutes ago. Apparently, they made too many or something, so they brought them all here," Elliott said, gesturing behind him.

Kate leaned forward to look past Elliott, and sure enough, there were pastel green boxes all over the station. "Wow."

"Yeah. The only problem is, they're all one kind," Elliott said as he opened the lid of the box. "Hope you like chocolate frosted."

Kate's face lit up as she gazed at the donuts nestled in the box, and as Elliott walked away, she reached in and pulled one out.

"Oh, crap. I almost forgot," Elliott said, patting himself down before turning back around. "This came for you about the same time."

"Thanks," Kate said, taking the small blue envelope from his hand.

"No problem. Enjoy your breakfast."

As soon as Elliott walked away, Kate ripped open the envelope and read the card inside.

Kate –

I love Sichuan.
See you at 7.

B

PS – Don't ruin your dinner.

***

Brodie had torn up, crumpled, or shredded more than two dozen notes before settling on the simplest of them all. A short affirmation to confirm her attendance at dinner was all that was needed because the words she needed to say weren't going to be delivered with boxes of donuts. They were going to be spoken in person...whether Kate wanted to hear them or not.

Somewhere between anxious and frustrated, Brodie drove to the restaurant. The smile Kate's donut delivery had produced had stayed on her face Wednesday morning, but toward the afternoon, it began to waver, and by the time Brodie arrived home that night, it had disappeared. What was she doing? After seeing Kate at the Hirshfeld's, Brodie had finally moved on. The Loft had reopened, and Brodie returned to what she knew, and while shagging Talia in the bathroom would never be more than just that, it was a step in the right direction. It was who Brodie was, and until she had met Kate, it had been enough.

Brodie parked her car, and turning off the ignition, she sat in the dark and drummed her fingers on the wheel. She'd never dined at this restaurant before and located on the other side of town, Brodie had planned her route carefully, so carefully she had arrived early, and that was a mistake. It gave her too much time to think, too much time to consider whether she should just cancel and go home. Did it really matter what she had to say? Would it change anything? Brodie let out a ragged breath. How many times had she told herself *this* was the last time only to let Kate bewitch her again? What the *fuck* was she doing?

***

Kate sat at a corner table, taking sips of her wine in between fidgeting with the silverware and keeping one eye on the entrance. She hoped tonight would be the first of many spent with Brodie, but as the day turned into night, and Kate found herself sitting alone in a romantic restaurant, her insecurities returned. What if Brodie wanted to move too fast or worse yet, what if Brodie didn't want to move at all? What if tonight wasn't about starting a relationship, but merely a way Brodie could put the final nail in the coffin Kate had built?

Kate reached for her wine as she looked toward the door again, and when she saw Brodie walk into the restaurant, an undeniable sense of pride swept over Kate. The heat of an unusually warm summer had demanded lighter colors, and Kate couldn't help but admire her guest as she made her way to the table. With her skin bronzed by the sun and wearing white jeans and a tea green long-sleeved linen top, Brodie looked stunning, and Kate shifted in her seat when she felt her body react to the view.

Brodie reached the table, and Kate beamed. "Hiya, Brodie."

"Hi, yourself," Brodie said, placing a butterfly kiss on Kate's cheek. "You look lovely."

Kate was wearing a breezy, pale peach crepe dress, wrapped in the front and tied with a belt in the same fabric, and if the truth be known, it was brand new just like everything else Kate had on right down to her knickers. She hadn't intended to shop for clothes until Brodie had accepted her dinner invitation, and after that, nothing Kate owned was good enough. Having worked over her allotted hours for the week, Kate had left work early and headed to a few of her favorite boutiques. She wanted something casual and bright, something feminine and soft that wouldn't overwhelm the evening, but rather blend with the ambiance of friendship and hopefully something more.

"Thanks. So do you," Kate said, watching as Brodie sat down. "And I'm glad you accepted my invitation."

"I was a little surprised by it, actually."

The waiter approached, interrupting their conversation long enough to take Brodie's drink order. Once he walked away, Kate leaned a smidge toward Brodie. "You were saying?"

"Oh, right. I was saying I was surprised. I thought Friday night dinners were set aside for boyfriends."

Kate rested back in her chair. "I don't have one of those."

"No?"

"No."

Brodie sized up Kate while she thought back to the Hirshfeld's party. "But I thought...I mean, you said it was serious between you and Fitzgerald."

Kate's smile wavered, and she handed Brodie a menu. "Why don't we order something, and then we can talk. Okay?"

***

They shared a dinner of Bang-Bang shrimp, stir-fried pork, and crispy duck, both preferring the tasting plates offered instead of separate entrees. As they ate their food and sipped their wine, they shared a few stories about their week, but it wasn't until the table was cleared of empty plates when Brodie finally said what was on her mind since she'd sat down. "Why am I here, Kate?"

"I asked, and you accepted."

Brodie's nostrils flared, but before she could speak, the waitress returned with their tea. Resting back in her chair, Brodie waited, using the time to curb her annoyance. Her eyes never left Kate's, and as soon as the young Asian woman walked away, Brodie sat up straight again. "Now is not the time to be coy."

Since making the reservation, Kate had looked forward to this moment almost as much as she had feared it. The time had come to finally say the words they both wanted her to say, and nervous didn't even come close to what Kate was feeling. Her heart was racing, and her mouth had gone dry, and under the table, she could not calm her bouncing knee. Kate took a deep breath. "I know. I'm sorry. I didn't mean to be evasive," she said, forcing a weak grin.

"Then answer the question."

"It's complicated."

Brodie leaned back and took an audible breath. She wanted answers, and she wanted them now. "Where's Fitzgerald?"

"I told you. I don't have a boyfriend."

"What happened?"

Focusing on her tiny cup of tea, Kate ran her fingertip around the china edge. "Um...I don't really want to talk about it."

"Kate, I'm tired of your games," Brodie said, crossing her arms. "I'm tired of thinking one minute you like me, and the next you don't. Now, either you start talking, or I'm leaving—for good. So, what's it going to be?"

Kate raised her eyes. "I've missed you."

"Great! Next time, send me a card," Brodie said as she stood and tossed her napkin on the table.

"Brodie...wait."

"I'm done waiting, Kate," Brodie said, eyeing the woman. "Why can't you just admit you like me?"

"I *do*," Kate blurted.

"Say that again," Brodie said, raising her voice.

Kate noticed several heads in the restaurant turn her way. "Brodie, please," Kate said as a modicum of color was added to her cheeks. "Please just sit down, and we'll talk about it."

Brodie had no intention of moving. She didn't even blink. "I said, say it *again*."

"Fine, I like you!" Kate shouted and quickly shrinking in her seat, her voice dropped to a whisper. "Now, will you please sit down?"

Brodie's face spread into a smile. She slipped back into her chair, and gazing at Kate, she pondered her next question. "So, did you lie about you and Fitzgerald? About it being serious?"

"Yes."

"Why?"

Kate nibbled on her lip for a second. "I...uh...I don't know."

Brodie jutted her jaw to the side. "Should I stand up and threaten to leave again?"

"Please don't," Kate said, her shoulders drooping.

"Then talk to me, Kate. Tell me why you lied about Fitzgerald."

For several seconds, the only sounds were those of the patrons around them chattering to their dinner partners as their silverware clinked against the plates.

Under the table, Kate ran her hands over her dress to dry her palms. "I was jealous."

"What?" Brodie said, furrowing her brow. "What do you mean, jealous?"

"I saw those...those marks your girlfriend left and —"

"Talia isn't my girlfriend."

"No?" Kate said, her eyes meeting Brodie's.

"No. She's just someone I know. Just a shag. Nothing else."

"Oh, I see," Kate said, slumping even further into her chair.

All emotion left Brodie's face, the lines caused by tension smoothing to an unreadable palette. Where it concerned Kate, hope had been Brodie's enemy. Lying in wait, it sprang up time and time again, only to dash her to the rocks days, weeks, or even hours later, and by now, Brodie knew all the signs. The flutter in her belly, the feeling of lightheartedness that would put a spring in her step, and that damned belief that everything would be okay were forever her companions when Kate had been in her life...just like they were doing now. Yes, hope had been her adversary, and once again, Brodie was going to lose the fight.

"I'm not going to see her again," Brodie said, gazing at Kate. "That is, in case you're wondering."

"No?" Kate said, popping up in her seat.

"No."

Kate hesitated and fiddled with her teacup. "And I'm not going to be seeing Julian anymore."

"Can I ask why?"

A faint twinkle appeared in Kate's eyes. "Because he's a wanker."

Brodie's laughter rang through the restaurant, and Kate smiled. The tension she had felt throughout the meal had finally eased, and taking a slow, steady breath, Kate dug deep. "I'm scared."

"Of what?" Brodie said softly.

"Of this."

"What do you mean by *this*?"

Kate shrugged. "You...me...us."

"Is there an us?"

"Oh, Brodie," Kate said, sighing. "This is really hard for me."

"Kate, just tell me what's on your mind," Brodie said, leaning toward Kate. "I promise I won't judge you. I won't rant or rave, but we can't go on like this. *I* can't go on like this. I have to know what you're thinking...what you want. Just tell me why you're so scared."

"I'm scared because...because my entire life's about to change."

"Why?"

Kate swallowed hard. "Because...because I want to date a woman."

"Really?" Brodie said through a smile that reached the next table.

"Yes."

It was one hell of a confession, and Brodie's body reacted in one hell of a way, yet she could sense something was off. Kate hadn't maintained eye contact for more than a few seconds before looking away, and if the woman didn't stop biting on her lip, she was going to do some damage. "Okay, what's wrong?"

"Huh?"

"Why do I think there's a but coming?"

Kate shook her head. "There isn't...not really."

"Not really?"

"Brodie, can I ask you a question?" Kate said quietly.

"Of course."

"How many women have you been with?"

Brodie flinched back her head ever so slightly. "Why does that matter?"

"Can you just...just answer the question?"

Brodie picked up her tea and took a sip. "To tell you the truth," she said, placing the cup back on the table. "I have no idea."

"That's what I thought," Kate said, staring down at her hands.

"Kate, what's this all about?"

"Brodie, you've been..." Kate stopped, taking a deep breath before trying again. "Brodie, you've been with a lot of women, and I haven't been with any, and that's a bit unnerving."

"How many men have you been with?"

Kate's eyes widened. "What?"

"How many men have you slept with?"

"Um…five."

Brodie held up her hands. "Well, I haven't slept with any."

"That's not the same thing, and you know it."

Cute comes in all forms. Puppies and kitten fill the bill, as do babies and the occasional pout, but for Brodie, cute was Kate off her axis. She was fidgeting, and Brodie had lost count how many times the woman had crossed and re-crossed her legs, and while her cheeks weren't flaming crimson, they did have an adorable cherry hue about them.

Brodie pressed her lips together, quieting her grin as it was about to escape. She could have sat there all night, observing Kate in all her floundering glory, or she could save her from herself. It didn't take long for Brodie to choose.

Brodie inched her chair a little closer to the table, and it wasn't until Kate looked her in the eye, that a sliver of Brodie's grin appeared. "What I know is that I adore you," she said, her tone soft as a feather. "It doesn't matter to me who you have or haven't slept with. It's not about quantity or experience. It's about feelings. It's about my day being made when I hear your voice or closing my eyes as your perfume invades my bloody senses. It's about looking in a shop window and picking out something for you, and it's about going slow if that's what you want, because I'll do anything for you, Kate. Anything at all."

A hint of humor danced in Kate's eyes. "If we go any slower, we're going to go backward."

"Somehow, I don't think that's what either one of us wants."

"It isn't."

Brodie drew in a breath and sliding her hand across the linen tablecloth, she held it open for Kate to take. "Then, we won't. We'll just take it day by day and see what happens. Okay?"

Kate slipped her fingers through Brodie's, and they sat there while their tea grew cold. One minute passed and then another until Kate said, "You want to get out of here? Get some coffee or something?"

Brodie motioned for the waitress, and when Kate pulled out her wallet, Brodie reached over and shooed it away. "My treat."

"But *I* invited you."

"As far as I'm concerned, you're now officially my girlfriend, and I'm going to pay for dinner. Unless, of course, I'm mistaken. Am I?"

Kate heard the challenge in Brodie's voice and smiled. "No…I think you're spot-on."

***

Like they had after all their Friday night dinners at Calabria, when Brodie and Kate left Chengdu Empress, they decided to walk off a bit of their dinner. They meandered down the street, but before they had gotten very far, Brodie leaned closer to Kate. "So…um…since I don't know the rules, is it all right if I hold your hand while we walk?"

Kate cast a quick glance down the sidewalk before lacing her fingers through Brodie's. "Yes, and what rules?"

"The *slow* rules."

"I don't remember mentioning anything about rules," Kate said, squeezing Brodie's hand.

"No?" Brodie said, smiling shamelessly. "Good to know!"

Kate lightly swatted Brodie on the arm and nearing a shop window, Kate tugged Brodie toward it. "So…you see anything you like?"

"Yes, I do."

Out of the corner of her eye, Kate saw Brodie looking in her direction. "I mean in there, silly," she said with a laugh.

"Oh, right," Brodie said, focusing on the display.

The store specialized in kitchen gadgets, dinnerware, and the like, and Brodie took her time before answering. "Yes," Brodie said, tapping on the glass. "The red apron over there."

"Really?" Kate squeaked. "I never pictured you as the apron type."

"Who said it was for me?"

Kate's mouth dropped open. "Wait. You expect *me* to do the cooking?"

"No, I just expect you to wear the apron."

"Sorry?"

Brodie bent, so her lips were but a few millimeters from Kate's ear. "I didn't say you'd be wearing anything else, now did I?"

Without saying another word, Brodie sauntered to the next shop while Kate tried to convince her cheeks to return to their natural color.

Jogging to catch up a moment later, Kate quickly slipped her hand in Brodie's. "I'm starting to rethink the rules part. Maybe I *should* make some."

"Oh yeah?" Brodie said. "Let me guess. The first would be something about keeping my hormones in check?"

"Is that possible?"

"I don't know. I never had to before."

"Ouch," Kate said quietly.

"Kate, I'm just joking, but for both our sakes, I think a few guidelines would be helpful. Don't you?"

"I don't know," Kate said, stopping for a second. "Like what?"

Brodie pondered the question as they continued their stroll. "Well...can I kiss you good night?"

"Yes."

"Can I kiss you good morning?"

Kate's blush returned instantly. "Eventually."

Brodie stopped, the street lights paling to her glowing face. "Do you have any idea how happy I am right now?"

"Yeah," Kate said in a breath. "I think I do."

***

Brodie followed Kate home, and pulling up behind her, Brodie quickly parked her car and then jogged to Kate's in time to open the door. Kate slipped her fingers through Brodie's, and hand-in-hand, they walked to the house.

"I had a great time tonight," Kate said as they stood on the porch.

"So did I."

"Do you want to come in for a drink?"

Brodie looked over at the door like Eve staring at the forbidden fruit. "Um...not tonight," she said, offering Kate a soft smile. "If that's okay."

"It's fine."

"Can I call you tomorrow?"

Kate's face lit up. "I'd like that."

"Then you'd best give me your number," Brodie said, grinning.

Resigned to the fact she'd never have to buy makeup to color her cheeks again, Kate waited while Brodie pulled out her phone before quickly rattling off her work, home, and mobile numbers. After

Brodie was done and slipped her phone back into her pocket, she looked over at Kate, and Kate's heart began to race. Their eyes met, and no words were necessary as Brodie leaned down for a good night kiss.

Kate had forgotten the finer points of being kissed by Brodie, and she marveled in the softness of her lips as they brushed against her own. Mingled with coffee was a flavor intrinsic to Brodie, and the combination took Kate's breath away. True to her word, Brodie didn't try to plunder or demand. Instead, she moved casually, tenderly kissing Kate again and again until Kate felt Brodie's tongue ask for entry. Losing herself in the luxury of being in Brodie's arms, Kate allowed the kiss to deepen, and as their tongues tasted and danced, hands began to wander, and bodies began to throb.

Brodie pulled away, knowing if she didn't, she'd break a promise only a few hours old. "I should go."

"I know."

"I'll call you tomorrow," Brodie said, sliding her hands into her trouser pockets.

"Okay."

"Are you all right?"

Kate reached up and touching Brodie on the cheek, she said in a breath, "Never been better."

Chapter Twenty

"So how many cold showers does that make so far?"

Brodie was exiting her bathroom when the unexpected voice interrupted her thoughts. Brodie jumped, and a second later, she was scrambling to hold onto the towel wrapped around her torso. "Christ, you scared the shit out of me."

Devon giggled. "Sorry. I guess you didn't hear me come in," she said, watching as Brodie went to the dresser and began rummaging for lingerie.

Brodie pulled out a matching set of black, lace-trimmed undies and set them on the dresser. "Do you mind?" she said, looking over at Devon.

"What? I've seen you naked before," Devon said with a wave of her hand. "Oh, wait...let me guess. Now that you're dating my sister, you've turned into a prude."

"I am not a prude. I just don't want Kate to get the wrong idea."

"And what idea would that be?" Gina said as she sailed into the bedroom and plopped next to Devon on the bed.

"Bloody hell, what are *you* doing here?" Brodie said, holding onto the loosening towel.

"Devon had some proposals she wanted to drop off, and since I didn't have to work today, and it's bucketing down outside, I volunteered to be her taxi," Gina said, giving the room a quick once over. "Nice place, by the way."

"Thanks, now if you two don't mind, I'd really like to get dressed."

"We don't mind at all," Devon said, resting back on her elbows. "So, where are you going tonight?"

Brodie picked up her watch from the dresser and glancing at the time, she muttered, "Fuck it."

In unison, Gina and Devon whistled their appreciation as Brodie dropped the towel to the floor, and after stepping into her knickers, she fastened her bra and turned back around.

"I'm going to Kate's. She's cooking dinner," Brodie said, opening the door to her wardrobe.

"So, are you going to stay the night?" Devon said.

"You know I'm not."

Devon sat back up. "It's been what...two weeks since you started dating?"

"Yes," Brodie said, stepping into a pair of jeans. "Exactly two weeks tonight. Why?"

"You must be going crazy."

Brodie frowned. Crazy wasn't the word. She could manage to keep her libido in check through dinner, coffee, and their nightly walk, but the good night kiss got her every time. Chaste was next to impossible when it came to kissing Kate, and one always seemed to turn into two and then rapidly into three and four...and more.

The promise of taking it slow was proving to be more difficult every day. Even though they had seen each other a dozen times in the past two weeks, Brodie had made it a point to arrange for their dates to be in public places. They had visited restaurants for lunch and dinner, had taken walks down busy streets or through crowded parks, and had even met at an art gallery opening, but a private dinner—*alone*—could prove disastrous.

Brodie knew her limits. She knew she loved Kate, and she also knew in the privacy of Kate's flat, it would be far too easy to forget her promise. The night before had been a repeat of many others, except when Brodie tried to leave, Kate refused to stop kissing her unless Brodie agreed to come to dinner. Kate pulled out all the stops, over and over ravaging Brodie's mouth with her tongue until, with passion soaking her knickers and her heart pounding in her ears, Brodie knew she'd either have to agree or risk climaxing on the porch.

Brodie tugged a vest out of a drawer, and pulling it on, she zipped her jeans and grabbed a pair of trainers from the wardrobe. She glanced over at the two women sitting on her bed. "So, do I look all right?"

Gina and Devon exchanged looks. "That depends," Gina said. "Are you going on a run or on a date?"

"It's just a casual dinner at Kate's," Brodie said, looking down at her clothes. "And this is casual."

"You don't do casual," Devon said. "Hell, you don't even go to the market dressed like that."

Brodie squinted at Devon. "Behave."

"Well, it's true!"

"What's true is that you're a pain in the arse," Brodie said, the tone of her voice directly opposing her stern expression.

"Yes, but you love me," Devon said, climbing off the bed. Offering Gina her hand, she pulled her up and then walked over to Brodie and kissed her lightly on the cheek. "We're going to leave now so you can change your clothes in private. I hope you have a great night. Catch you later, Brodie."

***

Brodie placed the last dish in the cabinet, and rolling down her sleeves, she fastened the buttons at the cuffs. Picking up the tray filled with coffee and biscuits, Brodie headed for the lounge where she found Kate reclining on the sofa. "I made us some coffee. I hope you don't mind."

"How come I invited you over for dinner, and you're doing all the work?"

"All I did was wash a few dishes and make some coffee. You prepared the feast," Brodie said, setting the tray on the coffee table.

"I'd hardly call a chicken and rice casserole a feast."

"Well, it was delicious."

"Thank you."

"You're welcome," Brodie said, looking at the woman stretched across the sofa. "So, are you going to slide a cheek, or shall I sit on the floor?

Kate grinned as she pulled up her knees, and once Brodie sat down, Kate placed her socked feet on Brodie's lap.

"What's this?"

"You offered me a foot rub once," Kate said, wiggling her toes. "And this is me taking you up on your offer."

"Oh, I see," Brodie said as she began the massage. "I've never actually done this before, so if I'm too rough, just let me know."

"You'll be the first," Kate said as she closed her eyes.

It hadn't been her idea to take it slow, but when Brodie had suggested it, Kate didn't think twice. She thought it was what she wanted. She thought it was what she needed. Kate thought wrong. She had no idea how chivalrous Brodie could be, and it was beginning to get on her nerves.

In her own small way, Kate had tried to take things further. Although on their first official date, she had asked Brodie in for a drink because it was the polite thing to do, Kate's manners rapidly gave way to feelings she couldn't deny. After Brodie refused the next two invitations to come in for a nightcap, Kate changed it to invitations for dinner, and when Brodie shot them down, Kate suggested takeaway and a movie, and again, Brodie politely declined. And every single time their kisses became so passionate their hands crept under each other's blouses, Brodie had backed away.

Kate opened her eyes just a little, gazing at the woman rubbing her feet. Brodie was stunning. She was smart, and she was charming. She was funny, and she was kind. A bewitching, stylish beauty whose eyes sparkled when she laughed, who cared not a bit about the gray at her temples, and Kate couldn't have asked for more. No one could have asked for more, yet like a pendulum, Kate's confidence swung the other way, and she closed her eyes.

Gina, Devon, and Brodie were living the life. They were walking the walk and talking the talk of out and proud lesbians, and Kate took a ragged breath. Would they make jokes about her naiveté? Would they make fun of her because she was the new kid on the block? Would their conversation be laced with innuendo, the occasional double entendre tossed in just so they could watch it soar over her head? Kate set her jaw. Maybe tonight wouldn't be the night.

"I was nervous about coming over this evening."

Kate opened her eyes. "I...uh...I didn't think you did nervous."

"Neither did I," Brodie said with a snort.

"Can I ask why?"

"Being here with you...alone."

"I just thought it'd be nice to spend some time together without waiters and crowds."

"It is," Brodie said, breathing deeply as she glanced around the room. "I just don't want to do anything to make you uncomfortable."

Kate could feel her nerves beginning to settle. It didn't have to be tonight. "You haven't, and you won't," she said softly. "You've been great, Brodie. Really great."

"The trick is lots of cold showers," Brodie said with a wink. "They work wonders."

"You're taking cold showers?"

"Yep," Brodie said with a quick bob of her head. "At least one a day and on date nights, usually one before and one after. I actually think I might be getting used to them."

Kate's face fell. "I'm sorry."

Brodie squeezed Kate's feet. "Don't worry about it. It's not your..." Brodie stopped and let out a laugh. "I was about to say it wasn't your fault, but actually, it is."

In a nanosecond, Kate's mood went from being somewhat relaxed to totally enraged. Snatching her feet away, she shot off the sofa and stomped into the kitchen, yelling over her shoulder as she went. "Well, I'm sorry to be cramping your style. Why don't you give Talia a call? I'm sure she'll be *more* than happy to fuck your brains out!"

"Shit," Brodie said, and dropping her chin to her chest, she pinched the bridge of her nose. A few seconds passed before she pushed herself to the sofa, and going to the kitchen, she stopped in the doorway. "I'm sorry."

Standing at the sink, Kate whipped around. "About what? About the fact you can't keep your bloody hormones in check or the fact you've probably fucked every lesbian in London?"

"That's not fair," Brodie said, taking a step in Kate's direction. "Before you, that's who I was."

"And now?" Kate said, jamming her hands on her hips. "Who are you now, Brodie?"

"Kate, you know how I feel, and it's been two weeks—"

"Oh, *I'm* sorry. I didn't *know* we had a schedule," Kate bellowed, waving her arms about. "Tell me, how long do I have before you go out and fuck a nameless stranger because you haven't fucked me?"

Brodie's entire being went tense, and in three long strides, she was standing within inches of Kate. Grabbing her by the arms, Brodie held Kate firmly against the counter.

"I don't want to fuck you, Kate. I want to love you," Brodie growled, staring Kate square in the eye. "I want to hold you in my arms and kiss you until we both can't breathe. I want to touch you— *all* of you—and discover those places that make you moan. I want to hear you scream my name and beg for more, and I'll give you more…more than you've ever had, more than you've ever imagined, more than you've ever dreamed possible. I don't want to fuck you, Kate. I want to make *love* to you…because I'm *in* love with you!"

Brodie maintained eye contact for a few more seconds before she released her hold on Kate and stormed from the room.

Kate couldn't move. She was frozen in place by a declaration spoken with more passion and honesty than she thought possible. The front door slammed, and Kate's heart began to race. Enough time had been wasted on worrying about what others would do or what others would think. Too many nights had ended in a kiss when Kate had wanted so much more. Falling in love with Brodie was no longer a question. It was a reality.

The sun wasn't supposed to set for another hour, yet when Brodie marched out of the house, black clouds filled the sky, choking out most of the light. The rain was coming down in sheets, and before she was halfway to her car, Brodie was soaked to the skin. Her khaki trousers had darkened three shades, and the russet hue of her blouse no longer hid the black bra underneath, and Brodie couldn't have cared less. She welcomed the feel of the cold rain, praying it would cool her anger and ice the frustration pulsing between her legs. She traipsed through the puddles on the walk until, through the slamming of the rain, she heard Kate call to her. Brodie whipped back around, water cascading down her face as she glared at the woman on the porch.

"Brodie," Kate hollered over the storm. "Please…please come back."

"Why?" Brodie called out, spreading her arms wide. "Why, Kate? So we can argue some more? So we can be uncomfortable and nervous? Well, you were right, Kate. I don't do nervous. It's not who I *am*!"

"Please come back inside. You're getting soaked."

"I don't *care*," Brodie shouted. "I don't bloody care! Don't you get that? All I care about is you. All I want is you. All I need is you, but you can't get past your....your doubt...your insecurity."

"Yes, I can."

"*No*, you can't!"

"*Yes*, I can, Brodie," Kate said, her voice loud enough to invade her neighbor's homes. "Because I'm in *love* with you!"

Around them was a storm, dark and loud, and up until that moment, it had matched Brodie's mood, but when Kate saw the rage drain from Brodie's face, her mouth gaping as she stood frozen in place, Kate knew she finally had the woman's undivided attention. A smile touched Kate's lips. "Now, come back inside...and take what's yours."

Chapter Twenty-One

Kate walked into the lounge, and making her way across the room, she waited in front of the fireplace. Even though there was no fire blazing in the hearth, it felt to Kate as if the room was growing warmer with every second that passed. When she heard the front door close, Kate's center pulsed.

Brodie stood just inside the entry. Her heart was racing, and her mouth had gone dry, and taking a few deep breaths, she ran her fingers through her hair, sending droplets of water everywhere. She barely noticed the puddle at her feet as she kicked off her shoes, and filling her lungs again, Brodie headed into the lounge. "Say it again," she whispered as she came to stand behind Kate.

"I love you," Kate said in a breath.

"Say it again."

"I love you."

"Say it—"

Kate spun around and stopped Brodie's words with a kiss. Rough and demanding, lips parted and tongues tasted as their mouths ground together in a hungry show of need that seemed to go on forever.

Brodie showered Kate's face with kisses before returning to again revel in the sweetness of her mouth, and when she felt Kate's hand slip under her blouse, a sensual rumble rose in Brodie's throat. She pulled back slightly, and in Kate's eyes, Brodie found her answer. There was no fear or doubt. There was only hunger gazing back at her, and as soon as she pulled the ribbed knitted top from Kate's body and tossed it aside, Kate frantically fumbled with the buttons on Brodie's blouse.

A flurry of thoughts swirled in Brodie's mind. She had wanted their first time to be something cherished and remembered and romantic. She had envisioned roses and chocolates, and in a room lit by a hundred candles, while soft music played, they'd move in slow motion, neither willing to risk rushing the moment. But fantasies don't always play out as imagined, and by the way Kate was kissing her, and by the way Kate was touching her, their first time would *not* be slow. It would be greedy. It would be wanton. It would be carnal...and it would be *now*.

As soon as Brodie was free of her blouse, they came together. They blazed trails of kisses down necks and across shoulders, and when their lips met again, so did their tongues. Fingers threaded through hair and breathing grew ragged, and relentless about what they wanted, minutes went by unnoticed until they both had to come up for air.

Brodie licked her lips to replace moisture stolen by Kate, and when their eyes locked, Brodie reached around to unclasp her bra. A moment later, Kate pulled away, and like an invisible sucker punch, the air was driven from Brodie's lungs. She fisted her hands, prepared to storm out of the house for the last fucking time in her life...and then she saw Kate's expression. It wasn't apprehensive, and it wasn't apologetic. It was quite the opposite.

Kate knew what Brodie was thinking. She could see the shock, fear, and even a hint of anger in her eyes. Like the night in the hostel, Brodie had ignited something in Kate as terrifying as it was bewitching, but unlike *that* night, Kate's anxieties had finally taken a back seat to her passion. "Let me," she said, closing the space between them.

Brodie held her breath when she felt Kate's fingers work the clasp of her bra and when it loosened, and Kate drew the straps down her arms, Brodie's knees went weak.

Kate couldn't help but stare. Brodie's breasts were full and firm, and with nipples pebbled by desire and tips hardened by want, Kate had never seen anything more beautiful or more sensual in her life. Until Brodie, she had never looked at another woman. She had never wanted to touch another's breast, or feel the weight of it in her hand, but now Kate's body sizzled at the possibilities of what the night was going to bring.

Kate placed her hand over Brodie's heart for only a moment before lowering it to cover her breast. It was warm and soft, and guided by instincts she didn't know she had, Kate began to caress the bronzed orb. It was amazing. Simply and *utterly* amazing.

Brodie sucked in a sharp breath. The ache between her legs had become raw and need pulsed from her body, soaking through her knickers in an instant. The intimacy of Kate's touch had set her on fire, and it was all Brodie could do to force words through her ragged breathing. "Bedroom...where...where is it?"

Kate's mouth dropped open as she pulled in air. She thought she knew what desire was up until that moment. She thought she knew what it was to crave and covet, to yearn for someone's touch, their closeness, their body, but *this* was something new. *This* had erased all but the most primitive of urges...and *this* was not going to wait.

"No...here...now," Kate said between breaths. "Please, Brodie...here...now."

In a blink of an eye, Brodie pulled Kate to the sofa, and falling back onto the cushions, as soon as Kate straddled her, Brodie wasted no time in ridding Kate of her bra. She barely had time to admire before Kate's lips pressed against hers again, and Brodie consumed what she was given, probing with her tongue while she cupped one of Kate's breasts in her hand.

Kate squeezed her legs against Brodie's thighs, moaning into the kiss as she felt Brodie's hand on her breast. The sensual massage was making Kate squirm, and when Brodie rolled the erect tip between her fingers, tugging at it gently as it grew even harder, Kate broke out of the kiss, panting for air. "Oh my...God."

Kate had only shifted a few inches, but it was enough for Brodie to slip her leg between Kate's, and as their eyes met, Brodie pressed her thigh against Kate's center, and Kate's reaction was immediate. She began to wantonly grind herself against Brodie's muscled thigh.

Brodie was mesmerized by the feel of Kate rubbing against her leg, and placing her hands on Kate's waist, she urged her to bend closer. Covering the puckered center of one breast with her mouth, Brodie suckled against it, pulling it into her mouth again and again while she teased and tweaked the other nipple between her fingers. In an instant, Kate's hands were in Brodie's hair, holding her firmly against her breast in a silent plea to continue. Brodie stepped up her attack. Torturing both peaks with her fingers and lips, it wasn't until they were rock hard when she slowly moved her free hand downward.

Kate was beginning to spiral out of control, and when Brodie cupped her sex, a sound, husky and lustful spilled from Kate's lips a second before she buried her face in Brodie's neck. The need for release pounded in her core and clenching her inner walls to squelch the pang was no longer working. Kate sat back for a moment, her eyes never leaving Brodie's as she unsnapped her jeans and drew down the zipper. Taking Brodie's hand, Kate guided it toward the opened denim. "Touch me," she whispered, and raising herself on her knees, Kate leaned forward and placed her hands on the cushions behind Brodie's head. "Please touch me."

Brodie pushed her hand into the gaping fabric, her fingers slowly traveling through dampened curls until they reached the source of the want now coating Brodie's skin.

"Oh...Brodie," Kate said in a breath, her eyes closing as she felt Brodie's finger slip inside. Kate bowed her head, relishing the feel of one gentle stroke after another, and as Brodie's plunges grew slightly harder, Kate began to move against the glorious intrusions. The sensation of having Brodie inside of her was like nothing Kate could have imagined. Exquisitely erotic, she was doing to Kate what no one had ever been able to do before. Brodie's strokes were stirring impulses so natural and primal that Kate reveled in what was building inside of her. Brodie was making Kate *want* to lose control. She was making her want to surrender to it, *need* to surrender to it, and opening her eyes, Kate gazed down at Brodie.

For almost a minute, they were still, each peering into the depths of the other's eyes, connected in a way that no words could define until Brodie began to dip her finger gently into Kate again. "Let it go, Kate," Brodie said softly. "Do what you want. Do what you need."

Kate drew in a breath and then slowly began to move against Brodie's hand again. Over and over, she accepted Brodie's thrusts, and as they came faster and faster, Kate's need grew feral. She arched herself into Brodie, lifting her hips to take Brodie's plunges even deeper inside of her, but it wasn't until Brodie began rubbing her finger around Kate's swollen clit, encircling the distended organ again and again, when Kate's passion crested. Throaty moan after throaty moan slipped from Kate's lips as endless spasms rocked her from within before she finally slumped against Brodie's chest, fighting for air.

Brodie smiled into Kate's dampened hair as she held her close. She kissed her head and gently ran her hand up and down Kate's back, saying not a word as Kate's breathing slowly returned to normal.

***

In her early teens, Kate and her girlfriends discovered romance novels, and one summer, they whiled away the hours reading about heroines dressed in gowns with tightly laced bodices and heroes with chiseled features and crotch-driven charm. They tittered in the privacy of their bedrooms, blushing at the descriptions and yearning to be the women in the books. They wanted to feel the waves of passion that would leave them breathless and satisfied, but at seventeen, in the basement of her boyfriend's home, the only thing Kate had felt was pain and embarrassment. The captain of the football team, he was the one that every girl wanted, but he had chosen Kate. He said he loved her—he lied. She thought she loved him—she was wrong. And so, amidst boxes of old clothes and athletic equipment, on a lumpy, threadbare couch, Kate lost her virginity to a boy who, after all was said and done, scoffed at her inexperience and told her to find someone else to practice with.

It had taken a few years before another man caught Kate's eye. They dated and laughed. They danced and drank, and when he asked her to spend the night, Kate said yes. He was gentle and caring, and his kisses made her quiver, but trust wasn't something Kate gave easily. She opened her legs, hoping to experience an orgasm of the magnitude described in gothic romances, but Kate refused to open her mind. Over the next several years, other lovers came and went, a few even managing to extract from her honest murmurs of satisfaction and small climaxes, but afraid of losing her self-control, Kate had always held something back. With them, it was easy. With Brodie, it was impossible.

Kate took a deep breath, and opening her eyes, she smiled at the woman smiling back at her.

"Hi there," Brodie said, pushing a few strands of hair from Kate's sweaty brow.

Kate stretched for a kiss, and as she greedily took what she wanted, all Brodie could do was hungrily reply in kind. There wasn't a nerve in Brodie's body that wasn't on fire, and the more Kate kissed her, the more Brodie's body flamed. In all of Brodie's fantasies about Kate, a modicum of bashfulness had always existed, but the way Kate was kissing her wasn't shy. It wasn't even close.

Kate mimicked what had happened earlier, and placing her leg between Brodie's, she pressed hard against the woman's apex. In an instant, Brodie flexed her hips to increase the pressure. Kate cupped a breast, squeezing and kneading it until the tip was pebbled and swollen, while underneath her, Brodie ground herself into Kate's thigh, rising and falling against it in utter abandon.

For months, Kate's dreams had been filled with images of this moment, but reality was so much sweeter. She had never imagined Brodie could feel so soft or that her curves would be so sensual. She had no idea that her breasts pressed against Brodie's would feel so incredible, and the mere sounds of pleasure Brodie was making would take Kate to a place, libertine and free.

Kate pulled out of the embrace and standing, she waited for Brodie to look at her before Kate pushed her jeans down her legs. She didn't want the feel of denim. She wanted the feel of Brodie.

Brodie swallowed hard. Kate stood before her, her body shimmering in the light. Her breasts heaved with excitement, and the dark triangle between her legs glistened with want. Brown eyes met those of blue, and for a few seconds, the world ceased to exist before Kate broke the silence in a voice, raspy and thick with need. "Take them off," she said, pointing to Brodie's trousers. "Take them off now."

As Brodie unfastened the dampened khakis, she was thankful she had changed into something more forgiving than jeans when soaked by rain. She lifted her bottom, quickly pushing the trousers and knickers from her body, and as she lowered herself back to the sofa, she saw the way Kate was devouring the sight of her nudity. Brodie's body throbbed, and her words came out in a plea. "I need you."

Kate wasted no time in returning to Brodie, their bodies becoming one as their legs tangled, and their hands skimmed over heated flesh. Their lips touched again, and their tongues danced again, and when

Kate's hand traveled south, Brodie pulled out of the kiss and drew in air as if she was drowning. "Oh...God, yes."

There was no hesitancy as Kate's fingers moved across skin as sleek as silk, nor did she stumble when curls *weren't* discovered, for she was on a quest. For a split-second, it did feel odd to be in a place foreign yet so familiar as her fingers glided through Brodie's soaked folds. They were as petal-soft and warm as her own, but that blip in time came and went in the blink of an eye for Kate wasn't on a mission to discover the unknown. She was on a voyage to grant Brodie the release she so desperately craved.

Ever so slowly, Kate's finger entered the warmth and wetness of Brodie's body and captivated by the feel, Kate paused, lost in the sheer bliss of the moment. Brodie was tight and drenched with passion, and as Kate unhurriedly began to stroke, Brodie arched her back.

"Yes. Oh...yes."

Brodie was so slick with want that Kate's plunges were effortless, and when Brodie spread her legs, thrusting her pelvis upward to take all Kate wanted to give, Kate didn't think twice. Slipping another finger inside, she filled Brodie completely.

"Oh...dear...God."

Just as Brodie had done, Kate varied her lovemaking, sheathing her fingers for a few seconds before circling Brodie's clit, applying more and more pressure each time she did. Under her, Brodie's breathing was coming in short, harsh gasps, and Kate knew she was close. Oh so close.

Brodie fisted the cushions of the sofa. Deep inside of her, the inner trembling of her orgasm had begun, and within seconds, the shuddering contractions forced an uninhibited cry of pleasure from her lips. Her body pulsed and then pulsed again, pushing need from her center as spasm after spasm rocked her body, and it wasn't until the demand for air became too great when Brodie finally filled her lungs again.

Hypnotized by Brodie's release, it wasn't until the woman quieted that Kate relaxed by her side and rested her head on Brodie's breast. She listened as Brodie's breathing slowed, and as their heart rates returned to normal and sleep began to overtake them again, Brodie whispered, "Say it again."

Chapter Twenty-Two

Devon walked into the kitchen, setting her cup of takeaway coffee down as she looked around. Noticing that the coffee maker on the counter was off, she said, "Looks like I won the bet. No coffee means she's still asleep."

"I can't believe she's not ready," Gina said, coming into the room. "When I talked to her yesterday, she said she'd be up bright and early."

"Kate doesn't do bright and early."

"She did in school."

"Was she happy about it?"

"No."

Devon snickered as she wrapped her arms around Gina's waist. "Well, you should have remembered *that* before making a bet, honey."

"You weren't actually *serious* about that, were you?"

Devon held Gina at arm's length. "You bet your cute arse, I was. You, woman, owe me breakfast in bed. So, should I tell you what I want right now, or wait until tomorrow morning?"

"Why do I think I'm going to need to make a shopping list?" Gina said, laugh lines appearing on her face.

"You don't," Devon said, her eyes twinkling. "All I want is bacon and eggs, some coffee and juice, and…oh…a bit of jam."

"You forgot the toast."

"No, I didn't," Devon said as a devilish leer spread its way across her face.

It took only a second for Gina to understand Devon's inference. "Oh, so after slaving all morning over a hot stove to fix you breakfast, you think I'm going to allow you to *slather* me with jam?"

Devon pulled Gina close and kissed her without holding anything back. Her tongue slipped inside Gina's warm mouth, and it wasn't long before both allowed the kiss to intensify. Almost a minute passed before they came up for air, and when they did, Devon grinned. "And don't forget, strawberry is my favorite."

All week, Gina had been eagerly awaiting the arrival of Saturday. Since college, Kate and Gina made a point of spending one Saturday every few months shopping for clothes. They'd meet in the morning, have some coffee, and then hit the streets. Going from one shop to the next, they'd spend the day trying on outfits and testing perfumes. They would model dresses neither could afford, prance around stores wearing pumps and high heels costing more than they earned in a week, and tee-hee like schoolgirls as they sat at counters having makeup applied by saleswomen. They never came home weighed down with packages, and many times they'd go home with nothing more to show for the day other than the smiles on their faces and the memories they'd made. As Gina looked into Devon's eyes and saw smoldering passion staring back at her, Gina's center fluttered. Shopping was going to be fun, but Sunday breakfast was going to redefine the word.

***

Brodie had been awake for a while, quietly lying next to Kate and breathing in the scent of her perfume and the aroma of sex still heavy in the air. They had climbed the stairs in the wee hours of the morning, and falling into bed, they made love again. It was still rushed and hungry for, after months of pent-up passion and erotic dreams, slow had yet to be found. Brodie felt Kate stir, and she smiled at her body's reaction. The throb was immediate, and slickness formed before she took her next breath.

Kate pressed closer, possessively placing one leg over Brodie's as her eyes fluttered open. "Hiya," she cooed, feeling Brodie casually began to rub her back.

"Good morning," Brodie said, her voice raspy from sleep.

Kate took a long, slow breath and tipping her head, she placed a light kiss on Brodie's lips. It was meant to say hello, just a feathery brush of lips against lips to start the day, but when Brodie returned the kiss with her tongue, stopping wasn't an option. Lips tasted, hands groped, and within a few minutes, Kate was pushing aside the sheets and straddling Brodie's lap.

In less than twenty-four hours, Kate had become someone she didn't even recognize. Having always preferred darkness in the bedroom, she now craved only light. With the morning sun streaming through the blinds, she sat atop Brodie's thighs, marveling at the beauty of the woman below her. There was no self-consciousness as her eyes raked over Brodie's naked form. There was no need to be covert, hiding her admiration behind heavy-lidded eyes, and there was no attempt to cover her own nudity. Kate didn't have to look down to know her nipples were hard. She didn't have to look down to know her breasts were rising and falling in time with her breathing, because Brodie was doing all the looking for her. Her stare was bold and hungry, and when Kate saw Brodie lick her lips, her core fluttered.

Kate shifted slightly as Brodie sat up, and when her hands covered Kate's breasts, Kate wrapped her legs around Brodie's middle. She tucked her head into the crook of Brodie's neck and exhaled, "I love you," before drawing her tongue around Brodie's ear.

Brodie buried her head between Kate's breasts, kissing one and then the other while she rolled the hardened tips of Kate's nipples between her fingers. Kate breathed a sensual groan of pleasure in Brodie's ear, and the sound of it sent a ripple of pleasure through Brodie's body. She turned her attention to the pale pink centers, and circling her tongue around the delectable pebbled rosiness, she captured an erect tip in her mouth.

Kate threaded her fingers through Brodie's hair, silently urging her on. The night before had been fast and frantic, but this morning Kate wanted slow. She wanted to experience everything, see everything...taste everything.

Out of the corner of her eye, Brodie saw a shadow in the doorway, but before she could react, Gina walked into the room.

"All right, Sleeping Beauty. Daylight's wasting, and we have shopping to—"

Gina's words died in her throat. She couldn't see Kate's partner, but between Kate's position and her naked back, it was obvious what Gina had just interrupted. Her eyes bulged, and with her cheeks flaming, Gina spun toward the door. "Oh, shit. I'm sorry."

Kate dove under the sheets, and Brodie rushed to grab just enough of the duvet to cover herself. "Get out of here, Gina."

Recognizing the voice instantly, Gina whipped back around. "Brodie?"

"Gina, please. Just give us a minute, will you?"

"Oh...um...right," Gina said, stumbling to the door. "Sorry."

Brodie waited until Gina closed the door to lift the sheet, and seeing Kate hiding under the linen with cheeks the color of crimson, Brodie laughed. "You can come out now."

"I cannot *believe* that just happened," Kate said, burying her face in a pillow.

"That'll teach you to give your flat keys to a friend," Brodie said, kissing Kate on the back of the head. "And what's this about going shopping?"

Kate flopped onto her back. "Devon, Gina, and I had an outing planned for today, but I'll go down and tell them I can't make it."

"No, don't do that."

"Oh..." Kate said, propping herself up on her elbows. "I thought we'd be spending the day together. I mean...I just thought..."

"Darling, trust me, I would like nothing more than to spend the entire weekend making love to you, but I have to meet a client later this morning, and it's an appointment I can't cancel."

Kate pouted as she sat up. "But it's the weekend."

"I agree, but when I made the appointment, I didn't know I'd be waking up in your bed this morning."

"Yeah, I guess you didn't," Kate said as she fell back onto the pillow.

Kate's adorable pout could have easily changed Brodie's mind about almost anything, except the appointment was regarding something she'd been working on for months. "Look," she said, pushing a few strands of hair off Kate's face. "Why don't you go shopping, and once I'm done, I'll ring you up and meet you wherever you are. How's that?"

"Is that the best you can do?" Kate said with a long face.

Brodie chuckled as she climbed on top of Kate. "No, it's definitely *not* the best I can do," she said, casually running her fingers over Kate's breasts. "But we both have things to do. So, you go do your thing, and I'll go do mine, and afterward, I promise to make it up to you...in as *many* ways as you'd like."

Kate's gulp was audible. The intensity swirling in Brodie's eyes was unmistakable. She knew in an instant that Brodie had *every* intention of keeping her promise. Kate cleared her throat. "So, what now?"

"Well, I'm going to get dressed, and you, my darling, get to go down and face the inquisition."

***

Devon looked up for a second as Gina came back into the kitchen. "Is Kate awake?" she said, returning to buttering her toast.

"Most definitely."

"She almost ready to go?"

"If I hadn't walked in, I'm thinking—yes."

Devon wrinkled her brow, and stopping what she was doing, she turned around to see almost every tooth Gina owned shining in the woman's grin. "Okay, Gina, what's going on?"

"She wasn't alone."

"Huh?"

"She *wasn't* alone."

"Who?"

"*Kate.*"

"What do you mean, she wasn't alone?"

Gina planted her hands on her hips. "What do you *think* I mean?"

It took a few seconds for Gina's words to sink in, and Devon's eyes flew open. "Really?"

"Yep."

"Wait," Devon said, shaking her head. "She went out with Brodie last night."

Gina adored Devon. She loved every inch of the woman, inside and out, so instead of continuing the verbal tennis match, she cocked her head to the side and waited. It didn't take long.

"Oh, shit," Devon said, her eyes bugging out even further. "Are you saying she was with Brodie?"

"Yep."

"Are you sure?"

"No, Devon, come to think of it, maybe Kate was sleeping with another woman," Gina said, rolling her eyes. "Of course, I'm bloody sure."

"Sure about what?" Kate said as she ambled into the kitchen and began setting up the coffee maker.

Gina glanced at Devon, and when Gina's only reply was a slow, subtle shake of her head, Devon looked over at Kate. "Um...I was just asking Gina if she was sure...well, if she was sure—"

"Sorry to break this up, but I really have to get going, or I'll be late," Brodie said, coming into the kitchen.

Brodie paid no attention to the two women who were standing in the middle of the room with their jaws touching the floor. Her focus was solely on Kate, and striding over, Brodie kissed her full on the mouth, leaving no doubt in anyone's mind who had been in Kate's bed.

"I'll call you later," Brodie said softly.

"I'm counting on it."

"Are you going to be okay with them?" Brodie said, dipping her head in the direction of Devon and Gina.

"I'll be fine."

Brodie grinned and placed a light kiss on Kate's forehead before turning to face Devon and Gina. Giving them a wink, she walked out of the room without saying another word.

***

After successfully managing to avoid their questions in the kitchen, Kate grabbed a quick shower to wash away the aroma of the night's activities. A short time later, the three women piled into Gina's sedan and began their excursion.

While clothes shopping, especially in the stores Kate and Gina wanted to visit, held little interest for Devon, she found herself enjoying the morning. Admiring their taste in feminine frocks, Devon sat back and watched as they'd emerge from behind draped doorways, checking themselves in mirrors and twirling around as they asked for her opinion. At one point, Devon found herself smiling, wondering how two women, so different, could have become such good friends.

Gina leaned toward flamboyance, gravitating in the direction of tighter dresses with plunging necklines and jersey fabrics that fit her body like a second skin. Kate preferred power suits and loose-fitting dresses with muted patterns and modest necklines, drawing enough attention for a second glance, but not enough for an over-the-top gawk. The only two dresses Kate owned that didn't fit the pattern had both been purchased by Gina as gifts, and even though Devon had seen her sister wear the black jersey once, as far as she knew, the red satin had never come out of Kate's wardrobe. But sitting in the corner of yet another dressing area, waiting for them to emerge from behind yet more curtains, Devon was having a hard time trying to keep her amusement contained. It seemed Kate's taste in clothing was changing.

At their first stop, Kate had walked from the dressing room wearing a dark brown dress, and while the color was sedate, the style was not. Made of a polyester/spandex material, the frock hugged her form in all the right places, and Devon immediately noticed that the length of the skirt was shorter than anything in Kate's closet. The scoop of the cowl neck was still reserved, but the short-capped sleeves and the show of leg made the dress more than just a little provocative.

Much to Devon's dismay, Kate didn't buy the dress, even though Devon had watched Kate hesitate no less than three times before finally returning it to the rack. So, they strolled from that shop to the next and then to the next, and in each, Kate began her browsing at the fixtures filled with business suits and ended it, modeling dresses meant for drinks, dinner, and maybe more.

Devon and Gina had agreed to wait until Kate brought up the subject of Brodie before peppering her with questions. However, if curiosity indeed killed the cat, Gina and Devon would have needed a defibrillator by the third store. Now, standing in the fourth, as Gina watched Kate gaze at yet another come-hither frock, Gina decided she either needed to say something or internally combust. "You'd look marvelous in this," she said, fingering the scarlet fabric in Kate's hand.

"I have a red dress."

"There's nothing to say you can't have two."

"No, I suppose not," Kate said, considering the dress. "But it's a bit showy, don't you think?"

"As long as you're showing *it* to Brodie, I doubt there will be a problem."

Kate's mistake was to shoot Gina a quick look. As soon as she did and saw Gina's disarming smile, Kate's cheeks began to burn, and she hastily returned the dress to the rack.

"Oh, no you don't," Gina said, stepping in front of Kate. Grabbing the provocative dress and a few more, she turned around and pushed the clothes into Kate's hands. "Try these on and stop pretending you aren't shopping for her."

The heat on Kate's cheeks traveled to her ears, and she huffed out a breath. "Fine, maybe I am, but I don't even know what she likes, Gina."

"She *likes* you. This is all just pretty wrapping," Gina said as she held up another dress and then placed it in Kate's hand. "But I think between the two of us, we should be able to find something to make Brodie believe it's Christmas."

***

"So, you ready to talk about it?"

"Talk about what?" Kate asked as she perused the menu.

Gina filled her lungs with air, and reaching across the table, she yanked the laminated sheet out of Kate's hand. "Oh, I don't know. How about the fact you slept with Brodie?"

"There's nothing to talk about."

"How can you say that?"

"Gina, what would you like me to say?" Kate said, snatching back the menu.

The restraint Gina had shown all day was gone in an instant. Annoyed, she didn't think twice about shouting, "Well, it's not often a woman gets to lose her virginity *twice*! How about we talk about that?"

The noise level in the pub dropped dramatically as Gina's voice carried across the room, and if Kate could have crawled under the table, she would have already been there.

"Keep your bloody voice down," Kate said in a rushed whisper.

"What?" Gina shrugged. "What did I say?"

"That Kate lost her virginity again," Devon said, placing three mugs of ale on the table. "And the blokes at the bar seem *really* interested in finding out how."

"Did I say it that loud?" Gina said, looking back and forth between the two women.

"*Yes*," Kate and Devon replied in unison.

Gina slid further into the booth so Devon could sit down. "Sorry. I guess I'm just a bit frustrated as to why you don't want to talk about it. I mean, from what I saw this morning, you two obviously hit it off—yes?"

"Yes, we did," Kate said quietly as she picked up a drink and took a sip.

Devon and Gina exchanged confused glances before Gina took the lead. "What's wrong, Kate?" she said, leaning slightly over the table. "Wasn't it what you expected?"

Kate sighed. "It was amazing. She was..." Kate stopped, allowing the memories of the night to flood her brain and warm her blood. "Brodie was wonderful," she said in a breath.

"But?" Gina said, arching an eyebrow.

Kate took another sip of her beer. "I'm just not sure I'm ready for all of this."

"I thought you were in love with her."

"I am," Kate said, locking eyes with Gina. "I'm not talking about...about being with Brodie. I'm talking about...I'm talking about..."

"Being out?" Devon said.

"Yes," Kate said, her shoulders drooping. "Seeing you two today, holding hands and being together, I realized that even if I didn't know you, if I saw you on the street, I'd know you were partners."

"And you don't want people to know that you're involved with a woman?" Gina said.

"It's not that, not really," Kate said, staring off into space. "When Brodie and I go for walks after dinner, we always hold hands, and I've never felt uncomfortable, but today I couldn't help but notice how many people stared at you and Devon...and then I started thinking about my job and the men I work with—"

"Kate," Gina said, reaching across the table to take her hand. "You need to take a breath and relax. I'm sure Brodie won't have a problem with you two taking things slowly when it comes to the out and proud department. The important thing is that you want to be with her."

"I do."

"Good," Gina said, squeezing Kate's hand. "So stop worrying about all the other crap, finish your bloody beer, and let's go do some more shopping."

"More?" Devon said, sliding down in her seat. "Honestly, Gina, haven't you two bought enough clothes today?"

"Clothes, yes," Gina said, flashing a knowing grin a second before kissing Devon on the cheek. "Lingerie...no."

***

Standing amidst chrome fixtures filled with brassieres of every style and color, Kate pondered the shades in her hand. Already choosing a matching set in dark green and another in chocolate brown, the remaining would either be royal blue or pale pink. Unable to make up her mind, she was about to return both to the rack when she heard a familiar voice.

"If it matters, I like the blue."

Kate's face creased into a smile, and she turned around. "Hi, Brodie."

"Hi yourself," Brodie said, taking a step closer.

As if bewitched by the other's gaze, for a few moments, they just stood there like enamored teens on a first date until a passing customer jostled Kate and brought her back to the planet. "How'd you find me?"

"I texted Devon a short while ago, and she let me know where you'd be. I have to say, though, I'm a little surprised your arms aren't full of packages."

"They're in the car."

"Oh, I see," Brodie said, unable to break eye contact with Kate. "Hopefully, not a large car."

"It's large enough," Kate said, her cheeks turning rosy. "So, how'd your meeting go?"

"Good. He asked for a few changes, so it took longer than I expected, but the contract is now signed, and Ethan will start work next week."

"I see you found us," Devon said, walking from between the rows of lingerie.

"And I see Gina likes to shop," Brodie said, watching as Devon struggled with the bags she was carrying.

"These are Gina's," Devon said, holding up the bags in her left hand before shoving the bags in her right hand in Brodie's direction. "These are Kate's."

Brodie took the packages and then looked back at Kate. "I thought you said *yours* were in the car."

"Okay, so maybe not *all* of them," Kate said with a laugh.

"So," Brodie said, adjusting the bags in her hands. "Are you done here, or should I find a comfortable chair and take a kip?"

Kate's need to shop any further was lost and holding up the blue lingerie set, she said, "I just have to pay for these, and we can go."

A short time later, all four met at the entrance to the store, two loaded down with bags, and two discussing their plans for the evening. It was a tradition that all their shopping extravaganzas ended with dinner at a Chinese restaurant, but today's spree was ending earlier than usual.

All Kate wanted to do was to return to her flat and continue where she and Brodie had left off. Unfortunately, she knew her reasoning would be transparent. She had put up with more than enough playful banter and sexual innuendo at lunch to last for one day, and she wasn't about to add fuel to the fire. After everyone tossed ideas about, Brodie finally suggested they meet at her flat later that night for Chinese takeaway, and once Kate's purchases were transferred to Brodie's car, Devon and Gina headed for home.

Brodie climbed into her car, glancing at her watch before looking over at Kate. "So...your place or mine?"

Without missing a beat, Kate said, "Yours. It's closer."

Chapter Twenty-Three

Kate would have never described herself as oversexed, but while they rode the lift to Brodie's flat, Kate was beginning to have her doubts.

She had spent the better part of a day in opulent department stores and small, eclectic shops, trying desperately to keep her mind on the business at hand, but every time Kate ran her hand over silken fabrics or fingered the lace of a bra, her mind returned to the night before. A frantic hour on the sofa and then several more in her bed hadn't begun to quench the thirst she had for the woman who was standing beside her. The chime signaled the end of their ride, and as they exited and approached the door to Brodie's flat, Kate's core pulsed.

Brodie was a consummate professional when it came to dealing with her clients. She was always polite, always attentive, and changes they'd suggest were always—*always*—taken into consideration, except today, when her client asked for a few revisions, it was all Brodie could do not to huff out a breath. Brodie didn't want to work. She wanted to play, and she wanted to play with Kate. She had yet to savor all that Kate had to offer, and that thought created damp knickers each time it entered her brain. More than once, Brodie had to ask her client to repeat his question, and more than once, she mentally scolded herself for the titillating thoughts running through her head.

Brodie unlocked the door and ushered Kate inside, and both dropped the bags they were carrying on the floor. The flat was cool and quiet, and when their eyes met, questions not asked were answered. Taking a deep breath, Brodie slipped her fingers through Kate's and led her to the bedroom. As they neared the bed, Brodie felt Kate squeeze her hand, and when she turned, she was met with a kiss.

Neither tentative nor hungry, but rather somewhere in between, they melted into each other, the flavors of coffee and ale blending as their passion grew. Brodie found the buttons of Kate's blouse, deftly unfastening them as Kate did the same with Brodie's, and when their shirts fell away, fingers found clasps and bras of black and ivory followed. They came together again, and as breasts, with nipples dimpled and erect touched, they consumed each other with kisses passionate and probing until, fighting for air, they parted. Overwhelmed by their need for each other, they stepped out of their jeans and knickers and fell on the bed, legs intertwining and hands touching all that could be reached.

Kate's lips traveled over Brodie's face and down her neck, stopping to suck and taste as she slowly made her way down Brodie's body. She cupped Brodie's breasts, their plumpness so perfect in her hands, she could effortlessly sweep her thumbs across the dark centers, and watching as they grew pebbled and stiff, they became too tempting to resist. She pulled one into her mouth, and Brodie's reaction was instant. Grabbing Kate's bottom, she squeezed the roundness again and again as Kate nibbled and sucked until Brodie's breathing grew shallow.

Driven by something stronger than she could have ever imagined, Kate slithered upward. She captured Brodie's mouth in a ravenous kiss, and using her knee, she nudged Brodie's legs apart, grinding her pelvis into Brodie's to further fuel the fire building between them.

As Kate's slickness began to mix with her own, Brodie opened her eyes and more want pulsed from her center when she saw Kate, on outstretched arms, above her. Brodie stared in amazement. Kate, with eyes closed and lips parted, seemed lost in the eroticism of the moment. Absorbed in the feral nature of the act, concentration lines were etched into Kate's forehead. Her face was flushed, and her body shimmered with sweat, yet over and over again, she arched into Brodie until finally, her eyes fluttered open.

Kate's breath caught in her throat when she realized Brodie was watching her, and freezing in place, streaks of heat colored her face.

"Don't," Brodie said, reaching out to touch Kate's cheek. "You're beautiful, Kate. Please don't stop." When Kate didn't move, Brodie cupped her chin. "Do what you want, darling. Do what you feel."

Kate gazed into Brodie's eyes and taking a ragged breath, she returned to the tempo she had set. Slow and deliberate, she rubbed herself against Brodie, and Brodie met each stroke by lifting her hips. It was sheer carnality, and it was *almost* perfect. It was missing only one thing and slipping her hand between their bodies, Brodie pulled up on the fold of skin above her clit to expose it in all its engorged glory.

"Oh..." Kate said in a breath, her tempo increasing instantly. Her mind went blank as instincts took over, and thrusting harder into Brodie, she was unforgiving as below her, Brodie struggled to breathe.

There was nothing Brodie could do to stop the urge any longer, and as her soul-shattering climax claimed her, she bucked one last time, sending Kate over the same precipice.

Low, guttural moans were all that could be heard as both crested at the same time, and as Kate fell to the side, surrendering to every spasm that swept over her, Brodie clutched at the sheets, riding each glorious wave right to the end.

Time didn't exist until ragged breaths calmed and rolling her head to the side, Brodie gazed at Kate. "Are you okay?"

Kate opened her eyes, her cheeks coloring again. "Um...yeah."

"What's wrong? Why the blush?"

"I...uh...I don't even know where that came from."

"I would hope from your heart."

"That goes without saying," Kate said, propping herself up on her elbow. "But...but..."

"Are you embarrassed?"

"No, well, yeah. I don't know. Maybe."

"Why? You obviously liked what you were doing."

Brodie smiled when Kate's cheeks grew even darker. "Kate, what you did, what *we* did, was natural and beautiful, and there's nothing to be embarrassed about."

Kate rested her head on Brodie's arm. "I suppose."

Brodie flicked her gaze to the ceiling. "Come here," she said, crooking her finger at Kate. "Afterglow isn't nearly as nice unless you get to hold the person you love."

Kate inched closer and snuggling against Brodie, she let out a contented breath. "This is nice."

"Yes, it is."

"I could stay like this all night."

"Me, too," Brodie said, unconsciously running her hand down Kate's arm. "But unfortunately, we have guests coming over."

"I forget. What time are they supposed to be here?"

"Um…seven."

"Oh."

Brodie looked at the clock on the nightstand. She quickly did the math, and then rolling Kate to her back, she began placing butterfly kisses across Kate's shoulder and up her neck, allowing her tongue to taste as she went.

"What are you doing?" Kate murmured, closing her eyes.

"Like you have to ask."

"Didn't you just say we have guests coming over?"

"I did," Brodie said, climbing over Kate. "But that's a whole three hours away."

Kate's eyes flew open when she suddenly felt herself being pulled to the edge of the bed, and seeing the look on Brodie's face, Kate knew exactly what was about to happen.

For a second, Brodie waited, but when she saw Kate's breasts begin to rise and fall as she sucked in one quick breath after another, Brodie knelt by the side of the bed and gently moved Kate's legs apart. "And three hours means I don't have to rush this, not one…little…*bit*."

***

A room without doors, and a shower without walls, no longer concerned Kate. The oversized showerhead allowed water to fall like rain, gently washing away the lather that took with it the smell of sex and sweat. They embraced time and again, unable to resist the need to touch and to feel amidst the steam and the foam, both knowing they couldn't take things further, but nonetheless, wishing they could.

Shutting off the valve, Brodie handed Kate a towel. "How you doing?"

Kate sat on the tiled bench to dry her legs and chuckled. "Well, given the fact twenty minutes ago I couldn't stand *or* form a complete sentence, I think I'm doing much better."

Brodie laughed and knelt at Kate's feet. "A bit of an exaggeration, don't you think?"

"You're amazing," Kate said in a breath. "I'd ask you where you'd learned how to do that, but I don't think I want to know."

Brodie cupped Kate's chin in her hand. "That's in the past, Kate. All they did was teach me how to love *you*...for the rest of my life."

Kate's eyes misted over. "I love you."

"I love you, too," Brodie said, placing a light kiss on Kate's lips before standing up. "But now I'd best get dressed and get ready for the girls. Are you going to be okay?"

"I'll be fine, Brodie."

"Good," Brodie said, wrapping her towel around her torso. She made her way across the room, only to stop and turn around when she reached the doorway. "By the way, your blouse is probably a bit wrinkled. There are T-shirts in the second drawer and blouses in the wardrobe if you want something clean to wear. Oh...and knickers are in the top drawer."

"You don't mind?"

"Of course not," Brodie said through a toothy smile. "Nothing says love like sharing one's knickers."

***

While Brodie readied the flat for Gina's and Devon's arrival, Kate finished in the bathroom and then began gathering her clothes. After making the bed, she tossed her crumpled shirt on a chair and took one of Brodie's Oxfords from the wardrobe. Enjoying the feel of the soft cotton against her skin, Kate sat on the edge of the bed and took a deep breath.

It had been less than twenty-four hours since she'd become Brodie's lover, and Kate knew her life would never be the same. Before she met Brodie, Kate had been convinced the road she was to travel would be straight and narrow, but now she wasn't sure, nor was Kate sure she cared. Earlier in the day, she had witnessed the slack-jawed faces of strangers, shocked to see Gina's and Devon's open displays of affection, and Kate was bothered by their rude reactions. She wasn't yet prepared for that kind of attention, although in time, she told herself it wouldn't matter. After all, she was happy, and she was in love. She'd get past this. She just needed some time.

Kate ran her hand over the duvet. Her thoughts returned to Brodie's lovemaking when, with her fingers and tongue, she had taken Kate to orgasms that had left Kate unable to speak or even to move. With delicious strokes, Brodie had tasted every crevice of Kate's sex, and as promised, when Kate begged for more, Brodie gave it...time and time again.

Kate blushed as her body reacted to the memories, and filling her lungs with air, she tried to push the thoughts from her mind. It would be hours before they'd be alone again, but when they were, Kate hoped to show Brodie exactly how quick of a study she was.

Jumping off the bed, Kate rolled up the sleeves of the borrowed Oxford as she headed to the kitchen, just in time to see Brodie filling two glasses of wine. "Are one of those for me?"

The sight of Kate wearing one of her Oxfords brought a smile to Brodie's face. "Of course," she said, handing Kate a goblet. "Come on. I want to show you something."

Kate slipped her fingers through Brodie's, and a minute later, they were ascending the circular stairway in the back of the flat. Climbing the iron treads, Kate admired the sway of Brodie's bottom until they reached the top, and Brodie pushed open the metal door.

Brodie stepped out onto the roof and waited until Kate joined her before flipping on the light switch mounted on the brick.

Kate gaped in astonishment as the entire rooftop became alive with the soft twinkle of fairy lights. Planters of every shape and size were everywhere. Ordinary terracotta sat alongside glazed ceramic vessels decorated in vibrant colors, and each container overflowed with greenery and flowers. "Oh, Brodie, this is amazing."

"Thanks. It took Devon and me months to carry all this stuff up here, but it was well worth it, I think."

"It certainly was," Kate said, her eyes darting here and there. Noticing a wooden chaise lounge in the center of the roof, she inclined her head. "Is that where you got your tan?"

"Yeah. I come up here on the weekends and relax with a book or some music. It's my way of escaping the world for a bit."

"I...uh...I noticed you don't have tan lines."

The glint in Brodie's eyes outdid the fairy lights. "The walls around the perimeter give me a bit of privacy, and the only buildings taller than this one are way over there."

Kate looked in the direction Brodie had indicated and then clearing her throat, she concentrated on the flowers surrounding them.

"Let me guess," Brodie said, inclining her head to look Kate in the eye. "You don't approve of sunbathing in the nude?"

"I never really thought about it," Kate said, her voice trailing off as she focused on another planter filled with greenery.

"Well, you could always try it sometime. You might just like it."

Kate sighed. It had taken her months to come to terms with her feelings toward Brodie, and after finally admitting them, in only a few short weeks, most of her insecurities had fallen to the wayside. But never in her life had she been involved with someone as confident as Brodie. That, coupled with the fact the woman enjoyed what some would call a self-indulgent lifestyle, began to weigh on Kate's mind.

Kate took a deep breath and let it out slowly. "You are *so* totally different than anyone I've ever dated."

"Because I'm a woman?"

"No, that's not what I mean," Kate said, shaking her head. "I used to think you were cocky, but that's not it at all. You're just comfortable being who you are."

"It's all I can be," Brodie said, placing her glass on a small iron table. "I can't worry about what others think. Life's too short for that, and since I've only got one life, why shouldn't I enjoy it as much as I can? So, if I want to lie out under the sun, nude, who's to say that I can't? If I want fancy cars and high-tech gadgets, why shouldn't I have them? I don't want to look back one day and wish for something I *could* have had, but didn't, just because I was too afraid to try."

"That's an admirable trait," Kate whispered. "But I'm not sure I possess it."

"You are who you are, Kate, and I love you," Brodie said, wrapping her arms around Kate and holding her close. "That's all that matters."

Their lips met, and Kate's fears waned. Running her fingers through Brodie's hair, she stroked the back of her neck as the kiss deepened, and it wasn't until they heard the squeak of the steel door that they moved apart.

"Oh, shit...sorry."

Kate laughed, burying her face in Brodie's chest for a second before turning toward the door. "Is this becoming a habit with you?"

Gina chuckled. "Christ, I certainly hope not."

"Me too," Brodie said through a grin. "And where's your other half?"

"She's searching for the takeaway menus."

"Well, I'd best go help her, or she'll empty all the drawers, and I won't find anything for weeks," Brodie said, loosening her hold on Kate. After giving Kate a quick peck on the lips, Brodie headed for the stairs. "See you two down there."

As the door closed behind Gina, she took in her surroundings. "Wow, this is great."

"Yes, it is," Kate said into her glass as she brought it to her lips.

Surrounded by possibly one of the most romantic places Gina had ever seen, Kate's pensive look worried her. "Hey, you doing okay?" she said, walking over.

"Yeah," Kate said, forcing a smile. "I just need to get used to a few things."

***

Kate's anxieties vanished as soon as she and Gina went back downstairs. Brodie and Devon were in the kitchen joking about the amount of food they were going to order, their laughter reminding Kate that tonight she was among friends who wouldn't judge or condemn. Before too long, she was joining the others at the table, and as Kate, Gina, and Devon popped open all the red and white containers of Chinese food, Brodie refilled their glasses.

Beer had always been Devon's drink of choice, but in her rush to get Kate back to her flat and into her bed, Brodie hadn't stopped to buy any. After turning up her nose at the taste of the bold, dry red the others were having, Devon was about to fetch some water when Brodie returned with a bottle of Riesling. She filled Devon's glass and pushed it in her direction, and once Devon sipped the crisp, fruity liquid, water was no longer needed.

Their feast began with spicy spare ribs, spring rolls, and wonton soup, and as they sampled, they sniggered at innuendo and cackled at smartarse retorts. Kate was on the receiving end more than once.

Whenever Brodie gave her a certain look or dared to send a knowing gaze in her direction, Kate's cheeks would darken three shades, and Gina and Devon would twitter like little girls or tap their silverware on their glasses, insisting the two women kiss.

Before the last slurp of soup had been swallowed, Devon's glass was empty, and once she scooped portions of Kung Po chicken, curried beef, and fried king prawns onto her plate, Devon refilled her glass. Having never developed a tolerance for alcohol, Devon had always limited herself to two beers. The Riesling, however, tasting more like watered-down juice than wine, caused Devon to forget her limitations, and halfway through dinner, she poured another splash into her glass…and then another.

Two hours later, with empty containers scattered across the dining room table, Brodie got up, picked up the two wine bottles, and headed into the kitchen. "Who wants dessert?"

Brodie snickered when she heard the loud, collective groan coming from the dining room, and placing the empty bottles on the counter, she pulled another from the rack.

"You may want to put on a pot of coffee, too," Kate said, dropping some empty cartons into the rubbish bin.

"For Devon?"

"You noticed?"

"Between her tittering and her 'whoopsie' whenever she dropped her fork, it was kind of hard not to," Brodie said, smiling as she handed Kate the bottle and corkscrew. "If you can handle that, I'll set up the machine."

"Thanks," Kate said, watching as Brodie began scooping out beans to put into the grinder. "She doesn't drink wine that much."

"Darling," Brodie said, looking up. "You don't have to apologize for her. Devon's just having some fun. No harm done."

"Okay."

They worked alongside each other quietly, and by the time the coffee was brewing, and the wine was opened, Gina had already cleared the table and deposited Devon onto the sofa in the game room. Once everything was cleaned up, with drinks in hand, Kate and Gina joined Devon, and Brodie followed shortly after with a tray piled high with biscuits and foil-wrapped chocolates.

As soon as Brodie walked into the room, Devon popped into a sitting position. "Whaz happening?"

"We're just having some coffee and dessert," Brodie said, sitting down.

"Iz that wine?" Devon said, pointing to the bottle next to Kate.

"Yes, and it's red," Kate said, handing her sister a cup of coffee. "So, drink this instead."

Devon stuck out her lower lip. "I don't want that."

"Too bad, drink it anyway."

"You're not my mother," Devon said, wiggling her finger in the air. "Oh…*thaz* right. I don't have one of those anymore. *Whoopsie.*"

In unison, Kate, Gina, and Brodie pressed their lips together to stifle their amusement, and when Devon stood up and swayed, all three women braced for impact.

"Honey," Gina said, patting the cushions on the sofa. "You really should sit down."

"Not interested," Devon said, waving her off. "But you know what? How 'bout we shoot some pool? Come on, Brod. Let's do it!"

Brodie looked at Gina and Kate for guidance, and when both shrugged in reply, she said, "Looks like we're shooting some pool."

"*Yes!*" Devon said with a fist pump before making a somewhat wobbly beeline to the rack of cues on the wall.

"What do you want to play, ladies?" Brodie said, directing her question to Kate and Gina.

"You and Devon decide," Kate said, picking up her wine. "It doesn't matter to us."

Brodie glanced at Devon, watching as she struggled to remove one of the cues. "Devon, it's your choice then. What do you want to play?"

The rack Brodie had mounted on the wall was designed like a thousand others. There was a narrow shelf on the bottom where the cue would rest and toward the top another equally narrow shelf with holes drilled every few inches. To remove a stick, one only had to lift it, pull it out to clear the bottom shelf, and lower it to free the tip from the hole at the top, but for Devon, it had become a Chinese puzzle box. She had no idea all eyes were on her, and she had no idea all three women were struggling not to laugh.

Devon lifted a cue and then rested it again on the shelf, staring at it for a few seconds before lifting it again. She repeated the same steps three more times before she finally solved the mystery. Letting out a squeal of delight, she whipped around with the not-so-firmly-gripped prize in her hand, and a second later, the lacquered stick slipped from her fingers and fell to the floor with a clatter. "Whoopsie," she said, giggling as she snatched it up. "Now, what were you saying?"

Brodie's eyes crinkled at the corners. "I was asking you what you'd like to play. Gina and Kate said for you to pick."

"Oh cool," Devon said, snagging a piece of chalk from the table. "Well, let's see. There's eight-ball, nine-ball...um...cutthroat, and we can*not* forget strip, now can we, Brodie?"

The heads of the two women sitting on the sofa popped up like moles in a carnival game, and after giving each other a quick glance, they spoke as one, "*Strip?*"

Brodie winced, and if Devon were paying attention, she would have seen that Brodie had sent her a look to kill. But absorbed in merrily chalking the end of her cue stick, Devon had no idea her loose, albeit drunken lips had just lit someone's fuse.

Kate jumped up and headed for Brodie, the weight of her stare forcing Brodie to look her in the eye. "Care to explain *strip* pool?" she said, putting her hands on her hips.

Brodie tried to put on a sweet smile, one to appease and calm, but it slipped off her face when she saw the veins in Kate's temples straining against her skin. "It's really nothing, darling," Brodie said quietly. "Just something we did once."

"Oh, come on, *Brod*," Devon said with an exaggerated eye roll. "We played it *lots* of times."

Kate tightened her jaw, and tilting her head to the side, she stared at Brodie. "So...who won?"

"What?" Brodie said.

"I said...who won?"

"We both did," Devon chirped. "Brodie's *really* good, but the more clothes I lost, the worse she played."

Gina instantly jumped up and trotting over, she snatched the cue stick from Devon's hand and laid it on the table. "I think I need to get you home," she said, grabbing Devon's arm. "Come on."

"What? What did I say?" Devon said, pulling her arm away. "I can't help it if she gets all distracted by tits."

Kate's entire body went rigid, and after staring at Brodie for a very long moment, she turned toward Gina. "Did you drive?"

"What?" Gina said.

"Goddammit, Gina. Did you take the Tube, or did you bring your bloody car? The question's not that difficult," Kate said, her face growing redder by the second.

"Kate...please don't..." Brodie's words died in her throat when Kate spun around, the blue of her eyes darkening with fury.

"Don't what, Brodie?" Kate said, invading the woman's personal space. "Don't get bothered because you played strip pool with my sister? Or how about the fact you think nothing of sunbathing in the nude on the roof of this bloody building?"

"She does," Gina blurted.

"Yeah, baby," Devon said with a fist pump. "*All* the time."

"Shut the fuck up, Cassidy," Brodie said, glaring at Devon.

"Don't tell her to shut up," Gina said.

"Enough!" Kate screamed as she stormed toward the door. Gathering as many packages as she could carry, she whipped around. "Gina, will you and Devon please grab the rest, and I'll meet you at the car."

Brodie jogged to the door. "Kate, please...I can explain."

"Don't bother," Kate said through clenched teeth. "I can't do this. I'm not *like* this. I don't sunbathe in the nude. I don't play strip billiards, and I don't treat sex like it's...like it's...like it's part of my fucking workout plan!"

"Kate—"

"That woman over there is my *sister*. Don't you get that?"

"*Yes*, I do," Brodie said in a tone calm and reassuring. "And if you'll just give me a chance—"

"Sod you, Brodie," Kate said, yanking the door open. "Better yet...fuck off!"

Chapter Twenty-Four

Kate paced on the sidewalk near Gina's car, white-knuckling the bags in her hands until she saw Gina exit Brodie's building. "It's about bloody time!" she yelled.

Gina moseyed down the walk and pressing the button on the remote in her hand, her car chirped in response. She opened the back door and snatching the bags from Kate, she tossed them inside. Quickly slamming the door, Gina set the alarm.

"What in the hell are you doing?" Kate barked. "And where the hell is Devon?"

"She's having a cup of coffee and trying to sober up," Gina said, pocketing her keys.

"*What*? I told you I wanted to go home!"

Gina poked her tongue against her cheek. "Since when do you tell me what to do, and I seriously think you need to calm down."

"Calm down?" Kate said, flinching back her head. "She played *strip* pool with my *sister*!"

"So what?" Gina said, holding up her hands. "Over the years, you and I have seen each other without clothes dozens of times."

"That's not the same thing, and you know it. We didn't ogle each other."

Gina lowered her chin, and the tiniest of grins appeared on her face.

Kate's mouth dropped open. "Oh, fucking great," she said, throwing her hands up in the air. "My best friend checked me out. That's just *fucking* great."

"Relax, Kate. It was only once or twice," Gina said as whimsy danced in her eyes. "I am a lesbian, after all."

"I really don't need to hear this," Kate said, trying to open the car door. "Will you please unlock the bloody car and take me home?"

"I would if I thought you were being rational."

"I am rational!"

"No, you aren't," Gina said, raising her voice just a bit. "You're angry, and you're jealous, and you have absolutely no reason to be either."

"How can you say that? How can you *possibly* say that?"

Gina crossed her arms and grinned. "Because Brodie didn't know Devon, or should I say *Cassidy* was your sister at the time...now did she?"

If Kate had been a hot air balloon, she would have plummeted to earth, every ounce of her anger dissolving in the crisp night air. "Shit."

Gina smiled. "Light bulb flickering, is it?"

Kate leaned against Gina's car and pinched the bridge of her nose. "I must have looked like a *bloody* idiot."

"I'm thinking more like a really, *really* jealous girlfriend," Gina said, going over to rest against the car next to Kate. "You know, I don't remember ever seeing you jealous before. It's rather a nice change of pace."

"Seeing me act like a stupid cow pleases you, does it?"

"No," Gina said softly. "Seeing my best friend in the whole wide world finally head-over-heels in love pleases me. I was beginning to think it was never going to happen."

Kate snorted. "You and me both."

***

Devon sat slumped on a bar stool, nursing a cup of coffee. She occasionally looked up as Brodie tidied the flat, but it wasn't until Brodie came back into the kitchen when Devon found the courage to speak. "I'm sorry," she said, raising her eyes. "I royally fucked things up, didn't I?"

Brodie grabbed the coffee pot and refilled Devon's cup. "No, you didn't fuck anything up, Devon. No worries."

"So...so you're not mad at me?" Devon said before taking another sip of her coffee.

Having been given the time to replay the events in her head, Brodie's anger had disappeared almost as quickly as Kate had run from the condo. Throughout Kate's tirade, Brodie found herself wanting to apologize and beg for forgiveness, yet once she was alone with her thoughts, and her drunken friend, Brodie realized that doing either would have been a lie. She neither needed nor wanted forgiveness for something as innocent as playing a bit of strip pool. Apologizing for that would have been the same as apologizing for being who she was, and that was something Brodie simply would not do.

Brodie placed the coffee carafe aside. "At first, I wanted to bloody strangle you," she said through a faint smile. "But then I came to my senses and realized you didn't do anything wrong."

"What do you mean? If I hadn't opened my gob about the billiard games, Kate wouldn't have stormed out of here."

"Oh, your timing sucked. I'll give you that, but all you did was tell the truth. And as for Kate leaving, I think she'll come to her senses once she calms down."

"I hope you're right," Devon said, staring down at her coffee cup.

"Me, too," Brodie said, pushing a strand of hair away from Devon's face.

The door to the flat opened, and Brodie looked up while Devon, not ready to face her sister or Gina, remained focused on her coffee.

Gina walked in, followed a second later by Kate, and pausing, Gina glanced back and forth between Kate and Brodie. Kate seemed unable to raise her eyes, while Brodie appeared to be staring Kate down, and Gina quickly came to the conclusion that standing in the middle of a firing range wasn't the smartest thing to do. In no time at all, Gina was across the room and hooking her arm through Devon's. "Come on, Minnesota Fats. It's time to get you home."

Gina guided Devon to the door, and as they were about to leave, she looked over her shoulder. "Brodie, thanks for everything. It was a blast."

Brodie nodded her acknowledgment, saying not a word as she focused on Kate. She had breathed a small breath of relief when Kate returned to the flat, but that was then, and this was now. When the door closed, Brodie walked from the kitchen, and leaning against the bar top, she decided the next move belonged to Kate.

Kate focused on the floor while she chewed on her bottom lip. Three times she had tried to look at Brodie, and every time, the intensity of the woman's stare forced her to look away. Taking a deep breath, Kate raised her eyes. "I overreacted."

"Yes, you did," Brodie said, her tone as calm as a supine lake.

"I have a bit of a temper at times."

"I've noticed."

Kate stared at the floor again. "And I was jealous."

Brodie crossed her arms. "I told you there was never anything between Devon and me."

"I forgot," Kate whispered.

"Perhaps you should write it down."

Kate raised her eyes, and when she saw Brodie smiling back at her, the corners of Kate's mouth lifted just a smidge. "You're not angry with me?"

"The weekend is almost over, Kate, and I don't want to spend it arguing, do you? Besides, I kind of liked the jealousy bit. It means you care."

"I do," Kate said in a breath.

"So...what now?"

Kate thought for a moment and then looked toward the game room. "Oh, I don't know. Feel like shooting some pool?"

***

More than willing to play a few games of pool with Kate, a little over an hour later, Brodie was having a hard time keeping her mind on the game.

Being the dedicated student during her days at college, Kate had always chosen her holidays carefully. Long breaks were spent at home with her mother, and short ones were spent on campus poring over her lessons. But when her studies were done, or she was too tired to think any longer, Kate would travel to a nearby pub where she'd order a pint and shoot some pool. Having learned the game in her youth, she honed her skills at the pub, and before long, she was returning to her dorm room with a small roll of money in her pocket.

Petite and feminine, there wasn't a man in the pub that believed the wee lass could win a game. With bravado fueled by drink, they'd offer Kate a wager, and most, if not all, she promptly won.

Not having played for a few years, Kate had lost the first three games, and her shoes, socks, and jeans had been removed. Since she had chosen eight-ball, the slower pace gave her the time to remember the basics, and like riding a bike, by the start of the fourth game, Kate's skills had returned, and she easily won the next three.

Kate was beginning to think Brodie was getting tired, and as she leaned down for her next shot, she glanced over at her opponent and almost burst out laughing. True to Devon's drunken admission, even though Brodie could hold her own playing pool, the sight of breasts, or rather *tits*, was her undoing. Kate was still wearing Brodie's Oxford, and one quick peek told Kate what she already knew. Each time she bent down, the shirt would gap, and that gap gave Brodie more than ample view of breasts trying their best to escape Kate's bra.

Kate quickly told herself it wasn't *really* cheating, and she began choosing her shots more prudently. Whenever there was more than one choice, she'd pick the one directly in line with Brodie's point of view, and as she sunk the eight ball on their seventh game, Kate stood straight and smiled.

Brodie frowned. With her shoes, socks, and jeans already piled on a nearby chair, she thought for a second before taking off her watch.

"That's not clothing," Kate said, picking up a cube of chalk.

"Sure it is."

"No, a watch is jewelry, not clothing, and you said the rules were the loser had to remove a piece of *clothing*."

"I didn't know you were such a fashion guru," Brodie said, setting her watch aside.

"I'm not, but since you buy watches in the jewelry department and not off the racks, it doesn't count. Choose something else."

Brodie was not bashful. When playing a game of strip pool with Devon, removing her clothes hadn't been a problem, yet tonight was different. The woman across the way would most likely be sharing her bed tonight, and if Brodie got her wish, Kate would be doing it for the rest of her life. As if slowly stripping in front of Kate wasn't enough to light Brodie's fuse, the glimpses she'd been afforded of Kate's breasts had caused that fuse to spark and sizzle.

"Well?" Kate said with her hands on her hips. "You going to stand there all night?"

Standing wasn't the position Brodie had in mind, and thinking for a moment, she upped the ante. Taking off her shirt, she tossed it on a chair. "Satisfied?"

"Yes," Kate said, gesturing toward the table. "And I believe you need to rack because it's my break...again."

While Brodie gathered the balls, Kate stood at the opposite end of the table, admiring the view. Although still wearing her underwear, the minimal black cloth did little to hide Brodie's attributes, and when she leaned over to adjust the triangle, Kate had to hold back a gasp.

Kate couldn't remember ever being affected like this. Her center throbbed, her mouth watered, and her mind was overflowing with things that would make any adult blush. Kate was totally turned on, and she liked it.

Brought back to reality when she heard Brodie call her name, Kate looked up. "What?"

"You've been cheating."

"I have not."

"Yes, you have," Brodie said, picking up a piece of chalk. "You remembered what Devon said earlier, and all night, you've been making sure to give me a view of your chest, or are you going to deny it?"

Humor sparkled in Kate's eyes as she shrugged. "I can't help it if you get all distracted by tits."

"Is that so?" Brodie studied Kate for a second, and then reaching around, she unclasped her bra and dropped it on a chair. "Well, let's just see how well you play now."

Kate told herself not to look. She told herself she'd seen Brodie's breasts before, and holding her head high, she told herself she *would* prevail. Kate walked around the table, and swallowing to clear the excess moisture in her mouth, she took aim on the cue ball...and promptly missed. Kate's cue skittered off the side of the white orb, and as the ball rolled a few inches to her left, Brodie's guffaw filled the room. Kate's cheeks flamed instantly.

In all her glory, Brodie strutted around the table, giving her time to get her mirth under control. "It seems like I'm not the only one distracted by tits, DI Monroe," she said, waving Kate away. "Now, if you don't mind, I believe it's my shot."

Presented with no less than three opportunities to re-enter the game, Kate failed every time. She couldn't concentrate on anything except a pair of beautiful breasts attached to the woman she loved.

Quite comfortable in her state of undress, Brodie began slowing down the game, casually leaning over the table to line up shot after shot. She was no longer in a hurry to rush what she knew was inevitable because this had become foreplay, and Brodie adored foreplay. Whether Kate knew it or not, the woman's breathing had changed. Her face was now flushed, and Brodie had lost count how many times Kate had cleared her throat or licked her lips.

Brodie leaned down again and called the corner pocket. The eight ball dropped solidly, and standing straight, Brodie grinned. "I believe that means you lose."

Kate cleared her throat again as she debated on which piece of clothing to forfeit, but instead of tossing the borrowed shirt on top of the growing pile, Kate reached underneath it. Seconds later, she pulled her bra down one of the sleeves, tossed it aside, and then re-racked the balls. "There you go, sweetheart," she said, removing the triangle. "And don't forget to concentrate."

Much to Kate's surprise, Brodie began running the table, calling pockets and making shots like she was a pro, and as each ball disappeared, Kate's core throbbed harder. With only the eight ball remaining, Brodie walked around the table, applying a bit of blue chalk to the end of her cue, and Kate backed away to allow Brodie the room to take her shot.

Brodie leaned over the table, prepared to sink the eight ball yet again when she felt the slightest hint of fabric belonging to an Oxford shirt graze her hip. Brodie froze.

Kate was all about self-control. She had quit smoking cold turkey, had always tried to limit herself to a few glasses of wine or the occasional fruity cocktail, and could walk past the most decadent chocolate shop in all of London without batting an eye. But Brodie had brought a whole new meaning to the word decadent. Actually, Brodie had brought a whole new meaning to almost everything.

Kate had known envy, but full-blown jealousy resulting in downing shots of tequila to kill the pain was a road she had never traveled until Brodie. Kate had also experienced physical attraction, yet the fierceness of the lust now flowing through her veins didn't compare. Simply put, Kate wanted Brodie...and she wanted her now.

Kate reached around and cupped Brodie's breasts, and a second later, the cue in Brodie's hand dropped to the table. Her throaty purr was like music to Kate's ears and smiling into Brodie's naked back, Kate pinched and rolled the stiffened tips of Brodie's nipples between her fingers.

Brodie's first instinct was to turn around until Kate pressed herself against Brodie and rubbed her pelvis against Brodie's bottom. It was Brodie's turn to swallow hard. She was a prisoner in Kate's embrace, and as the woman caressed, her lips traveled across Brodie's shoulders and down her spine, leaving a trail of wet kisses atop skin now growing hot and damp. Brodie's breaths grew short as her smoldering passion flared and unable to stand it any longer, she spun around. She wasted no time in tearing open the cotton shirt Kate was wearing, revealing the creamy flesh underneath, and for a split-second neither moved.

As if reading the other's mind, each threaded fingers through hair and pulled the other close. Their lips met in a hungry and demanding kiss, and as tongues plunged with urgency, hands groped, cupped, and fondled.

"I want you," Kate said in a breath. "Oh, my God, I want you so much."

Kate pushed Brodie's knickers down her legs, and as Brodie stepped out of them, Kate was instantly awash in the heady aroma of Brodie's desire. Their eyes locked for an instant, and no words were necessary. Brodie widened her stance, and Kate slipped her hand between Brodie's legs, burying her finger to the hilt into Brodie's heated center.

Wonderfully impaled, Brodie grabbed Kate by the hair and capturing her mouth in a savage kiss, Brodie lifted her hips, a sensual, silent plea for Kate to match her movement, yet Kate's hand remained still. Her finger was deep, and with her palm pressed hard against Brodie's clit, the sensation was more erotic than Brodie could have imagined. She was being possessed. She was being claimed...and the effect was dripping down her thighs.

Brodie broke out of the kiss, and the look in Kate's eyes was lustful and bold. It promised Brodie a night that would blend into morning and taking Kate by the wrist, Brodie urged her to remove her hand. "Let's go to bed," she said, her voice thick with passion.

"No," Kate said, pushing Brodie up against the table. "Here. Now."

A strained laugh slipped through Brodie's lips, and reaching behind herself, she placed her hand on the table and locked her elbow. "Kate, darling, I appreciate your adventurousness, but while this felt is soft to the touch, there's a very flat and a very *hard* piece of slate under it. We'll be...um...much more comfortable in bed."

"Who says I want comfort?" Kate said, stripping out of her knickers. "Now get on the table, Brodie, because the only memory you'll ever have about playing strip pool on this table again...is going to be *this* one."

Chapter Twenty-Five

A week after they consummated their relationship, they had cuddled on the sofa in Brodie's flat, and Kate voiced her concern about making their relationship known to her friends and work colleagues. Having never been one to hide her sexuality, at first, Brodie tried to argue the point until Kate finally told Brodie how her mother had reacted when Kate, like Devon, had come out to her. The ugly tirade her mother had spewed had been filled with vile words and disgusting analogies, and as Kate began to cry, Brodie held her close and reluctantly agreed.

So, for the next two months, behind the locked doors of their homes, they were partners in every sense of the word. Whether fixing a meal, relaxing in front of the television, showering, or making love, they were as one. However, when they ventured out into the hustle and bustle of the real world, things would change.

In dimly lit eateries or on darkened avenues, hands would be held, voices would become hushed, and words would be laced with innuendo, but when they walked the streets of London during daylight hours, Kate acted more like a friend than a lover. She'd amble alongside, but would never touch. If Brodie sent a lascivious grin in her direction, Kate would pretend not to notice, and when Brodie would suggest they stop by G-Street for a drink, Kate would offer a lame excuse and change the subject.

At times, Brodie's posture would slump, the lack of Kate's enthusiasm to allow their relationship to flourish outside their homes pressing down on her, except today wasn't like that. Today, Brodie was lighter than air when she walked into Kate's house.

"You're quite bubbly," Kate said as Brodie strutted in the door.

Brodie removed her coat, and tossing it on a chair, she pulled Kate into her arms. "I missed you," she said, giving Kate a quick kiss.

"It's only been two days," Kate said before she was silenced by another kiss, and this time, it was filled with passion and heat.

Almost a minute passed before Kate could finally come up for air, and when she did, she eyed Brodie and cocked her head to the side. "What's going on?"

"Whatever do you mean, darling," Brodie murmured as she went to kiss Kate again.

Kate held Brodie at bay. "You're either very horny, or something has happened. Now, which is it?" Brodie waggled her eyebrows, and Kate laughed. "Okay, so you're *always* horny, but this is something more—yes?"

Brodie's smile lit up the room. "We got the Cardinal Avenue school conversion."

"What!" Kate squealed.

"I signed the contract this morning. There's still a lot of work to do before Ethan can begin pulling permits, but the job is now officially ours."

"Oh, Brodie, that's great," Kate said as she gave her a hug. "Congratulations, sweetheart."

"You know it's going to mean a lot of work *and* a lot of long hours," Brodie said, holding Kate at arm's length.

"I'm sure it will, and that's fine. We'll manage."

Brodie hesitated for a moment. "And...um...and I'd like to celebrate."

"I would think so. What do you have in mind?"

"I'd...I'd like to take you dancing on Friday night."

Brodie already knew what Kate's reaction would be, so she wasn't surprised when all the gaiety on Kate's face dissolved in an instant.

"Kate, look," Brodie said, gazing into Kate's eyes. "I know you say you're not ready for everyone to find out about us, and you know I don't agree with hiding behind doors, yet I've honored your wishes. What your mother did was truly shit, but I'm not asking for you to put my photo on your desk at work or...or wear a placard saying 'I shag women.' All I'm asking is that you take this one small step."

"It's not small to me."

"I am not asking for the world here. Okay? This is a huge, huge contract, and all I want to do is celebrate it with you," Brodie said, placing her hands on Kate's shoulders. "We can have dinner at Calabria and then head over to Outskirts. You know it's a nice place, and seriously, do you really think anyone you work with goes there?"

Kate looked at the floor. "Brodie, I'm...I'm really not sure—"

"Please, Kate," Brodie said, lowering her head to look Kate in the eye. "Please...just do this for me."

Over the years, Kate had seen the true colors of many of the people she worked with. She knew the ones who had hearts of gold and the ones who'd go out of their way to help victims no matter the cost. She knew the ones who possessed not one ounce of prejudice, and those whose scales were tipped by the weight of their own bigotry. Kate knew the ones who would be her allies should she ever choose to come out, and Kate also knew the homophobes. Countless times she'd heard them pepper their conversation with words like fag or dyke, and her reaction had always been the same. She'd shake her head, chalk it up to sheer ignorance, and then get back to work, but it was different now. Now, they pointed to her. Now, they meant something, and now, they hurt.

Kate looked at Brodie, prepared to once again turn down her offer, except when she gazed into the woman's eyes, there was impending heartbreak looking back at her. Heartbreak that would be all Kate's fault, and in that moment, Kate's tunnel vision cleared. Brodie *wasn't* asking for the world. She *wasn't* asking for the impossible or the improbable or the impracticable. She was merely asking for an evening out on the town with the woman she loved. Kate sighed. "Okay," she said, managing a thin-lipped smile. "So...what time are you going to pick me up?"

***

After leaving work a little early, Kate had spent the last two hours primping and preening for her evening out with Brodie, and her nerves had finally given way to excitement. Already knowing what dress she planned to wear, Kate had spent an hour in the tub and another hour, picking out jewelry, applying makeup, and brushing her hair until it shined. Perfume was dabbed in all the appropriate places, lingerie was fastened, snapped, and adjusted, and shoes purchased for both looks *and* comfort were slipped on.

Kate pulled her dress off the hanger, and stepping into it, she zipped it up before going over to stand in front of the mirror in the corner of her bedroom. Pleased to see it fit her exactly like she remembered, Kate turned this way and that, admiring the dress until she noticed a smudge under her eye. She returned to the bathroom to touch up her makeup, and a few minutes later, as Kate set aside her mascara, she glanced at her watch. "Oh, shit."

Kate rushed back into the bedroom, trying her best to tidy up the mess she'd created when she got home. Work shoes were kicked under the bed and gathering up the clothes she had worn to work that day, Kate tossed them into the basket in the wardrobe seconds before she heard the doorbell chime. Taking a deep breath, Kate shut off the light and went downstairs.

It wasn't until Kate reached the entry when a bit of her anxiety returned, but pushing aside the feeling of a knot forming in her stomach, she opened the front door. "Hi there."

"Wow," Brodie said in a breath.

Purchased on the Saturday shopping spree a few months before, if ever there was a dress made for Kate Monroe, it was the one she was wearing. Soft jersey in a dark emerald hue, it was trendy and snug, and with a neckline plunging just short of being indecent, it wasn't until Kate was closing the door behind her when Brodie could force more words to come out. "You look amazing."

Kate beamed, her cheeks reddening slightly when she noticed Brodie's lustful stare. "Easy, stud," she said, giving Brodie a quick peck on the cheek. "That is unless you've changed your mind about going dancing?"

Brodie drank in the beautiful woman in front of her as if savoring the finest of wines. "Tempting," she said, placing a light kiss on Kate's lips. "But I think I'd enjoy a bit of foreplay if it's all the same to you."

Brodie's voice was low and carried in its undercurrent things that made Kate's body flutter. They had danced twice before, and while her recollection of one was fogged by alcohol, the other was crystal clear. Alone on a dance floor at Harrison Shaw's birthday party, they had swayed to a love song, and the feeling of Brodie's body pressed against hers was something Kate would never forget. *Foreplay*...was putting it mildly.

Kate shifted in her stance and took Brodie by the hand. "Then, let's do this."

***

For nearly two hours, they had sat sipping drinks and chatting while the club pulsed around them. Even though Brodie had come to dance, she couldn't fault Kate for wanting to wait until the crush of people moving to the music diminished. Toward eleven o'clock, the crowd finally thinned, and without saying a word, Brodie took Kate's hand and led her to the dance floor. Brodie was walking on air, her face glowing with happiness as they approached the ebony tile, and then suddenly, Kate snatched her hand away.

Brodie's face went slack. "What's the matter? I thought we came here to dance." Brodie waited for a moment before she realized that something else was holding Kate's attention, and following her line of sight, Brodie saw a tall, broad-chested man lumbering their way.

"Frank, what are you doing here?" Kate said through a false smile.

"I was about to ask you the same thing," Frank Daggett said, his eyes darting back and forth between Kate and Brodie.

Kate suddenly felt as if an elephant was sitting on her chest, and it was all she could do to maintain eye contact with Frank while her brain raced to come up with something to say. It finally did, and it would be the first of many mistakes Kate would make that evening. "I'm just having a drink with...with a friend. And you?"

"Right," Frank said, eyeballing Brodie for a second. "I'm here because my divorce was final yesterday. My mates thought they'd show me a good time and take me to all the new clubs in the area. I doubt I'll be coming back here, though. A bit too queer for my tastes, if you know what I mean."

Brodie went rigid. Having heard stories about Kate's arse of a partner, meeting him in person gave Brodie a whole new definition to the word arse. The man was an obnoxious, small-minded moron, and Brodie found herself struggling not to slap the smirk off his craggy, heavily-veined face.

Kate could sense Brodie's tension, but she told herself there wasn't anything she could do about it. After all, it had been Brodie's idea to go dancing, and in Kate's mind, she had made her reluctance crystal clear. She wasn't yet comfortable with having their relationship known, something else Brodie was more than aware of, and nothing had changed in the past week. Nothing at all. "I hadn't really noticed," Kate said with a shrug. "I come here for the wine and the music, not the clientele. They don't bother me, and I don't bother them."

Brodie's hands turned into fists, her neck growing corded as she stared at the floor. All she had wanted to do was dance with the woman she loved, hold her in her arms and sway to the music until the wee hours of the morning, but in the time it takes for a thought to form, Kate had ruined everything. Just like that. Their celebration of Brodie getting the largest contract of her career was gone. Just like that. Dancing the night away was gone. Just like that. Intimate conversation over wine was gone...just like that. And to add insult to injury, Kate's flippant statement made it sound as if she agreed with Daggett's homophobic observation. Brodie took a deep breath. She needed to say something. She *wanted* to say something, and she would have if two more men hadn't walked over and stood next to Daggett.

"Kate, you know Bill and Larry, right?" Frank said, draping his arm across the shoulders of one.

The dam broke, and Kate's doubts, insecurities, and phobias flooded her mind in a torrent of fear and shame and guilt. The two that stood before her were the most arrogant, opinionated, and prejudiced in the station and one wrong move or one wrong word, and her secret would be out. In an instant, her night on the town with Brodie became a charade, and it was one Kate would play to the hilt.

***

Along empty roads, dampened by an evening shower, they drove in silence back to Kate's house. One was trying to find something she could say to ease the other's mind, while the other grappled with an anger that had a life of its own.

Brodie had spent the last two hours sipping her scotch, hoping the aroma of the blended malt would drown out the stench of

Daggett's cheap cologne. Once the introductions had been made, Frank and his mates ordered another round of drinks, and much to Brodie's dismay, they yanked over a few unoccupied stools and plopped themselves down at the high-top table with Brodie and Kate. They began talking shop, complaining about their colleagues, whining about their workload, and pontificating on what they'd do if they were in charge as Brodie said nary a word. Kate interjected a nod when appropriate or flashed a smile if required, and more than once, she had joined the conversation, leaving Brodie feeling more alone than she thought possible. *That* was until the clock struck twelve.

At midnight, a handsome man with an athletic build and chiseled features swaggered up to the table and asked Kate to dance, and a few seconds later, Brodie watched as the woman she loved danced in the arms of a stranger. The song ended, and another began, and then another, and then another until Brodie could no longer watch the parade of men dancing with Kate. She lowered her eyes and stared at her empty glass, barely acknowledging Frank and his buddies when they left to go to another club. Brodie sat there for over an hour before Kate finally came back to the table, and by that time, Brodie's anger was raging.

Brodie pulled into the driveway, and shutting off the engine, she walked around her sports car and opened Kate's door. She knew if she said a word, it would be loud and most likely contain enough venom to kill an army, so she followed Kate silently up the walk, the click of Kate's high heels on the concrete infuriating Brodie even more. Those shoes were meant for their date. That dress was meant for their date. The perfume, the earrings, the whispered words that were never spoken were all meant for a *date* that wasn't.

They went into the house, and after flicking on some lights, Kate tossed her coat onto a chair. Out of habit, Brodie did the same, but as Kate headed for the kitchen, Brodie didn't move. Instead, she looked around at her surroundings and shook her head. This was the last place she wanted to be.

"I'm going to fix some tea. Would you like some?" Kate said as she reached the kitchen door.

"Actually, I think it would be best if I just leave," Brodie said, picking up her coat.

"What?" Kate said, doing an about-face. "I thought we were planning to spend the weekend together."

Brodie gritted her teeth as she threw her coat back onto the chair. "Well, it seems that plans change, Kate, or didn't you notice? *We* had a plan to go dancing tonight to celebrate the largest contract in my entire bloody *career*, but instead, I had to sit with a bunch of wankers and watch as you allowed yourself to be manhandled by strangers."

"I wasn't manhandled."

"They had their hands on your *arse*, Kate," Brodie shouted. "I saw them, and more importantly, I saw you do absolutely *nothing* to stop them."

"They had their hands on my *hips*, Brodie. It's what men and women do when they dance, but you wouldn't know that, now would you?" Kate said, and spinning on her heel, she headed for the kitchen.

Brodie went rigid, and clenching her hands, she marched after Kate. "Exactly, what is *that* supposed to mean?"

Kate was filling the kettle with water when Brodie came into the room, and slamming it onto the stove, Kate whipped around. "I wasn't *manhandled* by them, Brodie, but if you and I had danced tonight, exactly what were *your* intentions—eh? They didn't do anything you wouldn't have done if given half the chance."

"But I have the right."

"The *right*?" Kate yelled, throwing her hands in the air. "You have the *right*? Who the fuck do you think you are, believing you have the *right* to fondle me in public? What gives you the right to force me to be something I'm not yet comfortable being?"

"Exactly what aren't you comfortable with, Kate?" Brodie said, folding her arms. "Because if memory serves, two nights ago, you were *more* than comfortable with having my head between your legs."

Kate charged across the room, her anxieties morphing into fury as she swung at Brodie. Well aware of Kate's tendency to lash out, Brodie grabbed her arm, twisted her around, and pressed her against the wall.

"Not this time, sweetheart," Brodie said, pressing her body against Kate's. "And here I thought those visits to the counselor were helping."

"Yeah, well, he never met you."

"Oh, so your temper is *my* fault?" Brodie said with a laugh. "Nice try, darling."

"Sod you, Brodie," Kate said, fighting to get away. "Let me go!"

After spending almost the entire night in the role of a voyeur, the more Kate squirmed, the more aroused Brodie was getting. Sex had been the furthest thing from her mind, but it was quickly becoming just the opposite. Kate was warm and soft, and her body was molding against Brodie's so flawlessly, Brodie had to smother a groan as her libido announced itself.

"I said, let me *go!*"

Brodie smiled into Kate's hair, and she lowered her lips to Kate's ear. "You're quite the spitfire, aren't you, darling."

Brodie wasn't the only one getting turned on. Between Brodie's breath washing down her neck and the woman's body nuzzled against hers, Kate was caught in the middle of her own emotions. In one direction was lust, hot and lascivious, the idea of being taken standing against the wall as lewd as it was exciting. However, in the other direction, was Kate's rage. Rage about being pushed to do something she was not yet ready to do. Rage about her mother's repulsive tirade. Rage at the friends she knew she'd lose. Rage at her work colleagues for words they'd yet to utter. Rage about a fear she could not best...and rage at the woman standing behind her.

Kate's nostrils flared. "I'll show you spitfire," she said. With all her might, Kate jammed her elbow into Brodie's ribcage, and as soon as she heard Brodie's grunt of pain, Kate winced at her own actions.

Despite the fact the force of the jab had taken her breath away, Brodie was not yet willing to let Kate go. Kate's breathing had changed, and more than once, she had pushed her bottom into Brodie instead of hugging the wall to avoid any contact. Brodie grinned. Their heated argument had lit more than one fire.

Once again, Brodie lowered her mouth to Kate's ear. "I thought you didn't approve of bruises, darling."

"Let me go, and I'll *show* you bruises."

Brodie chuckled. "I think I prefer you this way, darling."

"*Stop* calling me darling!"

"Why? It's not like there's anyone else here, and besides, I already know you're a dyke."

"Fuck you, Brodie."

Brodie spun Kate around and looked her in the eye. "If I'm not mistaken, I believe that's exactly what you *want* to do right now. Isn't it?"

Kate swallowed hard. Brodie was right. It *was* what Kate wanted to do.

Before Brodie knew what was happening, she was being grabbed by the hair and pulled into a kiss. It was punishing and wet, and when Kate thrust her tongue between Brodie's lips, Brodie returned the kiss with equal ferocity. After hours of watching Kate in the arms of men and after hours of living a lie, Brodie's frustrations, anger, and desire melded into something undisciplined and carnal. She didn't want to make love to Kate. She didn't want romance and soft words. Brodie wanted to pillage Kate like she would a stranger in a seedy club. She wanted the savagery that comes from lust, and breaking out of the kiss, she shoved Kate up against the wall.

When Kate saw the hunger in Brodie's eyes, her heart skipped a beat. She barely had time to take a breath before Brodie's mouth was on hers, and for a fraction of a second, Kate tried to push away, and then the most basic of instincts took over. This *was* exactly what Kate wanted, and opening her lips, Kate returned the kiss as savagely as it was being given. Again and again, Kate captured Brodie's lips, and when Brodie placed one leg between Kate's and forced them apart, want oozed from Kate's body.

This was yet another road not traveled or even considered until Brodie had come into her life, and Brodie was again destroying signposts and presenting detours too tempting not to take. Kate had never wanted to be so totally possessed by another. To be taken forcefully and greedily was so alien, yet so erotic, and while there was a small part of Kate that wanted to run from the brutality of the moment, another part thirsted for the sheer domination it presented.

Brodie ravaged Kate's mouth as her hands began to do the same with her body, roughly squeezing breasts and tweaking nipples, and inflicting as much pleasurable pain as she could upon the woman who owned her heart. Brodie was mad for Kate, mad like an animal starving for food, and lifting the green jersey dress out of her way, Brodie grabbed Kate's rounded cheeks, squeezing them so tightly the force almost lifted Kate from the floor. Kate's sensual moan was all Brodie needed to hear, and a second later, she thrust her hand between Kate's thighs and cupped her center.

Kate was wet, so wet that her excitement had drenched her lacy knickers. Brodie ran a finger down the middle of the fabric, and as Kate's breathing increased, so did the friction Brodie was creating.

Through the silk, Brodie could feel the thickened folds, and urged on by Kate's gasps, she continued to rub, and it wasn't long before Kate began arching her hips toward Brodie's hand. It was a plea, an urgent plea that Brodie had no intention of answering. Instead, she rubbed Kate through the cloth, wiggling her finger this way and that, applying more and more pressure precisely where it was needed until Kate grabbed her wrist.

"I need you," Kate said, holding Brodie's hand in place. "I need you now."

Brodie looked Kate squarely in the eye. "This isn't about what *you* need, Kate. This is about what *I'm* going to take."

Kate's eyes flew open when, in one violent tug, Brodie ripped Kate's knickers off, and a second later, Brodie dropped to her knees and lifted the fabric of Kate's dress.

The sight of Kate's black garter belt and shimmering nylons almost pushed Brodie over the edge. She had never worn them before, and then Brodie remembered that tonight was *supposed* to be special. Brodie snickered to herself. This wasn't the special she had wanted, and this wasn't the special she had planned, but tonight would be special…nonetheless.

Brodie inhaled the intoxicating aroma of Kate's scent as she leaned in. A few weeks after they became lovers, Kate had shaved herself smooth, so there was nothing between Kate's skin and Brodie's tongue as Brodie licked the cleft between Kate's legs.

"Oh, God…" Kate said, her arms flailing wide in search of something to hold on to.

Kate's fashionable, high-heeled shoes were slipping on the tile floor as Brodie kept up her assault, and while Kate had managed to find the counter with one hand, it wasn't enough to keep her steady. Fully aware of the consequences of her actions, Kate had no other choice but to lift one leg and drape it over Brodie's shoulder.

Brodie was already enthralled with the heady taste and aroma of Kate's arousal, so when Kate opened herself up even further, Brodie wasted no time in devouring all that was now in full view. She tantalized and teased with her tongue, nearly drowning in the taste of Kate as she stroked and licked, while Kate helplessly writhed above her. With skills honed over the years, Brodie drew her tongue again and again through the moist petals, and when she reached Kate's clit, she'd circle it once or twice before returning to the crevices coated in nectar. Refusing to give in to the insistent throbbing between her own legs, Brodie continued to toy with Kate, and parting the swollen folds with her fingers, Brodie licked and sucked against the engorged nub until Kate grabbed her by the hair.

"Oh, God, Brodie," she cried out, her core pounding for release. "Oh…yes."

Brodie stopped what she was doing, and yanking out of Kate's grasp, she looked up. She waited until Kate's eyes fluttered open, and when they met hers, Brodie plunged one finger inside.

"*Yesss,*" Kate hissed, expecting the welcomed punishment to continue, but instead, Brodie was ever so slowly drawing her finger in and out. "Don't you dare tease me," Kate said, looking down at Brodie. "Don't you *dare.*"

Tease. In one way or another, their entire relationship was built around that word. For months, Kate had teased Brodie, offering her crumbs when Brodie wanted a feast. Walking in and out of her life, Kate had tugged at Brodie's heartstrings until they were stretched to the breaking point, and then she'd offer a glimmer of hope, and all was well again. Tonight had been like so many others, save for the fact that tonight their argument had erupted into the feral act now being committed in Kate's kitchen under the bright whiteness of fluorescent bulbs.

When she had walked into the house earlier, Brodie was angry, and even though heated words had driven Kate to try to strike her, raising a hand in return was unimaginable to Brodie. Instead, when her anger turned into lust, Brodie decided to inflict the only punishment she could. She would drive Kate to a point where she'd beg for climax, and then Brodie would gladly give it, but not before bringing Kate's dignity to its knees. Brodie needed Kate to feel what it was like to have her self-respect pummeled by the person she loved. To know what it's like to be forced to bow to Brodie's control, just as Brodie was forced to bow to Kate's at the club.

But Kate's throaty utterance wasn't a plea. She hadn't begged for release. She had demanded it, so Brodie continued to tease, tormenting Kate with leisurely strokes that had the woman squirming.

"Goddammit, Brodie," Kate said, taking a labored breath. "I'm begging you. Please…oh, God, please…"

Brodie was on her feet in an instant, sucking in air as she glared at Kate.

"What the hell are you doing?" Kate said, her eyes opening wide. "Don't st—"

"Take off your clothes."

"What?"

"I said, take off your clothes," Brodie said, giving Kate a slow once-over. "Every...last...*stitch*."

Kate didn't have to think twice. She kicked off her shoes, and scrambling for the zipper on her dress, the green jersey fell to the floor within seconds, followed by her bra, the garter belt, and nylons. Kate's breasts rose and fell in time with her breathing as she stood naked in her kitchen, waiting for Brodie to make a move. "Well, what are you waiting for? I did as you asked."

Brodie moved until she was almost right on top of Kate. She looked her in the eye, and when Brodie saw defiance staring back at her, a ghost of a grin appeared on Brodie's face. Sliding her hand between Kate's thighs again, Brodie pushed one finger inside where it remained motionless.

"Damn it, Brodie," Kate whimpered. "Stop playing these games."

"Say it, Kate. I want to hear the words."

Kate grunted in frustration as she tried to move against Brodie's finger, and each time she tried, Brodie followed her lead, keeping her finger firm, deep, and still. "Damn you, Brodie."

"Just say the words, Kate. Tell me what you want."

Over the past months, they had made love dozens of times, yet Kate never truly had to request what Brodie always gave so willingly. On occasion, she'd utter words of encouragement, but when it came to giving instructions or rather *direction*, that wasn't something Kate had in her vocabulary, or so she thought. Although Kate never believed herself capable of vocalizing her needs, Brodie had driven her to a point where Kate had no choice. "Make love to me, Brodie. Is that what you want to hear?" Kate blurted. "Then *fine*, make love to me."

Brodie snorted out a laugh. "This isn't about love tonight, and you know it," she snarled, extracting her finger. "Now, tell me what you want me to do, *Kathryn*, or you can do it yourself."

Kate's face was flushed, and her body was on fire, and grabbing Brodie's wrist, she squeezed it as tightly as she could as she jammed it between their bodies again. "Fuck me. Is that what you want to hear me say? Well, I'm saying it, Brodie. Now...*fuck* me."

A rumbling growl rose in Brodie's throat, and before Kate knew what was happening, Brodie had lifted her leg to rest on her hip. A moment later, Brodie's finger plunged into Kate again, and this time, there wasn't anything leisurely about Brodie's tempo.

"Yes," Kate said in a breath. "Oh...yes."

Brodie pressed into Kate again and again. Deliciously tight and warm and wet, she effortlessly sank her finger to the hilt with each stroke before tending to Kate's clit, continually repeating the pattern as Kate's breathing turned ragged.

Kate was caught in a riptide, and with each stroke, Brodie was taking her farther out to sea. Away from sensibilities, away from decorum, away from rights, and away from wrongs, Kate was being pulled to a place lewd and unchaste. A place where bodily urges reign supreme, where the most salacious thoughts are welcomed, and the most primitive of needs are met, and Kate couldn't fight the current any longer. She knew what she wanted. She knew what she needed, and this time Brodie wouldn't have to force the words from her lips.

"Brodie," Kate said, sucking in air as she stilled Brodie's hand. "I want your mouth on me. Go down on me, Brodie. Please...go down on me."

Erogenous zones are areas, which if given the proper attention, can produce sensations stimulating one to do the unthinkable, say the unimaginable, and cause desire to flow thick from bodies. Much to Kate's chagrin, Brodie had discovered many over the past few months. She knew that the back of Kate's neck, if tenderly kissed and tasted, would make Kate purr in delight. A nipple nibbled and sucked, would cause Kate to gyrate in anticipation of what she craved, and a kiss, deep and seeming to go on forever, would dampen Kate's knickers every single time. The list seemed endless, and for the most part, somewhat identical. Brodie enjoyed having her nipples tweaked and tasted, and kisses filled with wetness and tongues could make her squirm as well, but when Kate's request caused an animalistic growl to rumble in Brodie's throat, Kate knew she had just found another of Brodie's erogenous zones. Words.

Brodie froze. Lowering her chin, she closed her eyes for a long moment, and when she opened them again, her stare was bold and possessive. Locking eyes with Kate, Brodie licked her lips. Sweat was beading on her forehead and dripping down her back, and without giving it a thought, Brodie tore off her blouse, tossed it aside, and then fell to her knees. "Come here," she said, grabbing Kate's bottom.

Kate did as she'd been ordered, and draping her leg over Brodie's shoulder, she arched her hips. In an instant, she was once again prisoner to Brodie's mouth, held an obedient captive by each lick, each probe, and each lash. Kate could feel the orgasm building inside of her. There wasn't a nerve in her body that wasn't on fire, and as shuddering sensations fanned out from her core, she grabbed Brodie by the hair and pressed herself into Brodie's awaiting mouth.

Kate tensed for a split-second before the sound of her release, uninhibited and feral, filled the room. The spasms deep within all but crippled her, and raspy cries fell from her lips as she shuddered again and again...and again.

Brodie rested back on her haunches, watching as Kate became lost in a crescendo that seemed endless, and when Kate slowly began to slide down the wall, Brodie gently guided her to the floor. Kate's chest was heaving, and her skin was gleaming with sweat, both of which were adding more than a little discomfort to Brodie's situation. She had already orgasmed once, a few words pushing her over the edge minutes earlier, and Brodie knew she was close to doing it again. Brodie was also still angry.

Kate slowly opened her eyes. Her first thought was to smile, except when she saw Brodie's hardened expression, Kate's smile ended before it began. "What's wrong?"

"How does it feel to be someone's puppet?"

"What?"

"In the club, you were pulling my strings, and I went along, not wanting to cause a scene," Brodie said, her tone eerily flat. "And this, what we just had, was me pulling yours. I wanted you to know how it felt."

"I'm not sure I under—"

"Yes, you do," Brodie said through a knowing sneer. "You know *exactly* what I mean because a short time ago you were livid. You were *enraged* that I wouldn't give you what you wanted...and that's exactly how I felt earlier tonight sitting in that club watching you on the dance floor. I felt helpless, like a puppet dangling from strings, and you were controlling every last one of them. And it hurt, Kate. It bloody hurt."

"I'm sorry," Kate said, her voice sinking to a whisper.

"I don't want your apologies. I want you to promise me that after tonight, there will be no more strings and no more puppets in our relationship. If you need a bit more time to acknowledge us in public, then I will do my best to honor that, but don't you ever—*ever*—treat me like that again."

Kate took a deep, shaky breath. "I promise. No more puppets. No more strings."

"Good, and I'll promise the same in the morning," Brodie said, and getting to her feet, she took off her bra and tossed it aside. "But tonight isn't over, Kate. Not by a long shot."

Chapter Twenty-Six

Five weeks later, Brodie sat at the drafting table in her office, staring off into space. After the heated argument that had ended with both of them naked on the kitchen floor, Brodie thought things would change. She had voiced her concerns that night and again the next morning over coffee and toast, and Brodie honestly thought Kate was listening. She honestly thought Kate would start taking baby steps toward acknowledging their relationship, but she hadn't. Instead, Kate continued the charade.

Each day she went to work single and straight, and each night Kate returned to Brodie anything but. Each time Brodie brought up the subject, Kate would use her mother's rejection as ammunition to end it, and Brodie would. It wasn't long before Brodie realized arguing wasn't helping the situation, so she stopped. She decided making love was better than making war, and when they ventured out to a restaurant, Brodie made sure it was dark and secluded where sensual stares would go unnoticed. Walks in the park were done as friends, lightly bantering as they traveled down garden paths or watched children playing on the swings, yet behind the locked doors of their homes, they were lovers, and their love was insatiable.

Brodie blew out a breath, shaking her head at the exhaustion that now seemed to be her norm.

"Is it me, or are you plummeting?" Stevie said, sailing into Brodie's office.

"What?" Brodie said, turning around.

"You don't look like you're on cloud twelve anymore."

"Don't you mean cloud nine?"

"Oh, sweetie, you passed nine months ago," Stevie said, placing a cup of coffee on the table. "This is fresh. Thought you'd like a cup."

"Thanks," Brodie said, and picking up the coffee, she took a sip.

Stevie covertly sized Brodie up and then down. "Okay, so maybe this isn't my place, but that's never stopped me before, so why should it now. What's going on? You look like the weight of the world is on your back. Too much work?"

"No such thing," Brodie said, swiveling the chair around. She took another taste of her coffee, and as she put down the cup, she looked over at Stevie. "Have you ever dated someone not yet out?"

"Oh, Lordy," Stevie said with a wave of his hand before flopping into a chair and throwing one leg over the other. "Back before I found my own fashion sense, I dated quite a few. Why?"

"How long did it take before they came out...if they came out?"

"A couple of them did, and I don't remember it taking that long actually. I think once you get a taste of what you really want or who you really are, it's damn hard to keep that secret. And again—why?"

"Kate...Kate doesn't appear to be in any rush to do it, and I feel like a total prat. I mean, I know she's uncomfortable with the whole coming out part, but I'm not asking her to put placards on the damn lawn for Christ's sake," Brodie said, rocking back in her chair. "And then the more I think about it, the more I think I'm the one being selfish. I told her I'd be patient, and I'm trying, I'm *really* trying, but it's running thin, Stevie, and I don't know what to do. Dwelling on the subject makes me look like I don't care about what she needs, but we've been together for nearly three months, and nothing—*nothing*—has changed other than me. Kate knew who I was and how I lived my life before we ever got together, and it's like she expects me to change for her instead of meeting somewhere in the middle. Taking small steps toward...toward living a normal life is all I want, but she refuses to do it."

"Refuses?"

Brodie bit off a laugh. "There's a laundry list of excuses or reasons or whatever you want to call them. Christ, I can't even keep clothes in her wardrobe."

"What?"

"Sometimes I spend the night at her place, and sometimes she's at mine, but other than a damn toothbrush, whatever I'm wearing goes home with me. Heaven forbid I leave something behind."

"So, moving in together apparently is off the table."

"It's *under* the table and the rug…*and* the bloody floorboards," Brodie said, throwing up her hands. "Stevie, I love my place, and Kate's house is rather small, but I told her I was willing to lease my condo so we could live together. You would have thought I was asking to have a three-way in the middle of Trafalgar Square, for Christ's sake. She said she likes things the way they are, and she doesn't have enough closet space, yadda, yadda, yadda, and again, I feel like an insensitive cow if I try to argue, so I don't. I just keep waiting and hoping and praying, and it's wearing me out."

Stevie's ordinarily pristine posture slumped like Brodie's. "I wish I had some words of wisdom for you."

"Actually, I think just talking about it helps," Brodie said, sitting straight. "Since she's Devon's sister and Gina's best friend, I didn't want to bring it up to them. It just didn't seem like the right thing to do, so I've been holding it all in."

"And by the way you looked when I walked in a few minutes ago, it's still gnawing at you."

"Yeah," Brodie said with a huff. "I love her to death, Stevie. I really do, and I keep telling myself I'd do anything for Kate, but that's a lie because I can't keep doing *this*."

"She shouldn't expect you to."

"Tell her that."

The chime of Brodie's mobile interrupted their conversation, and snagging it off Brodie's desk, Stevie glanced at the display as he handed it to Brodie. "Speak of the devil," he said, popping up from his chair.

Brodie waited until Stevie left the room before taking the call. "Hey there," she said, her smile as automatic as breathing. "This is a surprise."

"Hi Brodie," Kate said, raising her voice enough to be heard over the street traffic.

Brodie moved the phone a little away from her ear. "Where are you?"

"Oh, um…I'm outside the station. I just wanted to call and give you some news."

"Yeah? What's going on?"

"There's an opening for a DCI, and it seems yours truly is in the running for the job."

"What?" Brodie said, jumping off the chair. "Kate, that's great!"

"Thanks."

"We need to celebrate."

"It's a bit too early for that, I think."

"Okay," Brodie said, pausing for a second. "Then at least let me take you out to dinner tonight."

"I would, except you forgot, I've got to make an appearance in court this afternoon, and once that's over, I'll have to come back to the station and wrap up the paperwork. I honestly don't know when I'll get out of here."

"Damn, you're right. I did forget," Brodie said, sitting down.

"Can I have a rain check?"

"You can have anything you want." Brodie grinned when she heard Kate's sexy chortle come over the line. "So, I guess I'm not going to be seeing you tonight—eh?"

"Probably not, but if things change, I'll call you. Okay?"

"All right."

"I'd best be going back in now," Kate said, glancing at her watch. "I just wanted to give you the news."

"And it's awesome news, Kate. I couldn't be prouder."

"Thanks."

"I love you, darling."

Kate looked at the people milling about before answering. "I love you, too, Brodie. Talk to you later."

After slipping her phone back into her pocket, Kate let out a long breath as she pushed aside the feelings of guilt. As soon as she had arrived at the station that morning, Kate had been told about the possible promotion, but it wasn't until she could escape the confines of the building to stand amidst the noise of the busy street that Kate dared to give Brodie the news. The plan Kate had so carefully mapped out for herself had taken a detour when Brodie came into her life, but now it was getting back on track. With her pristine work record and her file filled with commendations, Kate knew that even though she was younger than most clambering for the position, if she kept her nose to the grindstone, the job could be hers. All she had to do was dot every *I*, cross every *T*, and keep Brodie in the background.

Kate knew in her heart what she was doing was wrong, but she wasn't ready to risk losing this chance. Her private life had always been private. She had never flaunted the men she dated or adorned her desk with a photograph of someone tall, dark, and handsome, and Kate saw no need to change now, *especially* now.

As Kate made her way back into the station, she thought about the framed photograph of Brodie that was wrapped in tissue paper in the bottom drawer of her desk. It had been there for weeks, or was it months? She saw it every time she put her handbag away, and every time she lifted it out, the crinkled white paper would stare up at her waiting to be unwrapped, and that's where it would remain. Kate had already lost her mother's love because of her feelings for Brodie. She wasn't about to lose anything else…least of all, her career.

***

Kate juggled a stack of manila file folders as she walked down the stairs toward her office, and when she heard her stomach growl, she glanced at the clock on the wall. Seeing that it was indeed lunchtime, Kate quickened her pace, and rounding the corner, she planned to rid herself of the files, grab her handbag, and go get something to eat. Her plans changed in an instant when she saw Brodie leaning against her desk, and Kate stuttered to a stop. She took a few seconds to regroup, and adjusting the files in her arms, Kate strode over and dropped them on the desk. "What are you doing here?"

"I'm here to see you, of course," Brodie said as she went to give Kate a kiss on the cheek.

Kate took a quick step backward and scowled. "What the hell do you think you're doing," she said in a rushed whisper.

Brodie's face fell, and she glanced around to see if she was breaking any rules. Several people were roaming about, and none of them seemed to be paying her any attention, so her focus returned to Kate. "I thought I'd surprise you and take you to lunch…to celebrate."

"I told you on the phone it was too early for that."

"Um…okay," Brodie said quietly. "But I can still take you to lunch."

"I'm not hungry."

Brodie drew in another long, deep breath. Kate's tone was curt, and her scowl had yet to waver. If anything, it had become even more venomous. "Kate, what's wrong with you?"

"You shouldn't be here."

"Why?" Brodie said, looking around. "Nobody seems to care."

"*I* care, and I want you to go."

"Not until you tell me what this is all about," Brodie said softly. "Why are you so angry with me?"

"Brodie, I have things to do, and I am *not* prepared to stand here and discuss this. Now, please go, and we will talk about it later."

"Kate—"

"Brodie," Kate said through clenched teeth. "I asked you to leave. Now *do* it."

***

Brodie left the station with her head bowed, and her heart broken. Her chat with Stevie had raised her spirits, and Kate had just shattered them like a china plate thrown against a wall. She no longer had the strength to glue all the pieces back together again, and with each step she took, the shards of Brodie's compassion, patience, and hope were crushed under her feet. She climbed into her car, and running on autopilot, she headed back to her office.

She spent the rest of her day at her computer, filling her mind with absolutes. Geometry, algebra, trigonometry, and calculus were things Brodie could always depend on to give her the answers she sought, and in a way, they provided her comfort. This was something she knew. This was something she understood, and *this* was something Kate would never be able to give her. Brodie needed a solid foundation on which to build their lives, where doors and windows led out as well as in. A roof to weather any storm for it was constructed with trust and compassion, each beam fortified by mutual respect and understanding, and below that would be rooms and hallways filled with warmth. True, the walls built would divide the spaces, providing areas of privacy and places to hang photos, artwork, and high-end televisions, but they weren't there to hide behind. They weren't there to block out the reality of life that lived just outside the door. Their purpose had never been to barricade what one couldn't face...from what one could.

It wasn't until everyone else had left for the evening, that Brodie trudged from her office, loaded down with as much work as she could carry. She put a note on Stevie's desk with instructions for tomorrow, and after shutting out the lights, she locked the door and left the building. She made a few stops as she drove around town, buying things she didn't need but merely craved, and when she pulled into Kate's driveway and didn't see her car, Brodie turned off the engine and waited. It was the right thing to do, and it was the wrong thing to do. Without math to keep her company, Brodie would be alone with her thoughts for almost two hours.

***

Brodie cracked the window again to let the smoke of another cigarette escape. Rain coated the windshield and tapped against the roof, and even though the chill of the night invaded the car, Brodie's anger had kept her warm. How many times had she told herself to be patient? How many times had she reined in her temper or kept her feelings hidden to appease Kate? How many times had she allowed herself to be Kate's dirty little secret?

Headlights lit up Brodie's car as Kate pulled into the driveway, and taking one last drag of her smoke, Brodie rolled up the window and climbed out of the car. She flicked the cigarette into the grass and then slowly made her way toward the woman who supposedly loved her.

Kate smiled when she saw Brodie in the mirror, and gathering her attaché and handbag, she opened the door and stepped out into the drizzly night. "This is a nice surprise."

"We need to talk," Brodie said in a tone flat and lifeless.

"Of course," Kate said. "Let's get out of the rain. Shall we?"

Once inside, Kate dropped her things onto a chair and shaking the water off her raincoat, she hung it on the tree just inside the door. Turning to Brodie, Kate tilted her head slightly. "Have you been smoking? I thought you said you quit."

"I did, and I'll do it again," Brodie said, blankly staring at Kate. "Just not right now. It's been a rough day."

"I know what you mean," Kate said, regarding Brodie for a second. "So, I suppose you're here to apologize."

Brodie stiffened, and it was all she could do to speak without screaming. "Apologize for what?"

"For what you did today, of course."

"I didn't *do* anything today I need to apologize for, Kate."

"Sweetheart," Kate said, touching Brodie on the arm. "You came to the station."

"Yes, I did," Brodie said, pulling her arm away. "So what?"

"You know how I feel about those men finding out—"

"Jesus Christ, Kate, it wasn't like I was wearing a name tag saying 'Hi, my name is Brodie. I shag Kate.'"

"Don't be so crude," Kate said, and whipping around, she stomped to the kitchen. Stopping at the doorway, she looked back at Brodie. "I didn't ask you to come there, and I do *not* want you to do it again. Is that understood?"

Brodie clenched her fists and trotted after Kate. "Just who the fuck do you think you are talking to me like that? I'm not your bloody child."

"Then stop acting like one!"

"What the hell are you talking about?"

"I keep telling you I'm not ready, and you keep pushing, just like you did today. You waltzed in there, and in front of everyone, you tried to kiss me!"

"I was going to kiss you on the cheek, Kate. I wasn't trying to shove my tongue down your throat," Brodie yelled. "And if you could have pulled your homophobic head out of your arse for one bleeding second, you would have known that."

"I am *not* homophobic! Just because I don't feel the need to advertise who I sleep with like the rest of you, doesn't make me a homophobe."

"Maybe not in the true sense of the word, but you're just as scared of straights as some of them are of us," Brodie said, taking a step in Kate's direction. "You're absolutely terrified if people find out about us your world will crumble, but I'm a part of that world, Kate, and *I'm* crumbling. I can't do this anymore. I have never, *ever* been ashamed of what I am. I have never hidden it, and I can't, not even for you. Not anymore. Today you treated me like I was something disgusting, something that needed to be kept hidden, and that hurt, Kate. You tore my heart out this afternoon. Don't you get that?"

"Brodie, how many times do I have to tell you I just need time?"

"I am so *bloody* tired of you saying that," Brodie said, raising her voice again. "Why is it always about what *you* need, Kate—huh? *You* need time. *You* need privacy. *You* need me to be patient. It's always you, you, you. Well, *need* is a two-way street, Kate, and *I* need to be who I am. *I* need to be loved for what I am, and *I* need *you* to get off this fucking carousel. Make a decision, Kate. Either I'm a part of your life, or I'm not, but I am *not* hiding anymore. Do you get that? I am *not!*"

Thinking back to the arguments they'd had over the past several weeks, Kate knew this one wasn't going to end with unbridled sex on the floor, sofa, or stairs. This one was coming dangerously close to words that no apology would undo, and knowing she needed to defuse the bomb that was Brodie Shaw, when Kate spoke, her voice was soft. "Brodie, sweetheart, this promotion means a lot to me. All I need you to do is just wait—"

"Christ, you haven't heard a single word I've said."

"You're not *listening* to me," Kate said, taking a step closer to Brodie.

"Yes, I am. I hear you, Kate, loud and clear," Brodie said, her voice cracking with emotion. "You've got a plan for yourself, and it doesn't include me, not in the way I need to be included. You want a road easily followed, with no potholes or speed bumps to get in your way, and I'm a bump. Aren't I? Hell, I'm a bloody sinkhole."

"Brodie—"

"Kate, I need to *live* life, not hide behind walls and watch it pass by. I had no intention of doing anything today that would have given *anyone* in your office cause to question our relationship. All I was trying to do was take the woman I love out to lunch because I was *proud* of her, and that's where you and I differ so drastically. You see, I'm proud to have you in my life, Kate…and you're humiliated for me to be in yours."

Brodie turned and schlepped from the room. It took all the strength she had to put one foot in front of the other, and hanging her head, she headed for the door.

Kate gave chase, and catching up with Brodie, she grabbed her by the arm and spun her around. "Please don't do this, Brodie. Please just stay. We can talk."

Brodie slowly shook her head. "It's over, Kate. I've never been in love before, but I'm fairly certain it shouldn't hurt this much."

"But I love you."

"No, you don't," Brodie said, her eyes luminescent with unshed tears. "I was just a detour, Kate. A roundabout that you took by mistake, but now you're back on track and traveling down a one-way street toward a promotion which I truly hope you get." Brodie leaned down and placed a light kiss on Kate's cheek. "Goodbye, Kate. I wish you all the best. I really do."

Chapter Twenty-Seven

Kate sat alone in her lounge, thinking whoever said silence was golden was full of crap. There was nothing golden about listening to the thrum of an empty house. There was nothing golden about a phone that wouldn't chime with a text saying Brodie got home all right. There was nothing golden at all.

Her tears had started and stopped a dozen times over the past two hours, and wads of tissue littered the coffee table and floor. Kate looked over at the mess, but she didn't see it for what it was. She saw it as shrapnel, bits and pieces of a relationship destroyed...but by whom?

Kate picked up the bottle of wine and tipped the remaining few drops into her glass. Giving the spoonful of Chardonnay an evil look, Kate pushed herself off the sofa and went to the kitchen to open another bottle. She didn't really need the alcohol's ability to numb because Kate had already been anesthetized by Brodie's words and paralyzed by her actions. She had walked out the door, and she had walked out on them. So, was this Brodie's fault?

With a freshly-opened bottle of wine, Kate returned to the lounge and sank onto the sofa again. She filled her glass to the rim, and after taking a gulp, she leaned back and sighed. It wasn't Brodie's fault. Not totally. Not really. Not at all? She simply wanted something Kate saw as impossible, or rather...unnecessary?

Why was it so important to wear it on her sleeve? Just because others draped themselves in rainbows, why did Kate have to do the same? In the heat of a moment, Kate had found the strength to tell her mother, but if she could go back in time, would she do it again? Kate nodded to herself. Yes, she would do it again for Devon. Not for Brodie though. It hadn't been for Brodie, and it surely wasn't for herself...or was it? When do lies become truths?

If logic were applied, would the finger of fault indeed point toward Kate? It wasn't as if Brodie didn't know about Kate's fears. It wasn't as if it had been a secret recently uncovered. And why couldn't Brodie understand how important Kate's career was to her? Kate had never complained about Brodie's, never whined when a few hours on nights or weekends were spent with Brodie at her drafting table while Kate puttered about. It was what partners did, wasn't it? When does the rational become the irrational?

The answer was easy, yet Kate couldn't see it. The truth is always invisible when you're looking to blame someone else.

**

Stevie sprang to his feet when Devon walked in the door. "It's about bleeding time! What did you do, take the slow boat from China?"

Devon pursed her lips as she took off her coat. "We weren't in China. We were in Madrid on holiday, which you know, and we didn't get back until late last night."

"Didn't you get my text?"

"Yes," Devon said, holding up her phone. "'*Get to the office now. 999.*' I saw it as soon as I woke up, and here I am. So what's the problem? What did you do to your computer now?"

Stevie took a step in Devon's direction. "This isn't about my computer. It's about Brodie."

"Brodie?" Devon said, glancing at the door leading to Brodie's office. "What about her? What's wrong?"

"I don't know," Stevie said, lowering his voice. "While you were down in New Milton wiring up the Hirshfeld's cottage a couple of weeks ago, she worked from home, and last week, while you guys were on holiday, she did the same thing. She's churning out designs, don't get me wrong, but today's the first day she's actually been in the office for two weeks...and she looks like shit."

"Has Ethan seen her?"

"With the school conversion contract signed, he decided to take a ten-day holiday before all hell breaks loose with it. He won't be back for a few more days," Stevie said, moving even closer to Devon. "And honestly, Dev...she doesn't look like she has a few more days. Someone needs to talk to her, find out what's going on because—"

"All right," Devon said, holding up her hands. "All right. Make us some tea, will you? I'll go talk to her."

Before Devon reached Brodie's door, she had a feeling she knew exactly what was wrong. Other than one phone call from Kate telling Devon about a possible promotion a couple of weeks back, Devon hadn't heard from her sister. A few texts had been exchanged, simple touching-base words to let the other know they existed, and thinking back on those, Devon frowned. There hadn't been a mention of Brodie in any of them, and there hadn't been any talk of plans or dinners or restaurants or movies. They had only contained one or two words. Yes. No. Fine. Okay. All right.

Devon took a deep breath and opened the door. She walked inside and closing the door behind her, her eyes remained glued on the back of the woman sitting at the drafting table. "Hey, boss. How's it going?"

"It's going, Devon. What do you need?" Brodie stayed focused on the dual monitors in front of her for a few more seconds before she pushed the keyboard away and spun her chair around. "I said, what do you need?"

Devon took a half-step backward, giving herself a moment to regroup. Brodie usually didn't need any makeup to enhance what came naturally to her, and what she did use was minimal, but right now, Brodie needed a hell of a lot more than minimal. The deep shadows under her eyes made them appear sunken, and the hollows of her cheeks were even more pronounced due to the weight Brodie had lost. Her face was pale, and her hair was dull and mussed as if she'd climbed out of bed, put on her clothes, and left her house without ever looking in a mirror.

"I need you to tell me what's going on," Devon said, walking across the room. "Because you look like crap, Brodie. You look worse than crap."

"I've just had a couple of bad weeks," Brodie said, staring at the floor. "That's all."

"Bad, how?" Devon said, resting her hand on Brodie's arm.

Brodie pulled in a shuddering breath and raised her eyes, hating herself for the tears that appeared in them. "I ended it with Kate, and it's for good, this time. No going back. No trying again. It's over."

"Are you sure? Maybe—"

"Devon, I'm sure. We're at an impasse, a stalemate. I've already given all I can give and Kate…Kate can't get past her fears," Brodie said quietly. "I thought maybe she'd try to call, try to convince me to change my mind, give her yet another chance, but when a week went by, and she didn't, that told me all I needed to know. So, now I'm just trying to move on."

"She could still call."

"She won't, Devon. Trust me. We've been a dog chasing this tail for way too long, and I think she's finally realized that."

The despair in Brodie's voice cut Devon like a knife, and she blinked back the tears trying to form. "I'm so sorry, Brodie. I really, really am."

"There's nothing for you to be sorry about. You're awesome…and so is your sister. She and I just can't be awesome together. We see the world differently, opposite-sides-of-the-spectrum differently, and I got tired of fighting a battle I could never win. Hell, I couldn't even come close."

"So, instead of calling me, you starved yourself for two weeks?"

"I wasn't in the mood to talk to anyone right after…right after it happened. I just needed space, and then you went on holiday," Brodie said. "And I didn't starve myself on purpose. I wasn't hungry. I just wanted to work, so I put everything I had into that…and into fags. Jesus, my place stinks."

A thin grin appeared on Devon's face as she considered Brodie's wrinkled, untucked Oxford and a pair of jeans that had seen much better days. "Well, you don't stink, but you're not exactly dressed for success."

"I don't have any meetings today."

"Maybe not, but I think a long, hot shower and some clean clothes may make you feel a little better."

"I doubt it."

"How about we go find out?" Devon said, gesturing toward the door. "Let's take you home, and you can get cleaned up. If you feel like coming back afterward, we will."

"Honestly, Devon, I think I just need..." Brodie stopped and then chuckled under her breath. "I just need some more time. Now, where have I heard *that* before?"

"It doesn't matter," Devon said, pulling Brodie to her feet. "What matters is Stevie is out there worried sick about you, and I'm in here doing the same thing. You need to eat, Brodie. You need to sleep, and you need to heal, and between Gina and me and Stevie and Ethan, we're going to make sure that happens."

"What about taking care of your sister?"

"I'll be there for her, too, if she needs me. I won't lie to you about that. I love her like I love you, except right now, you're the one standing in front of me looking positively dreadful," Devon said, guiding Brodie toward the door. "Now, let's go. Time to get you home."

Brodie pulled up as Devon opened the door. "I don't want to know."

"What?"

"About Kate. I don't want to know how she's doing or...or if she gets the promotion. I need to cut all the ties, Devon. If I'm going to get through this, I can't have things reminding me of her. I have a brain full of those. All right?"

"Where does that leave me...and Gina?"

"It leaves you where you've always been," Brodie said, placing her hand over her heart. "You're in here, Devon, and you're my best friend. When I look at you, I don't see Kate. I see you. I see your funny grins and that unibrow you make when you're concentrating way too hard. I see a woman who's become so much more over the past few years. She's smart, and she's kind. She's hardworking, yet she can be a real loafer at times, and she has a beautiful partner named Gina, who I hope to know better as the years go by. You do *not* remind me of your sister, Devon. You remind me of everything that's *right* in the world...not everything that's wrong."

***

"We need a bigger fridge," Stevie announced, sashaying into Brodie's office. "That tiny one in the corner out there isn't working anymore."

"It's broken?" Brodie said, looking up from her desk.

"No, it's too small. I almost had to butter the sides of the three casseroles to make them fit."

"*Three*," Brodie said, rocking back in her chair. "Look, I know everyone means well, but between the food Gina and Devon are bringing to my flat, and what you've brought here for me to take home, I'm starting to feel like a goose being fattened for a meal."

"You know I'm going to be out of town for...for the upcoming holiday, and since you refuse to go with me and you're not going to your dad's, I wanted to make sure you had plenty to eat."

"Me and what army?"

Stevie hung his head, and Brodie's shoulders fell. "I'm sorry. I know you mean well."

"I do," Stevie said, flinging himself into a chair. "I want you to be happy and sassy and—"

"Fat?"

"No, but at least fill out the arse of your trousers."

Brodie folded her arms, and the corners of her mouth eased up just a bit. "I'm sorry, but are you saying you've looked at my arse?"

"No, I'm saying I've looked at your saggy pants, which are still saggy. Your arse is of no concern of mine."

"Good. For a minute, I thought you were switching sides."

"Oh, heaven forbid," Stevie said, faking a shudder. "The thought of it gives me the willies."

Brodie broke into a full smile. "Well, if we are done talking about my arse and your willies, I have something for you." Brodie opened her desk drawer and handed Stevie an envelope. "Merry Christmas, Stevie."

Stevie's mouth dropped open, his cheeks darkening a shade as he took the envelope. Even though Christmas was right around the corner, he had never once broached the idea of decorating the office, nor had he dared to mention the name of the upcoming holiday. It was a time of love and gift-giving, and while Brodie seemed to be doing better, Christmas and New Year's Eve were going to be tough. He knew it. Devon and Gina knew it...and they all knew Brodie knew it.

"You always do so much. I wasn't expecting anything."

"Shall I take it back?" Brodie said, holding out her hand.

"Not on your life," Stevie said, clutching the envelope to his chest.

Brodie let out a laugh, and Stevie beamed. He liked the fact he could make her laugh. He liked it a lot. "Can I open it now?"

"Of course," Brodie said, waving her hand. "Have at it."

In the time it takes a hummingbird's wing to flap, Stevie had the envelope ripped open and was staring at a check, the amount of which caused his lungs to empty in a whoosh. "Oh my, God," he said, looking at Brodie. "This is too much, Brodie. This is...this is way too much."

"No, it's not," Brodie said softly. "Stevie, you're the face of my company...of *our* company. You excel at everything you do, you juggle more balls in the air than I could ever think possible."

"Well, I am gay, you know?"

"I am not talking about *those* balls, and now you're giving me the willies," Brodie said, faking a shiver of her own. "I'm talking about you keeping this place running while I was away for two weeks licking my wounds. I'm talking about you greeting every client so professionally and brilliantly, they're almost ready to hire me, even before they walk through *my* door. I'm talking about you keeping the books balanced to the penny and making sure our people are paid as are the vendors, and fighting tooth and nail whenever a supplier tries to pull a fast one."

"They are slimy bastards at times."

"Yes, they can be," Brodie said as she leaned forward and pointed to the check. "*That* is my way of saying thank you. Thank you for being *you*. Thank you for calling Devon a few weeks back. Thank you for worrying. Thank you for...for your lovely casseroles and for always making me smile no matter how badly I may be feeling."

"It's a gift," Stevie said with a shrug.

"I truly think it is. You're a great friend, Stevie, and I couldn't ask for a better employee, and that's my small way of making sure you know it."

"It's hardly small."

"It's just a piece of paper with a few numbers on it, but I couldn't think of how else to show you how much I appreciate you because I do...more than *all* those numbers on that check."

Stevie sniffled back his emotions. "Oh, crap. I think my mascara is about to run."

"Then you better go home and fix it."

"Huh?"

"It's Thursday, and Christmas is Tuesday, and I know you've been avoiding bringing up *that* subject for weeks, something else I appreciate," Brodie said, and standing up, she walked around her desk. "So take that check, go pack up your satchel, and I'll see you next year. All right?"

Stevie sniffled again and got to his feet. "Is it sexual harassment if you give your boss a hug?"

"Absolutely not," Brodie said, opening her arms. "I wouldn't have it any other way."

***

Even though Brodie had given Stevie an early reprieve, she did not afford herself the same luxury. Instead, every morning, she got up, showered, dressed professionally, and headed to the office. Brodie found the routine helped her keep her mind on what she could control and not on what she couldn't. Since everyone else was away, there was no one to question her being in the office on Saturday or Sunday or even the twenty-fourth of December, and that, in and of itself, gave her peace. She was just a woman doing her job. Nothing more. Nothing less. She wasn't heartbroken. She wasn't alone. She wasn't being watched or reprimanded for skipping a meal. She was a responsible adult acting responsibly. She was doing what she wanted to do...and that worked until she left her office and returned to her home on Christmas Eve.

Brodie sat on the sofa, drumming her fingers against her thigh. It was harder at night to silence her thoughts, to quiet her memories, to breathe. She always managed, though, and she thought she would tonight as well, but Christmas was tomorrow, and Brodie was struggling. She wouldn't allow the tears to fall. Too many had already streamed down her cheeks. She wouldn't allow her anger to awaken. There was nothing to be angry about any longer. Brodie picked at a loose thread on her jeans. She was the one who had chosen not to go home this Christmas. She couldn't bear to face her family like this. Broken, somber...alone.

Brodie bolted upright and then flew off the sofa like she'd been burned. "Oh, no, you *fucking* don't," she said, practically running to the door. "You are *not* going to feel sorry for yourself. No fucking way. That's not who you are. That's not who you've ever been, and

I'll be damned if *she's* going to turn me into that!" Brodie snatched up her wallet and keys, and grabbing her coat, she escaped out the door.

As soon as Brodie left the building, she felt better. The air crisp, and what was left of the rain that had fallen earlier had turned into shiny patches of ice on the sidewalk. Her breath steamed around her as she carefully made her way to the car, zipping up her jacket and pulling up the collar as she went. She forgot her gloves, but Brodie didn't care. The cold felt good, and even though she didn't know where she was going, that mattered about as much as the location of her gloves. Brodie just wanted to drive. She just wanted to control something instead of it controlling her.

Not long after Brodie pulled onto the road, she flicked off the radio, preferring silence over the endless holiday classics playing on all the stations. She cracked the window and lit a cigarette, a habit that would soon end once and for all. Brodie had already set her quit date to be on the second of January, the same day she had scheduled to have her flat professionally cleaned. She knew they'd remove the smell of nicotine. If only they could remove the memories, too.

The light at the intersection turned red, and while she waited for it to change, Brodie mindlessly looked around. Neon still beckoned in a few bar windows, and the distant thump of bass had made it to the street, the music loud enough to wake the dead or perhaps silence the haunts of those on stools sipping ale. Brodie hadn't been looking at anything in particular until she saw some fairy lights draped in a shop window. Tiny twinkling, happy-go-lucky fairy lights put there to add festivity, and atop white velvet was a display of jewelry nestled amidst baubles of silver and blue. The light turned green, and Brodie stepped on the gas, but the joyousness of the season followed her. Electric candles propped in windows, wreaths on doors, inflatable snowmen, and wire-framed reindeer covered in lights seemed to be everywhere...and Brodie pressed on the accelerator just a bit more.

She continued for a few more miles, and with even more decorations coming into view, Brodie turned off the main road onto a side street, hoping the darkness and solitude of a way less traveled would clear her mind. It didn't, and with her jaw quivering and her eyes becoming as glassy as the pavement before her, Brodie fought against the vision her mind had created. She could have handled visions of past Christmases with her family gathered around the tree.

She could have even handled visions of a Sugar Plum Fairy dancing to Tchaikovsky. What Brodie couldn't handle was a vision of a Christmas that wasn't to be, with gifts overflowing, maybe a ring, maybe not? Would it have been too soon? She'd never know.

Brodie tried and failed to blink back the tears that stung at her eyes. As they overflowed and streamed down her cheeks, she lifted her foot off the gas pedal. Everything was becoming blurry, smeared by the salty result of sadness and pain, and unable to stop the sobs now choking her, when her eyesight cleared for a second, Brodie didn't think twice. Seeing a place to pull over, she stepped on the brakes, and in an instant, her car began to fishtail. She had forgotten the temperature had dropped, and the thin layer of water left on the street wasn't water at all. It was ice.

Chapter Twenty-Eight

Kate poured herself a glass of wine, and shuffling into the lounge, she relaxed back on the sofa. She took a sip of her drink before reaching for her mobile only to realize she'd left it somewhere else. How things had changed.

For the first few weeks after Brodie walked out on her, Kate's phone had never left her side. In her pocket or in her handbag, and when she showered, just outside the vinyl curtain, she kept it fully charged, and the volume always cranked, not that it mattered. Brodie hadn't called, and Kate refused to do so. The world wasn't black and white. She was no more wrong than Brodie was right. Gray was a color, too.

Kate's pragmatism enabled her to head off to work most days with her head held high. She wouldn't allow her emotions to distract her from her goals, but alone in her house was another story. She had lost count of how many nights had been spent flip-flopping between grief and anger, mourning the loss of the woman she loved one minute and then damning Brodie's ideology in the next.

Kate picked up the remote and turned on the TV only to turn it off almost as quickly. It hadn't held her interest in weeks, and tonight was no different, so tossing the remote aside, she went in search of her phone. She plodded from one room to the next until finally finding it in her bedroom, and returning to the lounge, she got settled and stared at the mobile in her hand. It gave her comfort in a way for held in its memory were Brodie's words. Dozens of texts with tiny emoji of hearts and winks filled a perpetual screen, and unable to stop herself, Kate opened her text messages again. She scrolled to the beginning and started re-reading the words born from love, playfulness, and promises. Some made Kate smile, and some made her laugh, and others made her cry as the memories of what she had lost came rushing back.

The promotion had also been lost, given to a man with a few more years under his tightly-cinched belt, so still partnered with Frank Daggett, Kate made the best of her horrible days and struggled to get through nights and weekends that seemed so much worse. Devon and Gina had tried to cheer her up, and insisting on another Saturday shopping spree, they had dragged her into the city, but Kate no longer had anyone to buy for. It didn't matter how much cleavage showed if Brodie wasn't leering at it, and why care about the color or style of undergarments if Brodie wasn't there to remove them? And as she had stood on a street corner while Devon and Gina browsed an adult store for items to accentuate their love life, Kate grew jealous. How could it be so easy for them to hold hands in public? Couldn't they see the heads turn when they stole a quick kiss? Didn't they know what people thought when they walked through those doors? Why didn't they care?

Christmas came and went without so much as a fa la la. Like she had done the year before, Kate took on as many extra shifts as possible. There wasn't really any reason not to, and while she had managed to get through a Christmas Eve dinner with Gina and Devon, Christmas day became like any other. Go to work, come home, pour some wine, get lost in her thoughts, and cry...just like today.

Kate choked back her emotions and tossed her phone aside. It had been nearly two months since Brodie had walked out of her house, and Kate was no better now than she had been then. She thought it would get easier as the days went by, but she'd been as stupid about that as she had about so many other things. Stupid to believe Brodie would call, stupid to believe work could fill the void, stupid to believe time would stop her heart from bleeding, and stupid about the sheer doggedness of this thing called love.

Love wasn't a thing Kate could best by intelligence or cunning. Love wasn't an object casually tucked away in a drawer and forgotten. Love wasn't a place from which she could escape for it followed her wherever she went like a shadow lurking right over her shoulder, reminding her, mocking her, and pummeling her at every twist and turn. Kate hadn't been able *not* to fall in love with Brodie. How stupid was it to believe she would ever fall *out* of love with her no matter how much time she was given?

Kate took a sip of her wine and glanced at the clock. The New Year had apparently arrived an hour earlier, and she hadn't noticed. In a way, she had hoped it would bring with it some miraculous sense of closure, so she could move on, but Kate had yet to realize love didn't work like that. Love didn't own a wristwatch. Love had its own set of rules, and it did not play fairly. Love did *not* like to lose, and in one way or another, it was hell-bent on proving it to Kate.

***

Brodie stepped into the construction trailer at the Cardinal Avenue project, and taking off her hard hat and coat, she placed them on top of a file cabinet. Ethan was sitting at his desk at the other end of the trailer, talking over a schedule with one of the foremen, and Brodie waited until the man walked out before she turned to her brother. "Happy New Year."

Ethan pushed aside the schedule and looked up. "Happy New Ye—" Ethan's eyes bulged. Brodie was sporting two black eyes, and her right hand was in a cast. "What the hell happened to you?" he said, jumping to his feet.

"I had a bit of an accident."

"What? When?"

"On Christmas Eve."

"Christmas Eve?" Ethan said, rushing around his desk. "Why the fuck didn't you call us?"

Brodie shrugged. "There wasn't any point."

"It sure as hell looks like there was a point!" Ethan said, quickly guiding Brodie to a chair.

"Will you relax," Brodie said, chuckling as she sat down. "I'm fine. It looks a lot worse than it is, and once I got out of surgery—"

"*Surgery?*" Ethan shouted, waving his arms about. "What the hell happened? What kind of accident are we talking about?"

"I guess you could call it a car accident."

"A car accident? Were you drunk?"

"Don't be daft," Brodie said, shooting Ethan a look. "Of course, I wasn't drunk. I was driving around to clear my head. I hit a patch of ice and lost control of the car—"

"Jesus *fucking* Christ!"

"Will you *please* calm down?" Brodie said with a laugh. "I didn't crash the car."

"You just said—"

"Ethan, calm the fuck down. I didn't crash the car," Brodie said, holding up her casted hand. "This happened after I got it under control and pulled off the road."

"What the hell are you talking about?"

"I got out to...to just pull myself together before driving home. It was dark, and I tripped over a tree root."

"You did what?"

"Do I really need to repeat it?" Brodie said, eyeing the man standing next to her. "I feel stupid enough without having to repeat it."

"So, you didn't *wreck* the car?"

"Christ, you're like an old mother hen," Brodie said, laughing again. "I did *not* wreck my car. I wrecked my nose, my wrist, and a few bones in my hand, and once I realized I couldn't drive, I called for a tow, and they were nice enough to drop me off at the hospital on the way."

Ethan plopped down in the other chair and surveyed the damage. Brodie's hand was encased in plaster from her fingertips halfway up her forearm, and under both eyes were splotches of greenish-purple bruises. He leaned in and studied her a bit more closely. "Well, at least your nose is still straight."

"Yeah, it was a minor break. Unfortunately, my hand wasn't. They had to go in to fix the damage, which is why I needed surgery, but I was in and out the same day. So, like I said, it was no big deal."

"Dad is going to have a fit when he finds out."

"Then let's not tell him. At least not right now. The last thing I need is Dad hovering over me."

Ethan looked at his sister for another long moment before pushing himself out of his chair. "You want a cuppa?"

"Yeah, that would be great. Thanks."

"So..." Ethan said, going over to the coffee pot. "You said you were out trying to clear your head. Should I assume it was because of your break-up with Kate?"

"Yes," Brodie said quietly. "It was a rough night, and I thought some fresh air would do me good. Unfortunately, once I started seeing all the Christmas shit, my emotions got the better of me. I started to cry and knew I needed to stop so I could regroup...and you know the rest of the story."

"I'm sorry you're hurting."

Brodie held up her casted hand. "It doesn't really hurt, at least not anymore."

"I wasn't talking about that. I was talking about your heart."

"Oh."

"But maybe you two will get back together. You did the last time."

Brodie leaned back in her chair. A few weeks after she and Kate had returned from Bournemouth, Brodie told her family that she and Kate had broken up. It wasn't a lie because after the night in the hostel, their friendship had ended, and it quickly stopped her family from mentioning Kate in conversation. But lies have a way of taking on a life of their own...if you let them.

"Yeah," Brodie said, looking at Ethan. "About that."

***

They sat there for almost an hour as Brodie confessed her sins. There was only one in Ethan's mind, a tiny lie told about a make-believe relationship that eventually turned into a real one, and as Brodie spoke about that weekend at their father's, her emotions began to bubble to the surface. Before too long, through tears and sobs, she told Ethan everything. About a woman she loved more than she ever thought possible, about endless arguments behind doors always closed, and how, in the end, Brodie had to walk away or fear losing what Ethan had never realized was a privilege. Being yourself.

Thinking back over the years, Ethan tried to remember the last time he had seen his sister cry. Even though he was the oldest, Brodie had always been the strongest. Skinned knees, broken bicycles, and football losses all seemed somehow more manageable with Brodie by his side. Now the tables were turned, and Ethan didn't hesitate. As

Brodie had done for her brothers so many times before, he wrapped his arms around his sister and held her tightly.

Brodie's words spun in Ethan's head, and he damned the world, and he damned Kate. There was nothing wrong with his sister. There was nothing wrong with wanting to live your own bloody life. There was nothing wrong with being who you are. Ethan hung his head, and tears pooled in his eyes. What the fuck was wrong with some people?

Before too long, fearing he'd start blubbering like a little girl, Ethan sniffled back his tears and went about making another pot of coffee. The time gave them both a chance to regroup, and when he returned to Brodie and handed her a fresh cup, their eyes were no longer red, and their noses were no longer running. "Here you go."

"Thanks," Brodie said, taking the drink.

Ethan sunk into his chair and stared at the cup in his hands for a moment. "Not to continue beating this horse, but it's really hard to believe that when you and Kate were up at Dad's, you weren't...uh...you weren't..."

"No, we weren't," Brodie said, grinning. "It was just an act."

"I'm sorry."

"You have nothing to be sorry about. I'm the one who lied."

"Yeah, but it's because we were always trying to fix you up."

"You were just doing what you thought was right."

Ethan slowly bobbed his head. "So...were we ever?"

"Ever what?"

"Right about the women we pushed on you? Any of them ever turn your head?"

"No."

"Oh."

"But that's okay," Brodie said, and setting her cup on the desk, she spun it around so she could hold it properly. "You were doing it out of love. I know that."

Ethan mindlessly took a sip of his coffee while he watched his sister struggle with hers. "Oh, Christ. Is that going to cock things up?" he said, staring at Brodie's cast. "You're right-handed."

"I am, and that's another reason why I didn't call anyone. I didn't need you around while I fumbled with trying to zip my jeans."

"Oh, I don't know. We did bathe together when we were children. That's not too far of a stretch."

Brodie scrunched up her face. "Do you have *any* idea how many things are wrong with that statement?"

"I was just joking, sis," Ethan said, snickering. "The last thing I want to do is see your bits and pieces, but seriously, Brodie, are you going to be able to manage? I know you use CAD, but left-handed?"

"Tell me about it," Brodie said with a laugh. "The first time I tried to use the stylus, I definitely felt challenged, but once I switched over to the mouse, things got a little easier. So, the only thing I cocked up was my ability to drive a car and tie my shoes. When it comes to designing, I should be okay."

"Good," Ethan said, glancing at Brodie's work boots. Tickled to see the laces dangling, he leaned over and tied them, and when he popped up again, he was wearing a wide and toothy smile. "Because you're going to be a *very* busy girl."

"I know. I've got twenty-four flat designs I have to finish for this job."

"That's not what I'm talking about."

"Huh?"

"You remember that condo remodel we did for the Jacobs?"

"Of course. It was an investment property. They sold it shortly after we were through remodeling it."

"At twice what they paid."

"Seriously?"

"Yep, and Mr. Jacobs called first thing this morning. He and his wife want to hire us to do another job, which means it's time for me and you to either shit or get off the pot."

"What in the world are you talking about?"

"Brodie, they've been sitting on two empty buildings, and they've finally got the capital to convert them. One's an old church they want to turn into an upscale home, and the other is a factory they want to remodel into apartments. They're thinking four or possibly even six flats. Could be more depending on what you come up with."

"What!"

"So, all those chats we've had about expanding the business may need to be put into play. We don't have enough employees to do the work unless we hire more, and we can't hire more, unless we have someone to help with all the paperwork. I can't do the invoices, hire all the subs, handle the suppliers, and run the sites, too. We either turn this down or expand."

"Shit."

"Does that mean no?"

The past week had given Brodie a lot of time to think, and unlike the previous weeks when her thoughts would always return to Kate, that hadn't happened, at least not as much. Between recuperating from the accident and adapting to being left-handed, when Brodie's head hit the pillow at night, she fell into a welcomed dreamless sleep. Being busy was Brodie's friend, and Brodie needed a friend. She looked over at Ethan. "Do the Jacobs want to start right away?"

"No, not for a few more months. Why?"

"Because it looks like we're expanding."

***

That night, Brodie stepped out of the lift, her attaché slung over one shoulder, tubes containing blueprints tucked under her arm, and a bag filled with enough Chinese food to feed an army dangling from her fingertips. She noticed a box on the floor as she approached her flat, and after placing the bag down long enough to unlock the door, she picked up her dinner, pushed the box inside with her foot, and kicked the door closed behind her.

A short time later, after devouring a couple of egg rolls, Brodie retrieved the box sent by her father. Every few months, he would send her a care package filled with nibbles and the like, along with a few paperbacks he thought she'd like, so she wasn't at all surprised until she opened the box. Seeing the envelope on top, she ripped it open and read the words he had written.

My darling Brodie –

After all that's happened, I wasn't sure what to do with what was supposed to be your Christmas present, so I thought I'd let you make that decision. The other things I had forgotten to give you when last you visited, although I did keep a few. I hope you don't mind.

Give your father a call when you're up to it. I miss hearing your lovely voice.

Love, Dad

Brodie set aside the note, and removing some crumpled newspaper from the box, she pulled out a large brown envelope and dumped its contents onto the table. Brodie instantly beamed. The sketches and drawings that had hung on the walls of her childhood room were now in front of her, and picking up a few, Brodie ran her finger along the outlines of houses drawn in crayon and colored pencil. "Thanks, Dad," she whispered, setting them aside.

At the bottom of the box was a photo album, and Brodie flipped it open without giving it a second thought. A moment later, tears welled in her eyes for inside were the photographs Harrison had taken when Brodie and Kate had visited for his birthday.

One by one, Brodie looked at the pictures filling the pages. The posed ones made her laugh, remembering her father's order to repeatedly say cheese, and she grinned at the innocence and precociousness sparkling in the eyes of her nephew and niece. She gazed lovingly at the ones showing her and her brothers, three peas in a pod so different yet so alike, and all a spitting image of their father either in looks or in attitude...and then there were those of Kate.

Brodie took a deep breath, struggling not to stare, struggling not to care, struggling not to remember, but when she reached the candid shots, Brodie lost her battle. As she fought back the tears, Brodie gathered up the album and headed into her bedroom, placing it on her nightstand for safekeeping. Tomorrow, she'd put it away, tuck it into a closet or a drawer and try to forget it existed, but for tonight, it would remain close at hand...just in case she found the strength to look at it again.

Chapter Twenty-Nine

By the end of February, the business plan Brodie and Ethan had written up a year earlier was now well underway. Their initial idea included finding new office space large enough to hold their accounting and clerical staff as well as offices for the partners in the company. They both thought it would be the hardest part of the expansion when, in fact, it became the easiest. With the office next to Brodie's vacant, in less than a week, she had signed the lease, and a day later, Ethan and his crew showed up and got to work. Walls came down, and walls went up until finally, they had a conference room, an administrative area, his and her bathrooms, four more private offices, and a break room complete with a fridge large enough to hold as many casseroles as Stevie could carry.

Much to Stevie's surprise, he was given a promotion that Ethan and Brodie knew was well deserved. Although it meant he had to leave his post at the reception area behind him, the face of the company did not disappear behind drywall and studs. Instead, the outer walls of all the offices were now glass, and the Chief Financial Officer, in all his rainbow glory, could be seen by whoever walked into the offices of Spaces by Shaw.

A hiring melee followed with Stevie reviewing every application before they ever found their way to Brodie's desk until, eventually, they had an accounting clerk, a junior architect, and a new receptionist. It had been two hectic months filled with long hours, mountains of paperwork, endless interviews, not to mention visiting clients and jobsites, and as Brodie hoped it would, being busy helped.

Brodie leaned back, moving her head this way and that to work out the stiffness that had settled after spending the past few hours putting the finishing touches on another design. She let out a long breath as she got to her feet, and removing the splint she was still forced to wear, Brodie tossed it aside and walked from her bedroom. She snagged her coat from the back of a dining room chair, and tugging it on, she went into the kitchen to grab a bottle of lager from the fridge before she headed to the roof.

The air was crisp, and breathing it in, Brodie went over and sat on a bench, swinging one leg over the other as she took a few swallows of her beer. She let a rather large belch escape a few seconds later, and snorting out a laugh, she took another swig of her drink and looked up. The night sky was speckled by a thousand tiny lights, and Brodie marveled at the sight. Like her hand, the healing process had been slow, yet the ache in her heart *had* eased just a bit.

At first, whenever she found herself thinking about Kate, Brodie would get angry. She would spend the rest of the day taking it out on innocent friends and unsuspecting strangers until one night when she sat under the stars, she saw one shining brighter than the rest. It was then when Brodie realized her bitterness was poisoning the only thing she had left of Kate. Memories.

To be enraged, suddenly made no sense. Love was an amazing gift, and for a few short months, Brodie had shared it with an incredible woman, and to be angry at the loss of it was selfish. After all, she was still in love with Kate. Even though she was no longer in her arms, Kate was still in Brodie's life. She lived on the roof where they had once kissed and in the shower where they had made love amidst foam and steam. Kate was in the bedroom, lying across black sheets with her hair glistening in the candlelight, and she was in the game room, challenging Brodie to a game of eight ball that neither would win. It was impossible not to smile as the memories flooded Brodie's mind. She couldn't help it. She was in love.

Brodie finished her beer and pushed herself to her feet. She pulled out her phone and sighed when she saw the time. She felt like it was midnight, and it wasn't even ten.

***

Four weeks later, Brodie was running on fumes. She had pushed herself each and every day, rushing here and there and everywhere, and the workload had all but removed Kate from her mind. It had also taken its toll. Three designs were in the rubbish bin due to mistakes she would never have made before, and earlier in the day, she snapped at Stevie for no reason at all. The look on his face was all it took to convince Brodie that everyone needed a break.

"Where is everybody?"

"Well, hello to you, too," Brodie said, looking up from filling her attaché. "And don't I count?"

"Of course, you count," Devon said, walking to the desk. "But no one else is here."

"I sent them home early."

"All of them?"

Brodie grinned. "Apparently."

"Why?"

"Because it's Friday and everyone has been working their arses off for weeks. I thought it would be a nice gesture."

"How come I didn't get the memo?"

"I thought you and Gina were already on your way to spend ten days shushing down the slopes in France," Brodie said, closing her briefcase.

"Our flight doesn't leave for a few hours, so I'd thought I'd just stop by and drop off some purchase orders before I go pick her up. I put them on Stevie's desk."

"Okay," Brodie said, looking up. "And I didn't know you knew how to ski."

"I haven't been in years, but Gina found this terrific deal online for a small resort in Les Houches. It's more for beginners and intermediate skiers, so I should be okay. And if push comes to shove, I'll sit in front of a fireplace sipping cocoa while she plays in the snow."

"Well, I hope you both have a great time," Brodie said, picking up her briefcase.

"Thanks," Devon said as she noticed an insulated bag on the desk. "Let me guess. Another casserole from Stevie?"

Brodie glanced at the bag. "Yes," she said, pushing her chair under the desk. "Thankfully, I've finally got him down to bringing in just one a week, plus he's letting me slip him some cash to cover the cost, too. And I wasn't about to say no to his lamb casserole."

"Oh, I love his lamb casserole."

"Too bad. It's mine," Brodie said, picking up the cooler bag. "Is there anything else?"

"Wait," Devon said, glancing at her watch. "It's not even four. You're leaving early, too?"

"Yes, I am."

"You have a date?" Devon said without thinking.

Brodie smiled when she saw Devon's cheeks darken. "Yes, with an empty apartment and a lamb casserole," she said, giving Devon a quick peck on the cheek. "I think I've finally worn myself out, so I'm going to take the weekend and relax. No work. No computer. No designs. No contracts. Just me, some food, some books...and some wine."

"Are you okay?"

Brodie looked down her nose at Devon. "I thought we both agreed you'd stop asking me that."

"Sorry," Devon said, slumping her head forward. "Hard habit to break, I guess."

Brodie put her finger under Devon's chin and lifted her head. "I know you mean well, but I'm fine. I'm just tired. I'm not depressed. I'm not sad. I'm not anything...except tired. All right?"

"Okay."

"Good, now let's get the hell out of here."

***

"Come on, get a move on," Frank Daggett barked, yanking open the car door. "The weekend is right around the corner, babe, and the quicker we get back to the station, the quicker I can meet up with my mates at the pub."

Kate's posture drooped even further. Frank being in a rush for anything, was never good. With paperwork, it meant she would spend hours filling in all the blanks he left, and with driving, it meant yet another harrowing jaunt through the city.

She had spent practically the entire day in the car with Daggett, and as far as Kate was concerned, she didn't want to spend another— *ever*. Her personal life was already shit, and there was no reason to compound it with a professional one that followed suit. After trying for months to find a way to work with the man, Kate had come to the conclusion that Frank was a loathsome misogynist who had no intention of ever changing his ways. So, as much as she abhorred the race she was about to enter, getting back to the station in record time would mean Kate could request to rid herself of her partner that much quicker.

A sliver of a smile appeared on Kate's face as she walked to the car. With Frank's Mustang in the shop and his machismo preventing him from being seen in Kate's sub-compact, today they'd been driving around town in a standard-issue police vehicle. The BMW was a few years old, but it was clean. It didn't smell of cigarettes, and brightly checkered in yellow and blue, it could easily be spotted by naïve drivers who actually believed all police officers practiced what they preached.

Kate got into the car, slammed the door, and fastened her seat belt. She tugged at the restraint, and tightening its grip on her body, she waited for the inevitable. Frank started the engine, and with a jerk, they were off, the sounds of screeching tires behind them signaling Frank's chronic disregard for everyone else on the road, no matter what car he was driving.

As usual, Frank drove at lightning speed through the streets of London, weaving in and out of traffic and laughing under his breath each time he forced another vehicle to slow or swerve. Unconsciously, Kate yanked her seatbelt tighter as they narrowly missed yet another parked car, but it wasn't until a pedestrian walking too slowly to meet Frank's standard had to dart out of the way when Kate had reached her limit for the day. "Could you *please*, for the love of God, just slow down? There's too much traffic to drive like this. You're going to get someone killed."

"Christ, do you ever not whine?" Frank said, glancing at Kate. "You have been on my bloody back for months about my driving, and we're both still here, aren't we? So, do us both a favor, Kate, and just shut the fuck up about it already. All right?"

Kate wanted to unleash on Frank, let loose all the rage that had been building inside of her, but most of it didn't belong to him. Most of it belonged to Kate, and it had gnawed at her for months, so she bit her tongue. The less she talked, the more Kate prayed Frank would keep his eyes on the road. After all, the traffic *was* bad, and eventually, he'd *have* to slow down. No sooner had the thought crossed Kate's mind when she felt the BMW lurch forward.

"Son-of-a-*bitch!*" Frank snarled, slamming on the brakes to avoid a dark blue sedan that had pulled out of a side street. A moment later, he flipped the switch controlling the blue warning lights and gave chase.

"Frank, what in the hell are you doing?"

"He ran a stop sign, love. Didn't you see him?"

"*You've* run at least four of them today, Frank. Just call the plate into the traffic unit, and let's get back to the station. Shall we?"

Frank's lips twisted into a sneer. "Not on your life, Kate. That lad broke the law, and I'm going to make sure he knows it," he said, pressing the accelerator to the floor.

Kate watched as the speedometer began to climb, and as each hash mark came and went, the moisture in her mouth evaporated. "Frank, please, you need to slow down. This is crazy."

"Sorry, love, but that bloke's speeding," Frank said as he maneuvered the BMW across two lanes of traffic before returning to the first. "And I gotta catch him."

Kate looked up the road. They were approaching a busy intersection, and relaxing just a bit, Kate put her hand on the dash, preparing for when Frank would step on the brakes, but as they neared the junction, Kate stiffened. They weren't slowing down. They were going even faster.

"Frank, what in the hell are you doing," Kate yelled. "The light's red for God's sake. You have to *stop!*"

"I have no intention of stopping, Kate," Frank said as an arrogant smirk smeared its way across his face. "Don't you know? It's called going on red."

It was like a dream. A slow-motion kaleidoscopic minute of Kate's life filled with snippets of reality and sounds of terror. The front wheels of the BMW crossed the point of no return, and she heard the screech of tires, the crunch of metal, and the shrieks of fear. A horn blared and then another, and then the world spiraled out of control. They were hit in the side, the force spinning the car once, twice, and then Kate lost count. Her head hit the passenger window, but before the pain could register, she was being pushed back in the other direction, and suddenly, there was another scream. It was Kate's.

Brick, red and mortared, seemed to be chasing them, or was it the other way around, and then there was a force so strong it drove the air from her lungs. A deafening explosion followed, and for a split-second, Kate couldn't breathe...and then the world went black.

Chapter Thirty

Kate sat on the bed with her feet dangling over the side, staring at her torn nylons, bloodied legs, and the splotches of black and blue that had already begun to form. She drew in a breath, wincing as her lungs and chest announced their location, and ever so slowly, she buttoned what was left of her blouse. There wasn't a part of her that didn't ache, and she'd already been told by the doctors that it would get worse before it got better.

She had a concussion, courtesy of the window, and scratches, scrapes, and bruises seemed to be everywhere. X-rays and scans showed no breaks, punctures, or skull fractures, and when quizzed on her name, address, and phone numbers, Kate had passed with flying colors. She was told the dizziness and nausea would pass in a few days, as would the headache, and properly treated, the cuts she had received wouldn't scar...not that Kate cared. She was alive. That's all that mattered.

"How are you feeling?" Elliott said, peeking around the curtain.

Without thinking, Kate popped up her head and immediately regretted it as a bolt of pain shot down her neck and across her shoulders. "I'm okay," Kate said, trying to hide her grimace. "What are you doing here?"

"Are you kidding? Half the department is outside."

"Really?"

"We almost lost two of our own today. You really think we wouldn't be here?"

"Oh right," Kate said, lowering her eyes. "Sorry, I...uh...I wasn't thinking."

"Understandable," Elliott said, nodding.

"How's Frank?"

"Two busted legs, so he won't be putting the pedal to the medal anytime soon." As soon as Elliott saw Kate frown, he said, "Kate, it's no secret Frank likes to drive fast. We've all heard you two argue about it at the station."

"I suppose," Kate said, looking down at her hands.

Elliott's eyebrows knitted. He wanted to tell Kate he thought Frank was an arrogant prick. He wanted to tell Kate that none of this was her fault. He wanted to tell Kate all the details he knew about the accident, implant the truth in case some was lost in the fog of Kate's concussion, but like the woman across the way, Elliott had taken an oath. He had sworn to do his job with fairness, integrity, diligence, and impartiality, so Elliott bit his tongue...hard.

"You know what?" Elliott said a little louder than he intended. "We really shouldn't be talking about any of this until the investigators are done with their interviews."

"I'm surprised they're not in here already."

"The doctor told them to back off," Elliott said with a laugh. "Between the concussion and the drugs, they said your mind wouldn't be clear for a few days."

Kate drew in a slow breath. "Can you tell me if anyone else was hurt?"

"I'm not sure if—"

"Please? Please, Elliott. I need to know if anyone else was hurt."

Elliott's resolve wavered when he heard the emotion in Kate's voice, and he let out a long breath. "Yeah, a few," he said. "Five already went home. Two are still in surgery, and the other two are supposed to be released sometime later tonight after they're done with some tests."

"Shit."

"If it helps, I was told nothing was life-threatening."

"It doesn't help," Kate said, locking eyes with Elliott. "It doesn't help at all."

"You weren't driving, Kate," Elliott said, and then a split-second later, he held up his hands. "And I really need to stop interjecting and do what I'm supposed to be doing."

"Which is?"

"The Chief said your sister is out of town, so I volunteered to be your taxi since the doctors said you're refusing to spend the night," Elliott said, and taking a few steps, he looked Kate in the eye. "That is unless you've changed your mind about staying?"

"No. I hate hospitals," Kate said, wrinkling her nose. "They smell funny."

Elliott's eyes creased at the corners. "Yeah, I know what you mean," he said, glancing at the door. "Well, let me go find you some wheels, and we'll get you out of here. Be right back."

As soon as Elliott left the room, Kate closed her eyes in hopes the room would stop spinning. When she opened them again, Elliott was standing in front of her with a wheelchair.

"Look...um...you're a bit gray," he said softly. "Are you sure you don't want to stay the night? The doctors said you're pretty banged up and—"

"Please...please, I don't want to stay here," Kate mumbled. "I don't want to stay here."

"Okay, then let's get you into this thing," Elliott said, locking the wheels on the chair. Seeing a handbag on the bed, he picked it up. "Is this yours?"

"Um...yeah."

"All right, I've got it," he said, slinging the handbag over his arm.

Elliott watched as Kate, moving slower than he thought possible, stood and took a few baby steps toward the chair. Once she slumped into the seat, he let out the breath he'd been holding, unlocked the wheels, and began to push her from the room.

"Wait," Kate said, holding up her hand. "Is everyone still outside? I'm really tired, and I don't think I want—"

"You don't have to worry about that. Once I offered to be your driver, the Chief told everyone else to get out of here. The coast is clear."

"Oh...good."

Elliott didn't say a word as he pushed Kate through the hospital and car park, all the while smiling at the nurses, doctors, and orderlies he passed along the way. Kate's head remained bent until they reached the car, and it seemed to Elliott that it took every ounce of strength Kate had to get herself out of the chair and into the car. He shut the door, and handing off the wheelchair to an attendant, Elliott trotted to the driver's door and climbed inside just in time to hear Kate cry out in pain.

"Jesus, what's wrong?" he said, swiveling in his seat. "Should I go get someone?"

"No," Kate said, agony carved into her face. "I...I just can't buckle this. It hurts."

"Hold on. I got it," Elliott said, and taking the seat belt from her hand, he let it slowly retract. His eyes met Kate's, and he winked. "I won't tell if you won't."

"Thanks," Kate said, closing her eyes.

"So, where do you live?" Elliott said, starting the car.

"I...um...I don't want to go home," Kate said softly. "There's nothing there for me."

"That's not a problem. We can stop at a market on the way. Just tell me what you need, and I'll go in and get it."

"No," Kate said, opening her eyes. "That's...um...that's not what I mean."

"Okay," Elliott said, flashing a quick grin. "So, where would you like to go then? I'll take you anywhere you like. I just want to make sure you're safe."

Kate didn't even need to think about the answer. "Brodie's."

"Who's Brodie?"

"She's my..." Kate stopped, allowing the memories to flow freely. Easy banter and a suggestive glint in eyes brown and beautiful, whispered words and endless sighs, heated arguments and equally heated lovemaking, and then the sounds of a crash filled her head...a crash that could have ended her life.

Kate took a slow breath, grimacing at the pain in her chest as her lungs expanded. She slowly turned to look at Elliott, and the softest of smiles graced her face. "She's my partner."

***

Brodie placed what remained of the casserole in the refrigerator, and picking up the stress ball on the counter, she began her nightly routine. Walking through her flat, she tidied with one hand while she exercised the other with the soft rubber until Brodie finally ended up back where she started. She tossed the ball onto the sofa, and grabbing a beer from the fridge, she made her way through the flat.

She climbed the stairs leading to the roof, and as she opened the door, she heard what sounded like her doorbell. Brodie stopped for a second to listen, totally forgetting the door had an automatic closer until it slammed on her hand. "Fuck me!" she howled, and clutching her hand against her chest, she sat on the step, rocking as she waited for the pain to pass. "*Fuck* me."

It took almost a minute before Brodie was willing to inspect the damage, and she held her breath, praying she hadn't just broken her hand again. She held it out slowly, and seeing no bruising or cuts, Brodie flexed her fingers and wrist, finally daring to exhale when everything moved without incident. "Thank God," she said, getting to her feet just as the doorbell rang for the third time.

Brodie stomped down the stairs, her anger at her own stupidity about to be let loose on whoever was disturbing her peace. She took a quick drink of her beer as she marched through the flat, and slamming the bottle down on the kitchen counter, she went over and yanked open the door.

For a few seconds, Elliott and Brodie stared at each other. Both were trying to place where they'd met before, and while one was taking the time to connect the dots, the other wasn't so patient.

"Just who the hell are you?" Brodie snapped. "And what the hell do you want?"

"My name's Elliott. I'm a friend of Kate's," Elliott said, glancing to his left as Kate stepped into view. Without giving it a thought, he wrapped his arm around her waist as she began to sway.

The instant Brodie saw Kate, her anger faded, but when the handsome stranger put his arm around Kate's waist, Brodie went from zero to sixty in a split-second. "Well, I see it didn't take you long to find what you were looking for," she growled, glaring at Kate.

Brodie didn't know that Kate's escort now had his hands fisted, and she didn't know that his jaw was set because all her attention was on Kate. Blinded by her own annoyance, it took a few seconds for Brodie to notice Kate's appearance. Her coat was torn and dirty. Her face was chafed, and the look in her eyes was dull and blank.

"Kate?" Brodie said, moving a bit closer. She waited for a moment, and when Kate didn't reply, Brodie looked toward Elliott for answers. "What's going on?"

"She was in a car accident today."

"What? When? Is she all right?" Brodie said, looking back and forth between the two people standing in her doorway. "Kate...Kate, are you okay?"

"Do you think we can come in?" Elliott said, adjusting his hold on Kate.

"Oh, Christ," Brodie said, stepped back to let them enter. "Yes, of course. Come in. Please come in."

As soon as Brodie closed the door behind them, she leaned down to look Kate in the eye. "Kate, are you all right?" Again, Kate didn't answer, and again, Brodie looked at Elliott for guidance.

"They gave her something to help her relax, and something for the pain," Elliott said, putting Kate's handbag on the floor.

"Pain?" Brodie said, standing straight. "Wait. Should she even be here? Why isn't she in the hospital?"

"Her injuries aren't serious," Elliott said, keeping his voice low. "They did *suggest* that she spend the night, but she refused. I work with her, so I volunteered to take her home."

Brodie's eyes traveled from Elliott's zippered hoodie to his baggy sweat pants and back again. "You're a copper?"

"Yeah. I was just going for a run after work when the call came in. It sounded bad, so I jumped in my car and went to see if I could help."

Brodie barely managed a nod before her attention was drawn back to Kate. "Kate...can you hear me?"

Through the fog of muscle relaxants and painkillers, Kate managed to dip her head slowly, blanching at the ache the simple movement had caused. She raised her eyes, and when she found Brodie's, she whispered, "I'm tired. Can I...can I stay here tonight? Please...please, Brodie, can I?"

Brodie's heart was breaking. All she wanted to do was hold Kate, comfort her, and tell her she still loved her, yet she couldn't. Brodie knew all too well about Kate's fears of being outed, so when she spoke, she chose her words carefully. "Of course, you can, Kate. That's what friends are for." Brodie moved closer, and as Elliott removed his arm from Kate's waist, Brodie's took its place. "Now, let's get you into bed."

At a turtle's pace, Brodie guided Kate toward the bedroom, glancing back at Elliott as she did. "You said you were off duty?"

"That's right. For a few hours now. Why?"

"There's beer in the kitchen if you'd like some. Please don't leave yet, though. Okay?"

"Yeah, sure," Elliott said, unzipping his sweat jacket. "I'll stay."

Once past the dividing panels, Brodie turned on a light. Helping Kate to the bed, she gently turned her around and lowered her to the edge. Without asking, Brodie unbuttoned her coat, and her eyes misted over when Kate whimpered as Brodie eased it off her shoulders. "I'm sorry," Brodie said, tossing it aside. "I'm not trying to hurt you."

"I know."

"Would you like me to run you a bath?"

"No...no...I'm tired," Kate said in a breath. "I'm so tired, Brodie. All I...all I want to do is sleep. Is that okay?"

Brodie knelt in front of Kate. "Of course, it is. Let me just go find you something to wear."

Without waiting for an answer, Brodie went to her dresser and opening a drawer, she pulled out a set of flannel pajamas. She returned to Kate a moment later, and when she saw her sitting motionless on the bed with her eyes closed, Brodie paused. "Kate? Are you awake?"

"Yeah," Kate said, forcing her eyes to open.

"Then let's get you out of those clothes. Shall we?"

The fog was getting thicker, and it took a second for Brodie's words to register. "Yes, please."

Brodie painstakingly began to peel away the layers of what remained of Kate's clothing. The suit jacket was first, and moving slower than she had with Kate's coat, no murmurs of pain were heard. It was all Kate could do to get to her feet while Brodie loosened her skirt and allowed it to fall to the floor, and the ruined stockings were quickly pushed down Kate's legs before she sunk onto the mattress again. There were scrapes and cuts everywhere, but it wasn't until Brodie removed Kate's blouse that she had to fight back the tears. Although some were still hidden by Kate's bra, a swath of black, blue, and purple bruises crossed Kate's chest like a beauty contestant's sash, and another, brutally equal in color and width, ran from hip to hip. "Jesus Christ," Brodie muttered.

"Is it bad?" Kate said, trying to look down.

Brodie quickly placed her finger under Kate's chin. "No, it's just some bruises, Kate. Nothing to worry about."

"It hurts."

"I bet it does, darling," Brodie said, blinking back her emotions as she tenderly removed Kate's blouse. "I bet it does."

Brodie reached for the pajama top, and when she looked back at Kate, their eyes locked for a moment. While Kate's still seemed dull, there was just a hint of acknowledgment.

"Can you help me with this?" Kate said, touching the strap of her bra.

A weak grin appeared on Brodie's face. "I wouldn't have it any other way."

After gently removing Kate's bra, Brodie began to redress her in the flannel top. Like a child, Brodie guided her arms through the sleeves and then carefully fastened each button. It seemed every movement made Kate flinch, so when Brodie picked up the matching bottoms and saw Kate cringe, she quickly set them aside. "I don't think we need those, do you?"

"No...no, we don't."

"All right," Brodie said, bending down to look Kate in the eye. "So, would you like a cup of tea or...or maybe some water?"

"No...no, I just want to sleep."

"Of course," Brodie said, and cupping her hand behind Kate's head, she gently lowered her to the pillow. She drew up the sheet and duvet as she gazed at the battered woman, and unable to stop herself, Brodie leaned down and placed a featherlike kiss on Kate's forehead. "Get some rest."

Brodie didn't wait for an answer, but as she began to creep out of the room, Kate called out.

"Brodie?"

"Yeah?" Brodie said, turning around.

"I'm sorry."

Brodie rushed back to the bed. "Shhhh. No need to talk about that now."

"But I...but I want you to know—"

"Kate, hush. Whatever it is, it can wait. The only thing you need to do right now is get some sleep. We'll have plenty of time to talk when you're feeling better."

"But—"

"No buts, Kathryn," Brodie said, brushing a strand of hair from Kate's brow. "Sweet dreams, darling."

Brodie placed another small kiss on Kate's brow, and this time she reached the dividing panels before Kate called out again.

"Brodie?"

Amused that even in her exhausted state, Kate was still as stubborn as ever, Brodie looked toward the bed. "Yes, dear?"

"I love you."

It wasn't what Brodie had expected to hear, and hanging her head, she blinked back the tears. Almost a minute passed before she dared to look up again, and when she did, Kate had fallen asleep. "I love you, too, darling," Brodie whispered. "I love you, too."

***

Brodie exited the bedroom and made a beeline for the beer she'd left on the counter. Chugging it down, she glanced over at the man sitting on her sofa that was dangling an empty bottle from his fingertips. "Do you want some more?"

"Yeah, I think I could use another," Elliott said, getting to his feet.

"That makes two of us," Brodie said, striding into the kitchen as Elliott followed. Opening the fridge, she pulled out two more bottles and handed one to Elliott.

"Thanks."

"You're welcome."

"And I don't think we've been formally introduced," Elliott said, holding out his hand. "Sergeant Elliott Thackery, at your service."

As Brodie shook the man's hand, the connection was made. "Actually, we've already met," Brodie said, motioning toward the lounge. "It was about a year ago. I was a witness on a burglary case."

"That's where I've seen you," Elliott sat as they sat down on the sofa. "I knew you looked familiar. I didn't know you were Kate's partner though."

Brodie thought she'd done an excellent job of hiding her feelings, and her face went slack. "Partner? Why would you think I was Kate's partner?"

"Because it's what she said."

"It's what who said?"

"Kate," Elliott said, eyeing Brodie. "When I was about to drive her home, she asked that I bring her here instead. I asked who you were, and she said you were her partner. To tell you the truth, I didn't know Kate was gay, not that it matters, but I was a little surprised that she didn't call you from the hospital."

Brodie took a moment to come up with a plausible explanation, and then she realized she didn't have to. "We had an argument."

"Oh."

For a minute, Brodie stared at the bottle in her hand, trying to understand why Kate would have made such a confession. "Elliott," she said, looking up. "What about her injuries? Can you tell me anything?"

Elliott scratched his head. "Well, I know they poked and prodded her for a couple of hours, and all the tests came back fine. She's got a pretty bad concussion, but nothing's broken, and there aren't any internal injuries."

"Thank God."

"Oh, wait. I've got something for her," Elliott said, getting to his feet. Retrieving his sweat jacket, he pulled out a tube of cream, three medicine bottles, and a wad of folded papers, and handed everything to Brodie. "The pills are muscle relaxants, antibiotics, and painkillers. The papers explain what's to be expected from her concussion, and the cream is for the burns on her face."

"I was wondering about those."

"They're from the airbag," Elliott said, returning to his place on the sofa.

Brodie quickly scanned the instructions on the containers. "Do you know what happened?" she said, placing the medicine on the end table.

Elliott's lips thinned as a dark cloud settled on his features. "From what I've heard, and...and this needs to stay between you and me until Kate gives her statement, okay?"

"Of course."

"Well, it seems her partner went through a red light at an intersection. By the time I got there, they had Frank in the ambulance and were trying to cut Kate out of the car...or should I say, what was left of the car."

"Was it that bad?"

Elliott mulled over the question for a few seconds before pulling his mobile out of his pocket. Tapping on the screen, he handed it to Brodie. "I have no idea how fast Frank was going when he smashed into that building, but honestly, looking at the passenger side of his car, I still can't believe Kate wasn't killed."

The photos on Elliott's phone were far too real and far too scary, and the blood drained from Brodie's face as she swiped left again and again and again. Broken glass was everywhere, and the hood of the car was torn and crumpled like a piece of paper as it lay against what was once a windshield. The front wheels were gone, and fluids could be seen puddling under the mangled engine as they seeped from the cracks in the steel. The rear of the car had almost been shorn off, and the muffler lying off to one side was the last clue the pile of twisted wreckage had once been a car.

As Elliott took another swig of his beer, he noticed Brodie's hands were shaking. "Are you okay?" he said, setting the bottle down.

Brodie shoved the phone in Elliott's direction before jumping to her feet and running into the kitchen. She barely knew Elliott Thackery, and she didn't want to lose it in front of a stranger, but to Brodie's dismay, Elliott followed her, and his hand was now on her arm.

"I know you don't know me very well, but I've got pretty big shoulders, and I'm not afraid of tears," Elliott said, his voice growing hushed as he continued. "I care about Kate. She's my friend, and if she loves you as much as you obviously love her, then offering you my shoulder to cry on seems the least I can do. Don't you think?"

He was right. Elliott was a stranger, yet his voice was filled with so much compassion, Brodie's tears began to flow freely. She turned around, and when he opened his arms, she fell into them, burying her head against his shoulder as she sobbed. Racked by her wails, her body shook, and as Brodie's tears soaked through his shirt, she felt Elliott's hug grow stronger.

Chapter Thirty-One

Brodie refilled her cup and debated on whether to make another pot of coffee. She had spent the better part of three days hovering over Kate from the chair at the drafting table, intently watching the rise and fall of Kate's chest beneath the covers. She had made a dozen half-hearted attempts to sleep, but closing her eyes for more than a few minutes proved impossible. Even though coffee had become her beverage of choice since Elliott Thackery left her flat on Friday night, Brodie hadn't really needed the caffeine to keep her awake. Worry did that just fine. The bruises were horrid, and alone on the bed, Kate appeared so small and so fragile. It was almost too much to bear.

Brodie's mood lifted when Kate would awaken, the need for the bathroom causing her eyes to open, and with her arm gingerly wrapped around Kate's waist, they would snail-walk to the toilet and back again. Twice, nausea emptied Kate's belly, and afterward, Brodie would get Kate to drink some more. An obedient patient, Kate would sip some water and down the medication without saying a word, and after several spoonfuls of warm broth, sleep would take hold again.

By the time the sky turned from black to orange and then to blue on Monday morning, Brodie was running on empty, so tiptoeing from the bedroom, she went in search of coffee and her phone. Her calls were quick and hushed. The first was to Ethan to let him know what had happened and that Brodie would be working from home for the next few days, and the second was to Stevie. Asking him to step in and run things in the office until her return, before Brodie hung up the phone, her schedule for the day was rearranged, and files were uploaded, so she could access them from home.

Brodie took her mug to the lounge, and as she sat on the sofa sipping the steaming Columbian blend, she watched as the sun moved higher in the sky, its brightness slowly creeping over the room like a plague. Mornings had always been her favorite. A time when the world was still half asleep, she could enjoy her first cup of coffee while marveling at yet another beautiful sunrise or cloudy skies filled with nourishment for the earth. Today was different though. Today, Kate was still in her bed, and Brodie was torn between wanting her there and wanting her gone. Her heart rejoiced at having the woman she loved so close, yet her head told Brodie nothing had changed. Once awake and aware, conversations about time and waiting would start again...and Brodie's heart would break again.

Letting out a long breath, Brodie set her mug aside and resting her head back on the sofa, she closed her eyes. She told herself all she needed was a few minutes of sleep, and then she'd return to the bedroom to watch over Kate, but fatigue can be a greedy bastard...and it was.

***

As Kate fought her way through the medicating cloud that enveloped her, three words repeated in her mind. Going on red. Going on red. *Going on red.*

They were the last words Kate had heard before she was pulled into a terrifying vortex of tires screeching, horns blasting, and glass shattering, and when she crept toward consciousness amidst the smell of petrol and smoke, they had returned. Like a mantra, they repeated again and again in her head, and each time they did, Kate took another breath until finally, the sound of pounding forced her to open her eyes.

Strangers peered at her through the cobwebbed glass, excitedly thumping on the car and shouting muffled messages through the shattered windows. Emergency crews had been called, they said. She'd be okay, they said. Remain calm, they said.

Kate felt it an odd request, for she *was* calm. A peacefulness she had never known had wrapped its warmth around her, and she would wait as long as it took. She had time. She had nothing but time.

Buckled steel surrounded her, holding her captive and preventing all but the simplest of movements, and while others may have panicked, Kate did not. She didn't feel in danger. She didn't feel broken. Kate felt alive. Kate felt very *much* alive.

She heard the sound of sirens, and moments later, police and medics circled the car. Yelling through the glass, they cautioned her to close her eyes as they broke out what was left of the windows. They reached in, hands of strangers feeling for pulses and groping for injuries while their voices remained composed and reassuring, but their words fell on deaf ears. Kate didn't need to be convinced she'd be okay. She had far too much to live for to have it any other way.

She hissed as a needle was put into her arm, the medics insisting she needed an IV to help prevent shock, but Kate wasn't in shock. She was in awe. Her coat had opened on impact, and in the fading light of the afternoon, Kate stared at her green skirt, never noticing until that moment just how *green* it was. She could see blood on her hand, and it was more vibrant than any red she could remember, and the medic attending to her was wearing cologne that reminded her of a winter's day. It was crisp. Everything was *so* crisp.

A foam collar was placed around her neck. Kate didn't like it, her movement stilted even more by something they said was precautionary, but she didn't complain. Frank was doing enough of that for both of them, and then some. He was dropping numerous F-bombs as he groused and grumbled about the medic's inabilities and inadequacies, griping about the pain they were causing or the smell of their breath while they tried to do their job. Kate was impressed. Their voices held no hint of annoyance or sliver of frustration, their tones remaining forever compassionate and caring while they tended to someone callous and stupid.

Kate waited patiently as they eventually pulled Frank from the car, and then it was her turn. Covering her with protective blankets, they sawed through the twisted wreckage that had once been a car, every so often stopping to lift the cover and check on their patient, but they didn't have to. As odd as it was, it was giving Kate time to think, time to realize that life *was* too short to live it for others. And when they finally were able to remove Kate from the car and put her into an ambulance, there was only one thing on her mind. Brodie Shaw.

Kate's eyes popped open. Thin streams of light found their way into the room through tiny gaps in the drapes, and as Kate ran her tongue over her lips to moisten them, a ghost of a smile appeared. Thank God it wasn't a dream.

A few minutes passed before Kate dared to move. She knew what had happened, and she knew where she was. She also knew *this* was going to hurt. Kate took a slow, deep breath and ribs, bruised but not broken, announced themselves in an instant. She held her breath as she sat up, biting her lip to prevent a whimper from escaping as small bolts of pain shot through her body like fireworks exploding across a darkened sky. Taking a moment to catch her breath, Kate turned on the light on the nightstand and looking down at her legs hanging over the edge of the bed, she paled. Brush burns and scratches covered her knees and calves, and there was a bandage wrapped around her thigh. "Jesus," she said under her breath.

Although curious as to what was under the gauze, Kate's priority was the bathroom. As she got to her feet, she noticed a pillow on the drafting table, and she ran her hand across the indentation in the middle. Someone had rested their head there, and while the cotton was cool, the depression had remained.

***

Brodie awoke slowly, and opening her eyes, she lifted her head off the back of the sofa, only to let out a grunt at the stiffness that had invaded her neck. She rolled her head from side to side and worked out the kinks, and righting herself, Brodie picked up her phone and glanced at the time. She blinked and blinked again, trying to discredit the numbers displayed, and then she jumped to her feet. "Shit."

Brodie hurried to the bedroom, and then as quiet as the proverbial mouse, she tiptoed past the panels only to stutter to a stop when the bed came into view. It was empty, and panic punched Brodie in the stomach like a balled-up fist. She sucked in all the air in the room in one breath, and a split-second later, it exited her lungs much slower than it went in. She could hear water running, and puffing out another breath, Brodie made her way into the bathroom.

Wearing a rumpled pajama top that ended mid-thigh, Kate had her hands resting on the top of the vanity, and her body language screamed of pain and stiffness. She was hardly moving, just staring at her reflection in the mirror, and even though her hair was a mess and her legs were covered in scrapes and bruises, Brodie's heart did a flip. Kate was still the most beautiful woman she had ever seen.

***

Kate stood in front of the double sinks and pulled her toothbrush from the holder, warmed by the fact Brodie hadn't thrown it away. She was starting to feel a bit more human, and once her mouth was minty and her hair was brushed, Kate stared at her reflection in the mirror for a moment before she found the courage to lift the hem of her flannel top. "Shit," she said as the bluish-black bruise across her hips came into view, and the further Kate raised the top, the more she thanked God for sparing her life. Having seen enough, Kate let the flannel fall back into place, and resting her hands on the vanity top, she waited for a few seconds to gather the strength she'd need to make it back to the bedroom.

"What are you doing out of bed?"

Kate's lips took on a loving curve, the slightest hint of rose coloring her cheeks as she looked over at Brodie. "I had to pee."

Brodie grinned. "Acceptable answer," she said, bobbing her head. "Now, get back to bed."

"I will in a minute," Kate said, buying what she hoped was enough time to stop the room from spinning. "And thank you for letting me stay here. I really appreciate it."

"Not a problem," Brodie said, noticing a bit of color had drained from Kate's face. "Are you all right?"

"What? Oh, yeah. I'm fine. I probably just need something to eat."

"Well, how about I get you back into bed, and then I'll fix us something?"

"Um...actually," Kate said, hiding her grimace as she looked over at the shower. "I thought...I thought I'd try to get cleaned up if...if that's okay?"

"Of course, it's okay, but are you sure you can manage? You look more than a little washed out."

"Car accidents have a tendency to do that," Kate said, forcing a laugh. "I'm fine though."

Something told Brodie Kate wasn't actually fine, and she hesitated before answering. "All right," Brodie said, studying the woman. "Then you shower, and I'll scrounge us up some food."

"Sounds good."

Brodie smiled her acknowledgment, but as she turned to leave, her heart told her to stop. *This* wasn't what she wanted, and going over to Kate, she lightly touched Kate's chafed cheek. "Does that hurt?"

"No...um...not really. Why?" Kate said, gazing into Brodie's eyes.

"Because I didn't want to hurt you when I did this," Brodie said, placing a light kiss on Kate's cheek. "Now, get washed, and call me if you need me."

***

Brodie had listened to the shower running for twenty minutes before she walked into the winding hallway leading the bathroom and called out, "Are you okay in there?" When Brodie didn't hear a response, her heart began to pound, and raising her voice a little more, she tried again. "Kate, are you all right in there?"

"Uh...not really."

Brodie hissed in a sharp breath and rushing into the bathroom, her eyes were drawn to the shower where Kate sat slumped on the tiled bench. "Shit." Brodie rushed over, and without thinking twice, she stepped under the hot spray and squatted at Kate's feet. "What's wrong? Are you hurt? Should I call emergency—"

"No. No, I'm fine. I was just trying to shave my legs, but I dropped the razor."

Brodie tilted her head, mindless of the water cascading down her face as she stared at the woman bent over on the bench. "You...you dropped the *razor*?"

"It wasn't so much about dropping the razor, but when I bent over to get it, the room started to spin...and I felt like I was going to throw up," Kate said, keeping her head bowed. "So, I just closed my eyes and waited for it to pass."

"Oh, Christ. I'm sorry. That's the concussion talking," Brodie said, placing her hands lightly on Kate's thighs. "Are you still nauseated?"

"No, that's gone, but the straightening up part is kind of where I got stuck. Everything hurts."

"All right. What can I do?"

"Um...just push me up. I'll do the rest."

Kate bit her lip, forbidding any whimper or groan from escaping, and in no time at all, she was leaning back against the tile wall. She waited for a moment before opening her eyes, and when she did, they almost popped out of her head. "Oh my, God, Brodie, you're soaked. I'm so, so sorry. I didn't mean—"

"Don't worry about it," Brodie said, standing straight. "As long as you're all right, it doesn't matter. It's just clothes."

"I guess," Kate said, reaching for a washcloth. "But I don't want to be a bother."

Brodie dropped her chin to her chest. The tone of Kate's voice was barely audible over the sound of the shower, and even the heated water hadn't brought color back to Kate's cheeks. Confusion clouded Brodie's face. Why couldn't she just admit she needed help? A second later, Brodie wanted to kick herself. How in the hell had she forgotten about Kate's pigheadedness?

Huffing out a breath, Brodie knelt in front of Kate again. "Look, there's been a lot that's gone down between us, but right now, can we agree to just...to just forget about it for a while. You're hurt, Kate, and you shouldn't have tried to do this by yourself. I know it, and you know it, so how about I just strip out of these clothes, help you wash, and if you'd like, I'll even shave your legs. It's not like we haven't seen it all before—right? And honestly, the sooner I can get your cute, albeit bruised arse out of my shower, the sooner we can get something to eat."

***

With the last plate drying on the rack, Brodie filled a glass with water and returned to the lounge. "Here you go," she said, handing Kate the water as she sat down.

"What's this for?" Kate said, holding up the glass.

Brodie pulled three pill bottles from her pocket and tapping one tablet out of each, she held out her hand. "It's for these."

Kate stared at the pills. "What are those?"

"Wow, you really don't remember anything, do you?"

"I remember the accident just fine, but the last twenty-four hours are a bit fuzzy."

"The last twenty-four hours? Kate, it's Monday night."

"What?" Kate blurted. "It's Monday *night*?"

"Yeah, you've basically slept since you got here except for when you said you needed the loo. I'd guide you there and guide you back, and you'd fall asleep. I always managed to get the pills into you, though, which is why you're going to take them right now."

"But what are they?"

Brodie sucked in her cheeks. "The white one is a muscle relaxant. The blue one is for pain, and the massive one in the middle is an antibiotic," she said, moving her hand a little closer. "So, pick them up and swallow them down like a good girl."

Kate liked medicine about as much as she liked hospitals, and it showed on her face as she scowled at the pills. "Brodie—"

"Oh, don't even start," Brodie said, rocking back. "We were in the shower for over an hour, and if I hadn't helped you to get dressed, you'd still be trying to pull up the bottoms of those pajamas. Now, take the bloody pills and don't argue."

A glint of amusement crossed Kate's face as she took the tablets, and popping them into her mouth one by one, she followed each with a small sip of water. "Satisfied?" she said, handing Brodie the glass.

"I will be once I get you into bed."

"I really don't think I'm up for that, sweetheart," Kate said through a small smile.

Brodie's face lit up, and she laughed. "That's not what I meant, and you know it."

Ever since Brodie had kissed Kate on the cheek, their awkwardness had given way to the familiarity that comes with having been lovers, and while that kiss held no promises or words of forever, their comfort level had returned. Under a spray of hot water, Brodie had tenderly helped Kate wash, lathering away the remnants of dust and dirt and dried blood. After gently toweling Kate dry, Brodie carefully removed the bandage on Kate's thigh, revealing a gash too deep not to suture. Brodie bandaged it again, and with a touch softer than a butterfly's wing, she applied ointment to Kate's face on the areas still chafed. Neither had ogled nor leered at the nudity of the other, and giggles hadn't been uttered for when love is unconditional, when it is altruistic and unequivocal, the peripheral goes unnoticed.

Brodie placed the glass aside, looking back at Kate just in time to see her eyes close and then slowly open again. "Come on. You're tired. You need to get some rest."

Kate let out a slow breath. "As much as I hate to admit it, you're right." Kate gingerly got to her feet, and hiking up the long-legged pajama bottoms, she shuffled to the bedroom, doing her best not to trip on the excess material as it dragged on the floor.

Brodie faced a quandary as she followed one step behind. On the one hand, she was sympathetic to the pain Kate obviously was in, the woman walking slightly stooped and slower than a snail on a good day. However, on the other hand, she was more than a little tickled by the hunchback slogging herself toward the bedroom. "You're walking like my grandmother used to."

Kate came to an abrupt halt and looked over her shoulder. "You think this is funny?" she said, trying her best to appear angry even though she wasn't.

"No, of course not," Brodie said, reining in her mirth. "I was just making an observation."

"Well, how about this for an observation," Kate said, turning slightly. "If your legs weren't so bloody long, I wouldn't have to worry about tripping, now would I? And while we're on the subject, since when do you wear flannel pajamas?"

"I don't."

"Oh, so you just keep them around for accident victims?"

"No," Brodie said. "They were a Christmas present from Dad a few years back, and I hadn't the heart to give them away. And you should feel bloody lucky I didn't because if I had, you'd be wearing nothing but a smile right now."

Kate had to bite her tongue to prevent '*I love you*' from escaping. She was exhausted, and she knew the talk she wanted to have with Brodie would be a long one. There was so much to say, and Kate had no intention of rushing one word. Smiling softly at Brodie, Kate shuffled the rest of the way into the bedroom.

Kate climbed into bed, and as she reached for the sheet, Brodie did as well. Their hands touched, and instinctively, their fingers meshed, and for a few moments, all they could do was gaze at each other.

"You're tired," Kate said quietly.

"I'm fine," Brodie said, smoothing out the duvet. "I'll rest in the lounge once I've got you settled."

"Stay with me."

"All right," Brodie said, pulling the chair at the drafting table closer.

"No, not there. Here," Kate said, patting the other side of the bed.

Brodie's eyes began to sparkle. "I thought we already discussed the fact that you're not up for that."

"I'm not, and neither are you by the looks of it."

"I never said I wasn't tired."

"Then come to bed."

"I don't want to hurt you," Brodie said, shaking her head. "I could roll over and...and...bump into you."

Kate's face split into a grin. "Brodie, I'm bruised, not broken. Now please...for me?"

Brodie rubbed the back of her neck as she eyed the chair and then the bed and then the chair again. "Be right back."

Disappearing into the bathroom for a few minutes, Brodie walked out wearing her standard black tank top and knickers. She slipped under the sheets and turned toward Kate. "Satisfied?"

"Getting there," Kate said in a breath, snuggling closer. "Definitely getting there."

Chapter Thirty-Two

Brodie made her way back to the bed and climbed under the covers. Once again, Kate placed her leg over Brodie's, and laying one arm across her waist, Kate buried her face in Brodie's side. It was the same position she'd been in for the past several hours, and Brodie had adored every second of it.

It was as if nothing had changed. They had never argued. Ultimatums had never been given, and words yelled in anger had never been spoken. But they had, and it was those words and memories that ran through Brodie's mind as she unconsciously rubbed Kate's back.

Brodie didn't want this to end again. She didn't want Kate to exist only in her dreams. Brodie wanted the real thing, and breathing in the scent of the woman she loved, Brodie sighed. She didn't know what the next day would bring or the day after that, but for now, she had Kate in her arms, and that was enough.

"That feels good," Kate mumbled into Brodie's tank top.

"Are you okay? How are you feeling?"

"Don't know. I haven't moved yet."

Brodie grinned in the darkness and reaching for the bedpost, she ran her hand over the contacts, and the lights on the nightstands came to life.

"Give a girl a warning next time, will you?" Kate said, squeezing her eyes closed as she pressed her face further into Brodie's side.

With a snicker, Brodie broke free of Kate's grasp and got out of bed. She ran her fingers through her hair as she looked down at the woman in her bed. "Should I turn off the lights and let you go back to sleep?"

"That depends. Are you going to join me?" Kate said, rolling onto her back

"No, I'm going to grab a shower and then head over to work for a bit. I have a couple of meetings I can't afford to cancel, that is unless you don't think you'll be all right alone. I can always call Ethan and see if he can—"

"Of course, I'll be all right. Wait," Kate said, opening one eye. "It's morning?"

"Yes, apparently your laziness is contagious," Brodie said, opening a dresser drawer to grab a bra and knickers. "We both slept through the night."

"I am *not* lazy," Kate said, her face contorting as she pushed herself into a sitting position.

Concern etched Brodie's face instantly. "Are you okay?"

"Will you *please* stop asking me that?"

"Then stop making those god-awful faces," Brodie said, scrunching up her face to demonstrate. "They're positively dreadful."

"What's dreadful is I'm discovering a shiteload of muscles I didn't know I owned," Kate said, pushing aside the bedcovers. "And my feet have disappeared."

Brodie looked down at the legs of the pajamas extending well past Kate's feet. "You could try rolling them up, you know?"

"I have, and they just unroll. Do you any have pins?"

"Probably, but I think I have a better idea."

"Oh yeah, what's that?"

"After my meetings are done, I thought I'd grab a bit more work and bring it back here. That way I can get some things done while keeping an eye on you, and on the way—"

"I am not a child."

"No, although you are *seriously* exasperating at times," Brodie said, chuckling. "Anyway, like I was saying, on my way back, how about I swing by your place and pick up some of your stuff. You can make me a list, or I'll just call you when I get there, and you can walk me through what you want me to get."

"I don't want to be any trouble."

"That'll be a first."

Prescriptions for muscle relaxants and pain relief had absolutely nothing on Brodie Shaw. Sore muscles seemed to ease with each lighthearted retort, and the twinkle in Brodie's eyes had all but eliminated the need for painkillers, except all of a sudden, Kate realized she could be reading the situation all wrong. She hadn't had an invitation when she intruded on Brodie's privacy the night of the accident. Kate had merely shown up, bruised and battered, and Brodie had taken pity on her. She had taken over Brodie's bed, monopolized her time, and now, Brodie was rearranging her day all because of Kate. How many times had Kate been this thoughtless? How many times had she put herself first? How many times had Kate forced Brodie to do things for her?

Kate hung her head. "You know what? Maybe I should go. I can take care of myself."

"What?" Brodie said, dropping the lingerie back in the drawer. "Kate, I was kidding."

"Were you?" Kate said, lifting her eyes.

Brodie's brow creased, and going over, she sat on the edge of the bed. "Look, I'll be honest. All right?"

"Please."

"When you first got here, there was a small part of me that didn't want you here."

"Then it's settled," Kate said, attempting to stand.

"Let me finish," Brodie said, placing her hand lightly on Kate's knee. "I said *was*. Kate, you and I both know there's a torrent of water under our bridge, and it took me a little while to be able to fight that current, to be able to fight the anger and the hurt, but I have, and I want you to stay as long as you'd like."

"But if I'm making you uncomfortable—"

"What would make me uncomfortable *and* what would drive me *completely* insane is not having you here. I'd be worried sick if you were anywhere else, Kate. I really would."

Kate took a deep breath, trying her best to hide the pain in her ribs while doing so. "Are you sure? Are you really sure, Brodie?"

"Yes," Brodie said in a breath, placing a soft kiss on Kate's cheek. "Now, let me go wash, so I can retrieve some pajamas that actually fit you."

***

Brodie returned to the bedroom after taking Kate's breakfast tray into the kitchen. "Are you sure scrambled eggs and toast were enough for you?"

"It'll hold me for a while," Kate said. "I don't feel sick, but I don't want to push it either."

"It's got nothing to do with the food. It's got to do with the concussion," Brodie said, opening the tablet bottles and tapping out some pills.

"How did you get so smart?" Kate said, taking the pills.

"I read a pamphlet on the subject," Brodie said, handing Kate a glass of water. "When you were in the shower, you bent over. Blood goes to your head. Dizziness and nausea follow. Oh, and while we're on the subject, try not to think too much while I'm gone, and keep the drapes drawn."

Kate closed one eye and cocked her head to the side. "How *exactly* am I supposed to stop myself from thinking?"

"Oh, sorry," Brodie said with a laugh. "What I mean is don't play any brain games on your phone or try to read or work on any puzzles. No computer or TV either. The less work your brain has to do, the better. For the most part, you should just try to sleep."

"I've been sleeping for days."

"Do you like the feeling of being on a whirling carousel or that oh so marvelous sensation you have seconds before you're about to hurl?"

"No."

"Then stay in the bloody bed," Brodie said, hovering over Kate. "And promise me if you get hungry, or if you need to use the loo, you'll take your time getting up. You're not to rush to do anything. I mean it, Kate."

"All right."

"Promise me."

Kate let out an exaggerated sigh. "I promise."

"Good," Brodie said, smiling. "Now, take your damn pills."

***

The meetings took most of the morning, and after sorting out a few more things, by the time Brodie dared to leave the office, it was almost one o'clock. She made her way to Kate's house with a list of all the essentials needed, and after packing a small travel bag and watering some drooping houseplants, shortly before three, Brodie was letting herself back into her condo.

It was quiet, and with the drapes in the lounge closed, it took a few seconds for her to get accustomed to the dim lighting before she made her way to the kitchen. Brodie placed the two cooler bags on the counter and then went into the dining room to set down the work she'd brought home. Taking off her coat, she draped it over a chair before tiptoeing into the bedroom.

Brodie couldn't help but smile at the tangled bedcovers or at the lump underneath, and when she saw the pill bottles on the table with a half-empty glass of water, her smile broadened. "Good girl," Brodie said, her voice barely above a whisper.

"I'm glad you think so," Kate said, opening her eyes.

"I'm sorry. I didn't mean to wake you," Brodie said, taking a step into the room.

"You didn't. I woke up a little while ago. I was just doing the only thing I'm allowed to do. Relax."

Brodie walked nearer the bed. "Did you get something to eat?"

"Yes. I had some of the lamb casserole that was in the fridge. It was really good," Kate said, slowly sitting up. "I hope you don't mind."

"I don't mind at all. No nausea then?"

"Nope. Not a wave."

"That's a good sign," Brodie said, rearranging the pillows behind Kate into a pile.

"What time is it?"

"Um…a little after three. Why? You have someplace to be?"

"Not until Friday."

"What's happening on Friday?" Brodie said, sitting on the edge of the bed.

"I made a few phone calls while you were gone," Kate said, resting back on the pillows.

"Did you call Devon?"

"No."

Brodie pulled in a breath, holding it for a second before letting it out. "Kate, the last thing Elliott said before he left on Friday was that you had refused to allow anyone to call her, and I really think she and Gina should be aware of what's happened."

"Why? You and I both know they'll cancel their holiday if I call, and I don't want them to. It's not like I'm going to heal any faster if they're here, and I'm fine."

"You are most assuredly *not* fine."

"Okay, so I'm not a hundred percent, but those two fussing about isn't going to make a difference. Is it?"

Brodie wished she could argue the point, but she couldn't, and it showed on her face. "No, I suppose not," she said. "So, if you didn't call Devon, who did you call?"

"My Chief. I was trying to schedule a time when I could talk to the investigators about the accident, but he told me I couldn't do that until my doctor can confirm I'm thinking clearly. So, I called to make an appointment, and the soonest my doctor can see me is Friday."

"Oh, for what time? I have a conference call at nine."

"It's at eleven, but don't worry about it. I can call a taxi."

"Don't be silly. I spent part of my morning rearranging my schedule. Everything's covered this week except for that phone call, and I've brought enough work home to keep me busy for a few days." Brodie's eyes narrowed as she looked at Kate. "Unless…unless, of course, you don't want me to take you."

"It's not that I don't want you to, but if you have work to do, I don't want to get in the way of that. I'll just call a taxi. No worries."

"Right," Brodie said, slapping her hands on her thighs before she stood up. "Well, speaking of work, I have more than enough out there to keep me busy. Do you need anything before I go?"

"Uh…no. I'm good."

"Fine."

A cloud of confusion crossed Kate's face as Brodie marched from the room. Kate looked up at the ceiling, replaying their short conversation in her head, and the cloud grew darker. What had just annoyed Brodie so much that Kate had seen the veins throbbing in Brodie's temples?

***

A few hours later, Brodie came back into the bedroom just as Kate was pushing herself into a sitting position. "You look like an angry gargoyle. Should I take you to the roof?"

More than one giggle escaped before Kate shot Brodie a look. "It hurts."

"Sorry, I know it does," Brodie said, coming closer. "I just came in to see if you're hungry. It's almost six."

"Actually, I am," Kate said, dangling her legs over the bed. "But I'd like to take a quick shower. Did you get me any clothes?"

"Oh Christ, I left them in the car," Brodie said, clapping her hands to her head. "I was overloaded when I came home and totally forgot about them. I'll run down and get them now."

"Thanks."

"Are you going to be okay in there?" Brodie said, motioning toward the bathroom.

"Yeah, I think so."

"Okay, I'll be right back."

Kate scratched her head. A few hours before Brodie had seemed bothered and now, she was anything but. "Maybe it's just that time of the month," Kate muttered as she hiked up the legs of her pajamas and made her way to the bathroom.

Fifteen minutes later, Kate emerged from the steamy bathroom with a towel wrapped around her middle, and seeing an open travel case on the bed, she rummaged through the things inside until she found her pajamas. Without Brodie around to see it, Kate didn't hold back on her groans, winces, or hisses as she slowly got herself dressed, and after finger-combing her hair again, she left the room.

The preheat signal on the oven chimed just as Kate walked into the kitchen to find Brodie pulling two casseroles out of the fridge. "I thought you said you had work to do? When did you have time to make those?"

"Oh, I didn't," Brodie said, glancing at Kate. She had expected to see the same rosy-faced woman she'd seen a short time earlier, but instead, Kate's face was almost gray, and Brodie frowned. "Um...at the risk of you biting my head off, are you okay? You look a little pale."

"Between the shower and getting dressed, it kind of wiped me out. I'll be fine in a few."

"Maybe you should go back to bed."

"So, you're going to starve me then?"

"No. I can bring you a plate."

"Don't be ridiculous," Kate said with a wave of her hand. "I'm not an invalid."

Brodie arched an eyebrow, and when Kate squinted back at her, she laughed and held up her hands. "Fine, you're not an invalid. You're just bruised, not broken—right?"

"Exactly?"

"Okay, so what does your bruised self want for dinner? We have beef stew or Stevie's chicken with red peppers, sun-dried tomatoes, olives, and chorizo."

"Oh, that sounds heavenly. I vote for that," Kate said, leaning in to peek under the foil Brodie had lifted.

Kate watched as Brodie slipped the tray into the oven and then put the stew back into the fridge. "Okay, not that I don't appreciate the gesture, but why is your receptionist making me food?"

Brodie smiled. "Actually, he's my Chief Financial Officer now."

"What? When did that happen?"

"At lot has changed over the past four months, Kate," Brodie said, filling a goblet with wine. "Would you like water or tea?"

"Can't I have some of that?"

"Not with the medications you're on," Brodie said, putting the cork back into the bottle. "Sorry."

"Well, shit," Kate said, reaching for a glass. "Then I guess I'll have water."

"I've got it," Brodie said, taking the glass from Kate. "You go sit down."

By the time Kate reached the sofa, Brodie was right behind her, and waiting until they were both settled, Brodie handed Kate her water.

"Thanks," Kate said before taking a sip.

A second later, Brodie saw Kate screw up her face. "What's wrong? A problem with the water?"

"No," Kate said, setting the glass down. "I think I'm sitting on something." Kate shifted just enough to reach under herself, and a moment later, she pulled out a small, purple rubber ball emblazoned with a Chadwick Orthopedics decal.

"I've been looking for that one," Brodie said, taking the exercise ball. "Thanks."

"Chadwick Orthopedics? What's that about?"

"It helps strengthen my hand."

"Your hand? What's wrong with your hand?"

"Oh...um...I broke it a few months ago."

"What? How?"

Brodie's mind drifted back to the night when she was bested by a tree root, and she scowled. "It doesn't matter," she said, setting the ball aside. "I also sold my car."

Kate's shoulders fell. "Really? I loved that car."

"So did I, except every time I got into it, I remembered your face that first time at Calabria when you saw it...and it was like a snowball down a hill, and it was a hill I didn't want to travel," Brodie said before taking a sip of her wine. "And since I couldn't drive it for a while, I decided I may as well get rid of it along with the memories it held."

"Oh," Kate said, hanging her head for a moment. "I'm surprised you kept my toothbrush then."

"The car was a lot easier to part with," Brodie said softly.

A moment of silence passed between them until Kate noticed the aroma wafting from the kitchen. "Dinner smells good."

"Stevie's a good cook, and if you liked the lamb casserole, you're going to love the chicken."

"Why is he making you food?"

Brodie met Kate's gaze and paused to get her thoughts in order. "After you and I split up, I was having a hard time. I wasn't eating properly, and then I broke my hand. So, Stevie began bringing casseroles to the office to make sure I was eating, and Gina or Devon would stop by here to drop something off at least once a week."

"I didn't know they were doing that."

"I'm sure they thought there was no reason to tell you," Brodie said with a shrug. "They knew I didn't want to know what was going on with you, so they probably just assumed you felt the same way."

"Oh," Kate said, lowering her eyes.

"So...um...what about you? How's the new job?"

"I didn't get it," Kate said, looking up.

"Oh, crap. I'm sorry."

"It's okay. It's just a job."

Brodie leaned back ever so slightly. "I thought you wanted it. Part of the plan and all that."

"I thought I wanted it, too, but plans change," Kate said, eyeing Brodie. It was impossible not to notice that their conversation had become labored, weighed down by cautious words and careful looks, and Kate frowned. "Is it me, or have things suddenly become difficult between us?"

Brodie let out a long breath. "No, it's not you."

"What's wrong?"

There was a question that had planted itself in Brodie's gray matter days before. Like a weed with an endless root, it had dogged her for days until she finally came up with the only plausible explanation. Now, she just needed to hear it from Kate. "Why did you tell that man I was your partner?" she said, turning to Kate.

"Huh? What man?"

"Your friend Elliott. That first night, after you fell asleep, I came out and talked to him for a while, and he said you told him I was your partner."

Kate hesitated for a second. "That's right. I did."

"I'm confused."

"I'm not...at least not anymore."

Brodie settled back into the sofa, her eyes never leaving Kate's as she folded her arms across her chest. "Is that so?"

"Yes," Kate said with a slow nod. "You were right. Life's too short."

If Brodie had been a gambler, she would have just won a hefty sum with the wager she had placed with herself. Kate had stared death in the eye and won. Unfortunately, that didn't change the fact that some strangers would still gawk, some friends would still walk away, and Kate's relationship with her mother very well may have ended.

"Let me guess," Brodie said, swinging one leg over the other. "A near-death experience made you see the light?"

Brodie's remark was spot-on, but her rather flippant tone caught Kate's attention. "Please don't make fun of me."

"I'm not."

"Yes, you are."

"Kate, I appreciate what you must have gone through, but—"

"I don't think you do."

"How can you say that?" Brodie said, leaning away. "I saw the bruises, and I know you probably thought you were doing to die—"

"Please stop making this sound so trivial."

"Kate—"

"Will you *please* let me finish?"

If all things had been equal, Kate would have postponed this conversation for at least another day. She wasn't sure if it was the medication or the shower that had so successfully zapped her strength, except when she saw the look on Brodie's face, Kate's fortitude returned. Brodie was wearing a smug expression, not unlike the cocky one she had worn when they first met so many months before. Her chin was tipped slightly upward, and with her arms crossed, Brodie's body language said it all. Prove me wrong. I *dare* you.

There would be ample time to heal and plenty of time to sleep, but after everything she had put Brodie through, Kate knew this could very well be her last chance to make things right. So, if Brodie wanted an argument, that's precisely what Kate would give her. "Do you love me?" she said, looking Brodie square in the eye.

"What?"

"You heard me."

Brodie took several long seconds before she spoke. "Of course, I do, but that's not the problem. Love can only get us so far, Kate, and then it's up to us. We've got to be a *we*, and you aren't willing to do that."

"Yes, I am."

"Why? Because you thought you were going to die?"

"Yes, but it's so much more than that," Kate said, touching Brodie lightly on the leg. "When I realized Frank wasn't slowing down as we reached that intersection, I pleaded with him to stop. I *begged* for him to stop, and he just sneered at me. He was so bloody cocksure, you know? And then, seconds before everything went to shit, Frank said something…and when I woke up, his words were still in my head. Over and over and over again, it was all I could hear until my ears stopped ringing."

"Okay, I'll bite. What did he say?"

"He said…he said he was going on red."

"Going on red?"

"Yeah, it means to go through a red light after you've come to a stop."

Brodie snorted. "Kate, I know what it means. I'm just not sure why it's important."

"You know how they say that when you think you're going to die, your life flashes in front of you?"

"Sure."

"Well, it's not your whole life. It's just bits and pieces, little flashes of people and places that enter and exit your mind, one after another after another. But each of them…each of them is so clear and so real, it's as if you're looking through a picture book, turning the pages of your life. And when I turned mine, I realized most of them were filled with regret, and nobody else was to blame except me," Kate said quietly. "Brodie, whenever something or someone didn't fit into my plan, I walked away. Whenever a choice had to be made, I made it based on what was the easiest for me, never thinking about the other person's wants or desires. You said it yourself, it was always about me. I was so rigid in what I wanted for my life, I forgot that sometimes…*sometimes* it's okay to go against the grain, to think outside the box…to go on red."

"Kate, going on red almost killed you a few days ago."

"But it didn't," Kate said, straightening her backbone. "What Frank did was wrong, Brodie, but believing I was going to die was the wake-up call I needed. These past four months have been horrible, and I've been miserable. I kept trying to convince myself that you'd call, that *you* would change your mind, but that was wrong of me. That was *terribly* wrong of me because *you* don't need to change, Brodie. *I* do…and I *have*."

Brodie ran her fingers through her hair, and letting out a long breath, she got to her feet. "I need more wine."

A minute later, wearing a somber expression, Brodie returned with her goblet filled. "Kate, no offense, but I lost count as to how many times you said you'd change, and you never did. Why should I believe you now?"

Kate nibbled on her lower lip for a second. "Because now...because now, for the first time in my life, I know that the only thing standing between me and a life filled with happiness and love is my own stupid insecurity. So, I've decided that if friends walk away, I'll get new ones, and if things become too difficult at work, I'll transfer to another station because friends and jobs can come and go, but what I feel for you, Brodie...that's *never* going to go away."

Brodie let Kate's words sink in as she slowly sipped her wine, and when her thoughts were interrupted by the ring of the oven timer, Brodie got up to go turn it off. "Dinner's ready."

"Brodie, aren't you going to say anything?"

Turning around, Brodie stared blankly back at Kate. "I wish I could believe you, Kate. I really do, but you've cried wolf so many times. And if this is how you truly feel and what you truly *want*, you wouldn't have done what you did earlier."

"What are you talking about?" Kate said, getting up to follow Brodie into the kitchen. "What did I do earlier?"

"It doesn't matter," Brodie said, reaching for the oven mitts.

"Yes, it does," Kate said, grabbing Brodie by the arm and turning her around. "Brodie, I'm trying to save us here. If you think I did something wrong then—"

"If you've supposedly changed like you say you have, then why in the hell did you turn down my offer to drive you to the doctor—eh? I'll tell you why, Kate, because you didn't want to have to dream up some stupid excuse for me to stay in the bloody car."

Kate leaned back. "*That's* why you were upset this afternoon?"

"And for the life of me, I don't know why. It's not like I wasn't already used to you treating me like a leper."

"Brodie, I said I'd call a taxi because I thought I'd monopolized enough of your time. I showed up unannounced on Friday night, and you've taken care of me ever since then. You've fed me. You made sure I was taking my meds. Hell, you even washed me and shaved my legs, for Christ's sake. I was just trying to give you a bloody break."

Without saying a word, Brodie pulled out the tray of chicken and put it on top of the stove. "This needs to sit for a few minutes."

"Brodie, just give me a chance—"

"You know what, Kate," Brodie said, tossing the oven mitts aside. "Giving you another chance is right up there with giving you more time. It's the same old, same old."

"Then take me to the doctor on Friday, and I'll show you I've changed."

"It's too late for that."

"No, it's not, Brodie. I can't prove to you what you need to see if we aren't out and about. I can't do it here," Kate said, waving her arms about. "But I can do it out there. Just give me a chance."

Brodie bowed her head and closing her eyes, another mental tug-of-war invaded her mind. How many chances were too many? How much time was too much? How long would it take for the dreams to stop? Brodie opened her eyes and looked at Kate. "I don't know if I have the strength to do this again, Kate. I just don't think—"

"Would it help if I put it on a bloody billboard, let everyone know that Kate Monroe is head over heels in love with Brodie Shaw, because I'll do that Brodie. I'll do anything you want," Kate said, her voice cracking with emotion. "Just give me until Friday, Brodie. It's just a couple of more days. I'm begging you. I'll even get down on my knees if that's what you want. Just say the word, and I'll do it."

Brodie wanted to laugh, and it had nothing to do with Kate's offer. It had to do with love and the things you thought you'd never do...*again*. "You wouldn't be able to get back up if you did."

The flicker of mirth in Brodie's eyes was impossible not to notice, and Kate dared to take a breath. "So...um...does that mean...does that mean you'll give me until Friday?"

"You do know that if I agree to this, it makes me certifiable— right?"

Kate shrugged. "From where I stand, what some people define as normal is way overrated."

Chapter Thirty-Three

Brodie came out of the bathroom to find Kate grimacing as she stood by the bed wearing nothing but her underwear. "Something wrong? You're making one of those faces again."

"I haven't worn a bra since the accident and...um...it's kind of hurting."

"Then take it off."

"And go braless?"

"Kate, you're going to a doctor. I'm fairly certain he's seen tits before."

"Yeah, but..."

Brodie snickered. "Let me guess. It's not you?"

Kate cast the evilest look she owned in Brodie's direction and sliding the bra straps down her arms in record time, Kate whipped the bra around to undo the hooks and then tossed it on the bed. "I'll show you what's not me," she said, reaching for the long-sleeved T-shirt on the bed. A second later, Kate paled. "Fuck."

"Christ," Brodie said, trotting over. "Are you o—"

"Don't," Kate said, holding up her finger. "Don't say a word. Just help me put this bloody thing on."

Brodie pressed her lips together to smother her grin, and after assisting Kate in getting the shirt over her head, Brodie backed away while Kate straightened the fabric. "Um...Kate."

"Yes?"

"I know you said you've changed, but I'm thinking you haven't changed so much as to allow yourself to leave the house like that," Brodie said, pointing to Kate's chest.

Kate looked down, and her eyes bulged. Two certain somethings were at full attention and pointing back at Brodie like tiny arrows through the snug shirt. "Oh, crap. I can't wear this. Get it off."

"Put it on. Get it off. Make up your bloody mind," Brodie said with a laugh as she helped Kate out of the clothing. "And can I make a suggestion?"

"Sure. What?" Kate said, folding her arms across her naked breasts.

Brodie opened a dresser drawer and pulled out a flannel shirt. "How about this? It's large. It's warm, and it will hide your headlights."

Kate couldn't contain her smile, and taking the shirt, she put it on without further discussion.

On Tuesday, after Brodie had agreed to give Kate one more chance, the rest of the evening had gone by without another word about what tomorrow or the next day would bring. Instead, their conversation was light, and revolving mostly around the expansion of Brodie's business, Kate hung on every word. As Brodie promised, Stevie's chicken dish was scrumptious, and afterward, they relaxed in the lounge until eyes grew heavy, and they made their way to the bedroom. Kate slipped under the covers wearing her pink, floral pajamas and Brodie, her black tank top and knickers, and when Brodie turned out the light and draped her arm around Kate as she burrowed closer, Kate said a prayer. She didn't pray for time, and she didn't pray for strength to carry out her promise. Kate prayed for Friday to come quickly. She had something to prove, and by God, she was going to prove it.

***

Kate had spent Wednesday and Thursday resting while Brodie worked at the dining room table, popping her head into the bedroom every so often to check on her patient. Legs could now be shaved without the need of another, and Kate had begun taking short walks around the condo, gaining strength with every step she took. So, as they exited Brodie's building, Kate was feeling better than she had in days, and filling her lungs with the fresh morning air, she gazed up at the sky. It was a gorgeous April day, and with nary a cloud to block her view, the sky was bluer than any blue she could remember. Kate took another deep breath. Christ, it felt good to be alive.

When they reached the car park, Kate scanned the lot for Brodie's car for a few seconds before realizing her mistake. "Um...I was looking for the Jag, but I forgot you sold it. What are you driving now?"

Kate's answer came when Brodie pressed the remote, and the lights on a silver sedan flashed a second before the horn on the car blew. "Over there," Brodie said, gesturing with her head.

As Kate approached the non-descript automobile, she unconsciously wrinkled her nose. "This is yours?"

In three little words, Kate's voice had climbed the scale all the way to the top, and Brodie's eyes gleamed. "What? You don't like it?"

"Uh...well..." Kate said, eyeballing the family car. "I guess I was expecting something more...um...something more..."

"Now remember, *Kathryn*. We can't have a relationship if we aren't honest with each other."

Kate slammed her hands on her hips. "Fine, then no, I don't like it. It's...it's boring, and it's...it's—"

"A rental."

"What?"

"It's a rental. The dealership only had a limited selection when I walked their lot, but they have two shipments coming in today, so after I'm done running you around, I'll go over and pick something out," Brodie said, smiling. "But I have to say, seeing the look on your face was well worth having to drive that for the past few weeks. You looked positively appalled."

Kate pursed her lips and narrowed her eyes until they were slits. "I'll get you for that."

"That's what today is all about, isn't it?" Brodie said, opening the passenger door. "Now, in you go, or we're going to be late."

***

Brodie hadn't allowed herself any expectations on what the day was to bring. She had been down this road far too many times, so when they walked hand in hand out of the medical building after Kate's appointment, Brodie was trying not to stare at the woman by her side. For the past two hours, Brodie had waited for the shoe to drop...and the only thing that had dropped was Brodie's jaw.

Kate had held Brodie's hand while they sat in a waiting room overflowing with people. She had introduced Brodie to the receptionist, making it loud and clear Brodie was her partner, and when Kate was asked to update some forms, she changed her emergency contact to Brodie, printing in bold, block letters PARTNER in the space provided.

When Kate's name was finally called, she insisted Brodie come back to the exam room with her, and when her doctor walked in, Kate made the introductions, just as she had in the waiting room. She held her head high throughout the morning, and never once faltered as she outed herself again and again...and again.

Brodie hit the remote as they got to the car, and letting go of Kate's hand, she opened the door. "In you go."

Kate stepped toward the car and then stopping, she shaded her eyes as she looked up at the woman inches away. "You're awfully quiet."

"I'm trying to...um...I'm trying to *absorb* what just happened in there."

"What happened was my doctor said I'm well enough to talk to the investigators, so I'll call my Chief when we get home."

"I'm not talking about the diagnosis, and you know it."

Kate smiled. "I told you, sweetheart, I've changed. I don't care what anyone thinks anymore. If they want to stare, let them. If they want to curl their lips, they can knock their socks off. It makes no difference to me. I just hope I wasn't presumptuous."

"What do you mean?"

"Well, I did put you down as my partner. So...are you?"

Brodie hung her head for a moment. "I want to be..."

"But?"

"But, I need some..." Brodie snorted out a laugh. "*Fuck* that *fucking* word."

"Let me guess," Kate said, grinning. "You were about to say you need some more time, some more proof, maybe?"

"Kate, I love you with all my heart, but you really did a number on it. You've *got* to know that."

"I do, and all it means is that I just have to keep showing you that I've changed until you believe it. That's all."

"You're not angry?" Brodie said, flinching back her head.

"No, of course not," Kate said as she climbed into the car. "Proving it is going to be fun."

Chapter Thirty-Four

"You awake?" Brodie called out as she stepped into her flat.

"Yes, I'm awake. Smart arse," Kate said, coming out of the bedroom.

Brodie removed her raincoat, shaking it to dislodge some of the water before hanging it up. "If it keeps raining, we'd best find an ark."

"They say it's supposed to lighten up tomorrow," Kate said, placing a small kiss on Brodie's cheek. "How was your meeting?"

"It went well. The Jacobs have their eye on properties all over the place, so as long as these conversions are successful, it looks like Ethan and I will be busy for years," Brodie said while she gave Kate a slow once-over. "And how are you feeling?"

Kate sighed. "You know, you've asked me the same thing every day, and *every* day, I tell you I'm fine. Gina knows I'm fine. Devon knows I'm fine. Why can't you accept the fact that I'm fine?"

Since her visit to the doctor a week earlier, wearing Brodie's flannel shirts had become Kate's norm, and today she had on Brodie's favorite. The red and black checkered fabric had been washed a hundred times, so when Brodie hooked her finger in the collar, the cloth drooped easily. Exposing just enough of what remained of the bruise, Brodie said, "And what about that?"

"*That* is fine," Kate said, snatching the collar back up. "And unless you want to eat wearing those wet clothes, I'd suggest you change because dinner will be ready soon."

"You made us dinner?"

"We're having a picnic," Kate said through a smile.

Brodie glanced at the torrential storm outside the bank of windows in the lounge and then back at Kate. "Um...Kate, are you taking the painkillers again?"

"No. I haven't had any in days. You know that. Why?"

"Because you must be high if you think having a picnic in the rain is a good idea."

Kate's smile grew even wider. "How about a picnic by the fireplace?" she said, motioning toward the lounge.

Brodie took a step and looking around the corner, her face lit up when she saw a blanket on the floor, with silverware and plates at the ready.

"I hope you don't mind," Kate said, glancing at her makeshift picnic. "I was going to make a fire, but I didn't know how to work the vent."

"I don't mind at all. It's marvelous," Brodie said, gazing at Kate. "Do I have time for a quick shower?"

"Yeah, go ahead. I still have some things to do."

"If you need help..."

"Brodie, I'm *fine*. Geez," Kate said, and taking Brodie by the arms, she pushed her toward the bedroom. "Now, go take your shower already and leave me be."

"I'm going. I'm going," Brodie mumbled as she sauntered away. "Pushy wench."

Kate giggled to herself as she headed back to the kitchen to pull their dinner from the oven. Having received orders from her doctor not to return to work for yet another week, and not to drive for at least two, when Brodie suggested Kate stay at her place to recover, Kate didn't argue. The only place she wanted to be was with Brodie, so after a quick trip to her house to gather some more clothes, Kate had spent the better part of the past week catching up on sleep while her body healed.

As each day passed, aches and pains faded, and her nausea and dizziness were a thing of the past. Now, the only thing remaining from the accident was the memory, a few fading bruises, and a scar on her thigh where the sutures had been. They had slept in the same bed, eaten at the same table, and watched the same movies, yet through it all, Kate could sense Brodie was still cautious. She was still worried that Kate wouldn't follow through on her promises even though on more than one occasion, Kate had proven Brodie wrong.

On the way back from Kate's doctor's visit, Brodie said she needed to stop at the market for a few things, and while she thought Kate would stay in the car to rest, Kate wouldn't hear of it. Holding Brodie's hand, Kate meandered up and down nearly every aisle of the store, quietly chatting while they filled their cart. In the frozen food department, she didn't think twice when she slipped her hand in the back pocket of Brodie's trousers as they perused the selection, and while standing third in line to pay for their purchases, Kate gave Brodie a not-so-quick kiss on the lips.

Later that same day, when Brodie was about to visit the car dealership, Kate asked if she could go, too. It wasn't because she wanted to voice her opinion about whatever car Brodie would choose, and Kate hadn't cared about the color or the accessories either. Kate only cared about the people who'd be milling about. She cared that they saw. She cared that they knew. And Kate cared that she *didn't* if their reactions weren't pleasant.

Just as she had done in the market, as soon as they stepped from the car, Kate had taken Brodie's hand and refused to let go. In a way, Kate thought her attempt to prove she had changed was a small one, yet Brodie's smile told her differently. It was full, and it was bright, and it was proud. And when a few of the shoppers at the dealership had the nerve to shoot a condescending look in her direction, Kate returned her gaze to Brodie and beamed. The stupidity of others no longer concerned her.

***

After showering and donning a pair of jeans and a loose-fitting, bow-necked jumper, Brodie returned to the lounge, placing a few small logs in the fire pit before opening the vent. Lighting the kindling, she stepped back just as Kate came over carrying a bottle of wine and two glasses. "Are you allowed to have that?" Brodie said, pointing at the bottle.

"You know, for someone who doesn't want to have babies, you sure do have mothering down pat," Kate said, handing Brodie an empty glass. "And for what I can only *hope* will be the last time, I haven't taken any medication in almost a week, so will you please, for the love of God, stop coddling me."

Laugh lines formed on Brodie's face, and without saying a word, she held out her glass so Kate could fill it. After taking a sip, she discovered it was one of her better Cabernets. "So..." Brodie said, looking past Kate to the kitchen. "What's for dinner?"

"Lasagna."

"I didn't know lasagna was considered picnic food."

Kate playfully peered up at Brodie before setting the wine bottle and her glass on the end table. "And I didn't know you were such a stickler for details," she said, heading back to the kitchen. "Go figure."

No sooner had Brodie turned back to the fire to check its progress when the lights in her flat began to flicker. A few seconds later, the power went out, and with the fire in its early stages, it allowed Brodie only enough light to see a few feet in front of her. Then she realized Kate was in total darkness. "Kate," she called out. "Kate, are you all right?"

Kate chuckled under her breath as she stood in the middle of the kitchen surrounded by darkness. "No, sweetheart," she shouted back. "I've fallen into that *huge* hole in the floor, and I'll never be heard from again."

Carefully feeling her way through the kitchen toward the soft glow in the lounge, Kate stepped from the shadows and smiled. "Are you going to be like this for the rest of our lives? Because if you are, I seriously think you're going to need to get some counseling since you seemed to have forgotten what I do for a living."

A slight flush crept across Brodie's cheeks, and taking a step in Kate's direction, she dipped her chin. "I guess I've been a bit overprotective—huh?"

"I'm not made of porcelain, Brodie."

"You're not made of Kevlar, either."

Kate drew her head back quickly. "I didn't know my job bothered you."

"Honestly, it didn't until you got hurt. Not really." Brodie stopped and shook her head. "I mean, you're a copper, and you're bound to get into some...into some bad situations. I know that, but seeing you hurt, seeing you bruised, I guess it just put things into perspective."

"Meaning life's too short?"

"Meaning I love you with all my heart, and I'll do my best not to worry, not to dote, and not to coddle, but I can't promise I won't. It seems, when it concerns you, it's become as intrinsic to me as...as breathing."

Brodie's words brought a glow to Kate's face. "I can accept that," she said on a breath.

"So, you'll forgive me if I go too far occasionally?"

Before Kate could answer, her stomach announced itself like a rabid lion, and she laughed, "Yes, I can, but only if you light some candles so we can eat. It appears I need to be fed."

***

Brodie placed her hand on her stomach, groaning as she stared up at the ceiling. "I can't move. In fact, I doubt I'll ever move again."

"Well, nobody said you had to finish the whole tray," Kate said, coming from the kitchen carrying two cups of coffee.

"I know, but it was so good. I couldn't stop myself."

"I noticed," Kate said, handing Brodie a cup. "Here, this may help take the edge off."

Brodie propped herself up on her elbow and took the coffee. "Thanks."

"You're welcome," Kate said, sitting cross-legged on the floor next to Brodie. Sipping her coffee, she gazed at the flames in the hearth while she digested her dinner. Lost in her thoughts, Kate jumped when she felt Brodie's finger on her cheek. "What?"

"The cream worked. You can't even tell the burns were there."

"Yep, I'm fit as a fiddle," Kate chirped.

"So, I guess that means you'll be going back to work on Monday?"

"That's the plan, but I'll need you to take me back to my place on Sunday."

"Why?"

"Because I don't have any work clothes here," Kate said, setting her coffee down. "And I guess I should also refresh myself on the Tube schedules. It's either that or take a taxi since I can't drive for another bloody week."

"I'll take you to work and pick you up. That's not a problem."

"I can't ask you to do that."

"You're not asking. I'm offering, or is it because you don't want your colleagues to see us together?"

Kate's features softened, and empathy glistened in her eyes as she gazed at Brodie. Months before that question would have led to an argument, yet Kate couldn't fault Brodie for still having some doubts. Progress had been made in proving herself over the past two weeks, but two weeks of visits to the market or to the doctor or to the car dealership weren't enough to erase the damage she had caused. That was going to take a four-letter word called time.

Kate took a deep breath and climbed on top of Brodie, straddling her legs as she looked down at the woman. "I suppose I deserve that," she said as she took Brodie's coffee cup and put it on the floor. "But I'm more than willing to keep proving it to you...as long as it takes."

"Then, let me drive you to work on Monday."

"Will that do it? Will that prove to you, for once and for all, I've changed?"

"Yes...well, I mean, it's the biggest hurdle. Isn't it? What those blokes think? What they may say to you? It drove you to do...to do a lot of what you did."

Kate nodded slowly. "You're right. It did, but not anymore."

"No?"

"No," Kate said, looking Brodie in the eye. "Because, Brodie Shaw, if your offer is still good, will you do me the honor of driving me to work on Monday?"

"I'd be delighted to," Brodie said, her face brighter than the flames in the hearth.

"Good, then it's settled," Kate said, grinning as she leaned back and rested on Brodie's thighs.

"Are you comfortable?"

Kate looked right and then left. "Yes, as a matter of fact, I am. Why?"

"Because I'm a bit warm, what with the fire and all."

"Are you asking me to move?"

"If you don't mind."

Kate picked up her coffee and took a quick sip. "And if I do?"

"I guess I'll sweat."

"Well, then if you're going to sweat, I may as well give you something to sweat about," Kate said as she leaned in and placed her lips against Brodie's.

The first kiss was light, almost whimsical, and they both smiled into it. The second held a hint of need and passion, and when the third began, they both moaned as familiar flavors swirled together. It had been months since they had kissed like lovers, and time stood still as they rediscovered the sweetness of the other.

Brodie pulled away and held Kate at arm's length. "I think it's time for you to get some sleep."

"I'm not tired," Kate said, studying Brodie for a second. "And neither are you."

"Kate, I don't think you're ready…" The words died in Brodie's throat when Kate raised an eyebrow, a silent yet oh so deadly dare for Brodie to continue, and Brodie thought long and hard before she spoke. "What I mean to say is, and please don't get angry, but you're still recuperating, and I wouldn't want to hurt you."

"Then don't," Kate said as she began unbuttoning the flannel shirt. "Make love to me, Brodie…as only you ever will."

Brodie watched in silence as each button opened, and when the shirt gaped, showing just a hint of the creamy mounds still hidden by the fabric, Brodie swallowed the moisture building in her mouth. Her eyes were drawn to what remained of the bruise that ran from Kate's shoulder to her hip. Although impossible to miss, the colors had faded to pale yellows and greens, and gently, Brodie placed her hand between Kate's breasts. "Does that hurt?"

"No, sweetheart," Kate said in a breath, and taking Brodie's hand, she slid it over until it was cupping her breast. "And neither does this."

Brodie's guttural grown told Kate all she needed to know, and she bent forward, hovering over Brodie on outstretched arms. "You know what I like, Brodie," Kate said, lowering her breast to Brodie's mouth. "Please, don't make me ask, because I *will* ask…as I'm sure, you remember."

Brodie captured the swollen tip in her mouth. She heard Kate suck in a sharp breath, and when Kate threaded her fingers through Brodie's hair, silently urging her on, Brodie inwardly smiled. Yes, she knew what Kate liked.

Brodie tenderly sucked against the distended point, flicking her tongue over the bud again and again while Kate writhed over her. She ran her hands lightly over Kate's back, leaving trails of goosebumps wherever they went as she sucked and nipped until she finally rolled

Kate to her side, gently guiding her to the floor until they were lying face to face.

Awash in the glow of the fireplace, Brodie brushed a strand of hair from Kate's face before running her finger over her lips. "You are absolutely the most beautiful woman I've ever seen in my life," Brodie whispered. "And I'm totally in love with you."

"Then show me."

The naked longing in Kate's eyes took Brodie's breath away, and standing up, she offered Kate her hand.

"What?" Kate said, looking at Brodie's hand as if she was holding a snake.

"Let's go to bed."

"I told you. I'm not tired."

"I know," Brodie said, and taking Kate's hand, she pulled her to her feet. "Neither am I."

***

Hand in hand, they walked to the bedroom, their movements unhurried yet focused. As Brodie lit more candles, Kate turned down the bed, and piece by piece, clothing found its way to the floor. They slipped onto sheets smooth and cool, and in the dancing light of the candles, they came together like they'd never done before. Their foreplay had always been rushed; their need for each other undeniable, but tonight while their need was as strong as it ever was, their love was stronger.

As the aroma of bergamot and sandalwood rose from the melting wax, they dissolved into each other, their legs meshing perfectly seconds before butterfly kisses were bestowed. Tender and light, their lips met again and again, each holding the message of forever in its touch. Fingers, like feathers, brushed over skin warm and smooth, and they lazily traveled over naked backs, bottoms, and arms.

Their tempo was melodic, and like a slow-motion ballet, their bodies caressed each other's. Nipples aroused and hard met a matching pair as did breasts full and round, and lips supple and wet parted so tongues velvety soft and oh so welcomed could leisurely explore. They enticed with each kiss and coaxed with each touch, the gentle massage of their lovemaking slowly dampening their hairlines and making their skin gleam with sweat.

Their lips parted, and as Kate gazed at Brodie, her breath caught in her throat. There was a hint of fire in Brodie's eyes, born from lust and passion, but there was something else swirling in the brown. Unyielding, like invisible tears, love reflected back at Kate, holding in its shimmer tenderness, devotion, and eternity, and Kate's eyes shimmered, too. "I love you so much," she said, tracing Brodie's lips with her finger. "So, so much."

"I love you, too," Brodie said before she lowered her eyes.

For a split-second, Kate didn't understand why Brodie's brow had furrowed, and then she remembered the faint bruise across her chest. "Don't," Kate said, lifting Brodie's chin. "I told you, it doesn't hurt."

"It looks like it does."

"Well, I guess I'll have to prove it to you then," Kate said, and shifting slightly, she placed her knee against Brodie's center. "Now…where were we?"

Before Brodie could respond, Kate began pressing her knee into Brodie as she slowly started to rock. The sensual massage was to die for, and Brodie was transfixed. The sensations Kate was causing spread throughout her body like a million tiny specks of energy, they sparked and sizzled in every crevice of Brodie's being. Placing her hands on Kate's bottom, Brodie closed her eyes and enjoyed the ride, for she knew when those specks finally came together…the result would be soul-shattering.

Kate took her time. The slow grind, the unrushed slide, and the arch to press deeper were natural and instinctive, and while indeed carnal, they were also pure. The love Kate wanted to bestow on Brodie needed no intrusion, no probing or exploring for sometimes, especially *this* time, Kate needed to memorize everything she had almost lost. The beauty of a face flushed with passion. The sound of breathing growing ragged with each casual thrust. The way Brodie's hands felt on her bottom, possessive yet guiding. The slickness and scent of the desire coating her knee, and the way Brodie's body meshed so exquisitely against her own as they met again and again in an unceasing rhythm.

Perspiration dotted Kate's upper lip as she hovered on stretched arms over Brodie. Mesmerized, she fought against eyelids growing heavy with passion as she gazed at the writhing woman under her, and as if Brodie could read her mind, her eyes opened, and she looked up at Kate. One heartbeat later, she bent her leg and pressed her thigh against the apex of Kate's legs.

Air rushed from Kate's lungs at the feel, and the cadence of the tempo she had set quickened almost instantly. With her eyes locked on Brodie's, Kate arched into her, her nectar coating Brodie's thigh with each slide, and as their pace grew frenzied, so did their breathing. The thrum building within was growing more thunderous with each push and gasps spilled from lips as all was lost to this thing called love.

It wasn't long before liquid fire ignited their bodies. Brodie cried out first, her guttural, low groans filling the room as her body shuddered from release, and Kate followed soon after. Closing her eyes, she squeezed her legs tightly around Brodie's thigh, and gripping the sheets as she sucked in a breath, her climax brutally claimed her. Desire pulsed from her core as spasm after spasm pummeled her and helpless against the onslaught, Kate's uninhibited throaty sounds of pleasure went unchecked.

Neither opened their eyes until their breathing had slowed and still straddling Brodie, Kate smiled. "How you doing down there?"

"I'm doing well, and you?"

"Never been better," Kate said, her eyes creasing at the corners.

"I'll second that."

"Will you now?" Kate said, her gaze firmly held by Brodie's erect and pebbled nipples.

"Yes." Brodie gently rolled Kate to the mattress, and sliding her leg between Kate's, Brodie murmured, "So…are you tired yet?"

Brodie's answer came when Kate bent her leg and pressed her thigh against Brodie's soaked folds, and as Brodie lowered her mouth for a kiss, Kate whispered into it, "Absolutely not."

Chapter Thirty-Five

As planned, late Sunday afternoon, Brodie brought Kate back to her house to get ready for work the next day, and bright and early on Monday morning, Brodie returned. She was greeted by a sleepy woman with a puffy face and a to-die-for smile, and after having a cup of coffee together, Kate disappeared into her bedroom and left Brodie to her own devices. After finishing a second cup, Brodie made her way to Kate's room to wait, and sitting on the bed, Brodie was mindlessly glancing around when Kate emerged from the bathroom wearing nothing but her underwear.

"I thought you'd be dressed," Brodie said, standing up. "Lucky me."

The look in Brodie's eyes was unmistakable, and Kate waggled her finger as she went over and opened the door to the wardrobe. "Don't even think about it. The last thing I need is to be late on my first day back to work."

"I have no idea what you're talking about."

"Weren't you the one that said relationships need honesty?" Kate said, stepping into her skirt.

"I hate it when things come back to bite me in the arse," Brodie said through a frown.

"Then you are probably *really* going to hate this," Kate said, putting on her blouse.

Brodie paled instantly, and as her lungs emptied in a whoosh, she sunk onto the edge of the bed. "Let me guess," she said, staring at the floor. "You don't want me to take you to work."

Kate froze with her arm halfway down a sleeve. Hanging her head, she took a breath, pushed her arm through the sleeve, and then went over and stood between Brodie's legs. Putting her finger under Brodie's chin, Kate forced Brodie to look at her. "You couldn't be more wrong."

"No?"

"No," Kate said softly. "But a few months back, you told me you'd be willing to lease your place and move in here. Do you remember?"

"Yes."

"Well, I don't want you to do that."

Brodie slouched even further into the mattress. "Okay."

"Instead, I'd like to put this place on the market and move into yours. That is if it's okay."

"Are you serious?" Brodie said, straightening her spine.

"I've never been more serious in my life," Kate said, gazing into Brodie's eyes.

Before Kate could take another breath, Brodie pulled her into a passionate kiss, and it didn't end until Kate felt Brodie trying to unclasp the hooks on her bra.

"Oh, no, you don't," Kate said, struggling out of Brodie's grasp. "You're going to have to put your hormones on a leash because I can't afford to be late."

"Is this you calling the shots again?" Brodie said, crossing her arms as she fought to hide her smile.

Kate squinted back at Brodie. "Don't even start," she said as she buttoned her blouse.

"Right," Brodie said, getting to her feet. "Well, I guess I can start grabbing some clothes for you."

"What?"

"You're moving in—right?"

"Sweetheart, do you honestly think you can fit anything other than my houseplants in your car?"

"Damn," Brodie said, flopping back down on the bed. "I should have kept the sedan."

"The hell you should have," Kate said, taking her suit jacket off the hanger. "That was *so* not you."

"And you think the new one is?"

"Do you really have to ask?"

***

Brodie pulled into a parking space and turned off the engine. "So...you ready?"

"Ready as I'll ever be," Kate said, pressing the button to unlock her door.

"Wait. I have something for you." Brodie reached behind the passenger seat and pulling out a white paper sack, she handed it to Kate.

"What's this?"

"Chocolate frosted donuts. I heard they're your favorite."

Kate's heart doubled in size, and leaning over, she gave Brodie a quick kiss on the lips. "I love you," she said before opening the door. "But now I really have to go." Without waiting for a response, Kate climbed out of the car and shut the door.

Brodie hit the control for the passenger window. "*Oi!*"

"What?" Kate said, bending down to look into the car.

"Is that it?"

"Huh?"

"I pick you up at the crack of dawn, wait for hours whilst you get ready, buy you your favorite donuts, and all I get is a chaste little peck on the lips?"

"What did you expect?" Kate said with a laugh.

"A bit more tongue would have been nice."

Kate's smile reached beyond her ears. "Pick me up at five, sweetheart, and you just may get your wish."

***

When Kate walked into the station, she was greeted by smiles and handshakes. Uniformed officers, detectives, and superiors all made it a point of stopping by her desk to let her know how much she'd been missed. A short time later, she was called into her Chief's office and informed that since her driving privileges would not be returned for another week, for the next five days, Kate's duties would be more secretarial and less investigative. Upon hearing that a seasoned officer would be assisting them in doing their dreaded reports, almost every detective in her department began dropping off files and notes, and within two hours of her arrival, Kate's desk was overflowing with folders. Kate had never been one to back away from paperwork, so after grabbing a cup of coffee, she took off her suit jacket, rolled up her sleeves, and got to work, snacking on chocolate frosted donuts in between deciphering the handwriting of others.

Not quite eight hours later, Kate leaned back in her chair and blew an errant strand of hair from her forehead. She had spent almost the entire day at her computer and had yet to make a sizeable dent in the piles stacked on her desk. With only a few more minutes left of her shift, Kate grabbed a stack of reports she'd completed and headed toward the filing cabinets lined up along the wall on the far side of the room.

Kate had almost reached her destination when she heard a familiar voice, and looking over, her mouth dropped open when she saw Frank Daggett swing into the room on crutches. In an instant, three of Frank's gray-haired cronies surrounded him, and amidst all the glad-handing and slaps on the back he received, their gravelly voices rose in celebration. They whooped and hollered like middle-aged cheerleaders whose team had just scored the winning goal, but then Kate tilted her head. She covertly looked around the room and saw two of the most seasoned detectives still at their desks seemingly intent on whatever was on their computers, and a Superintendent, who had gone through the ranks with Frank, was standing at the coffee pot chatting with some officers nearby. It was impossible not to hear the ruckus, the voices booming their optimistic wishes, yet as Kate made her way to the filing cabinets, she couldn't help but wonder if some ears had suddenly turned deaf.

Frank had seen Kate as soon as he'd come into the station, and he also had seen her slack-jawed expression. Once his mates returned to their desks, he swung his way across the office to where Kate was busy filing. "Well now, Monroe. You seemed a bit surprised to see me back at work."

Kate looked over her shoulder, glancing at the plaster encasing Frank's legs. "Correct me if I'm wrong, Frank, but I doubt you're here to *work*, unless, of course, you're going to help with the filing."

"In your dreams, love," Frank said, setting his crutches aside as he dropped into a chair. "But you're right. I'm not working. I just stopped by to chat with the investigators about the accident and fill out some reports."

"Oh, I see," Kate said, and turning back toward the cabinets, she happily returned to the filing. Standing close enough to the window to see the car park, when a shiny new sports car caught her eye, Kate's face split into a grin.

Frank had been staring daggers through Kate's back for the last few minutes, and when he saw her face light up, he raised his chin. "You know, I can't ever remember anyone being so happy doing filing. You sure you don't want to change careers, Kate?"

Kate slipped the last folder into place, and closing the drawer, she turned around. "If you must know, I'm smiling because I just saw my partner pull into the lot, which means it's time for me to go." Kate took a step and then realized her path was blocked by Frank's crutches. "Could you please move those?"

"I didn't know you had a partner, Monroe," Frank said, ignoring Kate's request.

"There's quite a bit you don't know about..." Kate suddenly remembered something she had wanted to do all day. "Shit," she said, quickly pointing to the crutches. "Frank, for the last time. Move those bloody things so I can get by."

"What's your rush?" Frank said, unblocking the aisle. "We still have things to talk about."

As far as Kate was concerned, there was nothing she needed or *wanted* to talk to Frank about, and scurrying past, when she reached her desk, she opened the bottom drawer and removed a small package. Tearing off the tissue paper, Kate used the sleeve of her blouse to remove a few specks of dust from the glass, and shoving aside some folders, she placed the framed photograph in the center of her desk. She gazed at it for a few seconds, her eyes brimming with love, and then giving the picture of Brodie a wink, Kate put on her suit jacket, grabbed her coat and handbag, and turned to leave.

Frank had kept his eyes glued on Kate the entire time, so when he saw her preparing to go, he shouted from across the way, "*Monroe!*"

Kate let out a huff as she glared at the man. "What?"

"Bloody hell, woman," Frank said, waving his arms over his plastered legs. "Can I please talk to you for a minute, or should I just scream across the bleedin' room?"

Kate could sense heads were beginning to turn, and with a sigh, she strode back to where Frank was sitting. Tossing her things on a nearby chair, she planted herself in front of the man. "All right. I'm here. What do you want?"

"I just want to make sure we're on the same page."

Kate jerked back her head. "Sorry?"

"Look, when I'm finished with my report, they'll probably want to hear your version of what happened, so I thought we should compare notes."

"You did, did you?" Kate said, folding her arms across her chest.

"Come on, love. It won't take long, and the sooner we start, the sooner you'll be able to skip off to meet your partner. So what do you say? Take a load off, and let's get this done."

"I'm afraid it's too late for that, Frank."

"What are you talking about?"

"They already have my report."

Frank straightened in his chair. "That's impossible. I was told your first day back to work wasn't until today."

"You're right. It wasn't, but I guess the powers-that-be wanted to know what happened sooner, rather than later. I spoke to the investigators last week."

"Why in the hell wasn't I told?"

Kate's eyes sparkled with amusement, and she shrugged. "Well, Frank, I can't be sure, but my guess is they probably didn't think they needed your permission."

"Fine," Frank growled, rubbing his chin. "Then, just tell me what you put in your report."

"The truth," Kate said, unfolding her arms. "So, as long as you do the same, your report and my report *should* be identical."

Frank clenched his jaw and leaning forward in his chair, he kept his voice low. "Monroe, this is my bloody job we're talking about."

"Then you should have thought about that before you almost killed us, not to mention the nine other people who got hurt that day."

"It was an accident."

It had been a while since Kate's temper had gone from zero to sixty in a nanosecond, and slamming her hands down on the arms of Frank's chair, the man rocked back as she invaded his space. "*You're an accident, Frank,*" Kate said, her voice low and dripping with disdain. "You are a mistake this department needs to correct, and whether they do it by reprimand or dismissal makes no difference to me. All I know is that if they believe what I put in my report, and I have no reason *whatsoever* to think otherwise, you'll never sit behind the wheel of *any* car again."

Appearing to turn into a human pufferfish, Daggett's face ballooned as rage reddened his cheeks and mottled his face. The thought that a woman, *any* woman, could have bested him caused bile to rise in his throat. He had spent over twenty years on the force, and even though his file contained a few reprimands, Frank had managed to talk himself out of over a dozen more. With a round of beer or a round of golf, or even a round of both, he would lament about losing his children in the divorce, grouse about the long hours he had to work in order to provide for them properly now they were under *her* roof, and pile on the flattery to whatever superior he was currently chatting up. Frank had always ended with that, ended on a high note, so they walked away feeling appreciated, and it had *almost* always worked. Formal reprimands became merely slaps on the wrist, and Frank merrily went on his way...except the last time was different.

The last time he was given an ultimatum, to keep his nose clean and ride out the time to his retirement at another station or lose his job right then and there. Frank blustered and bewailed, especially once he found out he'd be saddled with a partner, but having a partner gave Frank the excuse he needed. To all his friends and cohorts, he made it crystal clear his *assignment* was to watch over some stupid twit in another borough until he and his superiors could put enough paper in her file to fire her. She was just another useless woman trying to do a man's job, and he welcomed the task of doing his part to rid the force of yet one more waste of time wearing a skirt. But Kate Monroe wasn't stupid, and while Frank had managed to push her around up until this point, after Kate's little show of temper a moment earlier, Frank decided to take a different tack.

Frank's demeanor suddenly softened, and taking a slow breath, he replaced his anger with charm. "Look, Kate," he said, resting his hands on top of hers. "You're talking about my livelihood here. I've got two kids to feed and an ex-wife to support, and if our versions of what happened that day don't match, it could really create some problems."

"Maybe for you, Frank," Kate said, snatching her hands away as she stood straight. "But not for me and not for anyone here who actually *wants* to be a good cop."

Frank opened his mouth to speak just as Kate's phone chimed, and pulling it from her pocket, she tapped on the screen as she strolled to the window. "Hiya."

"Hi yourself," Brodie said, smiling through the phone. "So, am I early, or are you late?"

"Both," Kate said, looking down at the parking area. "I saw you pull in a couple of minutes ago, but Frank wanted to have a few words with me, so I'm running a bit late. Sorry."

"Don't worry about it, and Frank? As in your partner?"

"Hopefully, not for long."

"Should I come up to protect you? Remember, I have two brothers, so I know how to wrestle."

"Oh, I do love you," Kate said as she placed her hand on the glass, and two stories below, Brodie instinctively looked up.

"Hey, there's a gorgeous woman checking me out," Brodie said, leaning against her car.

"Really?"

"Yeah, two floors up on the end."

"And what are you going to do about it?"

"Shag her silly when she gets home," Brodie said, grinning.

"I'm going to hold you to that, sweetheart," Kate said, her cheeks turning rosy. "I'll be down in a few minutes. Okay?"

"I'm not going anywhere without you."

Kate closed her phone and turning around, she couldn't help but notice the confused look on Frank's face. "Problem, Frank?"

"I'm assuming he's a doctor," Frank said, resting back in his chair.

"Who?"

"Your partner?"

Kate scratched her cheek, debating on whether to take the bait. She told herself she should just walk away, but there was something about Frank's supercilious expression that Kate couldn't ignore.

"Okay, I'll give," she said, looking Frank in the eye. "Why would you think that?"

"Because I'm a bloody good detective, Monroe. That's why," Frank said, steepling his fingers as his smirk stretched across his stubbly face. "You've never talked about any partner in all the months we've been working together, and all of a sudden, you're telling a bloke you love him? Plus, there's that picture you just put on your desk. I can't see it from here, but I'll bet you anything, it's a photo of some up-and-coming doctor, no doubt one you met in the hospital after the accident. That tells me it's true what they say about patients falling in love with their doctors, and honestly, Kate, I'm a little surprised. I mean, you never struck me as a genius, but I did think you were a *bit* smarter than that."

"Oh, Frank, Frank, Frank," Kate said, clicking her tongue. "I hate to disappoint you, but I am a *lot* smarter than you think I am."

"Is that so?"

"Yes," Kate said, giving the man a slow once over. "Because *I'm* smart enough to know when it's *safe* to go on red."

Kate snatched her things off the chair and tugging on her coat, she sashayed past Frank without giving him as much as a sideways glance. When she reached the door, Frank's voice rang out again.

"What in the hell is that supposed to mean?" he bellowed from across the room.

Kate stopped, chuckling to herself before she turned around. "You're the '*bloody good detective*,' Frank. *You* figure it out."

***

Kate walked across the lot, chuckling under her breath as she neared Brodie. "You're absolutely crazy."

Still leaning against the car with her ankles crossed, Brodie stood straight and grinned. "Why's that?"

"Because it's too cold to have the top down," Kate said, glancing at the cherry-red, convertible Jaguar now open to the elements.

"Where's your sense of adventure, DI Monroe?"

"I'm thinking it's standing right in front of me," Kate said with a laugh.

Only an arm's length from Brodie, Kate moved in for a kiss only to have Brodie turn her face at the last second, so Kate's lips landed on her cheek. "Hey, what's that about?" Kate said, stepping back.

Brodie's eyes darted from the building and back to Kate. "We're being watched."

"Huh?"

"A bloke is standing in the window where you just were, and he can't seem to take his eyes off of us."

Kate turned around, and seeing Frank staring down at them, she waved to make sure she had his undivided attention before pivoting back to Brodie and kissing her full on the mouth. Their lips parted a few seconds later, yet when their eyes met, Kate couldn't resist. She kissed Brodie again, and this time, Kate held nothing back. It was passionate, and it was wet, and almost a minute went by before they finally moved apart.

Pleasantly surprised, albeit a bit confused at such a hearty PDA, Brodie's smile was wide. "Kate, what are you doing?"

"I call it going on red, sweetheart," Kate purred, running her fingers through Brodie's hair. "Now, what say you take me back to your flat? I don't know about you, but I'm in the mood to shoot some pool."

Brodie's eyebrows disappeared into her hairline. "Is that so?"

"Yep."

"Well," Brodie said, opening the passenger door so Kate could get in. "How about we make a quick stop at your place first? Grab you some clothes so we can sleep in a few minutes tomorrow before I bring you to work."

"So, the time we'll be saving is so we can sleep in?" Kate said, watching as Brodie trotted around the car.

"Of course," Brodie said, and slipping into her seat, she started the car. "You don't think I have any ulterior motives, do you?"

"Absolutely none," Kate said, leaning in for another quick kiss.

"Good."

Brodie maneuvered the car through the lot, and as she neared the exit, she flipped on the turn signal.

"Oh, wait," Kate said, putting her hand on Brodie's arm. "You need to go left."

"Why?" Brodie said, quickly looking at Kate. "A left takes us back to my place. I thought we just said we'd go to yours first so we can pick up some clothes."

"We are," Kate said, her eyes twinkling as her lips parted into a smile as dazzling as it was playful. "But there's this billboard I need you to see."

The End

Thank you for reading Going on Red.

As an Independent author, I have no publicity department or publishing company to depend on to spread the word about my books, so if you liked Going on Red, I hope you can find a few minutes to return to where you purchased it and leave a comment or a review.

If you want to contact me personally, please drop me a line at Lyng227@gmail.com or catch me on Facebook https://www.facebook.com/lyn.gardner.587

Lyn

Acknowledgments

As always, I want to thank those who spent their days, nights, and weekends reading my words, diligently looking for typos, continuity errors, and so much more. They are my editors. They are my proofreaders...and they are my friends.

To Susan, Marion, Jan, Marian, and Bron, thank you for all your hard work. Words could never express my gratitude for the time spent and for all those marvelous "finds" that helped to make this story better. You speak your minds. You keep me in line...and you keep me sane. You are indeed the best!

Love you all,
Lyn

Other Titles by Lyn Gardner

Choices

SILVER MEDAL – 2019 Global Ebook Awards – Gay/Lesbian/LGBT Fiction
FINALIST – 2019 American Book Fest Awards – Fiction: LGBTQ

Robin Novak has made many choices in her life. She chose her career. She chose her friends, and she also chose to come out in college. Since that time, many women have walked in and out of Robin's life, but two had left indelible impressions. The first was a crush, and the second…almost destroyed her.

Mentally bruised and battered from an abusive relationship, in one short year, Robin has gone from being a successful author to someone struggling to breathe almost as much as she's struggling to write. With her confidence shattered, and her self-loathing at an all-time high, when an unexpected inheritance comes her way, Robin doesn't think twice. At the age of forty-four, Robin Novak packs up her life and her cats and moves to a place where she hopes to start fresh. But a change of location isn't the only thing Robin is looking for. After her last relationship, she knows this move will also drastically reduce the possibility of ever having another woman in her life.

Choices made create the paths on which we travel. Down some, friendships are born, and down others love is found, and during those journeys, lives change, truths are discovered, secrets are revealed, and high school crushes…can sometimes walk back into your life.

Born Out of Wedlock

WINNER – 2017 International Book Awards – LGBTQ Fiction
SILVER MEDAL – 2017 Global Ebook Awards – Gay/Lesbian/LGBT Fiction
SILVER MEDAL – 2017 eLit Book Awards – LGBTQ Fiction
FINALIST – 2017 National Indie Excellence Award – LGBTQ Fiction
DISTINGUISHED FAVORITE – 2017 Independent Press Award – LGBTQ Fiction
FINALIST – 2017 International Author Network Book of the Year – Romance
DISTINGUISHED FAVORITE – 2017 NYC Big Book Awards – LGBTQ Fiction
RUNNER-UP – 2017 Rainbow Book Awards – Best Lesbian Contemporary Romance

Two women. Two worlds. Two problems...and two attitudes.

Addison Kane does not want for much. With a touch equaling that of Midas and a confidence overstepping the borders of arrogance, Addison's ability is vast, yet her focus is narrow. Her vision tunneled by haunting memories of her youth, she is blinded to the peripheral. She doesn't care that life is passing her by. She doesn't notice as friends fall to the wayside, and the finery that comes from wealth holds no importance for Addison is single-minded. Her goal is the ultimate of paybacks. She needs to succeed like no other before her and prove someone wrong.

Joanna Sheppard lives a simple life because she can afford no other. At the age of seventeen, her father falls ill, and for the next eleven years, Joanna's sole focus is providing for the only parent she has ever known. For the man she loves with all her heart, she gives up her dreams and doesn't look back. She goes about her days with no complaints, working three jobs so she can pay off her father's creditors, but there is no light at the end of Joanna's tunnel...or so she thinks.

When an edict from the grave threatens all Addison holds dear, two women from two different worlds are brought together, and a deal is struck. In exchange for uttering a few words, both get what they need...but not what they bargained for.

There is a thin line, as they say, but when it is crossed, can love survive when more family secrets are revealed?

Give Me A Reason

WINNER – 2015 National Indie Excellence Awards – LGBT Fiction
SILVER MEDAL – 2014 Global Ebook Awards – Gay/Lesbian/LGBT Fiction
SILVER MEDAL – 2014 eLit Book Awards – Lesbian Fiction
FINALIST – 2017 – International Network Book of the Year – Romance
FINALIST – 2015 International Book Awards – Fiction: Gay & Lesbian
FINALIST – 2014 GCLS Ann Bannon Popular Choice Awards
FINALIST – 2014 GCLS Awards for Contemporary Lesbian Fiction

Intelligent, confident and beautiful, Antoinette Vaughn had it all until one night she went to help a friend and paid for it...with a life sentence in hell.

Four years later, Toni's judgment is overturned, but the damage is already done. She walks from the prison a free woman, but she's hardly free. Actually, she's hardly alive. A prison without rules can do that to a person.

She was raised amidst garden parties, stables and tennis courts, but now a dingy flat in a decrepit building is what Toni calls home. It's cold, dark and barren just like her heart, but it suits her. She doesn't want to leave much behind when she's gone, but the simplicity of her sheltered existence begins to unravel when a beautiful stranger comes into her life.

How does anyone survive in a world that terrifies them? How do you learn to trust again when everyone is your enemy? How do you take your next breath and not wish it were your last? And if your past returned...what would you do?

Ice

GOLD MEDAL – 2014 Global Ebook Awards – Gay/Lesbian/LGBT Fiction
WINNER – Indie Book of the Day – April 19, 2013
FINALIST – 2015 National Indie Excellence Book Awards – LGBT Fiction

Ice begins when a boy is kidnapped from a London park and Detective Inspectors Alex Blake and Maggie Campbell are brought together to work on the case. While their goal is the same, their work ethics are not. Intelligent, perceptive and at times disobedient, Alex Blake does what she believes it takes to do her job. Maggie Campbell has a slightly different approach. She believes that rule books were written for a reason.

Unexpectedly, their dynamics mesh, but when her feelings for Alex become stronger than she wants to admit, Maggie provokes the worst in Alex to ensure that they will never be partners again.

Three years later, fate brings them together again. Their assignment is simple, but a plane crash gets in their way. Now, in the middle of a blizzard, they have to try to survive...and fight the feelings that refuse to die.

***

Mistletoe

WINNER – Indie Book of the Day – December 28, 2013

Four-year-old Diana Clarke sends her wish to Santa Claus, but lost in the lining of a sack, it isn't discovered for thirty years. Now, Santa has a problem. No child's wish has ever gone unanswered, but the child isn't a child anymore.

Believing there is nothing in Santa's Village to satisfy the little girl's wish now that she's an adult, he calls on a Higher Power and is given a suggestion. Although most of Santa's workshops contain only toys for boys and girls, there is one that holds a possible solution to his problem. Learning that Diana will be attending three upcoming Christmas parties, Santa calls on his lead elf to deliver three sprigs of mistletoe, hoping that under one, Diana Clarke will find what she asked for thirty years before.

Made in the USA
Middletown, DE
15 July 2021

44256022R00243